John Macpherson

Critical Dissertations on the Origin

antiquities, language, government, manners, and religion, of the antient

Caledonians, their posterity the Picts, and the British and Irish Scots - Vol. 1

John Macpherson

Critical Dissertations on the Origin

antiquities, language, government, manners, and religion, of the antient Caledonians, their posterity the Picts, and the British and Irish Scots - Vol. 1

ISBN/EAN: 9783337125943

Printed in Europe, USA, Canada, Australia, Japan

Cover: Foto ©Andreas Hilbeck / pixelio.de

CRITICAL DISSERTATIONS

ON THE

ORIGIN, ANTIQUITIES, LANGUAGE, GOVERNMENT, MANNERS, AND RELIGION,

OF THE

ANTIENT CALEDONIANS, THEIR POSTERITY THE PICTS, AND THE BRITISH AND IRISH SCOTS.

By JOHN MACPHERSON, D. D.

Minister of SLATE, in the ISLE OF SKY.

DUBLIN:

Printed by BOULTER GRIERSON, Printer to the King's most Excellent Majesty.

M DCC LXVIII.

Charles Greville, Efq;

DEAR SIR,

MY Father, who was the Author of the following Differtations, would not, perhaps, have dedicated them to any man alive. He annexed, and with good reafon, an idea of fervility to addreffes of this fort, and reckoned them the difgrace of literature. If I could not, from my foul, acquit myfelf of every felfifh view, in prefenting to you the poft-humous works of a father I tenderly loved, you would not have heard from me in this public manner. You know, my dear friend, the fincerity of my affection for you : but even that affection fhould not induce me to dedicate to you, had you already arrived at that eminence, in the ftate, which the abilities and fhining

talents

talents of your early youth seem so largely to promise, left what really is the voice of friendship and esteem, should be mistaken, by the world, for that of flattery and interested designs. I am on the eve of setting out for a very distant quarter of the world : without asking your permission, I leave you this public testimony of my regard for you, not to secure your future favour, but to stand as a small proof of that attachment, with which I am,

Dear Sir

Your most affectionate Friend,

and most Obedient

Humble Servant,

John Macpherson.

PREFACE.

THE following Differtations are the production of the leifure hours of a clergyman in one of the remoteft of the Scottifh ifles. Excluded, by the pecufituation of the place of his refidence, from the fociety of the learned, he indulged his fingular paffion for literature among a few good books. Though the natural bent of his genius turned towards the belles-lettres, he fometimes amufed himfelf in difquifitions of a more ferious nature. Being mafter of the Celtic, in all its branches, he took pleafure in tracing other languages to that general fource of all the antient and modern tongues of Europe. From inveftigations of this kind many difcoveries in the ancient hiftory of nations arofe. This naturally led to the examination of the mafs of fiction, which almoft every nation of Europe poffeffes for the hiftory of their remoteft anceftors. The more he looked into thefe legendary fabrics of antiquity, the lefs he found them capable of bearing the teft of criticifm. He therefore refolved to write fome general differtations on that fubject,

a 3

which,

which, if they could not eſtabliſh a new and more rational ſyſtem, would at leaſt expoſe the abſurdity of the old.

It was not altogether from a partiality to his own country that Dr. Macpherſon gave the firſt place to Scotland, in his diſquiſitions. Though the Scots have as juſt pretenſions to a high antiquity as any nation in Europe, yet their origin is peculiarly involved in darkneſs. It was the misfortune of North Britain to have been almoſt totally deſtitute of letters, at a time when monkiſh learning, and thoſe religious virtues which aroſe from aſcetic auſterities, greatly flouriſhed in Ireland, and among the Saxons in England. This was the caſe in the ſeventh and eight centuries, the æra in which the Hibernian ſyſtems of antiquity were formed. The ſennachies and fileas of Ireland made then a property of the Scots of Britain, and, ſecure of not being contradicted by an illiterate, and I may ſay, an irreligious race of men, aſſumed to themſelves the dignity of being the mother-nation. The partiality of Bede for his holy cotemporaries of Ireland is well known. The good man believed and retailed whatever fictions were dictated to him by the religious of a nation for whom he had the greateſt regard for their orthodoxy.   The

THE almoſt continual wars and anomoſi-
ties which ſubſiſted between the Engliſh and
Scots for many ages naturally gave birth to
violent national prejudices on both ſides.
The learned of England could not diveſt
themſelves of that antipathy to their Northern neighbours which had ſeized their whole
nation. Though at variance with the Iriſh
in every other point, they agreed with them
wonderfully well in extenuating the national antiquities of the Scots. Some of thoſe
gentlemen had the cruelty to extirpate the
brave nation of antient Caledonians, leſt the
deteſted Scots of latter times ſhould derive
any honour from the military reputation of
a people who once poſſeſſed their country.

HAPPILY for the preſent times, thoſe
prejudices which blinded both nations have,
in a great meaſure, ſubſided. National a-
verſions are loſt in the antiquity of thoſe
national injuries from which they firſt aroſe.
Whatever may tend to do honour to either
nation is heard with candor, if not with
pleaſure, by both. They are, in ſhort, now
ſo much blended with one another, that
whatever throws luſtre upon the one, ought
to be reckoned an acquiſition of reputation
to the other.——If to throw a new and ſtrong
light on the antiquities of a nation, reflects

any

any honour upon it, the Scots of the prefent age are much indebted to the induftry and learning of Dr. Macpherfon. He travelled back, it is true, into the regions of anti-quity with more advantages than others have done, and therefore his fuccefs was propor-tionably greater. A few additional obfer-vations I am to make upon the general fub-ject of the differtations, arofe, if they have any merit, from the difcoveries he had made to my hand.

Some time before the total dereliction of Britain by the Romans, in the reign of Ho-norius, we find that the Caledonians were diftinguifhed into two capital nations, the Deucaledones and Vecturiones. By thefe two branches I underftand thofe, who, a fhort time thereafter, were known by the names of Picts and Scots. It was after the departure of the Romans, that the defence-lefs ftate of the degenerated provincials gave the Picts an opportunity of extending them-felves to the Eaftern counties to the South of the frith of Edinburgh. From the joint teftimony of all writers who examined the fubject, the Picts of the earlieft ages poffef-fed only the Eaft and North-eaft coaft of Scotland. From their fituation, with ref-pect to the Scots of Jar-ghael, their country

was

was naturally called by the latter *An Dua-chaeldoch*, a word compounded of *An Dua*, or *Tua*, North, and, *Caeldoch*, Caledonian country. Some of the South-weſt Highlanders of the counties of Perth and Argyle diſtinguiſhed to this day thoſe of Roſs, Sutherland and Caithneſs, by the name of *An Dua-ghael*, and their country by the appellation of *An Dua-ghaeldoch*. This appears ſo obviouſly the etymon of *Deu-caledones*, that nothing but a total ignorance of the Galic language could permit antiquaries to have overlooked it.

The etymon of *Vecturiones* is not ſo obvious. We learn from the moſt antient domeſtic records in Scotland, that a ridge of mountains, called Drum Albin, was the ancient boundary of the Scottiſh territories towards the Eaſt. The author of the Diſſertations has clearly demonſtrated that Drum Albin is the chain of mountains which runs from Lochlomond, near Dumbarton, to the frith of Taine, in the county of Roſs. This Dorſum Britanniæ, as it is called by Adamnan, abbot of Iona, runs through the Weſtern end of the diſtricts of Athol and Badenoch. That part of this ridge of hills which extends between theſe diſtricts, for a length of more than twenty

miles,

miles, is called *Drum Uachtur*. This circumstance is well known to many, besides the natives of that country, as the military road through the Highlands passes that way. If we should suppose that *Uachtur*, which is still retained as the name of a part of Drum Albin, was once the general appellation of the whole, the etymon of Vecturiones is at once decyphered. *Uachtur*, though now taken perhaps in a more confined sense than formerly, literally signifies *the upper country*. *Uachturich* is a word of the same import with Highlanders; and if the harsh Celtic termination is softned into a Roman one, Vecturiones differs only in a changeable vowel from *Uachturich*.

We have reason to believe, from the unfavourable climate, and sterile nature of the soil, in that part of Scotland which lies to the West of Drum Albin, that the ancestors of the Scots lived long in a very uncultivated state; as destitute of great national events as of letters to transmit them to posterity. Though the Scots of *Jar-ghael* must, in the nature of things, have been very barbarous and unpolished, as far back as the latter end of the fourth century, yet it is to be hoped they were less so than the Attacotti, their neighbours, or rather a

tribe

tribe of the Scots to the South of the Clyde, "In my youth," says the holy St. Jerome, "I saw in Gaul the Attacotti, a British people feeding on human bodies. When they found in the woods flocks of sheep or hogs, or herds of cattle, they used to cut off the buttocks of the herdsmen, and the breasts of the women, looking upon those parts of the body as the greatest danties*." I have such a veneration for whatever has fallen from the holy father, that I cannot entertain a doubt of the truth of this story, however incredible it might appear from an uninspired writer. The Irish nation, not content to deprive their posterity of Scotland of their antient bishops, abbots, presbyters and historians of any note, have also endeavoured to rob them of their barbarous and wild men. O'Connor, a learned dissertator on the history of Ireland, has, in the name of his nation, claimed a right to the Attacotti. I wish I could give them to the gentleman; for as the infamous label of St. Jerome is tacked to them, they can do little honour to the Scots of the present age.

It was in the fifth century that the incursions of the Scots, as a separate nation,

---

* Hieronym. con. Jovinian. lib. 2.

into

into the Southern Britain, rendered them
objects of attention to the writers of other
countries. It does not appear that letters
were any part of the booty which they carried home with them from the deserted Roman province. The seminary of monks
established by Columba, an Irishman, in the
island of Iona, in the sixth age, seem to
have been the only persons, within the territories of the Scots, that could record
events. If they kept any registers of transf-
actions, they were destroyed or lost, in the
Norwegian conquest of the Hebrides by
Harold Harfager, about the middle of the
ninth century.

The subversion of the Pictish kingdom
is the first æra in which it can be supposed
the Scots begun to have authentic records of
their own. Soon after the conquest of Pictavia, the Saxons found means to extend
their government to the frith of Edinburgh.
The Picts and Saxons had alternately poffeffed, for some time before, the counties
between the Forth and the Tweed. The
most of the inhabitants of those counties
were of the Saxon race, and no doubt, in
a great measure, they retained the language
of their ancestors. It was after the invasions of the Danes had totally broke the

power

power of the Saxons, that the Scots extended themfelves far to the South. The barbarity of thofe Northern rovers who in-
ceffantly harraffed England, as they themfelves were heathens, drove certainly a number of pious Saxon eccelefiaftics into Scotland. It was they that introduced the cuftom of recording events in monkifh chronicles; and upon the authority of Bede, they
all adopted the fyftem of the Hibernian extraction of the Scots nation.

THE Scots lament the deftruction of their
antient annals by Edward the Firft of England. Though Edward's policy in this cafe
was rude and barbarous, he did very little
hurt to the genuine antiquities of the Scots.
Many of the domeftic tranfactions of the
latter ages were no doubt loft; but what related to the origin of the nation was Bede's
tale re-told.——I fhall endeavour, in fome
meafure, to account, for that learned writer's miftake.——A miftake I call it, though
it is more than probable that the venerable
monk of Girwy had fome holy reafons for
giving eafy faith to the fennachies of Ireland.

THERE is reafon to believe, with Dr.
Macpherfon, that the gofpel was firft preach-
ed in Britain by miffionaries from the Leffer
Afia. The great zeal of Polycarp, bifhop

of

of Smyrna, who fuffered martyrdom in the year 170, it is certain, induced him to fend apoftles to Gaul. His difpute with the fee of Rome, about the very momentous affair of Eafter, is well known, The zealous fchifmatic preferred the tradition of the Eaftern church to the authority of St. Peter's chair.——An ardent defire of propagating his doctrine, occafioned his fending miffionaries to the very extremity of the weft, and of courfe to Britain. The opinion of the Eaftern church concerning Eafter, which prevailed among the Picts and Scots, is a corroborating argument on this head. The fee of Rome found means to recover the Southern Britons to the Catholic opinion upon this important point; but the barbarians of the North were obftinately tenacious of the faith of their anceftors.

Bede made many efforts to fave the fouls of his Northern neighbours, by endeavouring to bring them back to the true faith concerning Eafter and the Tonfure. Naitan, the great monarch of the Picts, was at laft overcome by the arguments of Ceolfrid, and, together with his nation, received into his religion thefe two articles fo neceffary to falvation.——But the wicked and abandoned barbarians of Jar-ghael would not, it feems,

be

be perfuaded out of their error. From their obftinacy, no doubt, arofe thofe prejudices againft them, which are very confpicuous in the writings of the venerable Bede. Ireland at that time was defervedly called the *Country of Saints.* The Catholic faith prevailed there in all its original purity. The momentous articles of Eafter and the Tonfure were received with that devotion which ought to attend the decifions of St. Peter's chair. —— The venerable writer, fo often mentioned, regarded the Irifh with that partiality which good men have for the beft of Chriftians, and gave great faith to their traditions and records.

BEDE was a very extraordinary perfon for the times in which he lived : pious and fervent, but calm in his zeal for religion, his writings throughout breathe the fentiments of humanity and devotion. He certainly had more knowledge than all his cotemporaries joined together. But it appears to me, that he was neither critically inquifitive, or knew much of national antiquities. The good man was much better employed. Miracles, vifions, dreams, martyrologies, Eafter and the Tonfure, and, above all, St. Cuthbert and the fee of Rome, engaged his whole attention,

attention, and diverted his mind from a ftudy more amufing than important.

THE few fcraps of antiquity which is contained in the firft book of his ecclefiaftical hiftory, the venerable prefbyter borrowed from Gildas, or from his own religious cotemporaries of Ireland. Before I proceed to Gildas, it may not be improper to give one inftance of the great partiality of Bede to the Irifh. Egfrid, King of Northumberland, had been, in the year 685, with the greateft part of his army, cut off by the Picts. This, fays Bede, was a judgment from God, upon Egfrid and his fubjects, for committing the year before this fatal event, unheard of barbarities and ravages among the Hibernians, *a nation very harmlefs and innocent, and of a moft friendly difpofition towards the Englifh.*

BEDE, however, muft be blamed for his fervile copying after Gildas, a writer not worthy of fuch attention. Gildas was one of the moft paffionate, peevifh, and querulous of mankind. He not only was immoderately angry with the Scots * and Picts,

---

* *Exin Britannia,* fo he calls that part of the ifland which had been fubject to the Romans, *duabus gentibus tranfmarinis vehementer fævis, Scottorum a Circio, Pictorum ab aquilone, calcabilis multos ftupet, gemitque per annos.* Gild. cap. 15. Bede explains, that Gildas gave the epithet of *tranfmarini* to the Picts and Scots, becaufe they came from beyond the firths of Forth and Clyde. Bed. Hift. Eccles. lib. 1. cap. 12.

who

who perhaps deferved very ill at his hands, but even his friends the Britons, and, above all, he was enraged againft the Saxons. From an expreffion in this author, fome Englifh * and many Irifh antiquaries, to their great joy, thought they found an unanfwerable proof that the Scots came originally from Ireland; and that in no earlier period than the fixth century. Gildas, fpeaking of the Scots and Picts, fays, *Revertuntur ergo impudentes graffatores Hiberni domus, poft non multum temporis reverfuri.*

The epithet *impudentes* applied to *Hiberni* is not fufficient to eftablifh the juftnefs of this reading, though it might have fome weight with men of wit. Bede was far from entertaining fuch an unfavourable opinion of the inhabitants of the *holy ifle.* In an edition of Gildas, given to the public by Dr. Gale, the paffage under confideration, is read in a more grammatical way, and lefs to the difcredit of Ireland: *revertuntur ergo impudentes graffatores Hibernas domus;* fo that Gildas meant no more than that the Scots returned home for the winter.

To juftify this reading, it is to be obferved, that the ancient Scots and their pofte-

---

* Lhoyd and Stillingfleet.

rity

rity gave the name of *winter houses*, the same exactly with the *Hibernas domus* of Gildas, to those more comfortable habitations to which they retreated when the warmer season of the year was over. In the summer they lived in the mountains and forests with their cattle, and to enjoy the pleasure and advantage of hunting. The Arabian Bedowins, the ancient Nomades and Scythians, and the present Tartars, give into the same practice. The Bedowins, in particular, gave the appellation of *winter houses* to the habitations to which they retreated from the autumnal rains. Bede, a Saxon, was perhaps a stranger to this characteristical practice of the Scots, and not knowing what sense to make of Gildas's *Hibernas domus*, he altered the old reading. This opinion seems decisive, as he had retained the word *domus*, instead of the more proper word *domum*.

THE times in which Bede lived, were the golden age of Ireland. That kind of learning which then subsisted in the world, flourished much in that country. No enemies invaded it from abroad, and there was an unusual tranquillity at home. National prosperity is the source of national pride. Averse to have themselves thought descend-

ed

ed from the Scots of Albany, who were far
from being a powerful nation at that time,
they began to search out for themselves,
anceſtors of a more dignified character. It
is probable that the ſchiſmatic diſpoſition
of the Scots, about Eaſter and the Ton-
ſure, had its weight in inducing the Iriſh
to inveſtigate their origin among a leſs per-
verſe people.

THAT the Iriſh ſyſtems of antiquity
were formed after the holy ſcriptures were
known in that country, is beyond all doubt.
All their fictions on that head are ingrafted
upon names in the old teſtament. This
ſubject is diſcuſſed at large, in the Diſſertations now given to the public. I only mention it now to aſcertain that the fable of
the Hibernian extraction of the Scots of
Albany was formed at the ſame time. The
preſent identity of language, and the ſimilarity of cuſtoms and manners which prevailed among the Albanian and Hibernian
Scots of antient times, made it evident that
they were originally the ſame people ; ſo
it became neceſſary to be very particular in
the time and manner of their ſeparation.
The Iriſh fabricators of antiquities furniſh-
ed Bede with that account he gave of the
firſt ſettlement of the Scots in Jarghæl.

If

If the British Scots had any national traditions of their own, which contradicted the
holy antiquaries of Ireland, Bede, from a
pious aversion to heretics, totally rejected
them.

FROM what I have said, it appears, that
the Scots have been hitherto, unfortunate
in the writers of the ancient history of their
country. There has been great expence of
erudition on the subject, both by foreign
and domestic antiquaries. But the grand
desideratum, in the disquisitions of those
learned men, was a thorough knowledge of the old Caledonian language,
which goes now under the name of the
Galic tongue. Dr. Macpherson happily joined a critical knowledge, in that
language, to his great learning in other respects. Something therefore, more satis-
factory ought to be expected from him
than from those who have gone before
him, and were not possessed of the same
advantages.

BEFORE the Doctor had thoroughly examined his subject, he paid great deference
to the opinion of Tacitus, concerning the
Germanic extraction of the Caledonians.
The colour of hair and size of body, which
distinguished them from the Britons of the

South,

South, were not conclusive arguments. These circumstances might depend more upon food and the peculiar nature of the soil and climate, than upon a different origin. The manifest difference in those dialects of the Celtic, which the Scots of the mountains and the Welsh speak to this day, seems more to argue their remote separation from one another. Their living as separate states, from the earliest times, could not have effectuated such a change: otherwise we cannot account for the identity of the Irish and Galic tongues, especially as the nations who speak those languages were in no period of antiquity that can be assigned, subject to the same government.

THIS was one of the arguments that must have influenced the judgment of the author of the Dissertations in his first view of the subject. But this difference of language is easily accounted for. The little progress that navigation must have made in the North of Europe when Britain was first peopled, is a convincing argument, that the first migrations into this island, was from the nearest continent, which was the Belgic division of Gaul. These migrations certainly happened in the earliest stage of society. The subsistence of a colony of sa-

vages

vages arifes entirely from hunting : it therefore may be fuppofed that the Gauls found firft their way to the Northern extremity of Britain, in purfuit of their game. In proportion as the original colony advanced Northward, other emigrants from Gaul trod on their footfteps. Thus for a courfe of ages Gaul poured into Britain a fucceffion of colonies. The manners and language of the Gauls, in the mean time, fuffered material changes at home. The arts of civil life gradually arofe among them, and naturally introduced new ideas and new words into their language. It is to this advancing civilization of Gaul that we muft afcribe the difference between the Northern and Southern Britons. The latter imported with them the changed manners, and adulterated, though improved, language of the more modern Gauls : the former tenacioufly retained the unpolifhed cuftoms and original language of their anceftors.

IT would be as prefumptuous, as it would be idle, to hope for the warm attention of the public to difquifitions of this kind. There are, however, fome who, could they be culled out of the mafs of mankind, have more enlarged ideas ; fome that are as impartial with refpect to times, as they are with regard to countries and individuals. For thefe, and thefe only, the author of the Differtations wrote. Difregarding the inattention of the many, could he but fecure the approbation of the judicious few.

THESE would be the fentiments of the author, could he fpeak for himfelf: but, I am forry to fay, he is now infenfible of praife or reproof. His death prevented his putting the laft hand to this work. His fon, to whofe care he left it, with a diffidence which ought to be natural to a very young man, chofe rather to give his father's differtations to the world as they ftood, than to attempt any amendments, which perhaps might injure the memory of a parent he tenderly loved.

THE moft of the nations of the modern Europe look back with a blufh, upon the ftrange fabrics of fiction they poffefs for their ancient hiftory. They confider them as, at once, the monuments of the puerile credulity and folly of their anceftors. The Scots of this age faw with unconcern, if not with pleafure, forty of their ancient lift of Kings expunged at once by Innes. This furious regicide, endeavoured to make amends to his countrymen, by giving them forty

great

great Pictish monarchs for the long lift of
the petty Princes of Jarghael, of whom he
deprived them. The offer was rejected with
that fcorn it deferved ; and the monarchs
of Pictavia, whofe exiftence depended upon
the fame, or even worfe, if poffible, authority, than that upon which the fiction of
the firft forty Scottifh Kings was built, funk
away into their original non-entity.

IRELAND, tenacious as it has been of its
ancient annals, begins to regard lefs the
indigefted fictions of her fennachies. Men
of fenfe fee the impoffibility of tranfmitting
events, through a feries of ages, without the
affiftance of letters. They could not poffibly affign an earlier æra for the introduction of letters than the apoftlefhip of St.
Patrick, and confequently, with Ware they
depended very little upon the accounts
handed down concerning ages prior to the
reign of Leogaire.

In this untoward fituation of the Irifh antiquities, ftept forth O'Connor to fupport
the falling fabric. The zeal of this gentleman can only be equalled by his dogmatifm.
He has crouded the bottoms of his pages
with the authorities of O'Flaherty, Keating,
and Buchanan, who had as few lights to
guide them through antiquity, as a writer

of

of the prefent time can be fuppofed to poffefs? The two firft are only remarkable for their confufed manner of compiling the indigefted fables of bards and fileas; and the latter has fcarcely any thing to recommend him but the elegance of his diction.

In vain has Mr. O Connor endeavoured to eftablifh an aboriginal knowledge of letters in Ireland. Innes had previoufly deftroyed the credit of that fyftem, and Dr. Macpherfon has thrown it down for ever. From an additional differtation publifhed lately by Mr. O Connor, he feems to have been extremely gauled by fome obfervations made by the tranflator of the works of Offian on the ancient hiftory and poems of Ireland. If a judgment can be formed from O Connor's intemperate rage, he feels very fore on that fubject. His perfonal abufe of Mr. Macpherfon feems to have proceeded from a very irafcible difpofition, or was intended to draw an anfwer from that gentleman, which might give importance to his own work. In this, it is to be feared, he will not fucceed. The tranflator of the Galic poems is not much in the humour of doing an honour of that kind to adverfaries who ufe low fcurrility in the place of argument and difpaffionate difquifition.

DOCTOR

DOCTOR MACPHERSON, in the course of the following Differtations, has shewn how ill-founded the fenachies of Ireland have been, in their pretenfions to the Britifh Scots. Before we proceed to a further difcuffion of that fubject, it may not be improper to examine a new claim, from the fame quarter, on another martial nation, who poffeffed a part of Caledonia.——Marcellinus relates, that the Attacotti, a warlike race of men, in conjunction with the Picts and Scots, laid wafte the Roman province in Britain, in the reign of Valentinian. St. Jerome gives a very extraordinary character of the Attacotti : " In my youth," faith the faint, " I faw in Gaul, the Attacotti, a Britifh people, feeding upon human bodies. When they found in the woods hogs and flocks of fheep, or herds of cattle, they ufed to cut off the buttocks of the herdfmen and the breafts of the women, looking upon thofe parts of the body as the greateft danties*."

IT would be perhaps thought uncharitable, if not impious, to call the holy Father's veracity in queftion, efpecially as he appeals to occular demonftration : but I muft

---

* Quid loquar de cæteris nationibus, cum ipfe adolefcentulus, in Gallia viderim Scotos (*Attacottos, Catacottos, variæ enim funt lectiones*) gentem Britannicam, humanis vefci carnibus, & cum per fylvas porcorum greges & armentorum, pecudemque reperiant, paftorum nates & fœminarum papillas folere abfcindere, et has folas ciborum delicias arbitrari. Hieronym. adv. Jovin. Lib. ii.

obferve, that it is fomewhat ftrange that the Attacotti, notwithftanding of their barbarity, fhould have been Canibals, at a time they had hogs, fheep and cattle before them. The policy of the Romans muft have been extreamly relaxed in their province of Gaul, when the buttocks of their fubjeds were fo much expofed to the barbarous gluttony of the Attacotti.

But leaving this fad on the authority of Jerome, it appears certain that the Attacotti were a Britifh people. Buchanan and Cambden prove, from the Notitia, that fome of that nation were among the mercenary troops. of the empire in its decline. In what part of Caledonia the Attacotti were fettled is difficult to determine. Buchanan, with great probability, places them between the walls; and in that cafe they muft have been a powerful tribe of the Mæatæ of Dion.

Stillingfleet obferves, that the etymon of Attacotti has not hitherto been underftood. The Dodor adds, by way of fneer on the whimfical etymologifts of Britifh names from the Punic, that he doubts much whether it ever fhall, unlefs fome learned critic chufe to trace it to the Phœnician language†. A tolerable knowledge

---

† Origines Britan. p. 387.

of

of the ancient languages of Britain, will, I think, enable a person, unacquainted with the Phœnician, to decypher the meaning of this word. Attacotti literally signifies *The men of the woods‡*.

THE Irish not contented to deprive us, their poor posterity in Caledonia, of our bishops, abbots and historians, of any note, have also endeavoured to rob us of our barbarians and canibals. A late dissertator on the history of Ireland claims a right to the Attacotti in the name of his country. I wish I could give them to this ingenious gentleman; for, under the aspersion of Jerome, they will do very little honour to any country. To use O'Connor's own words, " The *Attacotti* were originally a Belgian nation, who occupied the Western parts of Ireland. They were a motly aggregate of rebels, who, in conjunction with some other Septs of the same race, in the other provinces, were called *Abachtuata*, for their cruelties. They took up arms against the government about ninety years before Christ,

---

‡ In the Welch language, the particle *at* is a preposition of the same import with the English *at* or *about*. In the same dialect of the Celtic, *koed* signifies *wood*; *kuit* does the same in the Cornish, *coat* in the Armorican, and *coile* in the Galic. Young brushwood, and the twigs of any wood, are to this day called *coid* in the Galic. Attacotti may also be derived from *attich*, inhabitants, and *coed*, of the woods. Those who live in more woody parts of a country are still distinguished in the Highlands of Scotland, by the appellation of the *dwellers of woods*.

overturned

overturned it effectually, and had very nigh buried the whole Scottish nation, together with its memory, in one common grave*."

How the Irish were employed, what they acted, and what they suffered, about a century before the commencement of the Christian æra, their own faithful annals can only tell; and few in number are those chosen persons who have access to these mysterious and secret records.   That the Attacotti were upon the point of destroying the whole Scottish name, when the excellent Moran most opportunely interposed, those select persons will perhaps only believe.

The Attacotti, in the fourth age, were a British people.   That they came first from Ireland still remains to be proved. The Scots indeed have been long ago said to have been transplanted into Britain from that quarter; and had those learned Hibernians, from whom Bede and Nennius derive their information, ever heard that the Caledonians, Mæatæ and Attacotti had been once considerable nations in North Britain, it is highly probable they would have given all of them the honour of an Irish original.   But their traditions did not extend so high as the fourth century, when those names fell into desuetude.   The

* Differt. on the ant. hift. of Irel. Introduction.

Picts, it is true, were permitted to be of a different extraction : but the Picts, it seems, were vassals of Ireland, and unworthy of being descended from their Heremonian Lords.

Usher, no doubt with some degree of pleasure, found that, in the printed copies of Jerome, the British canibals of the holy Father were the Scots† The Primate remarks, at the same time, that some manuscripts called them Attiscotti, Catitti, Cattacotti, and Attagotti : but Cambden conjectures, with reason, that those names ought to be read Attacotti, according to the orthography followed by Marcellinus. Should we give the preference to the reading which Usher found in print, there arises a proof that the Scots, contrary to his own position, were settled in Britain in the fourth age.   If we adopt the opinion of Cambden, the Irish cannot possibly have any right to the Attacotti.——That the Attacotti possessed the county of Galloway, is highly probable : from a passage in Marcellinus, we may naturally infer, that they were more connected with the Scots than with the Picts ; consequently, that they possessed a part of the western coast, rather than that of the German ocean‡.

† Brit. Ecclef. ant. p. 307, 308.
‡ Picti, Saxonesque, et Scotti & Attacotti Britannos ærumnis vexavere continuis. Ammian. Marcell. l. 26.

CONTENTS

CONTENTS.

DISSER,

DISSERTATION I.

The remote Antiquities of Nations either entirely fabulous, or full of Uncertainty.

IN an age fo accurate as the prefent, it affords matter of fome curiofity to obferve thofe marvellous fabrics of fiction, which bards and antiquaries have erected as monuments of the antiquity and illuftrious origin of their nations.

Livy has obferved, that this credulous vanity of ancient times merits our indulgence rather than cenfure. The degree in which this indulgence is beftowed, and the readinefs with which belief is given, depend on the various opinions, and different fituations of mankind.

In rude times, before the love of property takes fuch abfolute dominion of the heart, that all its romantic and generous views are excluded, the moft exaggerated tales, which reflect honour on the antiquity and illuftrious defcent of a nation, are attended to with rapture, and regarded as genuine hiftory.

A

However

However abſurd the credulity and romance of antiquity may appear to us, it is both ungenerous and unfair to turn them to ſevere ridicule, without firſt attending to our own wcakneſſes : on a compariſon of both, it may be difficult to determine who is the greateſt object of contempt ; the brave Barbarian, intoxicated with the bloody atchievements, and ideal antiquity of his nation, or the civilized ſceptic, refined into a diſbelief of every truth, and equally removed from the partialities and ſuperior virtues of the heart.

National pride, an attachment to the marvellous, and eaſineſs of aſſent, are the ſtrong characteriſtics of mankind in their illiterate ſtate. Hence it is, that, in their earlier periods, almoſt all the nations of the earth have ardently vied with each other, in the invention and belief of the moſt pompous and incredible tales, with regard to their origin and antiquity. A ſhort ſurvey of the antiquities of the moſt conſiderable nations of antient and later times, will eſtabliſh the truth of this obſervation.

To begin with the Romans, a people whom national dignity and ſuperiority have deſervedly placed at the head of mankind.—Lucretius, Virgil, Horace, and what is more ſurpriſing, Saluſt, Livy, Dionyſius Halicarnaſſus, and almoſt all the ſucceeding hiſtorians, hold forth with one voice that the Romans were deſcended from Æneas : but the connection between that people and the Phrygian demi-god was no more than a perfect chimera. Homer's authority, together with the convincing arguments of a writer of great erudition [a], have ſet this matter in the cleareſt light.

---

[a] See Bochart's Letter to Segrois.

Homer

Homer gives us a prediction of Neptune, in which we are plainly told, that as Priam's whole family were hated by Jove, Æneas himself and his lateft pofterity fhould reign over the Trojans [*b*]. " This teftimony of Neptune, fays Mr. Pope, " ought to be confidered as an authentic act, the " fidelity and verity of which cannot be queftion- " ed."——Notwithftanding the prophecy of the earth-fhaking God, and in direct oppofition to pro- bability and true hiftory, the Roman poets made their court to princes, fenators, and a powerful nation, by drawing out their Phrygian defcent in all the beautiful colours of their art. Even thofe writers, in whom it was unpardonable to give a hearing to the moft plaufible romance, could not but patronize a tale, which, as hiftorians, they fhould have defpifed ; but which, as Romans, they fondly believed.

Ir we go from Italy into Greece, we fhall find that the learned and polite nations of that country, had a confiderable fhare of the fame vanity. Ac- cording to the earlieft accounts of time with them, their great Princes and heroes were fons or grandfons of fome one divinity or other. An ori- ginal fo noble, became at length too eftimable a blefling to remain the property of a few. It was fit that whole communities fhould partake of its benefits ; therefore the Arcadians gave fcope to their ambition, and ferioufly afferted that their predeceffors were older than Jupiter, or what it feems they thought ftill more honourable, older than the moon herfelf. The Athenians feeing no good reafon why any part of creation fhould take precedency of them in point of antiquity, affirmed

----

[*b*] Hom. Iliad. xx. ver. 306.

 that

that their progenitors were co-eval with the fun. Thefe two nations were the *Aborigines* of Greece, and the latter affumed the name of *Autochthones*, a name which ftrongly characterizes their pride and ignorance.

O n fhifting the fcene to the other divifions of the old world, the fame ambitious folly, and the fame anility of belief prefent themfelves to our view.

Egypt was reputed the mother of wifdom, and the kingdom of fcience and knowledge : but whatever degree of wifdom and learning the Egyptians had, they had alfo weaknefs enough to entertain the moft extravagant notions concerning their own antiquity. They carried up the age of their empire to an immenfe height, and reckoned it their peculiar honour and felicity to have been governed by gods, for ages immemorial. Thefe gods, through time, became indolent, and fo cloyed with power, that they thought proper to refign the adminiftration of Egyptian affairs into the hands of mortal kings. The mortality of kings was fupplied by the regularity and perpetuity of fucceffion. Accordingly, we are told that between the commencement of their government and the reign of the laft prieft of Vulcan who fat on the Egyptian throne, a feries of no lefs than three hundred and forty-one generations had paffed away. This period of *mortal monarchs* was fo intimately known to the literati of Egypt, that they fpoke with confidence of every trivial occurrence that happened, and could afcertain the exact duration of every particular reign. The courfe of things had very happily adapted this laft branch of the hiftory to their remembrance ; for it was demonftrable that the number of their monarchs correfponded

correfponded precifely with the number of generations in which they reigned. A circumftance of
this furprifing uniformity, though fo oppofite to
the common inequalities of the natural courfe of
reigns, muft have afforded the higheft gratifica-
tion to the puerile and fuperftitious fancy of an
Egyptian.

HERODOTUS relates this curious hiftory very
circumftantially, and feems to have been no lefs
convinced of its verity than he was impreffed with
its awfulnefs and grandeur. The priefts of Memphis gave him the ftrongeft affurances that, agreeable to this faithful and exact calculation, the
Egyptian empire had lafted eleven thoufand three
hundred and forty years; and how was it poffible
for a hiftorian of his character to difbelieve a relation, however miraculous, which was folemnly
attefted by fuch unexceptionable men. The infallible fervants of Jupiter had conducted him into
a large hall, where he faw with his own eyes the
ftatues of all the Vulcanian high priefts, who had
been enumerated to him. Every one of thefe facred perfonages was introduced to him in the very
order in which they had filled the chair; and,
what is a little remarkable, every one of them
was the fon of his immediate predeceffor in the pontificate.

THESE were the fentiments which the Egyptians entertained and profeffed concerning their remote antiquities. The extravagance of this paffion,
inftead of fubfiding through a feries of ages, was
conftantly rapidly increafing, until the unfortunate
reign of *Pfammetichus.* That wife monarch, and
his equally wife fubjects, found themfelves under
a neceffity of acknowledging, that the Phrygians
had exifted before all other nations, and, of con-

A 3

fequence,

fequence, had a right to take place of them. Herodotus relates this ſtory in all its ſtriking circum-ſtances. The profound gravity with which he carries on the relation, and his ſerious appeal to the prieſts of Vulcan at Memphis, ſerve only to eſtabliſh the conſiſtency of this hiſtorian's character *.

TROGUS POMPEIUS, another famous hiſtorian, informs us, that the Scythians were thoroughly ſatisfied that they themſelves had much juſter pretenſions to antiquity than either the Egyptians or Phrygians. The philoſophical arguments with which theſe barbarians ſupported their claim to ſo ineſtimable a dignity, appear to have had conſiderable influence over the faith of Trogus; and to do them juſtice, they were neither leſs convincive nor more frivolous than thoſe on which *Pſammetichus* and *Herodotus* had relied ſo much, in the diſpute againſt the Phrygians †.

HOWEVER ridiculous the Egyptian and Phrygian ſyſtems of antiquities may appear, it muſt be allowed that none of them was more pregnant with abſurdity than that of the Babylonians. *Beroſus*, a celebrated Chaldæan prieſt, ſaw the propriety of putting the antiquity of his own nation on a ſure and reſpectable footing. Accordingly, he applied himſelf to accurate and unwearied enq iry. The reſult of his labours was ſuitable to his moſt ſanguine expectations; for he found that the Babylonians had made aſtronomical obſervations for a hundred and ſeventy thouſand years before Alexander the Great made himſelf maſter of Aſia. Of conſequence, the Chaldæan nation

---

muſt have exiſted for a ſpace of time equal at leaſt to that number of years; and what reaſonable perſon could think of reſiſting the power of ſuch a demonſtration * ?

I t may not be improper to return now into Europe, and inquire how far the Celtic nations were blinded by the pleaſing deluſions of fable, and overpowered with national prepoſſeſſion. Thoſe *Celtes,* of whom the moſt conſiderable nations of modern Europe are ſprung, were originally ſo un-connected with the other parts of the world in which the uſe of letters prevailed, that their hiſ-tory, and in a manner their being, is later in pro-portion. It was only after their intermixture with the poliſhed part of mankind, that their manners became ſettled, and their notions of antiquity diſtinct. Formerly they, like all men in a bar-barous ſtate, aſſociated in detached tribes, and wandered over the common field as chance or choice directed. In ſuch uncultivated and uncer-tain ſituations, a tale might amuſe for a ſeaſon, and the bard might occaſionally ſing; but the varieties of a migrating life could never allow the one to form into a tradition, nor permit the other to take any laſting hold of the memory. It is even a conſiderable time after a nation is formed that they think of looking back into antiquity by determinate ſteps. Ages and centuries are never the meaſures of time for the barbarian. He may be of opinion that his tribe is as old as any other, or may have originally deſcended from the ſun †, or ſprung ſpontaneouſly out of the ground, like

---

* Diod. Sicul. lib. ii.
† Charlevoix's Hiſt. of Indians.

the

the wood in which he purfues his game * ; but without the aid of records, he can never trace back the origin of his diftant predeceffor, nor, were he in the humour of fiction, can he have any idea of framing a legendary one. On thefe accounts it is fruitlefs, and indeed fuperfluous, to fearch after the ideas or fyftems which the old Celtic nations formed with regard to their remote origin and hiftory.

THESE natural obftructions to the refearches of a barbarous people, after a fplendid origin, did not at all difcourage the nations of Europe. Spain, in particular, claimed to herfelf an extraordinary proportion of antiquity and genealogical honour. Strabo informs us, that the *Turdetonians*, a nation of that country, could produce written monuments to fupport their claim, together with many celebrated poems and laws couched in verfe, all of fix thoufand years ftanding. Our author obferves, that thefe *Turdetonians* were the moft learned people in Spain ; and we may very fafely add, that they were beyond comparifon the moft antient people on earth, if Strabo's account of them be juft : but that judicious writer acknowledges that the high antiquity of the *Turdetonians*, and the genuinenefs of their records, reft entirely on the credit of their own teftimony. It is a pity that thefe hiftorical records, poems, and verfified laws, fhould, after fo long and fuccefsful a ftruggle with time, have in the end perifhed fo prematurely, that not the fmalleft veftige of them could be difcovered for thefe fifteen hundred years paft.

---

* Tacit. de Mor. Germ. cap. 1.

THOUGH

THOUGH the Turdetonian archives have funk in oblivion, time out of mind, yet the antiquities of Spain have been preferved in the works of authors truly antient, and have been publifhed from thefe by a new *Berofus*. This faithful and moft enlightened hiftorian found, by what he thought unqueftionable evidence, that Jubal, the fon of Japhet, and grandfon of Noah, ought to be placed at the head of the Spanifh royal line. He alfo afferts, that the right of this grandfon of the patriarch, to the empire of Celtiberia, was founded on a donation of his grandfather, when he divided the world among his pofterity.

I T is idle to take any further notice of the many curious anecdotes which this hiftorian, if he deferves that name, has extracted from fictitious records. But one cannot help being furprized how *Mariana*, one of the beft hiftorians of modern times, fhould have given into the abfurdity of this ill informed and credulous author. The very firft fentence of Mariana's hiftory acquaints us, that Jubal was undoubtedly the perfon who introduced its firft inhabitants into Spain. In the next fentence we are told, that all men of great learning and extenfive enquiry, were of this opinion. He proceeds then to inform us, that Jubal, after having fettled many colonies, and built populous cities, applied himfelf to the arts of government, and ruled over his extenfive empire with great moderation and juftice *.

FRANCIO, an imaginary Trojan prince, the fon of the celebrated Hector, was once thought the founder of the French empire. An origin derived from fo illuftrious a fource, could not fail to ele-

---

* Mariana, Lib. 1.

vate an airy and fantaſtic people into the utmoſt intemperance of national pride. But the French of later times ſeem little inclined to believe their *Phrygian* pedigree, nor are they ſo injudicious as to avail themſelves of a paſſage in *Ammianus Mar-cellinus*, which might favour a pretenſion of this kind.

THE old Germans had bards eſtabliſhed among them as far back as our authentic accounts of them reach. Theſe bards, upon the authority of rhimes, venerable on account of their antiquity, affirmed, that they had the honour of being deſcended from a God. The name of that God was *Tuiſco*; and ſo univerſal was the reverence paid to his memory, that every diſtinct nation of Germany adored him as their progenitor *.

LONG after letters and chriſtianity had been introduced among the Germans, the ſame genea-logical enthuſiaſm remained, though under a dif-ferent form. No ſooner had the deformities of the old ſyſtem begun to appear, than the Saxons, Frieſlanders, and Brunſwickers, had the good for-tune to diſcover that they were originally ſprung from three renowned generals who ſerved under Alexander the Great. It was thought abſolutely inconſiſtent with probability, that the Pruſſians, ſo celebrated for bravery, ſhould be the offspring of Celtic or Teutonic barbarians; accordingly an able antiquary reſcued their reputation, by tracing them up to Pruſſias, king of Bythynia.

BUT of all the inhabitants of the North of Europe, the Danes were certainly the moſt roman-tic in their pretenſions to a remote origin and au-thentic records. Denmark was firſt inhabited by

---

* Tacitus.

giants,

giants, fays the eloquent Saxo Grammaticus. Thefe giants were of matchlefs ftrength of body and vigour of mind. There were local demonftrations of the one, and traditional proofs of the other. *Dan* was the father of the Danifh nations, and *Argul*, his brother, gave being to the Englifh. Thefe two great perfonages flourifhed an innumerable feries of ages before the birth of Chrift.

If any one fhould afk, how the hiftory of *Dan*, and of his immediate pofterity were preferved, *Saxo* will fatisfy his curiofity on that head. Denmark, according to him, produced a fucceffion of excellent bards ; whofe bufinefs as well as amufement it was to record the actions of its kings and heroes, in all the fublimity of heroic compofition : but as the productions of bards, however happy, may be deftroyed or effaced by time, our author affures us, that the works of the Danifh poets were liable to no fuch inconvenience, as they were engraved upon folid rocks and obelifks of the moft durable nature. He even affirms, that he himfelf extracted thofe numerous hiftorical rhimes, which crowd his work, from thofe permanent monuments of antiquity.

A learned archbifhop has traced the kings of Sweden all the way up to Magog, a perfon whofe clofe connection with Noah fitted him highly for fo eminent a ftation.

The Englifh were once enthufiaftically fond of an ideal predeceffor, and of an imaginary fuperiority derived from him. Brutus, the fon of Silvius, the grandfon of Afcanius, and great grandfon of Æneas, was, to their great happinefs, reputed the parent and founder of their nation. Brutus, happily for England, had the misfortune to kill his father ; fo that he found it neceffary to leave Italy,

and

and make his way into Gaul. There he performed many signal exploits ; but did not think it convenient to purfue his fortune long in that country,
as he was directed by the oracle of Diana to vifit
this ifland. Here he met with a monftrous race of
giants, who gave him a very hoftile reception : but
their enormous ftrength of body, and the greatnefs of their numbers, ferved only as a field for
Brutus to difplay his great military talents ; for
though a few battles were at firft fought with various fuccefs, yet in the end Brutus not only overcame, but exterminated this gigantic race. After
acting fo long in a military and victorious capaci-
ty, Brutus refigned himfelf to the lefs laborious,
but equally important occupation of a ruler and
fovereign. The greatnefs of his abilities was then
no lefs difplayed in the arts of peace than in his
former conduct in the field. He reigned long
over the extenfive empire of Britain, and at length
clofed a glorious adminiftration, by dividing his
territories between his three fons. Thefe were *Locrinus, Camber,* and *Albanactus.* England devolved on *Locrinus,* being his eldeft fon ; Wales
was the patrimony of *Camber,* and Scotland fell
to the fhare of *Albanactus.*

EVEN this tale had the good fortune to pleafe
an once credulous people. The Englifh of the
thirteenth and fourteenth centuries embraced it
with an enthufiafm peculiar to the romantic fpirit
of thofe times. Edward the firft claimed a fuperiority over Scotland, on account of his more
direct connection with Brutus. Accordingly, in
the heat of thofe difputes which enfued on the
death of Alexander the third of Scotland, Edward's agents urged ftrenuoufly before the Pope,
that in confequence of the divifion which Brutus
made

made of his dominions, Scotland was from the beginning, and of confequence fhould remain, a fief of England.

THE ftory of Brutus was far from wanting learned authority to fupport its credit. Geoffrey of Monmouth gave it all the aid which profound erudition and the warmeft zeal could beftow. He affirms, that he found it fully demonftrated, by the joint teftimony of old Britifh annals ; and it cannot be denied but an effential part of the ftory is found in Nennius, who wrote his *Eulogium Britanniæ* in the ninth century, about three hundred years before Geoffrey's time.

SELDEN has made fome attempts to defend the tale of Brutus ; and Cambden owns ingenuoufly that he himfelf had frequently ftrained his invention to the utmoft, in order to juftify the moft fufpicious parts, and reconcile the contradictions of this ftory : after all, he could not perfuade himfelf to believe it ; and it may be juftly prefumed, that all the Englifh antiquaries of the prefent and of fucceeding times will explode it for ever.

IT is now high time to examine the pretenfions which the Scots have to a remote antiquity : and after the foolifh appearance which the ancient legends of the greateft nations of the world have made, it cannot, without a miracle, be expected, that they alone fhould be well informed of their genuine origin, or free of national credulity. They had no doubt an equal claim with other nations to a renowned anceftry, and as remote an origin. A mountainous country, like Scotland, bids indeed the faireft for inhabitants of great antiquity. A plain and fertile country is always fubject to the inroads of their neighbours,

bours, and therefore often change their masters. The sterility of rocks, forests, and desarts, are far from being inviting to an enemy ; at the same time that their inaccessiblenefs enables the natives easily to repel invasions ——The Scots therefore had no cause to yield, in point of antiquity, to any other nation. If tradition had failed in handing down the particular æra and manner of their first settlement, they were ingenious to invent, and partial enough to give credit to a noble and fictitious origin. Accordingly, the procurators fent by the states of Scotland, to plead their cause against King Edward, before the court of Rome, contended strenuously, that the Scots were defcended from *Scota*, the daughter of Pharaoh King of Egypt.——That this Scota came into Scotland, together with her fon Erc, whom she had by Gathelus. That Argadia, or rather *Jar-ghael* *, derived its name from the progeny of that fon and father. In fine, That the old name of *Albania* was changed into that of *Scotia*, as foon as the Scots were fettled in that ifland ; and the Scots did ever fince that period retain their name and independence, while the Britons of the fouthern divifion changed their name and mafters frequently. This is in fubftance the genealogical account of their nation, which the states of Scotland transmitted by their agents to Pope *Boniface* the eighth, in the end of the thirteenth age.

ALMOST all the records and historical monuments of the Scots history have been destroyed

---

* Jar-ghael is that divifion of the Weftern Highlands which is partly comprehended within the county of Argyle. It plainly fignifies the Weftern Caledonians, in contradiflinction to the Picts or Caledonians who poffeffed the Eaft coaft of Scotland. *Jar*, Weft—*Gael* or *Gael*, *Celtes.*

through the barbarous policy of Edward Ift. of England of the Norman race, and the intemperate zeal of the Reformers. A few detached pieces, which have efcaped thofe revolutions, fatal to the antiquities of the nation, have been preferved by the induftrious Father Innes *. They throw little light on the genuine antiquities of Scotland, and ferve only to reconcile us more to the deftruction of thofe annals of which they are thought to be a part. The principal thing in which they agree, is, that Fergus, the fon of *Erc*, was the firft King of Scotland. One of thefe pieces, called the Chronicle, in rhime, fays, that the Scots came from Egypt into Spain, in the time of Mofes ; that of him fprung *Milo* King of Spain, whofe fon *Simon Bree* fettled in Ireland.—That fome of the pofterity of this Simon tranfmigrated from Ireland into Ergadia, about 443 years before Chrift ; and that the Scots lived there, in a moft uncultivated ftate, till Fergus, the fon of Erc, brought thither the *fatal marble chair* from Ireland, and begun his glorious reign. Another of thofe pieces fays, that the Scots came into Ireland, from Scythia, in the fourth age of the world ; that they and the Picts had one common origin ; and that thofe two nations were defcended from the Albanians †.

The Irifh, if we believe their antiquaries, are not inferior to either the Egyptians or Turdetonians, in the prefervation of the moft antient and minute events in their country, or in their claim to remote antiquity. The antient hiftory of Ireland is indeed fo characteriftical of the romantic extra-

---

* See his Appendix to his Critical Effay on the Scottifh Antiquities.

† Critical Effay, p. 774.

vagance

vagance of dark ages, and at the fame time fo connected with our fubject, that the pretended antiquities of that nation muft be indulged with a feparate difcuffion.

After the furvey which we have already made, it muft be fairly acknowledged, that the very remote hiftory of all nations is totally dif-figured with fable, and gives but little encourage-ment to diftant inquiry. At the fame time, it is to be regretted, how much of the early hiftory and antiquities of nations are loft, and how in-diftinctly fociety is feen in its rudeft form. The tranfactions of mankind, in the firft ages of fo-ciety, rife from the affections of the heart; of con-fequence, a knowlege of them would be highly interefting, and afford amufement, and even in-ftruction, in thefe polifhed times.

Though no nation in Europe has excelled the Britifh in other branches of literature, yet we muft acknowlege their deficiency in writing of hiftory. Our antient hiftorians, from the unfavourable times in which they lived, were ignorant, and full of prejudice. The few men of abilities who wrote of late years, haftening to thofe great events which croud the latter part of our annals, have left our antient hiftory in the fame obfcurity in which they found it: looking with too much con-tempt on the origin of focieties, they have either without examination, adopted the traditional tales of their predeceffors,, or altogether exploded them, without any difquifition. A writer of the greateft merit, who has lately favoured the world with an interefting part of the Scots hiftory, has likewife fallen into this error. He, with great gravity, be-gins his work with the migration of the Scots

from

from Ireland : a fiction in itself improbable, however venerable on account of its antiquity.

It were much to be wished, a writer of his abilities, both for elegance of diction and strength of judgment, had not been an absolute stranger to the original language of his country ; which would at least have prevented him from giving his authority to so idle a romance. The discussion of this popular error, which I am to give in the sequel of these dissertations, will justify these strictures on so eminent a historian as Dr. Robertson.

DISSER

DISSERTATION II.

General Obſervations on the firſt Migrations of Aſiatic Colonies into Europe.--
The Gauls the Progenitors of the ancient Britiſh.--Of the Caledonians.--The
Etymon of their Name.

IT was the opinion of the ancient poets and
philoſophers, that mankind and other animals
ſprung, like vegetables, out of the earth. Abſurd as a fiction of this kind may now appear,
it was believed by writers, who, on other occaſions, diſplayed an uncommon ſtrength of under-
ſtanding. Tacitus ſuppoſes that the firſt inhabitants of Britain * and Germany † were produced in this extraordinary way. The total ignorance of their own origin, which prevailed a-
mong them in the time of this celebrated hiſtorian, made him draw a concluſion, which requires no other refutation than expoſing it to public view.

Be this as it will, we learn, from the concur-
rent teſtimony of ſacred and profane hiſtory, that
Aſia was the firſt diviſion of the world that was

------

* Tacit. in vita Agric. c. 11.   † De Mor. Germ. c. 1.

peopled :

peopled : of courfe all the national migrations that have come to our knowledge move progreffively from Eaft to Weft. The northern parts of Europe, which of old went under the general name of Scandinavia, appear to me to have been as foon at leaft poffeffed by an Afiatic colony, as ancient Gaul, Italy, or Spain. Man, in a ftate of nature, was not capable to tranfport himfelf even acrofs the narrow firth of the Hellefpont. But as hunting has always been found to be the amufement, as well as fupport of barbarous life, we may conclude that the firft colonies of Scandinavia came gradually from the northern Afia in purfuit of their game. In the winter feafon, when the froft renders all the great rivers and fwamps of Ruffia and Poland paffable, thofe migrations might eafily have happened.

NAVIGATION, though a very early invention, is long before it arrives at that degree of maturity which is neceffary to give confidence to mankind to crofs an arm of the fea. We may therefore conclude that Scandinavia was in fome meafure peopled before thofe countries which border upon the Mediterranean. It is from this confideration we muft deduce the great difference we find between the Celtes of Gaul and the northern nations. Their manners and their language were in fome manner fimilar, and makes room for a conjecture that they were originally defcended from the fame ftock, though perhaps feparate nations before they left Afia.

THE firft race of Afiatics, in the progrefs of their migrations, were naturally feparated by the Cafpian Sea ; fome directing their courfe to Tartary, and others to Afia Minor. Of the Tartar race are defcended the Scandinavians, under which

name

name I comprehend the Danes, Swedes, weſtern Ruſſians, and Poles : the Celtes of Gaul, Italy, and Spain, were a colony from the leſſer Aſia. The Celtes extending themſelves to the North, and the Scandinavians moving towards the South, after, perhaps, a ſeries of ages, met on the confines of the modern Germany. The great diſtance of time from their ſeparation in Aſia, effected ſuch a change in their manners, language and cuſtoms, that their common origin was totally obliterated from their memory, and continual wars and animoſities ſubſiſted between them. This naturally occaſioned encroachments upon one another's territories, and that unavoidable mixture of people, which generally happens upon the frontiers of warlike nations, whoſe boundaries are often changed by the viciſſitudes of war. From this circumſtance proceed the mixed manners and language, and perhaps the very name of the Germans *.

THE Celtes of Gaul were, without doubt, the progenitors of the firſt inhabitants of Britain. The vicinity of the two countries, in a caſe of this kind, is a concluſive argument. At this diſtance it is impoſſible to form any conjecture concerning the time in which the firſt migration of the Gauls into Britain happened. It is equally impoſſible to find out by what national appellation they went at their firſt ſettlement in this iſland. Whether the firſt inhabitants of the northern diviſion of Britain were deſcended of the *Gauliſh* colony of the South, or came from the North of Germany, will fall to be diſcuſſed hereafter. I ſhall in this diſſertation confine myſelf to the Caledonians as

---

* *Allemans,* the ancient name of the Germans, obviouſly ſignifies a compoſition of different nations.

we

we find them in Britain, when their wars with the Romans made them objects of attention to the writers of Rome.

THE Caledonians were the moſt powerful, and, to ſpeak with Galgacus, the moſt noble of all the nations that were of old ſettled in that diviſion of Britain, which has ſince obtained the name of Scotland. By the joint conſent of all the writers who give us any account of them, the Caledonians were reckoned the *Aborigines* of that country. Lucan * is the firſt writer that mentions them, but he had but a very imperfect idea of what part of Britain they poſſeſſed. He places them in the neighbourhood of the *Rutupian ſhore*, near Sandwich, or ſome other part of the coaſt of Kent. Even Pliny and Florus, whoſe intelligence concerning the ſeats of the Caledonians, ought to be more preciſe, than any poetical deſcription given by Lucan, are far from being diſtinct on that head. Tacitus is the firſt of the hiſtorians of Rome that has aſſigned its proper place to Caledonia.

FROM the united teſtimonies of Tacitus †, Dio and Solinus ‡, we find, that the ancient Caledonia comprehended all that country to the north of the firths of Forth and Clyde. The *Mæatæ* ‖, whom ſome have reckoned a branch of the Caledonians, poſſeſſed all that tract of land which

---

* Luc. Phar. l. iii. v. 67, 68.   † Tacit. Vita Agric. c. 25.
‡ Solin. Polyph. c. 35.
‖ *Mæatæ* is probably derived from two Galic words *Moi*, plain, and *aitich*, inhabitants ; or as an ingenious friend of mine obſerved, from *mæan*, middle, and *aitich*, inhabitants ; alluding to their ſituation between the conquered Britons and the independant Caledonians.

inter-

intervened between Adrian's wall and the frontiers of Caledonia, properly fo called. It is not
now my bufinefs to enter into what has come to
our knowledge of the military hiftory of the Caledonians. The Roman writers who have given
us an account of them are in the hands of every
body. I fhall confine myfelf entirely to fome cri-
tical-remarks on the etymon of their name, as
this differtation is only intended to clear the ground
for an hypothefis, which I flatter myfelf fhall be
eftablifhed in the fequel of this work.

ANTIQUARIES are much divided about the
etymology of Caledonia. Buchanan *, though a
native of the Highlands, and of courfe converfant
with the Galic language, is not happy in his conjectures on that fubject. *Calden,* according to him,
fignifies a hazel tree. From thence proceeds the
famous Caledonian foreft, and the name of Caledonia. It is amazing to obferve how a man of his
learning, and great abilities, could give in to fuch
a puerile conceit. But had Buchanan confidered
properly his native tongue, he would have found
that *Caultin,* and not *Calden,* fignifies a hazel
tree ; and that there is no fuch a word as *Calden*
to be met with in the Galic language.

DR. LLOYD, bifhop of St. Afaph, derives Caledonia from *Cilydion,* a Britifh word, fignifying
borderers. The Caledonians, fays that learned
prelate, bordered on the Roman province in Britain, and therefore were with great propriety called *borderers.* The bifhop did not confider that
the boundaries of the province were often changed.
If we fuppofe the wall conftructed by Adrian,

---

* Buch. Hift. l. 2.

marked

marked out the limits of the Roman empire in Britain, then the *Brigantes, Ottadini* and *Mæatæ*, had a much better title to the name of *borderers* than the Caledonians. If the wall built by Antoninus Pius is to be looked upon as the boundary of the province, then it naturally fhould follow, that the Caledonians did not acquire the name of *Cilydion*, or *borderers*, till after the conftruction of that wall. But the paffage mentioned from Lucan proves, that the name of Caledonians made fome noife in the world as early as the reign of Nero. Thus the bifhop's etymon of Caledonia falls to the ground.

Camden, one of the beft antiquaries that the world ever produced, has endeavoured to give the etymon of Caledonia. *Kaled*, obferves that learned writer, is a Britifh word, which fignifies *hard*. In the plural number it makes *Kaledion*, and hence proceeds *Caledonii*, that is, a people, *hardy, rough, uncivilized*, as northern nations generally are: a people fierce in their temper, from the extreme coldnefs of their climate; a people bold, forward, and intrepid, from the abundance of their blood.

The feverity of this obfervation on the national character of the Caledonians does not at all favour the etymon produced by Camden. If the name of *Kaledion* was firft framed by the Britons of the fouth, it may be juftly queftioned, whether they themfelves, before the reign of Nero, were lefs *hard, rough*, and *uncivilized*, than their neighbours of the north, or of courfe lefs intitled to that name. But as every thing that falls from fo juftly celebrated a writer, makes a great impreffion: I confefs this etymon had fuch weight with me, that I long confidered the word *Kaled*

as

as the root of *Caledonii,* This led me further into the subject; and I submit to the world, with great deference to the great merit of Camden, the additional obfervations I have made.

KALED †, in both the antient Britifh and Galic languages, fignifies *hard.* In both thefe languages *in,* or *yn,* fignifies *a country.* From the monofyllable *in* comes the diminutive *innis,* which in the Welfh and Galic is of the fame import with the Englifh word *ifland.* By joining *Kaled* and *in* together, we have *Caledin, a rough and mountainous country*; which is exactly the fignification of *Alba* *, the only name by which the Highlanders diftinguifh Scotland to this day.—This etymon of Caledonia is at leaft plaufible : but I muft confefs that the derivation given by Mr. Macpherfon, the tranflator of the poems of Offian, is more fimple and natural.

The Highlanders, as he juftly obferves, call themfelves *Cael.* That divifion of Scotland which they poffefs they univerfally call *Caeldoch,* that is to fay, the country of the *Cael* or *Celtes.* The Romans, by a tranfpofition of the letter *l,* in *Cael,* and changing the harfh *ch* of *doch,* into an har-

---

† See Bullet's Memoires fur la lang. Celt. under the word *Kaled.*

* That this is the proper fignification of *Alba,* fhall be fhewn in the fequel of thefe differtations. If the etymon given here of Caledonia fhould appear a juft one, I fhall make no difficulty in fuppofing that the Calydonia of Greece is derived from the fame Celtic fource. Ætolia, of which the Græcian Calydonia was a part, was a very mountainous country. Three mountains in particular there, Taphiofus, Chalcis, and Corax, were, according to Strabo, immenfely high. The face of the country was very rugged, and the inhabitants hardy. Homer gives the characteriftical epithet of *rocky* to Calydon, the capital of that country. Hom. Iliad. xi. ver. 640.

monious

monious termination, formed the name of *Cale-donia*. From this etymon arifes an obfervation, of which we fhall make ufe in the fequel of thefe differtations.

DURING the invafions of the Romans, we find many other tribes, befides the *Caledonians* and *Mæatæ*, in the north of Britain; though probably they were no more than fubdivifions of thofe two illuftrious nations. Every one of thofe tribes were governed by an independent chief, or petty King. In Cæfar's time there were no lefs than four fuch chieftains in Kent, and each of them vefted with regal authority. The political government of Caledonia was, in Domitian's reign, much the fame with that of Kent during Cæfar's proconfulfhip.

WHEN the tribes of North Britain were attacked by the Romans, they entered into affociations, that by uniting their ftrength, they might be the more able to repel the common enemy. The particular name of that tribe, which either its fuperior power or military reputation placed at the head of the affociation, was the general name given by the Romans to all the confederates.

HENCE it is, that the Mæatæ and Caledonians have ingroffed all the glory which belonged in common, though in an inferior degree, to all the other nations fettled of old in North Britain. It was for the fame reafon that the name of *Mæatæ*, was entirely forgotten by foreign writers after the third century, and that of the Caledonians themfelves but feldom mentioned after the fourth.

THE *Mæatæ*, we have already obferved, were one of thofe tribes who were fettled to the fouth of the Clyd and the Forth. Ptolemy places the *Gadeni*, *Salgovæ*, *Novantes*, and *Damnii*, in the fame
divifion

divifion of the country *. To the north of the Firths the fame writer affigns their refpective places to the *Caledonii, Epidii, Carini, Cantæ, Logæ*, and feveral other fmall tribes. Without infifting upon the probability that Ptolemy, an Egyptian, was not fo minutely acquainted with the internal ftate of Britain as he pretends, at a time when the north of Europe was fo little known to men of letters, we fhall take it for granted, that all thofe nations he mentions were of the fame original ftock ; and to avoid confufion, I fhall, for the future, comprehend them all under the general name of Caledonians.

TACITUS divides the inhabitants of Britain into three claffes ; the Caledonians, *Silures*, and thofe who inhabited the coaft next to Gaul. He endeavours to trace thofe three nations to others on the continent, from whom he fuppofed they had derived their origin. The Caledonians he concludes, from the fize of their bodies, and the colour of their hair, were of a Germanic extraction. Though it muft be confeffed that this conclufion is far from being decifive, from thofe two circumftances ; yet there are many collateral arguments which corroborate the opinion of that great hiftorian. Thefe, in fome future differtation, I may throw together, and leave the whole to the judgment of the public.

⁎ This the author has done, in a differtation, intitled, A parallel between the Caledonians and Ancient Germans, which is printed in this work.

---

* Ptolem. lib iii. c. 10.

DISSERTATION III.

Of the Picts.---That they were the Posterity of the Caledonians.

VIRGIL's obſervation, that Italy often changed its name, is equally applicable to the reſt of the kingdoms of Europe. That migrating diſpoſition which poſſeſſed mankind in their barbarous ſtate, occaſioned, of old, ſuch revolutions and intermixture of nations, that no appellation of any country was permanent.

BRITAINS, Caledonians, Mæatæ, Barbarians, and unconquered nations, are the names conſtantly given to the old inhabitants of North Britain, by Tacitus, Herodian, Dio, Spartian, Vopiſcus, and other antient writers. The ſucceſſors of theſe Britains, Caledonians, Mæats, and Barbarians, are called Picts, Scots, and Attacots, by ſome Roman writers of the fourth century. The cauſe of this change of names is, at this diſtance of time, little underſtood. Some Engliſh antiquaries affirm, that the old Caledonians were gradually exhauſted in their wars with the Romans: that ſome foreign colonies occupied their almoſt depopulated country: and that theſe foreigners either aſſumed or received the name of Picts. If curioſity ſhould lead us to inquire from what quarter of the world theſe foreigners,

reigners came; Bi&shop Stillingfleet has already
affirmed, that the *Cher&sone&sus Cimbrica*, a part of
the modern Denmark, was their original country.
He has al&so told us, that they &settled fir&st in Caledonia about the middle, or rather near the end of
the third century.

THE que&stion now is, whether this &sy&stem is well
founded, or whether we have better rea&son to believe that the Pi&cts were the real off&spring of the
old Caledonians ?

BEFORE this que&stion can be fairly re&solved, it
will be proper to review the hi&story of North Britain, from the death of Severus to the reign of
Con&stantius. Several eminent antiquaries &say, that
it was under the reign of this emperor the Pi&cts,
Scots, and Attacots, began to make any con&side-
rable figure in this i&sland.

SOON after the death of Severus, Antoninus Caracalla, his &son, entered into a negotiation with
the Barbarians of Britain, and gave them peace
upon receiving ho&stages. This, in &sub&stance, is
the account given by Herodian, of the manner in
which Antoninus put a period to the Caledonian
war. He has not explained the conditions of the
peace. But as he &says, that Severus, oppre&ssed
with age, cares, and an inveterate di&stemper, had
not been able to fini&sh the war, and that his &son,
on whom the command of the army employed in
North Britain had devolved, was little &solicitous
about the further pro&secution or &succe&ss of that war,
it may be taken for granted, that the Caledonians
were far from being exhau&sted when the peace was
ratified.

IF we chu&se to follow Dio's account of this war,
we can hardly believe that the Caledonians &su&stained
any con&siderable lo&sses either before or after the

death

death of Severus. If it be true that Severus deprived the Caledonians or their allies of their arms, and some portion of their territories, it is no less so, that the Caledonians and Mæats took up arms with one accord, upon receiving the news of the emperor's indisposition.

After his death, Caracalla and Geta, his two sons, agreed in giving them peace upon very honourable and advantageous terms. This peace was ignominious to the empire in every article, excepting that relating to the hostages. For the two brothers resigned to the Barbarians all the advantages for which Severus and his predecessors had been so eagerly contending.

The affairs of North Britain were totally neglected for a long time after Antoninus and Geta had quitted this island. The empire was torn in pieces by tyrants; and those who assumed the purple wanted leisure, inclination, or spirit, to make any new attempts on Caledonia. The ablest men among them, Aurelian, Probus, and Diocletian, were too much employed elsewhere to execute such a design.

It is true, Carausius usurped the sovereignty of South Britain in that period: but it may be doubted whether he repaired the old Roman wall which stood between Clyde and the Forth; whether he fortified that wall with seven castles; whether he built that ancient edifice vulgarly called Arthur's oven, on the bank of the river Carron; or whether he erected a triumphal arch in the neighbourhood of that river, to perpetuate the memory of a signal victory which he had obtained over the Barbarians of North Britain. All these notable actions, together with the etymon given of

Carron †,

Carron †, reſt entirely on the authority of the fabulous Nennius ; or upon the credit of his equally fabulous interpolator.

After Carauſius and Alleɛ̄us, his ſucceſſor in the uſurpation, were ſlain, Conſtantius Chlorus, on whom Britain, together with the other Weſtern provinces of the empire, had devolved, upon the abdication of Diocletian and Maximian, came into this iſland. This Emperor formed a reſolution of ſubduing the Caledonians, though he had other affairs of much greater importance to mind ; but he died at York before he had time to carry his deſign into execution.

Constantine, who commonly goes under the name of Great, ſucceeded his father Conſtantius in the imperial dignity, and aſſumed the purple in Britain. But being, as it is natural to ſuppoſe, impatient to take poſſeſſion of the capital, it is certain that he loſt no time to acquire either new territories or laurels in Caledonia. The idle panegyrics of Eccleſiaſtics are the only authorities we have for ſuppoſing that he did either the one or the other in the beginning of his reign ; nor did he ever, after putting a period to the civil war, return into Britain.

The province of Britain fell, upon the death of Chlorus, to his ſon Conſtantine ; and it is certain that the Caledonians were neither exhauſted nor even moleſted by Roman legions under his ſhort

---

† To ſuppoſe that Carron comes from Carauſius is a very puerile conceit, though probably the only foundation of the curious anecdotes related by Nennius. The name of that river is a Galic one ; which ſignifies a *winding river*. Accordingly we find ſeveral Carrons in North Britain ; and one of them in the Weſtern diſtriɛ̄ of Roſsſhire, where Carauſius confeſſedly never was.

reign.

reign. His ambition infpired him with very different views. He made war on his brother Conftans, at no great diftance from the feat of the Roman empire, and was flain by his generals in battle near Aquileia *. This event fubjected Britain to Conftans; and it is allowed that he, accompanied by his brother Conftantius, came in perfon to vifit his new territories. But it does not appear that either of the brothers did penetrate as far as Caledonia. Two declamatory writers of that age, who fpeak of this expedition in a very high tone †, feem to refolve the glory of it into the victory obtained by Conftans and Conftantius over the Britifh ocean, during the winter feafon : a feat which, according to the opinion of one of thefe authors, was never performed before, nor ever to be performed afterwards.

CONSTANS was murdered in Spain, after a reign of feventeen years, by the party of Magnentius, who affumed the purple in Gaul, and drew over Britain to his fide. It is not probable that ever this ufurper had any difputes with the Caledonians. Conftantius made war upon him without any intermiffion, during the whole courfe of his fhort reign, and brought him at laft, after the lofs of feveral battles, to the neceffity of laying violent hands upon himfelf. Upon the death of Magnentius, Britain, together with all the other rebellious provinces of the empire, fubmitted to Conftantius.

FROM this review of the hiftory of Rome, in fo far as it is connected with that of North Britain, from the death of Severus to Conftantius, feveral

---

* Eutrcp. l. x.
† Livan. in Bas. Julius Firm. de error. profan. &c.

queftions

queſtions will naturally reſult. In what Emperor's reign were the Caledonians ſo exhauſted or degenerated to ſuch a degree as to yield up their country, their freedom, and their reputation, to a colony, or even an army of Scandinavian rovers ? In what period of time happened thoſe devaſtations by which they were exhauſted ? Were they either annihilated or reduced to a ſtate of incurable debility by Severus, or by his ſons Caracalla and Geta ? Did Macrinus, Heliogabalus, Alexander, or Maximinus, did any of the ſucceeding Emperors or thirty tyrants overcome them ?

As therefore there is no ground for ſuppoſing that the Caledonians were annihilated or even much weakened by the legions, generals and Emperors of Rome, it is far from being credible that an army ſufficient to overcome or extirpate them, could be tranſported from the Cimbrica Cherſoneſus, in the third century. Every body knows what little progreſs navigation had made at that time in the North of Europe. A few long boats, which were the only craft the Scandinavians could be ſuppoſed to have, were very inadequate for the purpoſe of carrying armies acroſs the German ocean.

The improbability of a great migration of this kind, at that period, is ſtrengthened by the ſilence of antient writers of credit on that head. It is therefore too precipitate in any modern antiquary, to give his authority to a fiction, ſo contrary to all the ideas we can form of the ſtate of the North of Europe, in thoſe times. The opinion of Camden, the moſt learned as well as moſt candid of the antiquaries of England, is deciſive on this ſubject. After mature conſideration of this new ſyſtem of Humphrey Lhud, he was far from believing that

the

the Picts were an upstart nation, or a colony of foreigners first settled in Britain in the course of the third century. Cambden's opinion was, that the Caledonians, so far from being extirpated by the Romans, or any other enemy, had multiplied to such a degree, that their own country became too narrow for them : and it is to this cause he attributes, chiefly, the frequent incursions they made into the Roman province *.

---

* Cambden's Brit.

C   DISSER-

DISSERTATION IV.

Of the Pictish Monarchy.

THE countries, of which the greatest monarchies in Europe are now compofed, were antiently divided into feveral fmall dynafties and petty republics. Men, whofe fuperior ftrength of body or mind raifed them, on fignal occafions, to the head of the community, were firft dignified with the pompous title of royalty. Their authority and power were originally, however, confined within limits extremely circumfcribed. Abfolute government is never eftablifhed in the firft ftages of fociety. It is after a feries of ages that the paffions of the human mind are fufficiently mellowed down to fubmit calmly to the dictates of defpotifm, and to wait with patience the tedious operations of an extenfive government.

MANKIND, in their uncultivated ftate, though averfe to that tyranny which fometimes attends monarchy, were incapable of any other form of government. A republican fyftem is too philofophical for the favage to comprehend it properly. I might have faid, though the obfervation is far from being favourable to the dignity of human nature, that it is too noble for even civilized communities long to preferve it among them. I fhall

not

not therefore hesitate to pronounce, that monarchy is the moſt natural government for mankind.— We accordingly learn, from the moſt antient accounts we have of every nation, in their earlieſt ſtate, that monarchy was univerſally eſtabliſhed among them.

We find, from Homer, that antient Greece was divided into an immenſe number of petty dynaſties. The ſame kind of government prevailed of old, in Gaul, Italy, Spain, and Germany. Britain, at the time of Cæſar's invaſion, was governed by a number of little independent Princes ; and from the accounts given of Caledonia by Tacitus, Dio, and Ptolemy, we may conclude with certainty, that it was compoſed of many ſmall ſtates, unconnected with one another, and without any one bond of union, excepting that which aroſe from their common danger.

Galgacus and Argetecoxus are the only Caledonian Princes expreſly mentioned in hiſtory. The firſt was no more than the Generaliſſimo of a powerful confederacy, though ſuperior in birth and renown to the other Caledonian Princes who fought againſt Agricola. The ſecond was little more than a petty King or Chieftain * ; for the ſpirited reply made by his wife to the Empreſs Julia ſeems to be the only thing that has preſerved his memory from oblivion.

To aſcertain that all the inhabitants or territories of Caledonia were governed by one monarch, in any one period of time before the beginning of the ninth century, is extremely difficult, if not abſolutely impoſſible. And if it were true that the Picts were a great people before the Scots were

---

* Xiphil. in Severo.

                                        ſettled

settled in Britain, it is far from being certain that those Picts were governed by general monarchs in any early period.

ADAMNAN, abbot of Iona, is the first that mentions any Pictish King, and the oldest author after him is Bede. We are told by these two writers, that St. Columba converted Brudius, King of the Picts, to the Christian faith; and we learn further from Bede, that Brudius was a most powerful prince, and that Columba came into Britain in the year of the vulgar æra five hundred and sixty-five. If there were any Pictish Kings before that period, Pictish Kings possessed of extensive dominions, or monarchs of Caledonia, we have no genuine record to ascertain their very names.

BUT the loss arising from the silence of antient writers is perhaps more than fully compensated by the accounts given of the Pictish Kings, and the antiquity of the Pictish monarchy, by the *Senna-chies* or historians of Ireland. We are told by them, that the Pictish monarchy began at the same time with that of their own country, that is to say, thirteen, or at least eleven whole centuries before the birth of Christ *. They assure us further, that the Picts had a succession of seventy Kings, from *Cathluan*, who was cotemporary with *Heremon* the first Irish monarch, to Constantine, who reigned about the end of the eighth century.

THOUGH the Scots historians took care not to do too much honour to the Pictish nation, yet it seems they found themselves under a necessity of granting that the Picts were settled early in Bri-

---

* Keat. Gen. Hist. of Ireland, p. 120, &c. Flaherty Ogyg. p. 190.

tain;

tain ; and that they had a fucceffion of fifty-eight, or at leaft fifty-two Kings *.

THE Pictifh nation was totally fubdued by the Scots in the ninth century, and their name has been fwallowed up by that of the conquerors with whom they were incorporated. Did any confiderable body of that people exift now, it is more than probable that fome of them would lay claim to the honour of remote antiquity, and boaft of a very long feries of monarchs, like the Scots, Irifh, and every other European nation. But though the Picts have been extinct for many ages back, they have found in Father Innes, the author of the Critical Effay, not only a moft zealous friend, but as able an advocate to plead their caufe, as perhaps any one their nation could have produced.

IT is well known that Innes has been at great pains, though born a Scotfman, to annihilate no lefs than forty Scottifh Kings. He was fenfible that many of the abettors of the high antiquities of Scotland would be difpleafed with the wanton attempt he made to rob them of their antient monarchs, to whom they had, at leaft, an old prefcriptive right. But he found out a method of making ample amends for this injury : inftead of forty or thirty-nine ideal monarchs, and thefe no more than petty Kings, had they actually exifted, he has given his country an indifputable right to forty powerful fovereigns of the truly antient Pictifh line ; and he has been at no little trouble to demonftrate, that the Scots of modern times are as much interefted in thefe Pictifh monarchs, as they could be in the antient Kings of their own nation,

---

* See Innes's Crit. Eff. p. 108.

who

who are placed between the firſt and ſecond Fergus.

INNES could not poſſibly believe that the antiquaries of Scotland were ſo blind as to be caught
in a ſnare ſo very viſible, or idle enough to be put
off with a compliment ſo vain and illuſory. That
writer could not have imagined, without a manifeſt
ſelf-contradiction, that the very names of ſo many
crowned heads, from *Cathluan*, the founder of the
Pictiſh monarchy, to *Dreſt*, in whoſe time the
goſpel was preached by St. Ninian to the Picts,
could have been preſerved without the knowledge
of letters, preſerved in the rhimes of bards, and
the traditionary ſtories of ſennachies.

HE could not have ſeriouſly entertained ſuch an
opinion, and at the ſame time ſee very good reaſons for deſtroying ſo many Scottiſh and Iriſh
Kings promiſcuouſly, and without any mercy,
whoſe exiſtence depended on a ſimilar authority.

BUT why were the Scottiſh Kings deſtroyed,
and the Pictiſh monarchs ſpared ? Why, becauſe
the annaliſts, hiſtorians, ſennachies and antiquaries
of Ireland are univerſally agreed that the Pictiſh
monarchy is coeval with their own ; and Iriſh
writers cannot be ſuſpected of diſhoneſty or ignorance in a matter of this kind. " They had no
private motives of their own, to invent this ſtory
of the antiquity of the Pictiſh ſettlement and
monarchy, They would not, without a neceſſity,
put a foreign people upon a level with their own,
in the two advantages upon which they chiefly
valued themſelves : and hence it follows, that the
Iriſh writers muſt have had good information in
this affair *."

---

* Inn. Crit. Eſſ. p. 140.

IT

IT is amazing how Innes could have prevailed with himfelf to follow Irifh guides through the impenetrable darknefs of the Pictifh antiquities. He himfelf has been at extraordinary pains to prove that thefe guides are, of all others, the blindeft and moft faithlefs : if fo, how can they who adopt their doctrine hinder themfelves from fufpecting both their honefty and intelligence ? There is no fmall difficulty in explaining the motives by which the inventors of hiftorical fable, in the feveral ages and countries of the world, are led to frame and publifh their fictions.

BUT the writers of Ireland had it feems a private view, though a fomewhat remarkable one, for carrying up the antiquity of the Pictifh monarchy to fo great a height. Keating affirms, that it was from Ireland the Picts got their wives when they went to fettle in Britain *. Other Hibernian hiftorians inform us, that *Cathluan* was married to one of thofe wives ; that the firft monarch of the Pictifh line, and all his Pictifh fubjects, fwore, in the moft folemn manner, to devolve the government of the country they were to fubdue upon the iffue of thofe Hibernian women, and to continue it with them for ever. Why an oath became neceffary in a cafe where the Picts muft, in the nature of things, leave their territories to their progeny by the Irifh ladies, as they had no other women, I fhall leave to the Milefian fennachies to determine.

INNES endeavours to perfuade us, that tradition, without the help of letters, might have preferved the names of the feventy Pictifh Kings. Why then could not tradition preferve at leaft the

---

* Gen. Hift. of Irel. p. 62.

	names

names of the Kings who governed the weſtern parts of Caledonia before Fergus the ſecond ? And what could hinder the Iriſh from preſerving, by means of the ſame oral chronicle, the names of all the monarchs or provincial Kings who reigned in their iſland before the time of *Leogaire* and *St. Patric ?* All theſe depend upon the ſame degree of authority, and muſt ſtand or fall together.

IT is to be obſerved, that the account given by the Iriſh ſennachies and annaliſts of the Pictiſh nation and Pictiſh Kings, differs eſſentially from that taken by Innes from his Pictiſh Chronicle, and the Regiſter of the Priory of St. Andrews *. According to the *Pſalter Caſhel*, quoted by Keating ‡, and according to the books of *Lecan*, quoted by O Flaherty ‖, Cathluan the ſon of *Gud* muſt be placed at the head of the Pictiſh royal line. But according to the catalogue publiſhed by Innes, *Cruithne* the ſon of *Cinge* was the founder of the Pictiſh monarchy. The *Pſalter Caſhel* and the book of *Lecan* are the two moſt valuable monuments of literary antiquity of which the Iriſh nation can boaſt ; and if any ſtreſs can be laid on the authority of theſe, Gud the father of Cathluan, and generaliſſimo of the Picts, after killing his maſter Policornus, came all the way from Thrace into Ireland, where he and his people were very kindly received by *Criomthan* King of Leinſter, and by *Heremon* monarch of the whole iſland. But Innes contends, that the Picts were of a Britiſh, and conſequently of a Gauliſh extraction : nor was he credulous enough to admit on the authority of

---

* Keat. Gen. Hiſt. of Irel. p 60, 61, 62.
‡ Crit. Eſſay, p. 134, &c. 798.
‖ Flaherty Ogygia Dom. p. 190.

Irish records, that Gud or Cathluan, Cinge or Cruithne, had been regicides, or come from Thrace.

Of the Pictish monarchs, whose names are enumerated in the catalogues exhibited by Innes, we have no less than five, every one of whom wore the crown of Caledonia longer by twenty years than the famous Arganthonius reigned over Tarteffus. Each of these Pictish monarchs held the scepter a whole century; and one of them had the honour of equalling a very celebrated Irish * King in prowess. He fought one hundred battles, or rather put a happy period to a hundred wars. His name was *Druft*. He reigned in the beginning of the fifth age, and in his time the gospel was first preached to the Picts by St. Ninian. The Kings who filled the throne of Caledonia before this Druft, had, for the most part, the good fortune to have reigned longer, by very great odds, than any other race of princes that ever existed since the days of the fabulous Egyptian monarchy.

The oldest domestic record that can pretend to throw any light on the history of Caledonia, is a small treatise published by Innes, in the Appendix to his Critical Essay ‡. This treatise must have been written about two hundred years before Fordun's Scotichronicon. The author had his materials from Andrew bishop of Caithnefs, who was cotemporary with King David the faint, and was a prelate of a very great reputation for sanctity, and historical knowledge. The treatise says, upon the bishop's authority, that the Picts reigned

---

* The famous Con Ceud-chathach of the Irish fennachies.
‡ The title of this little treatise is, De situ Albaniæ, &c. &c. See the Appendix to the Crit. Essay, Numb. I.

over

over all Albany, throughout a feries of one thoufand three hundred and fixty years, or at leaft one
thoufand and feventy. But the learned prelate
told the author of this treatife, that Albany was
of old divided into feven kingdoms, each of
which had a fovereign of its own ; and that every
one of thefe fovereigns had a petty King under
him. The moft antient of thofe fovereigns was
called *Ennegus,* if the bifhop deferves any credit.

IN fhort, the hiftory of thofe Pictifh monarchs
who reigned over Caledonia before St. Ninian's
time, is no lefs dubious than that of thofe forty
Scottifh Kings whom Innes has been at fo much
pains to eraze from the lift of Scots Kings. We
may therefore venture to affirm, that it is impoffible to prove, from any probable hiftory, that the
Picts were governed by any general Kings before
the time of Fergus the fon of Erc, fuppofing that
time to be the true æra of the commencement of
the Scottifh monarchy. If the Scots of modern
times will, at all events, have fpurious or nominal
Kings in the lift of their monarchs, Fergus the
fon of Ferchard, and his thirty-nine immediate
fucceffors, will anfwer their purpofe much better
than *Chruidne* and his ideal defcendants.

THE generality of the Scots hiftorians place
the beginning of the Scottifh monarchy in the age
of Alexander the Great. Every impartial judge
will allow, that Innes has totally deftroyed that
part of their fyftem *. But had Innes been confiftent with himfelf, or had he purfued thofe principles from which he argued fo fuccefsfully againft
the antiquity of the Scottifh monarchy, it feems
plain, that he would have likewife demolifhed

---

* See the Crit. Effay, p. 102, 103, 104.

that

that of the Pictish nation. The authority of the Psalter Cashel, the book of conquests, the book with the snowy cover, and other Irish chronicles, either imaginary or invisible, would have gone for nothing with him : and had those Pictish chronicles mentioned by Andrew bishop of Caithnefs been extant in his time, we have great reason to believe that he would have found himself under the necessity of admitting that they contained little more than ill-digested legends.

BRUDIUS, a prince cotemporary with St. Columba, is the first Pictish King exprefsly mentioned by any writer of credit. It is impossible to afcertain what figure his anceftors made in Caledonia, and who were his predecessors in the throne of Pictavia. We know little concerning those Pictish Kings who succeeded Brudius. Bede informs us, that during the reign of one of them, the Picts killed Egfred King of Northumberland in battle, and deftroyed the greateft part of his army. The venerable historian passes over in filence the name of the Pictish monarch in whofe time this great event happened. The continuator of Nennius calls him Brudius, and adds further, that he commanded the Picts in that glorious and decisive battle. Bede speaks of another Pictish King, for whom he had a particular regard, though for a very indifferent reafon. The name of that favorite monarch was *Naitan.* It was to him that Ceolfrid, abbot of Wiremouth, wrote his famous letter concerning Eafter and the Tonfure ; a letter in which Bede himself had very probably a principal hand. Roger Hoveden and Simeon of Durham mention two other Pictish Kings, under the disfigured names of *Onnuft* and
Kinoth * :

Kinoth * : and the fum total of their hiftory, as far as it has been recorded by thefe writers, is, that Onnuft died in the year 761, and that Kinoth gave a kind reception to Alfred of Northumberland, who had been expelled his Kingdom about the year 774. The accounts given by the Scots hiftorians of feveral other Pictifh Kings cannot much be depended on. Some of them were mif-informed or led aftray by inveterate prejudices, or too ready to believe legendary tales; while others, poffeffed indeed of a great fhare of learning, chofe to embellifh their hiftories with fictions of their own, or to make room for the fables which had been invented by their predeceffors. The ftories told by the Britifh hiftorians, Geoffrey of Monmouth, and the author of the Eulogium, concerning Roderic a Pictifh King, concerning Fulgenius, another prince of the fame nation, and concerning the three Pictifh colonies eftablifhed in North Britain, deferve not the leaft attention. The curious in ill-contrived legends of this kind may be amply fatisfied on that head, in archbifhop Ufher's antiquities ‡.

---

* Their true names feem to be Hungus, Angus or Innis, and Cineach or Kenneth.

‡ Chap. xv. p. 300, &c.

DISSERTATION. V.

Of the Pictish Language.

WE are told by Bede, that the inhabitants of Britain in his time, both studied and preached the gospel in the lauguages of five different nations, agreeably to the number of those books in which the law of God was written. These languages were the Saxon, British, Scottish, Pictish, and Roman *.

FROM this passage of that venerable author, some have concluded, and with some appearance of justice, that the languages of the Britons, Scots and Picts, were essentially different. Bede lived in the neighbourhood of the Pictish nation. The monastery of Girwy, to which he belonged †, stood near the mouth of the Tine. He could not have been a stranger to the British tongue, however much the Britons and Angles disagreed. He was personally well acquainted with many of the Irish Scots, and had a friendly partiality for their country. Besides, he has given us some specimens of his skill in the British, Scottish, and Pictish

---

* Bed. Hift. Ecclef. lib. 1. cap. 1.
† Now Jarrow.

languages;

languages ; fo that his authority fhould, according to the judgment of fome very learned writers,
weigh down all the arguments that have been
brought to prove that the Britifh tongue was
the fame with the Pictifh *, or that the
Scotch and Pictifh languages were effentially the
fame †.

CAMBDEN feems to have had a profound veneration for Bede, and accordingly calls him "the
" ornament of the old Englifh nation." But he
took the liberty to differ from him in the affair
now under confideration, and was at no fmall
trouble to prove, that the Britifh and Pictifh were
the fame identical language.

IT appears from that paffage in Bede, on which
fo much ftrefs is laid, in the prefent queftion, and
likewife from another part of his hiftory, that the
good man had great fatisfaction in finding that
the number of languages fpoken in this ifland
correfponded exactly with the number of books
in which the Mofaical law was written. Whether a pious inclination to juftify this very
edifying parallel may not have in fome degree influenced him to believe too haftily that
the Britifh, Pictifh, and Scottifh languages were
fpecifically different, we fhall leave undeter-
mined.

THE fpecimens which Bede has given of his
fkill in the Scottifh or Galic tongue will do him
very little honour. His explanation of the local
name *Alcluith* or Dumbarton, and his etymon
of *Dalreudini*, argue too ftrongly that his know-

---

* Cambden.
† Buchanan.

ledge

ledge of that language was extremely circumfcribed ‡.

It is unneceffary to difpute with vehemence
this pious writer's account of the languages which
in his time prevailed in Britain. If an author of
modern times fhould affert, that the gofpel is now
preached in Britain in five different languages, in
the Welfh, in Galic, in French, in the Englifh
of Middlefex, and in the Scotch of Buchan, it
may be prefumed that no reafonab'e objections
could be raifed againft the propriety of fuch an
affertion ; however true it may be that the two
languages laft mentioned are in fubftance the fame,
and underftood more than tolerably well by the
Englifh and Scots reciprocally.

It is univerfally known that the Irifh language,
and the Galic of Scotland were originally the
fame. But the pronunciation is fo different, that
a public declamation in the Irifh of Connaught
would be as little underftood by a Highland au-
dience, as a difcourfe in the Doric of Syracufe
would be by the Ionians of the leffer Afia,

If we allow that the language of the Picts and
Scots, of antient times, were as different from
one another as the Doric and Ionic dialects of the
Greek, we will do all reafonable juftice to Bede,
and fave the credit of his teftimony. To grant
more, would be too much indulgence, as fhall appear in the courfe of this differtation.

---

‡ *Alcluith*, according to him, fignifies the rock above Clyde,
and *Dalreudini* the portion of Reuda. But in the Galic neither Alcluith fignifies a rock, nor Dalreudini a part or portion,
though the learned author of the Archæologia Britannica fays
otherwife, upon the faith of Bede's authority.

It

It is evident, that the names of most of the places in the Eastern division of Scotland, which was of old the country of the Picts, have manifestly a Galic origin. This is so well known that examples are altogether needless. Almost every village, river, hill and dale there, will furnish a decisive proof on this head *.

If any one should beg the question, he may contend, that all these Galic names were framed by the Scots, after the extinction of the Pictish monarchy. And indeed the authority of Boece and Buchanan favour this opinion. These historians maintain that Kenneth, the son of Alpin, who subverted the monarchy of Pictavia, divided that district, which went once under the name of Horestia, between two brothers Æneas and Mernus. From the first, say they, the district which now is called Angus, derived its name; and the county of Mearns was so called from the latter.

But an author † much older than them, and even prior to Fordun himself, informs us, that Ennegus, the Æneia of Boece, and the Angus of our time, received its name from Ennegus, the first Pictish King: and were it true that the names of villages, rivers, and mountains, in the Eastern

---

* We learn from a very old register of the priory of St. Andrews *, that Kilrymont, which was the ancient name of St. Andrews, was in the days of Hungus, the last Pictish King of that name, called *Mukross*, and the town now called Queensferry, *Ardchinnechain*. But these two Pictish words are undoubtedly Galic; the first of them signifying, in that tongue, the wood, heath, or promontory of Swine; and the second, the peninsula of little Kenneth.

* See Dalrymple's Collect. p. 122.

† Andrew, bishop of Caithness.

parts

parts of Scotland were altered by Kenneth Macalpin, and his fucceffors, we beg leave to afk, How it came to pafs that the names of many Pictifh Kings were exactly the fame with others that were common among the ancient Scots, and continue to be fo among the Highlanders to this day ? Were thefe names too created after the extinction of the Pictifh monarchy ? Or did the conquerors give unheard of appellations to the Kings of the conquered nation, as well as new denominations to the feveral parts of their land ?

Any one who chufes to inveftigate this matter, may confult the two catalogues of the Pictifh Kings, publifhed by Innes ; and upon comparing their names with the true Galic names of the Scottifh monarchs, as exhibited by the fame author, he fhall immediately difcover a perfect identity in feveral inftances *.

It is impoffible to prove, from any faithful record, that Kenneth M'Alpin introduced a new language among his new fubjects, after he had united the Pictifh kingdom with that of the Scots. He was too wife a Prince to exterminate the brave and numerous people whom he had conquered, though fome Scottifh hiftorians have been injudi-

* * *

* *Cineoch* or Kenneth, *Oengus* Ennegus, Angus or Hungus, *E'pin* or Alpin, *Urfen* Eogen, Ewen or Eugenius, *Urghuis* or Fergus, Canaul or Conal, Caftantine or Conftantine, Demhnail or Dovenald. All thefe names were the proper appellations of Pictifh Kings : and the very fame names are found in the catalogues of the Scottifh monarchs, every one of them excepting Hungus, which is unqueftionably a Galic one, and very common among the Scots Highlanders, of thefe and former times. It is proper to obferve, that all the Pictifh names now mentioned belong wholly to thofe Pictifh Kings who reigned after Brudius, St. Columba's convert.

D

cious

cious enough to believe so improbable a fiction. Kenneth was too ambitious to confine his views to North Britain. He endeavoured to extend his empire farther; and for that purpose invaded England six different times *. For a Prince of such a disposition, it would have been extremely impolitic to extirpate a nation he had subdued, or to extinguish their language, had it differed from that of his own nation.

WITHOUT endeavouring to produce examples from remote ages, we may conclude, from the present state of the European tongues, that the inhabitants of mountainous countries are remarkably tenacious of the language of their ancestors. The Spaniards near the bay of Biscay, the French of Bretagne, the old Britons of North Wales, the wild Irish of Connaught, and many Highlanders near the heart of Scotland, still retain the languages of their remotest ancestors. Neither ridicule, contempt, or the power of fashion, which subdues every thing, have been able to extinguish those languages. From this obstinacy of all nations in retaining their respective tongues we may reasonably suppose, that if the Pictish language had differed much from the Galic, it would, like the Biscayan, Armorican, and old Scottish, have still preserved its being in some corner or other of those countries which belonged to the Pictish nation.

HENRY, archdeacon of Huntingdon, expresses his astonishment to find that the Pictish tongue was in his time totally extinguished, insomuch that the accounts given of it by writers of former ages had the appearance of downright fic-

---

* See Innes, Crit. Essay, p. 782.

tion.

tion. Henry wrote his hiftory within lefs than four hundred years after the Pictifh nation was incorporated with the Scots. It is therefore matter of great furprize, that no veftige of the Pictifh tongue remained in his time, if it differed at all from the Galic of the Scots. The arguments which may be drawn from the archdeacon's teftimony is not more unfavourable to Buchanan's hypothefis than it is to that of the learned Cambden.

John; prior of Hogulfted, another Englifh hiftorian, who had better opportunities of knowing the ftate of North Britain than the archdeacon of Huntingdon, relates * that the Picts made a very confiderable figure in the army of David the Saint, during his difputes with Stephen, King of England. The battle of Clitherbow, in which David obtained the victory, was fought, according to the prior †, by the Engifh on one fide, and by the Scots affifted by the Picts on the other. Before the battle of the ftandard was fought, the Picts infifted with great vehemence on their hereditary right of leading the van of the Scots army, and were gratified in their requeft by the King ‡. It cannot be imagined that thefe Picts who held the poft of honour in the Scottifh armies had been perfecuted out of the ufe of their native language; nor can we fuppofe that they themfelves held it in fuch contempt, as to abandon it voluntarily.

But fhould it be granted without any neceffity, that the Southern Picts had entirely forgot

---

* Hen. Hunt. Hift. lib. 1.
† Ioan prior Hoguif. ad annum, 1138.
‡ Rich. prior Hogulftad : ad annum, 1136.

or loft the language of their anceftors, through
the intercourfe they had for fome ages with the
Walenfes of Cumberland, the Saxons of Bernicia,
and the Scots of Jarghael, it may be prefumed
that the Picts of the North, the Picts of Murray
particularly, would have preferved their native language long after the time of Henry of Huntingdon. The Picts of Murray, the Moravienfes of
our old hiftorians, had frequent difputes with the
pofterity of Malcolm Canemore, in vindication of
the rights and privileges enjoyed by their Pictifh
anceftors; and it may be taken for granted, that
they would have likewife fought with great fpirit
for their language, if invaded or perfecuted : nor
was it an eafy matter to root that language from
among them, though totally reduced to obedience
in the thirteenth century, as the interior part of
their country was full of mountains and inacceffible
faftneffes.

It is certain that the Picts were in a refpectable condition after the Duke of Normandy's acceffion to the throne of England. The great charter granted by that conqueror to his Englifh fubjects affords an unqueftionable proof of this fact.
It is not therefore credible that either the Pictifh
nation or Pictifh tongue could have been entirely
extinguifhed in the time of the archdeacon of Huntingdon.

Innes, as well as Cambden, is of opinion that
the Picts fpoke the Britifh language. Thefe two
eminent antiquaries agreed in believing that the
Picts or Caledonians had originally migrated from
South Britain, and that the Scots were of Irifh extraction. To eftablifh thofe fyftems, it became
neceffary for them to prove that the Britifh was

the

the language of Scotland, and effentially different from the Gallic. But the arguments which
they produce are far from being conclufive.

CAMBDEN obferves, and after him Innes, that
Aber, a word denoting the mouth of a river, or
the confluence of two rivers, was frequently prefixed to local names, in thofe parts of Britain
which the Picts poffeffed, and that the fame word
is very common in Wales to this day. This cannot be denied. But the fame word *Aber* is found
in fome parts of North Britain to which the Pictifh
empire did never extend. *Lochaber* is the name
of a diftrict in the Weftern Highlands, which had
always belonged to the Scots.

SHOULD we fuppofe with Cambden, that the
Irifh went originally from South Britain, and alfo
agree with him and Innes, that the Scots of Britain are of Irifh extraction, what could have hindered either of thofe nations from ufing the word
Aber like the Picts or Caledonians? The Irifh might
have very naturally borrowed that word and thoufands more from their Britifh anceftors, and the
Scots from their Irifh progenitors. But if the
Irifh, and of courfe the Scots, muft be brought
from Spain, a notion which Innes inclined to believe, the *Cantabri* and *Artabri* of Spain might
have furnifhed the Irifh, and confequently Scots,
with the word *Aber*, a word in which the two
former nations, and therefore the two latter, were
peculiarly interefted.

STRATH is another word which Cambden
has gleaned up from among the remains of the
Pictifh tongue. It fignifies, as he juftly obferves,
a valley through which runs a river or brook.
But among all the local names in thofe Weftern

High-

Highlands and isles in which the Picts were never settled, there is hardly any one so common as those which have the word *Strath* prefixed to them. Nor is there any difficulty in finding the same initial part of a local name in Ireland *.

THE only specious argument urged by the two antiquaries in defence of their opinion, is founded on a discovery which Bede has made for them. We are told by that writer, that *penuahel* signifies, in the Pictish language, the head of the wall, and very fortunately that word bears the same meaning in the British. But it is to be observed, that both Cambden and Innes were of opinion that Bede committed a mistake, when he affirmed that the British and Pictish were different languages. The same mistake, which we may infer from them, arose from Bede's want of critical knowledge in the British tongue, might have led him to think that *penuahel* was a Pictish word, when in reality it is British.

THE author of the Eulogium Britanniæ informs us, that the same extremity of the Roman wall, which the Anglo-Saxon calles penuahel, went under the name of cenuahil in the Scottish tongue. Supposing then that Bede did not through mistake give us the British name of the wall's end, instead of the Pictish, the argument drawn by Cambden from pennahael proves with its full strength no more than this, that the Pictish and Scottish tongues differed in the initial letters of one word. And shall we infer from that immaterial difference that they were two distinct languages ? We might as well conclude that the Doric and Ionic dialects

---

* Strathbane and Strabrane, and a hundred others.

of the Greek had no great relation to one another. We muſt likewiſe maintain that the Latin authors who wrote Caius Cæſar, and Cneius Pompeius, uſed a language different from thoſe who wrote Gaius Cæſar and Gneius Pompeius.

Though I contend for the identity of the Pictiſh and Scottiſh tongues, I would be underſtood to mean no more than that theſe languages were reciprocally intelligible to the reſpective nations by whom they were ſpoken. The Iriſh of Ulſter differs in a conſiderable number of words from that of Connaught, as does the Galic of the weſtern iſles from that of Sutherland or Aberdeen ſhire. But the immaterial variations in theſe ſeveral idioms will never hinder one from affirming that the people of Connaught and Ulſter ſpeak the ſame Iriſh, and all the Highlanders of Scotland the ſame Galic.

By the Pictiſh tongue I mean, in the whole courſe of this diſſertation, the language of the old Caledonians. If in the ſequel it ſhall appear, that the Scots as well as Picts were the genuine deſcendants of the Caledonians, there will be no difficulty in ſuppoſing that they ſpoke the ſame language.

DISSERTATION VI.

Of the Scots.

THOUGH it is well known that the modern French and Germans are defcended of the antient Franks and Allemans, it is impoffible to affign the period of time in which they made the firft great figure in their refpective countries. Before the middle of the third century, their very names were unknown to the writers of Greece and Rome. It is therefore no matter of furprize, that the Picts and Scots, who poffeffed but a corner of a remote ifland, fhould remain equally unknown to hiftorians till that period.

EUMENIUS, the panegyrift, is the oldeft writer who fpeaks of the Picts, and Porphyrius, the philofopher, is the firft who makes any mention of the Scots. It is well known that Porphyrius was an implacable enemy to the Mofaic and Chriftian inftitutions, and that he wrote with peculiar acrimony againft both. In one of his objections againft the former, he took occafion to fpeak of the Scottifh nations. The words of that objection have been preferved by St. Jerome, who tranflated them into Latin, from the original Greek, and they run in Englifh thus: " Neither has Britain " a province fertile in tyrants, nor have the
" Scottifh

" Scottish tribes, nor has any one of the barba-
" rous nations, all around to the very ocean,
" heard of Moses or the Prophets *."

CAMBDEN, Usher, and several other eminent
critics, have quoted this passage, as the language
of the pagan philosopher, without ever suspecting
its authenticity. But Innes is positive that it is
Jerome's own invention. He says, " That this
" passage is not Porphyrius's, but Jerome's own,
" this the epithet he gives to Britannia, of *fertilis*
" *provincia tyrannorum*, seems to demonstrate.
" For when Porphyrius, about A. D. 267. wrote
" the book against the Christian religion to which
" St. Jerome alludes in that passage, there had scarce
" till then appeared from Britain any considerable
" tyrant, or usurper against the empire : whereas,
" betwixt that year 267 and the year 412, when
" St. Jerome wrote his letter to Ctesiphont, there
" had risen in Britain no less than seven tyrants or
" usurpers." After Innes had enumerated these
tyrants, and observed that four of them were cotemporary with St. Jerome, he concludes, that
Porphyrius had no real concern with the passage
now under consideration.

IT will appear hereafter, that Innes had particular reasons of his own for ascribing this passage
to Jerome. Had he acknowledged with other
critics, that it belongs undoubtedly to Porphyrius,
he would have pulled down his system with his
own hands. But whatever his motive may have
been for giving the words in question to the holy

---

* Neque enim Britannia, fertilis provincia tyrannorum, et
Scoticæ gentes, omnesque usque ad oceanum per circuitum bar-
baræ nationes, Moysen Prophetasque cognoverant. Hieronym.
Epist. ad Ctesiphont.

father

father, we shall in the mean time do full justice to his argument.

The ancient writer, whoever he was, calls Britain, a province fertile in tyrants. If Porphyrius was the real writer, it is certain that he wrote in Greek; and if he meant to say no more than that Britain was full of Kings, he surely wrote proper Greek in calling those Kings Τυραννοι, or tyrants; nor would he have given us a false account, had he affirmed that Britain was divided between many Princes. This was certainly the case, before the Romans subdued the best part of this island; and the very character that an ancient author gives of Britain is, " It abounds in nations, " and Kings of nations *."

But waving this consideration, Innes had no authority for maintaining that our author speaks of considerable tyrants or usurpers in the empire. There is not a syllable in the passage before us concerning tyrants from Britain who usurped the imperial dignity.

Some of the thirty tyrants who tore the Roman empire into pieces, after Gallienus had abandoned himself entirely to sloth and sensuality, had, it is true, been governors of Britain, and had assumed the purple there. Among these tyrants were Lollianus, Victorinus, Posthumus, Tetricus, and Maximus, whose coins were, in Cambden's time, seen more frequently in England than any where else. From that circumstance, that excellent antiquary concluded, with great appearance of reason, that these usurpers had been propraetors of Britain. He adds another to the number of tyrants now mentioned, that is, Cornelius Lælianus,

---

* Mela de Situ Orb. Lib. iii.

a pretended Emperor, whofe coins are found in Britain only *.

I T cannot be afcertained that Porphyrius wrote his book againft the Chriftian religion in the year 267. His mafter and friend Longinus, the critic, was put to death by Aurelian the Emperor, who died about nine years after that period ; and Porphyrius may have written the treatife, out of which Jerome quotes the paffage in difpute, fome little time before the death of Aurelian, or the year 275. But fuppofing the date of the philofopher's book to be precifely what Innes makes it, the learned infidel had a good deal of reafon to fay of Britain, that it had been fertile in Kings in former ages, or fertile in tyrants in his own time †.

HAVING thus eftablifhed the authority of that paffage, in which the Scots are mentioned for the firft time, we are to inquire next, where that nation, or the tribes who went under that name, were fettled.

I T muft be allowed that Porphyrius has not fufficiently cleared up this point. But archbifhop Ufher was furely too hafty in affirming that the philofopher places the Scottifh nation without Britain, that is to fay, fomewhere elfe rather than in that ifland ‡. The Scots were without Britain, in one fenfe, and within it, in another; at the very time when Porphyrius wrote againft Chriftianity. The very learned primate could not have been ignorant that the generality of Greek and Latin authors have appropriated the name *Britannia* to that part of the ifland which had been fubdued by

---

* Camden's Brit. Rom.
† See Tribellius Pollio's little book on the thirty Tyrants.
‡ Ufher. Antiquit. lib. xv. p. 380.

the

the Romans. Tacitus obferves, in the very beginning of his hiftory, that Britain had been loft
to the empire, and was foon recovered. Claudian
introduces Britannia to Stilicho, with a moft humble and grateful addrefs in her mouth, for the effential fervices done to her by that able general,
who drove away the Picts and Scots from her territories : and Bede has frequently confined the
name *Britanni* to the provincials, in contra-
diftinction to the Picts and their allies. All this
is undeniably true ; and therefore the Scottifh
nations mentioned by the philofopher may have
been within the ifland of Great Britain, though dif-
criminated from the provincial Britons.

AMMIANUS MARCELLINUS is the next author
who mentions the Scots : his account of them is,
that " In the tenth confulfhip of Conftantius, and
in the third of Julian, the incurfions of the Scots
and Picts, two wild nations who had broken the
treaty of peace, laid wafte thofe parts of Britain
which lay near their confines : fo that the provincials, oppreffed with a feries of devaftations, began to entertain the moft frightful apprehenfions.
Cæfar was paffing the winter at Paris, when the
Britons informed him of their diftrefsful fituation.
He was quite at a lofs how to behave in a conjuncture every way dangerous. He could not prevail with himfelf to leave Gaul, as the Alemans
at that very time breathed out cruelty and war
againft him ; nor did he at all think it prudent to
crofs the fea, in order to relieve his Britifh fubjects, as the Emperor Conftans * had done on a

---

* The Britifh expedition of Conftans happened in the year
343.

                                          fimilar

fimilar occafion.   He therefore judged it moft convenient to fend Lupicinus, an able general, into
Britain, to re-eftablifh the peace there, either by
force or treaty *."

As a learned Englifh prelate has given his opinion
that all thofe Scots who invaded the Roman Britain
were Irifhmen, he found himfelf under the neceffity of conftruing and expounding a part of this
paffage of Ammianus in a different fenfe.   To fatisfy the curious on this head, I have thrown at
the bottom of the page the bifhop of St. Afaph's
conftrution of this paragraph.

WHATEVER fuccefs Lupicinus had in his war
or negotiations with the Picts and Scots, it is cer-

---

* Lhoyd, bifhop of St. Afaph, far from allowing that the Romans had entered into a treaty with the Scots and Picts, would
have us believe that thofe two barbarous nations had previoufly
agreed among themfelves to invade the Roman frontiers, in fome
certain places which they had marked out, as moft fit for their
purpofe ; and thefe places, according to him, are the *condicta
loca* of Ammianus ; *condicta* being joined in the conftruction to
loca, and not to *rupta quiete*, according to our tranflation.   But
how came the hiftorian to learn that the Scots and Picts had
made an agreement concerning thefe certain places, and followed
with great exactnefs that plan of operations which they had concerted before the commencement of that war ? Suppofing that
Ammianus was privy to all their plans and compacts, what could
he mean by informing us, that the Picts and Scots difturbed the
tranquility of the province, when they laid it wafte ? Devaftations of that kind are never feen or felt, without a previous breach
of the public tranquility. *Gentium ferarum excurfus, rupta
quiete, condicta loca limitibus vicina, vaftabant.*   So Lhoyd
would have the words of the text pointed and conftrued.   But
in this difpofition they look very much like a folecifm in grammar
and fenfe ; while in the other, for which we contend, they are
perfectly confiftent with both.   Livy has *condicere inducias :* and
the fame great hiftorian oppofes *quies* to *bellum.*   Vid. Ammian.
lib. xx.

tain that they, as alſo the Saxons and Attacots, harraſſed the provincial Britons inceſſantly, during the ſhort reigns of Julian and Jovian *. In the reign of Valentinian, thoſe barbarous nations reduced the provincial Britons to extreme miſery, having killed *Tullofaudes* their general, and *Nectaridus* the warden of the maritime coaſt. In a word, they carried all before them, till, in the year 368, Theodoſius, the greateſt general of that age, marched againſt them, at the head of a numerous army, defeated their plundering bands in every place, recovered all the Roman territories which they had ſeized, and erected thoſe territories into a new province, to which he gave the name of *Valentia.* Having performed theſe exploits, he returned in triumph to court, no leſs eminent for his military virtues, ſays the hiſtorian, than Furius Camillus and Papirius Curſor had been in diſtant ages †.

Theodoſius, however victorious upon this occaſion, was either not able, or too much in haſte, to tame the wild nations of Britain, ſo far as to hinder them from renewing their incurſions and ravages. The mighty feats he performed in the Orkneys, Thule, and the Hyperborean ocean, are the poetical creation of Claudian, who flattered the grandſon of that general. The barbarous nations of the north were pouring in whole inundations of very formidable troops into the moſt fertile and important provinces of the empire ; of conſequence, the preſence of Theodoſius near the throne and principal ſcenes of action, became indiſpenſibly neceſſary. We

---

* Ammian. lib. xxvi.
† Ammian. lib. xxvii.

have

have therefore reafon to believe, that he contented himfelf with regaining thofe territories which
the Scots, Picts and Attacots, had wrefted from
the provincial ; and it was undoubtedly in thefe
territories that he erected the new province of Valentia ; though Gildas, Bede, and after them a
great number of modern writers, were of another
opinion.

WHATEVER the extent or boundaries of Valentia may have been, it is certain that neither the
Furius Camillus of the fourth century, nor Maximus the Spaniard, nor Stilcho's legions, nor walls
either new or repaired, obftructed or intimidated
the barbarians of North Britain, or confined them
within their native hills. Impatient of controul,
greedy of plunder, and thirfting for fame, they
refumed their former fpirit of conqueft and devaftation. They frequently invaded the fouthern divifion of the ifland, recovered the diftrict of Valentia, and continued their hoftilities, till Hono-
rius refigned all his pretenfions to Britain, and left
the provincials to fhift for themfelves. It was between the 420 and 435 of the Chriftian æra that
this inglorions, though involuntary, dereliction of
Britain happened.

EVERY one muft acknowledge, that the Scots
and Picts were by much too powerful for the Britons, after they were abandoned by the Romans.
The letter written by the degenerate provincials to
Ætius the conful, exhibits a moft lively picture of
their diftreffes. The following paffage of it has
been preferved by Gildas : " The barbarians drive
us back to the fea : the fea drives us back to the
barbarians : inevitable deftruction muft be our
fate, in either of thefe ways : we are either killed
or drowned."

SOME

SOME learned men, whofe prejudices have led them far in extenuating the national antiquity of the Britifh Scots, have found themfelves under a neceffity of allowing that the people who went under that name had fettlements of their own in this ifland, within lefs than a century after it was abandoned by the Romans. But no Greek or Roman writer has informed them that the Scots had no fettlements in Britain before the end or middle of the fifth century. Ammianus Marcellinus has not even furnifhed them with a dark hint, that the Scots who invaded the Roman province in the reign of Conftans, Conftantius, Julian, Jovian, and Valentinian, were Irifh. This is fo far from being the cafe, that he fays, in plain terms, " That he had, in that part of his hiftory which related to the Emperor Conftans, given the exacteft account of Britain, whether we regard its fituation or inhabitants ;—that it was therefore unneceffary to repeat that account in the hiftory of Valentinian ;—and that, of courfe, it was fufficient for him to fay, that, in the reign of that Emperor, the Picts, who were divided into two nations, the Deucaledonians and Vecturiones, likewife the Attacots, a warlike race of men, and the Scots, roamed about through different parts of the province, and committed many depredations *."

BUT, from the latter part of this very paffage, fome antiquaries of note have concluded, that the Scots of Valentinian's time were no more than vagabonds in this ifland, and confequently unpoffeffed of any fettlements. The hiftorian, after mentioning the Scots, adds immediately, *per di-*

---

* Ammian. lib. xxvii.

verſa vagantes, " a people without any fixed habitations."

. Before this criticiſm is admitted, we muſt
take the liberty to aſk, whether the Picts and Attacots had any ſettlements in Britain at this time ?
They certainly had. Yet ſo it is that the expreſſion from which the concluſion is drawn, relates
equally to them. The ſequel of the ſtory proves
this, beyond any poſſibility of contradiction.
" The Saxons and Franks ravaged thoſe parts of
" Britain which lay neareſt to Gaul. The Picts,
" Attacots and Scots overran, plundered and laid
" waſte ſeveral other parts. Theodoſius the Ro-
" man general formed a reſolution of applying the
" moſt efficacious remedy to all theſe calamities.
" Accordingly he divided his army, which was
" numerous, and conſcious of its own ſtrength,
" into ſeveral different bodies. This done, he
" took the field againſt all the hoſtile nations at
" once, and attacked their plundering bands with
" ſuccefs, in the ſeveral places which they ra-
" vaged †." Here is a deciſive proof that the
Scots were vagabonds only in the ſame ſenſe in
which the other hoſtile nations were ſo. Not one
of the five nations had a ſettlement in South Britain. But can it be reaſonably inferred from this,
that neither the Scots, nor any of the reſt, poſſeſſed
a foot of ground in the northern diviſion of the
iſland ?

Ammianus has ſaid, that the Franks, and
their neighbours the Saxons plundered the Gallican
or Southern parts of the Britiſh province, ſome-

---

† Diviſis pluriſariam globis adortus eſt hoſtium vaſtatorias ma-
nus. Ammian. lib. xxvii.

E

times

times by fea, and fometimes by land. But he has not fo much as infinuated that the Scots were fea rovers; neither has he favoured a certain tribe of antiquaries with a fingle hint, from which they could venture to infer, that the Scots were either mercenary troops or auxiliaries, muftered up by the Picts in Ireland. This was fo far from his meaning, that he makes the Scots principals in the war againft the Britons, under the reign of Conftantius.

In fhort, Ammianus, who holds a refpectable place among the hiftorians of Rome, found the Scots in Britain in the year 360, and left them there. He found them likewife in the fame country about the year 343. They had concluded either a truce or peace with the Emperor Conftans, in that year, and broke it in his brother's reign.— He found them a formidable people in Britain, and as well eftablifhed there as the Picts or Attacots, fifty years at leaft before any other author of tolerable credit has found the Scottifh name in Ireland.

But thefe Scots, according to fome, might have been adventurers from Ireland. This has been confidently affirmed by many able writers; and it has been the general belief of many nations, that the Scots of Britain have derived their origin from the Irifh. But as the bare authority of a thoufand learned men is not equal to the force of one folid argument, nor the belief of feveral great nations more, in many inftances, than a popular error, it is far from being impoffible that thefe writers and whole nations may have been miftaken in the prefent cafe. That they were actually fo, it is no crime to fufpect, nor an unpardonable pre-
fumption

fumption to affirm, when it can be evinced that their belief is ill founded.

WERE it certain, or even highly probable, that the Britifh Scots owe their name and exiftence to the ancient Irifh, it is difficult to fay why they fhould be afhamed of their origin. The Germans, South Britons and Caledonians were, before the birth of Chrift, nations of much the fame character with the old Hibernians, equally illiterate, equally unpolifhed, and equally barbarous in every refpect. About the latter end of the firft century, the difference between the Hibernians and the people of this ifland muft have been inconfiderable. In the fecond, third and fourth centuries, the Caledonians, Picts and Attacots, were undoubtedly wild nations, and no lefs fo than the Irifh. In the fifth, fixth and feventh, religion and learning flourifhed in Ireland to fuch a degree, that it was commonly ftiled the mother country of faints, and reputed the kingdom of arts and fciences. The Saxons and Angles fent thither many of their Princes and Princeffes, to have the benefit of a pious and liberal education. It ought likewife to be acknowleged, that fome of the moft eminent teachers of North Britain received their inftruction at the Irifh feminaries of literature and religion.

IF the Irifh of the middle ages became a degenerate race of men, we ought to confider that all nations have their dark and fhining periods.— The domeftic confufions of their government, and the cruel oppreffions of the Danes, very much contributed to their national depravity. Even the Englifh conqueft, for fome ages, rather fufpended than introduced government among them. Thefe misfortunes have, however, been for fome time

back

back removed, and we find that Ireland has gradually emerged from that cloud of national ignorance which involved it, and produced men who
would do honor to any nation in Europe.

BUT notwithſtanding all the national honor that
might accrue to the Scots, from an Iriſh deſcent,
yet that partiality I may be ſuppoſed to have for
my countrymen will never induce me either to believe or ſupport the venerable fiction of their Hibernian extraction. That my unbelief on this
head is not ill founded, will beſt appear from a
conciſe diſcuſſion of the antiquities of Ireland.

DISSER-

DISSERTATION. VII.

The Irish Antiquities peculiarly dark and fabulous.

TO thofe who confider the ancient ftate of Ireland, which, from its fituation, was little known to foreign writers, and was itfelf totally deftitute of the ufe of letters, till the introduction of chriftianity by St. Patrick, it will be little the matter of furprize, that very few of the domeftic tranfactions of that country have been handed down, with accuracy, to the prefent times. But Ireland has been peculiarly happy in its domeftic means of preferving its internal hiftory. Every thing material in its hiftory, from the very firft day of its population till it was conquered in part by the Norwegians, and in whole by the Englifh, has been preferved in the moft faithful records. Should any one afk what thefe records were ; the great hiftoriographer of Ireland furnifhed a lift of them taken from books of indifputable authority which were to be feen in his own time* : nor has the fame writer made any difficulty of affirming that the Irifh annals are of

---

* Keat. pref. to his Hift. of Ireland.

a

a fuperior fidelity to any other annals in the world

As the antiquities of Ireland have an infeparable connection with thofe of North Britain, it is hardly poffible to do juftice to the latter without examining the former. We are therefore under a neceffity of reviewing the Irifh antiquities with a particular attention : but the utmoft care will be taken to give no more unfair reprefentation of them than what is to be found in the writings of thofe who have pleaded the caufe of the Irifh nation with the greateft zeal and learning.

IRELAND, fays one of thefe zealous writers, lay uninhabited for the fpace of three hundred years after the flood. At the end of that period Partholanus, the fon of *Scara*, arrived there with a thoufand foldiers and fome women. He had killed his father and mother in Greece, his native country, and that was the reafon why he undertook this voyage into Ireland. If one is curious to know in what year of the world this adventurer took poffeffion of that ifland, in what part of it he landed, and as fome people are minutely inquifitive, about every thing in which great perfonages are interefted, in what month, and in what day of the month, the annals of Ireland will give him entire fatisfaction. Partholanus landed at *Tubberfceine*, in Munfter, on the fourteenth day of May precifely, and in the year of the world one thoufand nine hundred and feventy-eight.

— THE fame annals furnifh us with a moft circumftantial account of the lakes which broke out in Ireland during the reign of Partholanus, of the rivers which he found there, of his favourite greyhound, of his confort's moft fcandalous behaviour,

of

of his own death, and of that all-confuming plague
which fwept away in one week's time, all his pofterity, and all their fubjects ; fo that not a fingle
man or woman remained alive in the whole kingdom. This extraordinary event happened about
three hundred years after Partholanus had poffeffed
himfelf of Ireland ; and this total excifion of his
pofterity and fubjects, was a judgment inflicted
upon that wicked man for the double parricide he
had committed in Greece.

A F T E R the extinction of this firft Hibernian
colony, Nemedius, another Prince of Magog's race,
and the eleventh in defcent from Noah *, repeo-
pled the ifland, which had been a perfect wilder-
nefs for thirty years.   Nemedius began his voyage
in the Euxine Sea, and after a long and very
ftrange navigation, arrived at length in Ireland.
His fleet confifted of four and thirty tranfports,
and every one of them was manned with thirty
heroes.

T H E great improvements made by this new
fovereign in Ireland, the lakes which broke out
there under his reign, the battles he fought againft
fome African pirates, the grievous misfortune
which broke his heart, the moft cruel oppreffions
which his pofterity and people fuffered after his
death ; thefe and many other curious occurrences
are fet down at large in thofe annals to which we
have already referred.

T H E Nemedians were fo unmercifully ufed by
the victorious Africans, that after feveral ineffectual
efforts to recover their liberty, they found them-

-----

* Partholanus was the eighth.

felves

felves under a neceffity of quitting Ireland. They
equipped a fleet confifting of eleven hundred and
thirty tranfports, and put to fea under the command of three leaders. The firft of thefe was the
famous *Simon Breac*, who fteered his courfe for
Greece ; the fecond was *To Chatb*, another grandfon of Nemedius, who failed with his fquadron to
the Northern parts of Europe ; the third was
Briatan Maol, who landed in the North of Scotland. From this illuftrious leader Britain derives
its name, and the Welch their origin.

ABOUT two hundred and fixteen years after the
death of Nemedius, the defcendants of Simon
Breac, and of his followers, returned from Greece
into Ireland. They were conducted thither by
five Princes or Chieftains of a very high reputation ; and as a fifth part of the men who compofed this new colony fell to the fhare of each of
the faid Princes, it was agreed that the ifland
fhould be divided into five almoft equal parts, and
that one of thefe divifions fhould be allotted to
each of the five Princes. The Irifh hiftorians
have taken care to preferve the names of thefe
old provincial Kings, and their fubjects are the
men whom they ftile *Firbolgs*.

IF any one inclines to learn how thefe Firbolgs
were driven out of Ireland, or totally enflaved after the lofs of a hundred thoufand men in one battle, the Irifh hiftorians will inform him very particularly. They will let him know likewife that
the *Tuath de Dannans*, by whom thefe Firbolgs
were deftroyed, or brought under the yoke, were
a generation of Necromancers who came from
Attica, Bœotia, and Achaia into Denmark, from
Denmark into Scotland, and from Scotland into
Ireland.

THERE

There are two very remarkable circumstances in the history of these *Tuath de Dannans,* which we cannot pass over in silence: the first is, that they understood magic to such a degree of perfection, that they could restore life to those who had been slain in battle, and bring them into the field the next day: but in spite of their enchantments, the Assyrians were too many for them, and accordingly drove them out of Greece. The second circumstance that deserves our attention is this: from the four cities which the Tuath de Dannans possessed in Denmark, they carried away some noble reliques, a spear, a sword, a cauldron, and a stone. The last of these curiosities was called *lia fail,* and was that fatal marble chair on which the monarchs of Ireland first, and afterwards the Kings of Scotland were crowned. *Lia fail* was possessed of a very extraordinary virtue till after the birth of Christ. Whenever an Irish monarch was crowned, it made a strange noise, and appeared in a surprizing agitation.

But neither the wonder working sorceries of the Tuath de Dannans, nor the amazing virtues of their Danish reliques were able to deliver them out of the hands of the *Gadelians,* when they invaded Ireland. These Gadelians were the descendants of the celebrated Gathelus, and from him they derived their name.

Gathelus or Gathelglas was a great personage who lived in Egypt, and contracted a friendship with Moses the legislator of the Jews. His mother was Scota, the daughter of Pharaoh Cingris, and his father was *Niul,* a Prince of extraordinary learning and rare accomplishments. Niul was the son of the illustrious *Feniusa Forsa,* a

Scythian

Scythian monarch, cotemporary with Nimrod, and the same monarch that, by the assistance of two excellent scholars, invented the Hebrew, Greek, Latin, and Irish alphabets.

THE precise time in which the posterity of Gathelus came into Spain, after a long series of strange peregrinations by sea and land, the manner in which they possessed themselves afterwards of Ireland, and the means by which they at last conquered a great part of North Britain, are related fully and minutely by that Irish historian from whom I have borrowed every thing told in this section concerning the Partholanians, Nemedians, Firbolgs, and Tuath de Dannans *,

ACCORDING to the same writer, the Gadelians or Scots conquered Ireland about the year of the world two thousand seven hundred and thirty-six, or about thirteen hundred years before the birth of Christ. The chief leaders under whose conduct the Gadelians made that conquest, were Heber and Heremon, two sons of Milesius, King of Spain, who was married to a second Scota, the daughter of another Pharoah, quite different from him already mentioned. From either of these two Scota's, the Gadelians have been called Scots; and it is because all the Kings of Ireland, from the Spanish to the English conquest of that island, were descended from Heber and Heremon, the sons of Milesius, that the Irish historians call them the Princes of the *Milesian race.*

AN ingenious author who lately published some dissertations concerning the ancient history of Ireland, makes no difficulty of affirming that all the

* Keating.

antiquaries of that country are unanimoufly agreed in fixing the epoch of the Milefian colony's arrival in Ireland about a thoufand years before Chrift * ; but that gentleman could not have been ignorant that Keating, Kennedy and others had placed the fettlement of that colony in Ireland much earlier.

DONALD O NEIL, King of Ulfter, informs Pope John XXII. that the three fons of Milefius had come into Hibernia from Cantabria, more than three thoufand and five hundred years before that in which he wrote his letter to his Holinefs, which was in the year 1317. This hiftorical curiofity has been preferved by John de Fordun, and it may be prefumed that the King of Ulfter, and thofe other Princes who joined him in his epiftolary correfpondence with the Pope, would have

---

* Mr. O Connor's Differt. on the ancient Hift. of Ireland, p. 110 —This O Connor, fince Dr. Macpherfon's death, has publifhed another edition of his work, and has given an additional differtation to the world, with remarks upon Mr. Macpherfon, the tranflator of Offian's poems. He feems to have been fo galled with what that gentleman has faid concerning the antiquities of Ireland, in his prefatory differtations to, and notes upon, the works of Offian, that he has totally laid afide good fenfe and argument, for fcurrility and perfonal abufe. It is however to be hoped Mr. Macpherfon will not honour with a reply fuch an illiberal attack, which is as impotent as it is low and ungentlemanny. When a man appears extreamly angry upon a fubject, which can only be fupported by cool and temperate difquifition, it is a conclufive argument that he is fenfible of the weaknefs of his caufe, or extreamly diffident of his own abilities to defend it. But as the character of modefty is not very confpicuous in Mr. O Connor's works, it would feem to me that his intemperate rage had its rife from a narrow and irrafcible fpirit, thrown into confufion by the difcovery made, by Mr. Macpherfon, of the fabuloufnefs of the Milefian fyftem, which he himfelf had been at much pains to adorn. *Hinc illæ lachrymæ !*

confulted

confulted the ableſt fennachies, and moſt authentic records of the country, before they could venture to write ſo confidently on a matter of ſuch importance to the common father of all Chriſtendom.

But were it undeniably true, that all the antiquaries, hiſtorians, and bards of Ireland, have fixed the epoch of the Mileſian colony's arrival there in the very time aſſigned by Mr. O Connor, the queſtion is, whether we can ſafely depend either on his, or upon their authority, in a matter of ſuch antiquity ? How did it appear to him, or how can it be made clear to others, that a Spaniſh colony did actually ſettle in Ireland about a thouſand years before the birth of Chriſt ? Is it probable in any degree that one of the remoteſt countries in Europe could have found out the art of preſerving the memory of ſuch diſtant events before letters were known to any of thoſe Celtic nations who inhabited the ſame diviſion of the world ? And is there any one of thoſe Celtic nations that can, with reaſon, pretend to give a credible account of their anceſtors or their actions, at the diſtance of two thouſand and eight hundred years back ?

It may be aſked alſo, whether we have any better evidence for believing the ſtory of the Mileſian colony than for believing that of the Partholanians, Nemedians, Firbolgs, and Tuath de Dannans. If the Iriſh will give us leave to reject the ſtory of theſe more ancient colonies, how can they ſave the credit of the famous *Pſalter Caſhel*, *Pſalter nan-traun*, the *Book of conqueſts*, the *Book of the ſnowy back*, and that of all their other immortal manuſcripts and traditions.

Another

ANOTHER natural queſtion is, how it came to paſs that the Iriſh antiquaries and ſennachies found out the connexion of Partholanus, Nemedius, Gathelus and Mileſius, with Magog, Japhet, and Noah, when no Celtic nation in the world became acquainted with theſe patriarchal names befoie the promulgation of Chriſtianity? Did the Scots of Porphyrius's time know Moſes or the Prophets? And how came Moſes himſelf to forget his excellent friend *Gathelus* *, or *Cingris* his implacable enemy? The plain truth is this : That exact conformity which we find in the genealogies given by Moſes and the Iriſh annaliſts, from the beginning of the antediluvian world, down to the third generation after Noah, affords a clear demonſtration that the Iriſh annals and genealogies were framed ſome time after the books of Moſes were known in Ireland.

BUT we are told poſitively, " That the uſe of letters was known in Ireland from a very early period. The Mileſian colony imported the arts and ſciences into that country from Spain. The long intercourſe which the Spaniards had with the Egyptians, Phœnicians, Perſians, and Grecians, had humanized them and their poſterity to a very high degree. The Iberian or Spaniſh Scots who came into Ireland, under the conduct of Heber and Heremon, were, like their anceſtors, wiſe, brave, humane, and polite. Their genius was ſtrongly turned to literature as well as to arms. As they had ſeveral academies for martial exerci-ſes, ſo they had ſeminaries of learning eſtabliſhed among them, and theſe richly endowed. In theſe ſeminaries they employed able profeſſors of poetry,

---

* See Keat, Gen. Hiſt. of Ireland, p. 35 & 36.

eloquence,

eloquence, philosophy and hiftory. The philological parts of learning were in great requeft among
them. Philofophy was patronized by their Kings,
recommended by *Fileas*, and became the ftudy of
their great men, as without it no dignities could
be obtained in the ftate. The Irifh bards and
fennachies had hereditary fees fettled upon their
families ; and as they were obliged, by the ftanding laws of the kingdom, to confine themfelves to
the proper bufinefs of their profeffion, it muft be
prefumed that they made an extraordinary proficiency.

" But the Irifh hiftoriographers appointed by
authority muft have been peculiarly induftrious
and faithful. Their falaries were great ; and their
compofitions were to undergo a very ftrict and
impartial examination, in the public affemblies of
the ftates of the kingdom. The Irifh held trien-
nial parliaments at *Tara*. A committee of every
parliament was appointed to revife the work of
every hiftoriographer, before it could be publifhed : and as it was prudently confidered that the
fpirit of party might prevail in one of thefe com-
mittees and parliaments, it was ordained, that
the fame work fhould be re-examined by a new
committee of a fubfequent parliament."

All that has been advanced here concerning the
ufe of letters in Ireland, from the arrival of the Milefian colony, and concerning the flourifhing ftate
of learning there, has been copied from Mr. O Connor's Differtations. O Flaherty had likewife been
at great pains to juftify the pretenfions of his
countrymen to an early knowledge of the fciences : But O Connor has equalled him in zeal, and
exceeded him in dogmatical affertions.

I t

IT is needlefs to make any anfwer to the account of the learning of Ireland given by this writer, fimply on his own authority. The ingenious father Innes * has long ago convinced the candid and impartial, that the Irifh were wholly unacquainted with letters, till St. Patric brought them into their country, about the Year 432.

ONE of his arguments, and a very plaufible one, is, that the very words in the Irifh tongue which exprefs what in Englifh we call books, pens, paper, reading, writing, and letters, are manifeftly Latin ones Hibernized.

INNES has totally deftroyed all the proofs which O Flaherty had piled up in fupport of this abfurd doctrine, and evinced, in the moft fatisfactory manner, that the *Bethluis nion* of the modern Irifh is no more than the invention of a late age. All the Irifh letters may be feen in Latin manufcripts written in foreign countries, which had not the leaft Intercourfe with Ireland.

THOSE who defire to be more fully fatisfied in this matter, may confult Mr. Innes † ; and to his arguments I fhall beg leave to add one or two more, with a particular view to the doctrine promulgated by O Connor.

WERE it true that Ireland had been the feat of learning, and the mother of the fciences, long before the commencement of the Chriftian æra, it is abfolutely incredible that the old Hibernians fhould have been fo unfavourably characterized by Strabo, Mela, and Solinus. It is impoffible

---

* Mr. Innes's 2d part of his Critical Effay.

† Mr. Innes's 2d part of his Critical Effay, chap. 1. art 2, 3, 4.

to believe that no accounts of their extraordinary genius and passion for literature, their unexampled proficiency in philosophical knowledge, their most laudable munificence to the professors of eloquence, poetry, and theology, could have transpired, especially as the sea-ports of Ireland were better known than those of Britain, and more frequented by foreigners.—By what strange fatality has it happened, that the inhabitants of a country, so wonderfully well civilized, so early improved by their intercourse with Phœnicians, Carthaginians, Persians, and Egyptians, and so unconquerably tenacious of those excellent institutions which their ancestors transmitted to them, could have been represented by Strabo as savages more wild and unpolished than the Britons ? Or could they have been described by Mela, as the most uncultivated of all nations ?—The character which Solinus has drawn of them is equally unfavourable : he calls them a *nation void of humanity, unhospitable, and every way barbarous and atheistical.* These characters were certainly too severe : the vices and ignorance of the old Irish must have been cruelly exaggerated, and the writers now mentioned must not have been properly informed. But had the people of Ireland been that humane, generous, polite and literary people whom O Connor has described them, it is impossible to imagine that the world could have been so unjust to them, or that the writers now mentioned could have been so grossly mistaken.

Besides, if it be certain that Ireland was the grand Emporium of the North in the first century ;—that the Kings and armies of that country fought in Caledonia, against Agricola, before the

Scots were settled in North Britain ; that the Picts maintained a conftant intercourfe with the inhabitants of Hibernia, from the commencement of their refpective monarchies ; and that they frequently intermarried with their beft families :—If all this be true, how was it poffible that the old Caledonians and Picts could have been totally unacquainted with letters, and could have remained in their uncultivated ftate till the third or fourth century ?

If it is true, that Anglefey, on account of its vicinity to Ireland, then the country of literature and fcience, was the great Britifh univerfity for Druidical knowledge ; if it is certain that there was the metropolitan's feat, and that the philofophers of Gaul came thither to finifh their education * ; how could South Britain have been deftitute of hiftories, books and letters, till it was conquered and polifhed by the Romans ?

Sir James Ware, one of the moft diligent, and undoubtedly one of the moft learned antiquaries that Ireland ever produced, has, in feveral paffages of his works, given the fanction of his authority to the fyftem which we have been now defending. That learned gentleman, though very willing to do all poffible honour to his country, confeffes ingenuoufly, *that all the knowledge now remaining of what paffed in Ireland before the light of the gofpel began to dawn there, is extremely little* †. And for that very good reafon he has

---

* O Connor fays, that the reafon why learning flourifhed fo early in Anglefey, was on account of its vicinity to Ireland.

† Perexiguam fupereffe notitiam rerum in Hibernia geftarum ante exortam ibi evangelii auroram liquido conftat. Warius de Ant. Hib. in præfatione.

F   fpoken

spoken of those matters with diffidence and cau-
tion. He begins his account of the Irish Kings
no higher than Leogaire, who was cotemporary with
St. Patrick, and makes no scruple to acknowledge,
that almost all that is related concerning that King's
predecessors, is either mere fiction, or totally dif-
guised with fable. He defends Bolandus in his
opinion that the famous Apostle of the Irish was
the person who introduced letters among them,
and owns at the same time, that after the strictest
enquiry, he was not able to discover any one tolerable writer of the history or antiquities of his
own country more ancient than the *Psalter Cashel*,
which was wrote in the tenth or eleventh age.

THIS system of the aboriginal literature of the
Irish nation being subverted and ruined, the pretended accounts of their ancient colonies must together with it fall to the ground. In the differtation which immediately follows this, I shall endeavour to investigate the genuine origin of the
first inhabitants of Ireland.

DISSER-

DISSERTATION VIII.

Of the original Inhabitants of Ireland.----
That they went from Caledonia.---Why
the Irish and Britiſh Scots were called
Gaels.

THE unprejudiced part of mankind will allow, with Sir James Ware, that the domeſtic hiſtory of Ireland, prior to the time of St.
Patrick, which is the earlieſt æra that can be affixed for the introduction of letters, is irretriev-
ably loſt. Tradition might for a time have preſerved a confuſed ſhadow of great events. The
compoſitions of bards and *fileas* may have tranfmitted through a few generations, ſome occaſion-
al atchievements of their heroes ; but nothing is
more abſurd than to depend on either for the regular and continued hiſtory of any nation.

THE glow of poetry which animates ſome
of the compoſitions of the bards, the harmony of
numbers, and the elegance of thought and expreſſion, have, in ſome caſes, taken ſuch hold of
the human mind, that they have undoubtedly
been handed down through ſome generations
without the aid of letters. The poems of Oſſian
lately given to the public, may convince the world

of the truth of this obfervation, which, at firft fight, may appear paradoxical. But a number of circumftances have concurred in the prefervation of thofe monuments of genius. When the mind is impreffed by the boldnefs of poetical figures and metaphors the memory feldom fails. Thofe figures cannot be introduced into a hiftorical narration. The mind flags at the dull jingle of hiftory in rhime; and therefore no argument can be drawn to ftrengthen the hiftorical traditions of fennachies and fileas from the prefervation of the poems of Offian.—The period, moreover, to which Offian is fixed, is not fo much beyond the introduction of letters into the North, but their affiftance might have very early been received to perpetuate his compofitions. We have among us many ancient manufcripts of detached pieces of his works, and thefe may have been copied from manufcripts ftill more ancient.

But the tranfmiffion of merely hiftorical events, by the rhimes of a fucceffion of bards, cannot deferve the fame degree of faith. We know, in the Highlands of Scotland, how little our bards can be depended on in matters of fact, fince we had it in our power to examine them by the criterion of true hiftory. I therefore have rejected their idle tales concerning the antiquity of our nation, preferring the fmall, but more certain light we have from the writers of Greece and Rome, to all their incoherent and indigefted fables. But as the Irifh nation have not hitherto rejected the legends of their bards and fileas, we are not to wonder at the ftrange mafs of abfurdity which they poffefs for their early hiftory.

As

As it cannot be said that the Irish had the use of letters before the introduction of Christianity, so it is impossible to prove that they had any other infallible method of perpetuating the memory of events. The art of drawing hieroglyphics on pillars or rocks, notwithstanding their pretended intercourse with Egypt, it is certain they had not. Their wildest antiquaries do not even pretend it; and Keating absolutely disclaims it in the name of his whole nation.

From the accounts which that writer, and others who have adopted the same system, have given of the first inhabitants of Ireland, and its oldest colonies, it may be fairly concluded that the origin of that nation must be investigated any where rather than in its own annals.

Cambden, whose conjectures are plausible as his learning was immense, seems to have been persuaded that the first inhabitants of Ireland must have gone from Britain. But afraid or averse to provoke a whole nation, at that time desperately in love with their traditionary genealogies, he speaks too faintly and with too much brevity on that subject.

The arguments brought by that great antiquary to support his hypothesis, are in substance these * : " The vast number of British words found in the Irish tongue; the similarity of old proper names in the two islands; that conformity of nature and customs which point out the connection of the two nations with each other; the denomination of a British isle given by some ancient writers to Hibernia, and of Britains to its

---

* See Cambd. Hibernia, cap. 1.

F 3

inhabitants

inhabitants; and laft of all, the fhortnefs of the paffage from Britain into Ireland."

Had Cambden told us in plain language, that by that part of Britain from which the firft and earlieft colonies went over to Ireland, he meant the Northern divifion of it, his arguments with regard to the origin of the Irifh nation, would have been more if not perfectly convincing. The vicinity of the countries is a proof which pleads much more ftrongly for the Caledonians and *Mæatæ* of North Britain, than for the *Silures* or *Devices* or *Brigantes* of the South. The frequent vifits of the Hibernian Scots in the Northern part of the ifland, and their long alliance with the Picts, furnifh ftrong enough prefumptions that thefe two nations were united by the ties of confanguinity, or fprung at firft from the fame ftock. The two promontories now called the Mull of Galloway, and the Mull of Cantyre, lie more contiguous to Ireland than any part of England or Wales. The languages of the Caledonians and Scots were the fame, and from the fame principles it may be proven that the Pictifh and Irifh tongues were fo likewife. All thefe confiderations taken together will induce any one to believe that the oldeft inhabitants of Ireland were colonies from the Weftern parts of the modern Scotland.

Tacitus underftood, by converfing with Agricola, that the Hibernians cotemporary with that great man differed not much in their genius, manners, and cuftoms, from the Britains.

The bulk of the Irifh nation were a very different race of men from thofe on the Weftern coaft of South Britain. Their languages, though plainly related to one another, are far from being
reciprocally

reciprocally intelligible in both the countries : and till the Normans conquered some parts of Ireland, the people of that country had rather better opportunities than the Welsh to retain the language of their anceftors in its purity. Therefore as the Irish differs so effentially from the antient and modern Welsh, and is so nearly allied to the Galic or antient Scotch, it seems decisive that the Irish must have derived their language, and consequently their original from North Britain.

I SHALL endeavour in the sequel of these differtations to shew that the Scots of Britain are the genuine pofterity of the Caledonian Britains. If that attempt shall succeed, it will be readily granted that the Scots of Ireland went originally from Scotland. For it may be proved that a perfect fimilarity of genius, language, arms, drefs, manners and cuftoms, has fubfifted between the two nations from the earlieft accounts of time.

THERE is one argument more which may be confidered of some force, though of the grammatical kind.

THE Welsh to this day call the Irish and Scots *Guidhill* *. The Irish and Highlanders of this kingdom give themfelves this name reciprocally. We are told by a very able judge in such matters, that the Picts were called *Guidhill* by his countrymen of old. On the other hand, the Englifh, Welsh, and all who fpeak Englifh only, are diftinguifhed by the Highlanders and genuine Irish, with the appellation of *Gaul.*

---

* In the word *Guidhill*, the letters *dh* are quiefcent, fo that it is pronounced almoft in the fame manner with *Gael* or *Cael*, the name which the Irish and Highlanders of Scotland give themfelves to this day.

NATIONAL

NATIONAL prejudices and antipathies run much too high every where. From that source national reflections will flow very naturally : formerly an unfavourable idea was annexed to the name of Highlander, and the people of that country, in return, gave the name *Gaul* to every foreigner or enemy of their nation, and fixed to it the ideas communicated by the words, *stranger*, *ignoble*, *cowardly*, *penurious*, and *unhospitable*. But the true original meaning of the name is, a man from Gaul. The ancient inhabitants of Scotland thought themselves of a different race from the people of South Britain, a people who came at a later period from Gaul, and were of course strangers to them. It became therefore at last customary with them to call every foreigner *Gaul*, and every person who had his education in a remote country, or who affected to imitate the manners and fashions of other nations, *Gauldi*.

FROM the appellation of Guidhil or Gael given indiscrimately to the Picts, Scots, and Irish, by the antient inhabitants of South Britain, we may reasonably infer, that the latter were persuaded that these three nations had the same common original, and somewhat different from themselves. The Welsh, who are reckoned the genuine remains of these ancient South Britains, call themselves Kymre in their own language ; and had they been of opinion that the old Hibernians derived their blood from their own predecessors, it is probable that they would have confounded them with the Picts and Scots by giving the same national denomination to all ?

To strengthen the argument drawn from the appellation now before us, it may be observed,

that

that the Saxons who came from Germany into England, gave the name *Gaul*, with a fmall difference in the orthography, and lefs in the pronunciation, to thofe Britains of the South to whom they bore the greateft hatred. They called the Britains *Weales* in their own language, and *Gauli* in the Monkifh Latin of the times. The reafon why they affixed this mark of diftinction to thefe Britains was, that they were in their opinion defcended from the Gauls on the continent : a nation againft whom the old Germans, like their modern pofterity, had entertained ftrong national prejudices *.

As it will be afked why the genuine Scots call themfelves *Gael* or *Cael*, their country *Caeldocin*, and every thing that looks like them and their country *Gaeltich*, I fhall take the liberty to offer a conjecture which may tend to illuftrate the fubject under confideration.

Men of letters will allow that the Germans, as well as the people of Gaul, were called *Celtes* by the Greeks †. It is likewife true, that the power of the letter *G* was in a vaft number of words much the fame with that of *K* among the Greeks, and *C* among the Latins ‡. Thefe two

---

* The initial W of the Teutonic is commonly equivalent to the *Gu* and fimple G of the Britifh, Irifh, French, and Italian languages. Thus the Weales of the Anglo-Saxons is by the French pronounced and written *Galles*, as it is by the Irifh and ancient Scots *Gaullive*: it is unneceffary to produce more inftances. See Lhoyd's Com. Etymol. under the letter G.

† Suidas in his Dictionary.

‡ Thus the Romans wrote Carthaco and Carthago, pugna and pucna, vigefimus and vicefimus, and the Greeks inftead of the Latin Caius wrote Γαυος, &c.

obfervations being admitted, one may venture to fay that *Gaelti*, in the language of the ancient Scots and Irifh, is the fame with the *Celtæ* of the Latins.

I f we examine the changes made by the Greeks and Romans in the perfonal and local names of the Celtic language, the etymon now propofed can hardly be thought overftrained : at the worft it cannot be fo abfurd as that which deduces the name *Gael* from the Gallæci of Spain, with whom the Scots have perhaps lefs connection than with the *Galatians* of Afia and the *Galatæ* of Europe.

T h e etymon of *Gael* or *Cael* being thus eftablifhed, we have plainly the derivation of the *Caledonia* of the Romans. I have above obferved that the Highlands of Scotland is known, to this day, by no other name among the natives, than by *Cael-dochd*, a word compounded of *Cael*, i. e. *Celts*, and *Do-ich Country*. This obfervation was firft fuggefted by the tranflator of Offian's poems; and it is fo obvioufly the original of *Caledonia*, that it is matter of fome furprize it never was obferved before. The inhabitants of the Highlands of Scotland call themfelves emphatically *Na Cael*, i. e. *the Celts*. To the Irifh they give the name of *Cael Eirinach*, i. e. *the Irifh Celts*. Whether an argument could be drawn from this circumftance, that of old it was not the popular belief, that the Scots came originally from Ireland, I leave to others to determine.

I f any one fhould incline to think that the ancient Irifh and Scots had their denomination of *Gael* from their imaginary founder Gathelus, the fon or hufband of Scota, he may, while he pleafes, enjoy an opinion once popular and ftill harmlefs.

But

But it is fcarcely lefs credible that Gathelus ever had any real exiftence, than that he was miraculoufly cured by Mofes near the Red Sea. That young Prince had it feems the misfortune to be bit in the neck by a ferpent, and the whole mafs of his blood was immediately corrupted : but at the requeft of his father, Mofes interpofed very feafonably, and upon laying his wonder-working rod on the wound reftored the youth to a perfect ftate of health, mean time there remained a green fpot on that part of his body where the ferpent had fixed her teeth. From this green fpot he was ever after called *Gaidhil Glafs*, that is the green, or rather the grey : and Keating has inferted in his hiftory a dozen of verfes extracted from the faithful records of Tara, to prove that this illuftrious Prince derived his right to the epithet *Glafs* from the impreffion made on his body by the teeth of this monftrous fnake.

Upon the whole, it appears evident, that Ireland was firft peopled from Caledonia. The abettors of the high antiquities of Ireland have in fome meafure owned the exiftence of a Britifh colony ; but they were too much wedded to the indigefted fictions of a Spanifh extraction, to be convinced that all their anceftors went from this ifland. It would be no difficult matter to inveftigate the origin of the legendary fictions of the Irifh nation, and to fhew that they had not their rife in a very remote age. But a difcuffion of this fort is too unimportant in an age in which all but bigots to an abfurd antiquity, ought, in the judgment of fober reafon, to reject the Milefian fables; which bear about them the marks of their being invented fome time after Chriftianity was introduced into Ireland.

I N

IN the course of my reading on the subject of these differtations, I had an opportunity of examining all the Irish histories that have any pretensions to antiquity : I would have myself understood of thofe that have been given to the public : for though Ireland, as its annalists affirm, is crouded with ancient records, yet as they have been invisible to all but themselves, we may conclude, if they really exist, they throw very little advantageous light on the history of that country. The remarks I made I intend on some future occasion to throw together; though, as I above observed, the subject is unimportant, on account of the small degree of faith now given to the ancient domestic accounts of the Irish nation. But as in every age and country there are some enthusiasts that fondly believe the moft extravagant fictions concerning the antiquity of their respective nations, fo there are people that are ready to fupport that abfurd enthufiafm. I may therefore, by some drawcanfir of this fort, be called forth to fupport, with further arguments, the opinion I have advanced concerning the antiquities of Ireland; and it was from forefeeing that a circumftance of this kind might happen, that I made notes upon the fubject *.

---

* Thefe notes are now in the poffeffion of Mr. Macpherfon, of Strathmafhy, in the· county of Invernefs ; a very ingenious and learned gentleman, who has made the antiquities of Ireland his particular ftudy.

DISSER-

DISSERTATION IX.

Why the genuine Pofterity of the ancient Caledonians were called Picts and Scots.

FATHER Innes, fo often mentioned, and fome other antiquaries of note, fay, that " the occafion and rife of the name of Scots af- " ford a very probable conjecture that the own- " ers of it came, at firft, either from Scandia or " Spain *". Thefe are Innes's own words. According to him, the Scythæ and Scoti are names of a fimilar import and pronounciation ; therefore it is natural to believe that the latter is derived from the former, and that the original Scots of North Britain were a Scythian colony.

SHOULD we reafon from principles fo vague, we might infift on the clofe connection between the name *Scotus* on the one hand, and *Scotufa* of Theffaly on the other. And would any one, poffeffed of common fenfe, infer from this refemblance or even identity of founds, that the pretended conquerors of Ireland came from Theffaly, and were perhaps the fame with the myrmidons of Achilles ?

---

* Critical Effay, p. 536.

INNES

INNES and other writers add further, that the argument is founded, not fo much on the analogy of the names, as upon that conformity of manners and cuftoms by which the Scots and Scythians were diftinguifhed from all other nations.—It is difficult to fhew wherein the conformity confifted : if it lay in their barbarity and peculiar wildnefs of manners, the *Scotufæ* of Thrace might have fuited the comparifon as well as the moft unpolifhed parts of Scythia.

SHOULD a man of learning and abilities, even through humour, affert that the Scots came from Thrace, or the places adjacent, to the river Strymon, he might fupport his abfurd hypothefis with many plaufible obfervations. The Thracians have been very often called Scythians—Scotufa is nearly related to *Scotus*—the *Geloni* are not unlike the *Gael* in found ; the Geloni painted themfelves—The Geloni and the Bifaltæ, near Scotufa, drank the blood of horfes and milk curdled together : the Scots of Ireland have frequently eat of the fame compofition, if common fame has not belied them. A writer of great reputation fhews that the Geloni and Bifaltæ, and confequently the inhabitants of Scotufa, gave into this practice *.

NOT to infift on the conjectures of thofe who give a Scythian origin to the name of Scots, it is evident that at beft it is no more than an idle fancy to bring the Scots from either Scandinavia or Spain, till the learned are able to difcover the

---

* Bifaltæ quo more folent acerque Gelonus,
 Cum fugit in Rhodopen, atque in deferta Getarum,
 Et lac concretum cum fanguine potat equino.
       VIRG. Geor. iii.

Scots

Scots among the old inhabitants of thofe diftant countries. The geographers and hiftorians of ancient times condemn thofe two fyftems, by their total filence on that head ; and a hypothefis of this kind can never ftand on fo feeble a foundation as the diftortion of the word *Scythæ* *.

After all, it muft be confeffed, that it is extremely difficult to give any fatisfactory etymology of the name of Scots. It has puzzled the moft eminent antiquaries that Britain has produced ; and therefore I think it no difhonour to me to fail in a point where men of much greater abilities have not fucceeded.

Varro and Dionyfius Halicarnaffenfis difagree in their opinions concerning the etymon of Italia : nor are the derivations given of Gallia, Hifpania,

---

* It was on the fame falfe principles that the Irifh fhewed their connection with Spain ; but the affinity between the names Hibernia and Iberia is no more than the fhadow of a proof for fupporting their ideal genealogy. The Greek and Latin names of the ifland are to be derived from its weftern fituation, from the wintry temperament of its air and climate.—It may be likewife obferved, that the firft fyllable of the Latin word Hibernia is always long in the Latin profody, and the firft fyllable of Iberia fhort. From this circumftance it may, with fome fhow of probability, be inferred, that the poets were ftrangers to the relation between the Spaniards and the Irifh. To fuppofe that the Greek name of Ireland, that is Ierne or Iouerna, comes from the Greek word which fignifies *Holy*, is furely no more than a groundlefs fancy, though embraced by a learned gentleman. Had it come from that epithet, it muft have been written with an afpiration, like Hiera, one of the *Agates*, and Hiera, one of the OEolian iflands. One of the rivers in Spain is called Ierna by Mela. Ireland, like that river, was called Ierna, from the Celtic word *Iar*, that is Weft ; and the name of *Erin*, by which it has been always known by the Irifh and Highlanders of Scotland, is manifeftly a compound of *Jar, Weft*, and *In, Ifland*.

or

or Græcia, more certain. What shall we make of Europa, Asia and Africa? Cambden, with all his erudition and indefatigable induſtry, was greatly embarraſſed by the names Coritani, Silures, and many more nations, who made a very conſiderable figure in the country, which he illuſtrated with vaſt pains and equal ſuccceſs. Scaliger and Voſſius, Grotius, Bochart, and Menage, have been very often unſucceſsful in their endeavours to ſolve difficulties of this kind.

There is no reaſon why the Scots ſhould be aſhamed to acknowledge that the origin of their name is involved in darkneſs ; while that of Rome, the Queen of nations, remains utterly inexplicable. Plutarch found and left it ſo. Solinus gives no leſs than four different etymons, all equally unſatisfactory. Why the capitals of Britain, France and Portugal, have been of old called Londinum, Lutetia and Olyſippo, are queſtions which have not hitherto been ſufficiently cleared up, and probably never ſhall.

All we know with certainty concerning the appellation of *Scot* amounts to this, that it muſt have been at firſt a term of reproach, and conſequently framed by enemies, rather than aſſumed by the nation afterwards diſtinguiſhed by that name. The Highlanders, the genuine poſterity of the ancient Scots, are abſolute ſtrangers to the name, and have been ſo from the beginning of time. All thoſe who ſpeak the *Galic* language call themſelves *Albanich*, and their country *Alba*.

Contumelious appellations have been given in all ages not only to individuals, but to whole bodies of people, through ſpite, or a ſatirical pleaſantry natural to the human race. The *Pæ-*
ones

ones of Macedonia were a quarrelfome race of men, and therefore were called *Pæones.* The Proteftants of France and the Low Countries were nick-named Hugenots and *Gueux,* becaufe their adverfaries ftudied to make them ridiculous and contemptible. It is needlefs to multiply inftances. The fame ill-natured humour has been hitherto general, and will always continue fo.

THE Picts, who poffeffed originally the northern and eaftern, and in a later period, alfo the more fouthern divifions of North Britain, were at firft more powerful than the Caledonians of the weft. It is therefore eafy to fuppofe that the Picts, from a principle of malevolence and pride, were ready enough to traduce and ridicule their weaker neighbours of Argyle. Thefe two nations fpoke the fame language. In the *Galic* tongue *Scode* fignifies a corner, or fmall divifion of a country. A corner of North Britain is the very name which Gyraldus Cambrenfis gave the little kingdom which the fix fons of Muredus King of Ulfter were faid to have erected in Scotland *.

SCOT, in Galic, is much the fame with *little* or *contemptible* in Englifh; and *Scottan,* literally fpeaking, fignifies a fmall flock; metaphorically it ftands for a fmall body of men. For fome one of the reafons couched under thefe difparaging epithets, their malicious or fneering neighbours may have given the opprobrious appellation of *Scot* to the anceftors of the Scots nation.

THE Allemans of Germany were at firft an ignoble multitude, or a motley compofition of

---

* The kingdom of Argy'e, according to his information.

many

many different tribes and nations. For that very reafon, the reproachful name of *Allemans* * was framed by thofe who hated and defpifed them. But the deformity of that defignation was after-wards covered with laurels, like the blemifh which gave Cæfar fo much pain ; and the whole Germanic body is now proud of a title, thought at firft difhonourable. In the fame way it may be naturally fuppofed, that the people of *Albany* were, after a courfe of ages, reconciled to the once dif-paraging name of *Scots*, upon finding that all other nations agreed in diftinguifhing them by it.

I T is generally believed that the Picts derived their appellation from their characteriftical cuftom of painting their bodies. This opinion feems to be fupported by an expreffion of Claudian † ; who fhews, in another place, that the Picts continued the old practice of drawing the figures of animals on their limbs, after it had been abolifh-ed in South Britain ‡. But when the fafhion of painting in the fame way was univerfal in Britain, it may be afked, Why were not all the inhabitants called *Picts* by the Romans ? Why were the Caledonians of the Eaft diftinguifhed by a name to which thofe of the Weft had the fame right ; for it is certain they ufed the *Glaftum* of Pliny, and the *Vitrum* of Mela, in common ? *Picti* is no more than an epithet : and as Virgil would have been guilty of an impropriety, had he called ei-

---

* Allemans, q. *All mans*, a compofition of nations.
† Ille leves Mauros, nec falfo nomine Pictos,
Edomit.
‡ ———————————————— Ferroque notatas
Perlegit exanimes Picto moriente figuras.   CLAUDIAN.

ther

ther the Geloni or Agathyrſi, Piƈti, without ſpe-
cifying the particular nation to which he applied
that epithet, ſo the Romans in Britain would
have been guilty of the ſame ſolecitſm, had they
called the Eaſtern inhabitants of Caledonia *Piƈti*,
without annexing a noun ſubſtantive to the adjective.

UPON weighing theſe difficulties, I am apt to
believe that the name, out of which the Romans
framed the deſignation of *Piƈti*, was originally a
Britiſh one, and of a very different ſignification
from the Latin word, which is equivalent to *Painted* in Engliſh. The name was very probably
framed by the Scots to the Weſt, or the *Mæatæ*
to the South : and as it may have been impoſed
after the expedition of Severus, it is no matter of
wonder that it was unknown to all the Roman
writers till the very end of the third century.

AFTER the reign of Caracalla, the deſign of
conquering North Britain ſeems to have been totally laid aſide by the Romans. The frequent
competitions of rival Emperors, the public diſtractions
unavoidably attending ſuch conteſts, and a
long ſucceſſion of Princes, fooliſh, wicked and in-
active, muſt have diverted their attention to other
objeƈts. The barbarians of Caledonia had ſenſe
enough to avail themſelves of the advantages which
an adminiſtration, ſo feeble and uncertain, muſt
have afforded them. They made frequent incurſions into the Roman provinces, and met with
little oppoſition. Not long after, Conſtantius
Chlorus came from the Continent into Britain,
with an intention to make war upon them ; but
he died at York, before this deſign could be
executed. It was probably much about that time

that the Romans difcovered that the moft confiderable nation among the unconquered Britons
was called *Pictich*, a word correfponding in found
with the *Picti* in Latin : accordingly we find that
Eumenius, the panegyrift, is the firft Roman author who mentioned that people under this new
name.

In philological inveftigations of this kind, it is
much eafier to difapprove of the conjectures of
others, than to offer a more rational one to the
public. But as new opinions, which turn only
on verbal criticifm, are very innocent, though perhaps they may be ill founded, I fhall venture to
give a new etymon of the name of *Picti*.

The Highlanders, who fpeak the ancient language of Caledonia, exprefs the name of that
once famous nation, who were at laft fubdued
by the Scots, by the word *Pictich*. They could
not have borrowed this epithet from the Romans ;
for the illiterate part of the Highlanders have no
idea that the Romans were in this Ifland, or ever
exifted : yet the name now under confideration is
very familiar to their ears. One of the ideas affixed to the word *Pictdich*, or *Pictich*, is that odious one which the Englifh exprefs by the word
Plunderer, or rather Thief. Therefore it is not
improbable that their neighbours may have given
that title to a people fond of depredation : and
Dion gives us to underftand, that the barbarians
of North Britain took a peculiar pleafure in robberies ; nor was this character, in thefe days of
violence and ignorance, attended with much infamy : if the robber had the addrefs to form, and
the fpirit to execute his unjuft fchemes, he was
rather proud than afhamed of his conduct : all
the

the honefty required at his hands, was not to en-
croach on the property of a friend or ally *.

Among the Princes and chieftains whom Virgil has brought to the afliftance of Turnus, we
find fome who bear a perfeƈt refemblance to the
plundering heroes of Piƈtavia. The piƈture which
the poet has drawn of Ufens and his people may,
without any impropriety, be applied to the ancient Caledonian tribe now under confideration.

Et te montofæ mifere in prælia Nerfæ,
Ufens, infignem fama et felicibus armis:
Horrida præcipue cui gens, affuetaque multo
Venatu nemorum, duris Æquicula glebis
Armati terram exercent, femperque recentis
Conveƈtare juvat prædas, et *vivere rapto.*
　　　　　　　　　　　　Virg. Æn. 7.

The Brigantes of South Britain, the Brigantes
of Ireland, the Brigantii near the Alps, and the
inhabitants of Brigantium in Spain, derived their
names from *Brigand* †, a Celtic word, which fignifies a robber. The French have retained the
original word in their language; and the Englifh
have the word Brigantine, which properly fignifies a veffel ufed by pyrates.

Sextus Pompeius obferves, that thieves were,
in the language of Gaul, called *Cimbri*; and according to Plutarch, robbers went under the fame
name in Germany. The Cimbri had a ftrong

---

* Thofe who may imagine that robbery was efteemed more
honourable among the ancient Piƈts than among the other rude
nations of mankind, may confult Thucydides, p. 3. b. i.
† See Bullet. Diƈt. Celt. Fol. 2d, p. 211.

G 3

pro

propenfity to robberies of a private nature, as well .
as to that fpecies of depredation which goes under
the name of war and public conqueft. But if the
Cimbri of Germany, and the Brigantes of South
Britain, have borrowed their refpective names from
their defire of booty, or their fuccefs in plundering,
it is far from being incredible that a Caledonian people might have been called *Picidich* by their neighbours, for their uncommon dexterity in the fame
way.

EVERY one knows, that the Borderers of England and Scotland diftinguifhed themfelves for
many ages, by pillaging, plundering, and laying
whole countries wafte. In time of war thefe ravages may have been in fome meafure excufable.—
But even after truces and pacifications had been
folemnly ratified, the fame barbarous practices
were too fafhionable on both fides to be defifted
from; efpecially as they were attended with honour and encomium, rather than punifhment or
difgrace. It is hardly neceffary to add, that this
practice, though manifeftly incompatible with the
laws of all civilized nations, was tolerated, and
perhaps encouraged, till the acceffion of James
to the throne of England *.

THE explications I have ventured to give of
the names of Picts and Scots may be defective;
but they can hardly be more fo than thofe etymo-

---

* I am tempted to think that the ancient Selgovæ of Scotland,
who lay North of the Englifh Brigantes, were fo called from
the word *Sealg*, which, if literally taken, fignifies *Hunting*, and
metaphorically *Theft*. The Gadini, who were at no great diftance from the Selgovæ, feem to be nothing elfe than *Gadi-
chin* in Galic, that is to fay, robbers or thieves.

logies

logies which have been infifted on by men who may be juftly called the oracles of erudition in matters of this kind. It may be likewife faid that I have dwelt much longer on this fubject than its importance deferves. In the mean time, I leave it to the judgment of common fenfe to determine, whether it is not more probable that the Picts derive their name from a Britifh word, than from a Latin epithet *.

---

* Strabo, though a very judicious critic, hiftorian, and geographer, imagined, very inconfiderately, that the Germans received their name from their being as like their neighbours of Gaul as if they had been their Brothers-German. Bede, though a Saxon himfelf, and the moft eminent fcholar of his time, entertained a fancy that the name Anglus fhould be traced up to the Latin word Angulus, or a Corner. This conceit was little better than the puns of Pope Gregory at Rome, upon the words Angli and Angeli, Deiri and De ira, *Aella* and Alleluja †. And can it be matter of wonder that Claudian fhould have found the etymon of the Pictifh name in the Latin tongue, efpecially as thefe Caledonians were painted, and as the analogy between the Britifh word *Piɛtich* and the Roman *Piɛti* was fo very clofe?

† Bed. Hift. Ecclef. lib. 2. cap. 1.

DISSER.

DISSERTATION X.

The Highlanders Strangers to the National Name of Scots.----Call themſelves *Alba-nich*, or ancient Britons-----Gael, or Celtæ.---Obſervations on the Iriſh, Galic and Welch Languages.

FROM what has been ſaid in the preceding diſſertation, it appears, that the names of *Piƈts* and *Scots* were impoſed on the two nations into which the Caledonians were divided, ſome time before the Romans deſerted Britain, by the malevolence of their neighbours to the South, or roſe from the animoſities which ſubſiſted between themſelves. The indigenal name of the Caledonians is the only one hitherto known among their genuine deſcendants, the Highlanders of Scotland.—They call themſelves *Albanich* to this day. All the illiterate Highlanders are as perfeƈt ſtrangers to the national name of Scot, as they are to that of Parthian or Arabian. If a common Highlander is aſked, of what country he is, he immediately anſwers, that he is an *Albanich*, or *Gael*.

It

I T is unneceffary to produce authorities to fhew that the ifland, which now goes under the name of Britain, was in early ages called *Albion.* To fearch for a Hebrew or Phœnician etymon of *Albion* has been the folly of fome learned writers. In vain have fome attempted to derive it from the white cliffs near Dover, or from a Greek word which fignifies a certain fpecies of grain, or from a gigantic fon of Neptune.

I N the Celtic language, of which fo many different dialects were diffufed over all the European nations of the Weft and North, and let me add, the Scythians of Afia, the vocable *Alp*, or *Alba*, fignifies *High.* Of the Alpes Grajæ, Alpes Pæninæ, or Penninæ, and the Alpes Baftarnicæ, every man of letters has read.

I N the ancient language of Scotland, *Alpes* fignifies, invariably, an eminence. The Albani near the Cafpian fea, the Albani of Macedon, the Albani of Italy, and the *Albanich* of Britain, had all the fame right to a name founded on the fame characteriftical reafon, the heighth or roughnefs of their refpective countries. The fame thing may be faid of the Gaulifh Albici near Maffilia.

T H E Celtic was undoubtedly the language of the Belgic Gaul. For this we have the authority of Strabo. That from the Belgic divifion of Gaul the firft colony muft have tranfmigrated into South Britain, muft be readily allowed. The vicinity of the two countries, and the fhortnefs of the paffage, is an argument in this cafe equal to a demonftration. It was natural enough for men, who had been once fettled in the low plains of Belgium, to give the name of *Alba*, or *Albin*, to Britain, on comparing the face or appearance of it

10

to that of their former country. Men who had come from the Netherlands would moſt probably have called this new world *Albin* in an oblique caſe, and *Alba* in the nominative. And it is to be obſerved, that almoſt all the local names of the Celtic tongue are energetical, and deſcriptive of the peculiar properties or appearance of places.

THE Greeks became in ſome degree acquainted with Britain, and its original name, long before the Romans had any opportunity of knowing either. Agreeably to the genius of their language, the former naturally gave a new termination to *Albin*; and their Albion muſt have, in procefs of time, paſſed to the Romans. But the true Celtic name of the iſland having travelled gradually into the remoter parts of it, was there retained, by a race of plain, uncivilized men, who having no intercourſe with the Greeks, and very little with the Romans, adhered invariably to their mother tongue, and particularly to the local names which had been tranſmitted to them by their anceſtors.

THAT all the territories once poſſeſſed by the old Caledonians were formerly called *Alba* in Galic, and Albania in the Latin of latter ages, is certain, beyond contradiction. In the little ancient Chronicles of Scotland, publiſhed by Innes at the end of his Critical Eſſay, they go frequently under that name *; and Kenneth, the ſon of Alpin, who was the firſt Monarch of Caledonia, is called the firſt King of Albany, in ſome old Latin rhimes often quoted †. But had the Scots of Britain come

---

* Innes's Crit. Eſſay, in his Appendix, Num. 1, &c.
† Primus in Albania ſertur regnaſſe Kenethus,
  Filius Alpini, prœlia multa gerens.

originally

originally from Ireland, their Latin name would have been very probably Hiberni, and their Galic one undoubtedly remain *Erinich*.

AFTER the Germans had conquered the southern divifion of Britain, to thofe who remained of the old inhabitants they gave the name of Weales and Gauls, in their own tongue, and of Britonnes, in the Latin of the times ; while they themfelves thought it more honourable to retain their hereditary appellations of Saxons, Angles, and Jutes.

AMONG the moft illuftrious nations of antiquity, few have been equal, and fcarce any fuperior, to the Gauls, in military glory. Salluft makes ro difficulty of acknowledging, that in this refpect they were before the Romans *. Be that as it will, it is certain they had great merit in that way. Yet the Franks had too high a regard for their own genuine fame, and too profound a veneration for their anceftors, to affume the name of the Gauls, after they had poffeffed themfelves cf their country.

To ftrengthen the obfervation I am to make, it is almoft needlefs to mention the Ionians of Afia, the Phocæans of Gaul, the Boii of Germany, the Longobardi of Italy, the Belgæ and Atrebates of South Britain. All thefe, and other innumerable colonies, who left their native countries, and planted themfelves in foreign regions, made a point of retaining the proper names of thofe nations from which they were originally fprung.

HAD the Scots of Britain been a colony from Ireland, in fpite of all the hard things faid by Strabo, Mela, Solinus and others, to the prejudice

---

* Salluft in Catilina, cap. liii,

of

of the old Hibernians ; nay, if the univerſal conſent of mankind, inſtead of three or four ancient
writers, had agreed in calling the Iriſh ſavages,
cannibals, atheiſts, and ſtrangers to every virtue
under heaven, the Scots, notwithſtanding, would
have admired their anceſtors ſuperſtitiouſly, and
retained their name, rather than degrade themſelves into *Albanich*.   But no Britiſh Scot has ever
yet called himſelf an Hibernian in a learned language, nor *Erinich* in his own mother tongue.
Every Scot who underſtands the Galic calls himſelf, as I obſerved before, either *Gael*, that is, one
of the Celtæ, or *Albanich*, in other words, a genuine Briton.

No⊤ all the ſenſible and quaint obſervations
of civilized times will eradicate from the minds of
the bulk of a people the high opinion they entertain of themſelves, for their connexion with renowned national anceſtors ; and in every country
national anceſtors have a great deal of traditional
fame.   It is true, the merit of remote progenitors is ſometimes very ſmall, frequently dubious,
and always exaggerated by the partial fictions of
their poſterity.

Th⒠ founders of Rome were a very flagitious
race : the vagabonds that aſſociated with them an
ignoble and abandoned rabble.   Thieves, ruffians,
deſperadoes, bankrupts, cow-keepers, ſhepherds,
ſlaves, raviſhers of women, murderers of men,
oppreſſors and uſurpers, were the anceſtors of men,
lords of the world *   Yet the Romans were extra-

---

* Majorum primus quiſquis fuit ille tuorum,
 Aut paſtor fuit, aut illud quod dicere nolo.

					Juven. Satyr. viii. ad finem.

							vagantly

vagantly vain and proud of their origin. All other nations were in fome degree influenced by the fame puerile weaknefs.

But in the annals of mankind it is perhaps impoffible to find a nation more vain in this refpect than the old Irifh. To fay nothing of the antediluvian inhabitants of Ireland, and not to mention the Partholanians, Nemedians and others, the ideal connection they had with Scythian kings, Egyptian princeffes, and Iberian heroes, infpired them with a very high idea of their own dignity, and perhaps with a proportionable contempt for almoft every other people. Had the Scots of Britain been the real pofterity of a people fo extravagantly fond of their ideal national anceftors, is it reafonable to believe that they would have rejected the name of Hibernians or *Erinich* with fcorn, and preferred that of *Albanich*, a name which the Picts and old Caledonians muft have carried in common with them?

From the appellation Kymri, Cumri or Cumeri, invariably retained by the Welfh, it has been concluded, and with reafon, that, inftead of being defcended from the Romans, Saxons, Danes, Normans, or other interlopers into Britain, they are the genuine offspring of the ancient Gomerians or Cimbri. What therefore fhould hinder antiquaries from concluding likewife, the argument being exactly the fame, that the Scots of Britain, who without interruption retained through all ages the name of *Albanich*, are fprung from the ancient inhabitants of *Albany*, and confequently were genuine Caledonians? The Welfh have preferved their original Celtic name. The

Highlanders

Highlanders of North Britain retained the firſt appellation given to the inhabitants of the whole iſland. It will be aſked perhaps, why the Welſh have not retained the appellation of *Albanich*. I ſhall offer a few remarks to clear up that difficulty.

It is certain that the languages ſpoken by the people of North Wales, by the Highlanders of Scotland, and by thoſe commonly called the wild Iriſh, are the moſt genuine remains of the ancient Celtic tongue now extant. The Corniſh, Armorican, and Biſcayan dialeɛts, muſt yield the preference to the former three, however certain it is that in theſe dialeɛts ſome true Celtic words have been preſerved hitherto, which the Welſh, Highlanders, and Iriſh, have totally loſt.

By the ſuffrage of reaſon, and from the experience of nations and ages, we find that the language of a people out of the way of foreign invaſions, and unacquainted with the arts of commerce and civil life, has the beſt chance of continuing the ſame, or at leaſt of undergoing the feweſt alterations. Remote iſles, ſecured by tempeſtuous ſeas, and mountainous traɛts of land, environed with rocks, woods, and moraſſes, defended by a warlike race of men, and ſterile enough to diſcourage the avarice or ambition of ſtrangers, are the beſt means to fix and perpetuate a language.

It is true, no ſituation of country can ſecure a language altogether from the injuries of time, from the arbitrary power of faſhion, and from the common fate of every ſublunary thing. Some words muſt be imported by ſtrangers, ſome created by whim. Some will riſe out of new diſcoveries,

and

and others muſt be framed to expreſs new ideas conveyed by new objeꞔs. Language, in ſhort, even independent of the mixture of nations, muſt be in a ſtate of fluꞔuation. But after all that can be ſaid to prove the natural and accidental inſtability of language, rocks, ſeas and deſarts, ignorance, ſterility, and want of commerce, are its beſt preſervatives, next to valuable books, and permanent records.

Whether Wales, Ireland, or the mountainous parts of North Britain, have retained the Celtic the neareſt to its original ſimplicity, purity, or ſtrength, is a queſtion which, like all other matters of verbal criticiſm, is more amuſing than uſeful, and differently reſolved by the learned in that way. Of theſe ſome have declared for the country firſt named, others have determined the controverſy in favour of the ſecond, while the third, unfortunate in many reſpeꞔs, and particularly in its ſcarcity of domeſtic writers, has been entirely left out of the queſtion.

Every one knows that the Romans, Saxons, Danes, and Normans, had long and bloody corteſts with the ancient Kymri. In ſpite of all the brave ſtruggles they made for liberty, and the honour of their country, it is certain they were enſlaved by the firſt of the nations juſt mentioned, and brought under total ſubjeꞔion by the laſt. The intercourſe they had with the other two was too inconſiderable not to affeꞔ their language in ſome degree.

The Norwegians and Danes made ſtrong and ſucceſsful efforts in Ireland. By them were the principal towns or cities there built. Turgeſius
and

and his army made confiderable acquifitions there, and was cruelly oppreflive. The Eafterlings and Normans could never be totally exterminated out of that country. One of the braveft of the monarchs of Ireland, Brian Boroimbe, loft his life in the famous battle of Cluantarf, fighting againft thefe foreigners. The Hibernian antiquaries are agreed in complaining bitterly that the barbarians of the North made a dreadful havock of their churches, monafteries, feminaries of learning, and books. The wars, commerce, and intermarriages of the Irifh with the Eafterlings, muft have had fome confiderable influence on the language of Ireland.

THE Norwegians and Danes did likewife infeft Scotland for a courfe of ages, made a conqueft of the Weftern Ifles, and erected a principality there, called the Kingdom of Man, as that ifland was the feat of their fmall empire in North Britain. But fome of the Highland diftricts upon the Weftern continent of Scotland were never fubjected to any foreign yoke ; nor has the language of thefe diftricts been either exterminated, or till of late corrupted in any confiderable degree, by an intermixture of that tongue which has been prevailing in the more civilized provinces of this kingdom for feven centuries back.

IT will be readily granted, that the Irifh and Welfh dialects of the Celtic tongue are more copious than the Galic of thefe diftricts of North Britain which I have juft mentioned. I fhall allow likewife that the two former dialects were better polifhed, and rendered perhaps more harmonious. The countries in which they were fpoken produced many books, and encouraged men of letters. But

from

from thefe very confiderations, it may perhaps with reafon be inferred, that they receded farther from the fimplicity of the original language than thofe who had neither opportunities nor inclination to refine or enrich it. Is it not certain that one of the academies of France, and the many books publifhed by the members of it, have contributed much to deftroy what they call the old Gaulifh tongue in that country? And is is not equally true, that the modern univerfities of England and Scotland have, together with other caufes, almoft totally altered the language brought by the Saxons from Germany, and once common to much the greateft part of the firft of thefe kingdoms, and to the moft confiderable divifion of the laft.

I SHALL not carry the parallel between the Welfh, Irifh, and Galic, much farther. They only who underftand the three languages perfectly have a right to decide in this difpute. Let me only obferve, that the learned author of the Archæologia Britannica, one of the ableft judges the republic of letters has produced, made no fcruple to fay, though a Welfhman himfelf, that if the Irifh, Scotch, and Welfh, are compared with the ancient language of Gaul, the latter will be found to agree lefs with it than the other two. Certain it is that the meaning of many Celtic words which have been preferved by the Roman writers, and particularly names perfonal and local, the fignification of which has confounded the fkill of our beft antiquaries, may be eafily difcovered by thofe who are no more than indifferently converfant in the Galic.

To exemplify the general pofition laid down by the author of the Archæologia, the word *Ifca*,

once

once fo common in South Britain, *Ifca Silurum,*
Ifca Danmoniorum, Ifca Legionis Secundæ, and fo
on, common, I mean, in time of the Romans,
figrifies plainly *Water* or a *River,* in the Galic
and Irifh. The Welfh have loft the fignification,
and almoft the ufe of that word, which is *Uifce*
in the languages juft named. and *Wyfk* in that of
the old Kymri. For that reafon the learned Cambden was not able to find out the meaning of
Ifca, in the names mentioned above. But in all
the divifions of Britain were many rivers which
had no other names than the general appellatives
of *Uifk, Avon, Wy* and *Taw* *. In Scotland are
many fuch which are called *Efk,* though corruptly,
to this day. In England are feveral *Avons,* and
many fmaller waters which have *wy* for their final
fyllable, as there is a large navigable one diftinguifhed by the fame appellative. In the compound

---

* The largeft river in Scotland is called *Taw* in the Galic,
the moft noted rivers in Wales are called *Taff,* and the Thames,
the nobleft river in Britain, was undoubtedly called *Tamh* in
the old language of the country. *Tamh* fignifies the ocean, or
great fea, in Galic, and *Mor Tauch* has the fame meaning in the
Welfh I am perfuaded that thefe rivers obtained the names
now mentioned, becaufe they are ocean like, or feas, if compared to fmaller ftreams ; juft as the Hebrews, and fometimes
the Romans, gave the name of a fea to a large collection of
frefh water. For the fame reafon was the *Tagus* of Lufitania fo
called ; the Taio of the prefent times, a word which comes
nearer to the old Celtic name of that river. Here likewife it
may be obferved that the *Duriæ* of the Alpine regions, the
Durius of Spain, and the *Duranius* of Gaul, are all appellative
nouns, derived from the Celtic word *Dur* or water ; and I add
farther, that almoft all the large rivers in Europe have the vocables, *Avon, Ifc,* or *Dur,* either in the beginning or end of their
names, though much difguifed by the inflections of Greek and
Roman writers.

names

names of South Britain, we often find *Ex*; for example, Exeter, which anfwers to *Efk* of Scotland. In Yorkfhire is a rivulet called *Wyfke*, and in Monmouthfhire is a larger ftream which goes under the name of *Wyfk*.

CAMBDEN has been at fome pains to prove that the word *Braccæ*, which was undoubtedly a Celtic one, fignifying a party-coloured garment, is preferved to this day in fome manner by the Welfh, *Brati* in their language being the fame with foul tattered clothes. The learned antiquary made this remark, together with many more in the grammatical way, to prove that the language of South Britain was of old the fame with that of Gaul. How far he has fucceeded in the comparifon drawn between *Braccæ* and *Brati*, I fhall not fay. But in the Galic tongue, the word *Braccan**
is in common ufe to this day, and the idea affixed to it explains what the Gauls meant by their Braccæ much better than many learned critics had been able to do.

WE are told by Feftus Pompeius, that the father of Roman eloquence, and his anceftors, had the name *Tullius* from a cataract near the feat of the family. In the Galic, a flood or torrent like that which tumbles down from a cataract, is expreffed by the word *Tuille*. But I have not been able to difcover that the Welfh have preferved a word of the fame found and import in their language. It is hardly neceffary to obferve further that the Gauls were once poffeffed of many places

---

* Braccan is that kind of upper garment ufed by the Highlanders, which the Englifh call *Plaid*: it is derived from the adjective *Breac*, fignifying *party-coloured*.

in

in Italy, and muſt have left many local names behind them, ſome of which are extant to this day.

To conclude this tedious philological diſcuſſion : it is certain that many words in uſe to this day in the Highlands of Scotland, were once uſed in common by the Britons of the South, and the ancient Celtæ, though now diſcontinued in the language of Wales. From the whole I draw this concluſion : that the Welſh may have loſt in their language the appellation of *Albanich,* though once common in their country, in the ſame manner that they loſt the remarkable vocable *Uiſc,* and many others that could be ſpecified.

DISSERTATION. XI.

Of the Genius, Manners and Customs of the Caledonians, Picts and Scots.

THE Caledonians made war their great study, and the principal business of life. Agriculture was entirely neglected, or but faintly prosecuted, and the commercial arts were hardly known among them. The chace, an exercise manifestly subservient to a military life, was their favorite amusement. A peculiar attachment to the pleasures and advantages arising from such a course of life, gave them an uncommon degree of agility, vigour and patience to bear fatigue. Dio says, that they ran with extraordinary swiftness, and sustained cold, hunger, and toil, with an amazing constancy. Herodian calls the barbarians of North Britain, incomparably brave, and insatiably fond of slaughter. Let history determine, whether they were ever conquered, or whether the Lords of mankind, the Romans, were so bravely repulsed

　　　　　　　　　by

by any other nation, except the Parthians of the
East, and the Germans of the West. *.

I t must be allowed, that the particular situation of the Caledonian territories gave great difadvantages to any enemy that invaded them ; and
it is also certain, that the very same circumstance
inured the inhabitants to all the hardships incident
to a military life. The people of Numantia,
whose dominions were confined within the narrow
limits of a few mountains, gave much more trouble to the Roman arms than Antiochus the Great,
and the prodigious host which he collected on the
fertile plains of Asia. The genius of every soil
naturally transfuses itself into the souls and bodies
of its inhabitants. Caledonia was peculiarly
adapted to that kind of life which we call barbarous. Its forests and mountains produced game
in abundance. The severity of the climate, and
the rugged face of the country, tended to strengthen
the body, and inure the mind to hardships. These
circumstances, however disagreeable they may appear in this age, were highly favourable to that
martial spirit which subsisted among our ancestors ;
and what would render Caledonia but a poor ac-
quisition to the Romans, was the only means of
its defence against them.

---

* An author, who has done honour to the age in which he
lived, as well to the country which gave him birth, has touched
this subject with the usual felicity of his poetical genius.

    Roma securi geris prætendit mænia Scotis.
    Hic spe progressus posita Carrontis adundam
    Terminus Ausonii signat divertia regni, &c.
        BUCHANAN in Epithalamio Franc. Valef. & Mar.
    Scot. Reg.

I t

IT is impoſſible to ſay, with certainty, at what time the Caledonians began to cultivate the ground. Under the reign of Severus they were abſolute ſtrangers to agriculture. They thought, like their *Celto-Scythian* brethren of Germany, * " That he " who acquires, with the continual ſweat of his brow, what might be purchaſed all at once with a little blood, is deſtitute of ſpirit, genius and feeling.—One could more eaſily perſuade them to brave all the perils of war, than to toil at the ſpade, or wait for the ſlow returns of Autumn."

THEIR food was the natural produce of an uncultivated country, the fleſh of tame animals, veniſon, fiſh, milk, and the ſpontaneous growth of their fields and woods. We cannot believe, on the authority of Strabo, though a very exaɛt and judicious writer, that ſome Britons were barbarous enough not to have known the art of curdling milk : nor is it credible that they had an irreconcileable averſion to fiſh, though they had it in ſuch plenty in their ſeas and rivers. Solinus relates, that the inhabitants of the Ebudæ lived on milk and fiſh only.

IT is hardly neceſſary to obſerve, that the refinements of luxury were utterly unknown to the ancient inhabitants of Caledonia. One of their methods of preparing the fleſh of animals killed in hunting, is very exaɛtly deſcribed by Mr. Macpherſon, the tranſlator of Oſſian's Poems. The ſame method was praɛtiſed in Ireland. Nor is that ſpecimen of our ancient cookery much un-

---

* Tacitus de mor. Germ. c. xiv.

H 4

like

like that which hitherto prevails among the modern Highlanders, on their hunting parties *.

We learn from Cæsar, that the Britons of the South used brass plates and rings of iron by way of money : it is probable their neighbours of the North adopted the same custom. Herodian writes, that they held the last of these metals in the same degree of estimation which other nations placed on gold. Virius Lupus, one of the lieutenants or pro-prætors employed by Severus in Britain, purchased a peace from them with money. Agricola and his troops had probably taught them the use of coin.

---

* The Scots of the fourteenth century had not degenerated much from the simplicity of their forefathers in the article of living. In the reign of Robert Bruce, Randolph Earl of Murray, and Sir James Douglas, invaded the North of England, at the head of a select body of men inured to battles and fatigues. After these adventurers had penetrated farther than Durham, and committed dreadful ravages in their progress, Edward the Third saw the necessity of appearing against them in person. The two armies came at last very close to each other, being divided only by the river *Were.* They watched each other's motions for several days, without coming to a decisive action. At length, after Douglas, with a few men of approved resolution, had performed an extraordinary feat of prowess, the Scots quitted their camp, and marched off toward their own country. Some of the English, either to gratify curiosity, or in expectation of booty, took a view of the Scottish camp, and found there three hundred bags made of raw deer-skins, with the hair on them, and all these full of water and flesh, for the use of the men. The bags were contrived so as to answer the design of kettles. They found likewise a thousand wooden spits, with meat on them, ready to be roasted. Such was the luxury of the posterity of the ancient Caledonians, at the distance of little more than four ages back, and so well was their taste calculated for a military life. See Buchanan and Abercromby, under the reign of Robert Bruce.

THE

THE Britons of the South began to underftand the ufe of the mint foon after the Romans came firft among them.   There are extant to this day feveral coins belonging to their own native Kings, particularly Cunobiline and Caractacus.   The firft of thefe Princes was cotemporary with Auguftus, and the latter with Claudius.   If there were any pieces of money coined in North Britain within eight or nine centuries after that period, they are entirely loft or deftroyed.

THE riches of the Caledonians confifted wholly in cattle.   The cafe was much the fame in feveral other countries, long after the world had been fufficiently peopled.   An ancient author obferves, in his account of Geryon, King of Spain, whom Hercules plundered of his cattle, that in thofe times herds were accounted the only wealth *.   And Varro, the moft learned writer of his age, derives pecunia, the Roman word for money, from pecus, which fignifies cattle.

IT is, after property is long eftablifhed, and fome degree of commerce introduced, that money becomes the ftandard of wealth among nations. In the beginning of fociety, mankind do not think a piece of metal an equivalent for their flocks and herds.   Should I be permitted to give my opinion concerning the origin of coin, I would trace it to that fuperftition which is inherent in human nature in rude times.   The firft coin was probably a portable image of a Divinity, which was worfhipped by a community.   The beauty of the metal, and the facred awe arifing from the figure of a God, firft gave value to that kind of

---

* Juftin. Ep. lib. xliv. cap. 4.

medals

medals in the eyes of the favage ; and as enthufiafm often gets the better of the love of property, he would not fcruple to exchange his horfe,
or his ox, for that *Icon* of the power he adored.

AMBITION has been known, in every ftage of
fociety, to take advantage of the follies and weak-
neffes of mankind.—Kings, obferving the reverence
paid to thofe medals, by degrees fubftituted their
own image, inftead of that of the God, and by
their authority ftampt a value upon what we now
call coin. From that time forward money became,
as it were, the reprefentative of property ; and
the great convenience it affords, from the eafe
with which it can be carried, made mankind almoft univerfally adopt it as the ftandard of wealth.

IT is probable that the barbarous inhabitants
of North Britain imported the arts of hufbandry
from the neighbouring Roman province. The
advantages arifing from fo great an improvement
would have foon convinced them of their former
ignorance : but among men inured to idlenefs, ra-
pine and war, an art, cumberfome at firft, and
afterwards flow in rewarding the labourer's toil,
would have made no very rapid progrefs.

WHATEVER may be faid with regard to the
rife and improvement of agriculture in North Britain, it is certain that the inhabitants were numerous, robuft, high-fpirited, and martial, and confequently well fed. They muft have had therefore fome means of fubfiftence, with which we are
not thoroughly acquainted *. It has been already
obferved, that no country could be better adapt-

---

* See Sir Robert Sibbald's *Mifcellanea eruditæ antiquitatis*—
De Radice Chara.

ed

ed for an uncultivated life than the hills, vallies, rivers, woods and lakes of Caledonia. The inhabitants had no appetites of their own creation to gratify: happy in their ignorance of refinements, and by nature philofophers enough to reft fatisfied with a competency. If their fare was at fome times fcanty, that difadvantage was rendered eafy to them, by parfimony and patience, or was fufficiently compenfated by the abfence of luxury in all feafons. Want and toil could never enfeeble their bodies, or fhorten their lives, fo much as the exceffes arifing from affluence have done elfewhere. All the accounts of antiquity allow, that they were among the ftrongeft, and healthieft, and braveft men in the world.

In whatever degree the ancient inhabitants of Scotland poffeffed the neceffaries of life, it is certain that they were remarkably hofpitable Hofpitality is one of thofe virtues, which, if not peculiar to, is moft commonly met with in a ftate of barbarity. It is after property has taken abfolute poffeffion of the mind, that the door is fhut againft the ftranger. The Highlanders of our own time are beyond comparifon more hofpitable to ftrangers, and more ready to receive them into their houfes, than their more civilized country-men. Their manner of fhewing this generous difpofition may carry along with it, in the eyes of the polite part of mankind, a degree of rudenefs; but it is an honeft rudenefs, and expreffive of that primeval fimplicity and goodnefs of heart which they derive from their anceftors the old Caledonians.

" No people in the world, fays Tacitus, indulge themfelves more in the pleafure of giving a
kind

kind reception to friends, neighbours and ftrangers, than the old Germans. To drive away the ftranger from one's door, is accounted a grofs impiety. Every one entertains according to his wealth; and after the hoft has acted his part generoufly, he directs his gueft to the neareft good family, and attends him thither, without any previous invitation. This intrufion is fo far from giving offence, that they are both received with the greateft franknefs and civility. There is no diftinction made between the acquaintance and ftranger, as far as the laws of hofpitality are concerned *."

Any one acquainted with the manners and cuftoms of the inhabitants of the Highlands, would be tempted to think the celebrated writer drew this good-natured picture from them. It was once univerfally a cuftom among them, nor is it yet totally difcontinued, to accompany their guefts to their next neighbour's houfe, and there, as it were, to refign them to his care and protection.

So far were the old Highlanders from denying any man the benefit of their *roofs* and *fire-fides*, as they exprefs themfelves, that many of them made a point of keeping their doors open by night as well as by day. They thought it inconfiftent with the rules of honour and hofpitality to afk the ftranger abruptly, from what quarter of the world he came, or what his bufinefs was. This queftion could not be decently put till the year's end, if the family in which he fojourned was opulent, and the gueft chofe to ftay fo long.

---

* Tacit. De mor. Germ. cap. xxi.

IF it is an error to beﬅow too much praiſe on the good qualities of our anceﬅors, it is alſo unjuﬅ to deny them every virtue, becauſe we have taken it in our head to call them barbarous. Some people connect the vices and virtues of mankind with the periods of ſociety in which they live, without conſidering that what we call the barbarus and poliſhed ﬅages of ſociety, equally afford a field for the exertion of the good or bad principles of the human heart.——The only difference ſeems to be this : Among barbarians the faculties of the ſoul are more vigorous than in poliſhed times ; and of conſequence, their virtues and vices are more ﬅrongly marked, than thoſe of a civilized people.

THE old Caledonians were much addicted to robbery and plunder. Their poﬅerity inherited the ſame vice through a long ſeries of ages. Another high crime, of which the Caledonians and their poﬅerity of remote times ﬅood impeached, was, that they had their women, and brought up their children in common. The firﬅ of theſe vices was countenanced by neceſſity, the opinion of the times, and the ſituation of thoſe who were plundered. Property muﬅ be perfectly eﬅabliſhed, before the loſs of it can be hurtful, or an incroachment on its laws is followed by diſgrace. Beſides, as depredations took place only between different tribes and nations, they may be conſidered as a ſpecies of war.

WITH regard to the other ſpecies of immorality, with which Dion and Jerom * have impeach-

---

* Dion and St. Jerom.

ed

ed the old Caledonians, it is enough to fay, that it is a vice to which the civilized are more addict-ed than barbarians. It is only when luxury pre-vails, that irregularities of this kind tranfcend the bounds prefcribed by nature. Chaftity is one of the great virtues of rude life : when the foul is ac-tive, it feldom finks into fhameful enormities. Horace has given a very lively picture of thofe impurities which prevailed in his own time, and takes occafion to remark, that fuch criminal gal-lantries were very far from being fafhionable a-mong thofe Romans who defeated Pyrrhus, Han-nibal, and Antiochus the Great.

The Caledonians and Scots, like the ancient Germans, were remarkable for the virtue of con-jugal fidelity : " The men of that nation con-tented themfelves with one wife each, excepting fome few of their great ones; * nor were the laws of wedlock obferved with greater reverence and ftrictnefs among any people. The nuptial bed was defended on the females fide by an uncon-querable modefty, which neither public affemblies, nor private entertainments, nor love epiftles, had any opportunities of corrupting. Among the men, no one made a jeft of vice ; nor were matrimonial infidelities called the way of the world †."

The prejudice of Dion and Jerom againft the Caledonians or ancient Scots, concerning their

---

* Severa illic matrimonia : nec ullam morum partem magis lau-daveris. Nam prope foli barbarorum fingulis uxoribus contenti funt, exceptis admodum paucis.

Tac. De mor. Germ.

† Nemo illic vitia reddet : nec corrumpere et corrumpi fecu-lum vocatur.

Idem ibidem, cap. 19.

having

having their wives in common, has some plausible foundation. In those times of remote antiquity, it is very natural to suppose that the Caledonians were not very well lodged. The whole people of the family, with their occasional guests, lay on rushes, on the same floor, and in the same apartment. This custom, till of late, prevailed amongst the most uncivilized part of the Highlanders, and was once universal over Britain. If we may judge of the ancient inhabitants of North Britain, by the present rudest part of the Highlanders, this circumstance of sleeping in the same apartment was not productive of that conjugal infidelity mentioned by Dion and the holy father.

THE inhabitants of South Britain were, in Cæsar's time, equally unpolished, their domestic œconomy much the same, and their habitations just as mean as those of the rudest Highlanders. It was natural for a stranger, of any delicacy, who saw the whole family lying together promiscuously, upon one continued bed of rushes, fern, or leaves, to imagine that the wives and children belonged to the males in common. Hence it was, that Cæsar entertained that false opinion of the South Britons: and hence Dion and Jerom's opinion with regard to those of the North. But nothing could have been more rash than the conclusions which they drew from these appearances. The people of Germany lay almost indiscriminately together in the very same manner * : and we have been already told, by a very intelligent writer, that

---

* In omni domo nudi ac sordidi in hos artus in hæc corpora quæ miramur excrescunt. Inter eadem pecora, in eadem humo, degunt, &c.   Tacit. de mor. Germ. cap. 20.

there

there was not any country which produced fewer inftances of incontinence.

I⟶ is difficult to fay how far the Caledonians may have employed themfelves in cultivating the powers of the mind. The Druids *, thofe great teachers of all the other Celtic nations, were fettled among them ; and it may be prefumed that they reafoned like their brethren elfewhere concerning the nature and extent of the univerfe, the magnitude of the celeftial bodies, the power of the Gods, and the nature of the human foul.

I⟶ does not appear from hiftory that the Caledonians had any public games, or fchools of war ; but it is certain that their defcendants ufed exercifes perfectly fimilar to thofe of the Greek *Pentathla*. Thefe were leaping, running, *throwing the ftone*, as they exprefs it in the Galic, darting the launce, and wreftling. All thefe diverfions were peculiarly fubfervient to a martial life. And if to thefe exercifes we add that of hunting, it is plain, that though they wanted academies, their military talents were cultivated to very good purpofe ; and muft have been confiderably improved, before they had any opportunities of engaging an enemy.

I⟶ the Highlands and Iflands, where the old cuftoms of the Scots maintained their ground after they had been long abolifhed in the reformed parts of the kingdom, the moft of thofe exercifes were, till of late, held in high repute. They

---

* The author wrote a differtation on the Druids, and the rites of their religion, which he gave to the late ingenious and learned Sir James M'Donald, Baronet, and was unfortunately loft or miflaid among Sir James's papers.

reckoned

reckoned fwiftnefs of foot one of the moft confiderable accomplifhments. Nor was that manner of thinking peculiar to them.: Homer feldom forgets to mark out this characteriftical quality of his hero : and another eminent poet, in his lamentation over Saul and Jonathan, gives a peculiar praife to thofe Princes, on account of their fwiftnefs. In Homer and Virgil, we fee the champions of Greece, Phrygia and Italy, fometimes deciding their fingle combats, and the fate of battles, by throwing of rocky fragments.

THE old Britons had recourfe to the fame expedient on many occafions. To fit them for this method of fighting, a large round ftone was placed near the gate of every chieftain's houfe. The ftranger who happened to lodge there, or, if a man of rank, the ftrongeft man of his retinue, were regularly invited by the hoft to try the power of their fkill and ftrength on that fort of quoit.

LEAPING was another exercife in great efteem among the Scots of former days. Every chief, who had fpirit enough to fupport the dignity of his name and fortune, kept a band of young and active warriors continually about his perfon, one of whofe qualifications it was neceffary fhould be agility in this kind of exercife. Thefe warriors, or *Cathern*, were conftantly employed in manly exercifes and recreations in time of peace, and ferved the chief as a kind of body guards. Wreftling was their great and favourite exercife. Boys were inured to it early, and ftimulated to it by prizes fuited to their tafte and paffions. When one chieftain paid a vifit to another, after the firft civilities were over, the wreftlers retained by each came

firft

firſt to a trial of ſkill, and ſometi
blows, unleſs their maſters interpoſe

THERE were declared combatants
feſſion, who went about in queſt of
like Amycus, Caſtor and Pollux : t
arrived at a hamlet, than they chall
inhabitants, demanding a tribute to b
ly paid, or a fair battle, *without a*
they always expreſſed themſelves. T
men now living in the Highlands, v
theſe knights-errant ; and we are tolc
the moſt conſiderable chieftains in t
the diſtance of a few ages back, lo
fighting a champion of this order.
had affronted his whole clan : to
honour of his name, the chief encc
overcame him ; but by too violent a
his ſtrength, he broke a blood veſſel
ly expired.

IT is well known that the Cale
their deſcendants, had a particular
managing darts of every kind. The
men were famous, like the archers
The battles fought by theſe two nat
a ſtate of mutual hoſtility, were
either by the ſuperior ſkill of a bod
of the former, or that of the archers
Their dexterity in handling thoſe v
have deſcended to both nations from
anceſtors.

WE are told by Herodian and I
inhabitants of North Britain uſed ti
than any other weapon. The latte
cumſtance, omitted by every othe
thor : he ſays, that there was a piec

form of an apple, fixed to one end of their spears, which they shook, to terrify the enemy with its noise. I have conversed with old Highlanders, who have seen spears of that construction. The name they gave them was *Triniframma*. The critics are at a loss to find out what the *Framea* of the Germans may have been *. Tacitus shews that it was a spear; and it is highly probable that it was contrived like those used by the ancient Caledonians. The Galic name justifies this opinion. Dion's *Brazen Apple* was called *Cnap-Starra* in the language of the ancient Scots, that is, a Bofs, like that on the middle of a shield, studded with nails of brass †.

---

* Lipsius, in his notes on Tacitus de mor. Germ. cap. 6.

† Among the ancient Scots, the common soldiers were called *Catherni*, or fighting bands. The Kerns of the English, the Kaitrine of the Scots Lowlanders, and the Caterva of the Romans, are all derived from this Celtic word. The Gauls had a word of much the same sound and meaning. We learn from tradition, that these Catherni were generally armed with darts and *skians*, or durks. These were the weapons which the Caledonians used in Dion's time. The helmet and coat of mail were reckoned incumbrances by that people, according to Herodian; nor can I find out that they were in fashion among their posterity, till the Danes and Norvegians began to infest the coasts of Britain and Ireland. It was by these Northern invaders that this heavy sort of armour was introduced into Scotland, together with the weapons commonly called *Lochaber axes*. These weapons were well steeled, and extremely sharp, and destructive in the hands of strong men. Those who were armed with such axes, and with helmets, coats of mail, and swords, went under the name of *Galloglaich*, (by the English called *Galloglasses.*) They were generally men of distinguished strength, and commonly drawn up against the enemies cavalry. The designation of these soldiers proves, that the Scots and Irish borrowed their weapons from foreigners.

From the observations made on the military customs and manly exercises of the Caledonians, and their posterity, in the more early ages, it may be concluded, were history silent, that they must have been extremely well trained for war. They were certainly strangers to all the polish of fine life : commerce, its fruits and advantages, were absolutely unknown to them ; nor was a knowledge of these arts at all so necessary for them, as the virtues which they possessed, are for men in a civilized state. When a state is invaded, and is in danger of falling a prey to an enemy ;—when the freedom and very existence of a people are at stake; the warrior, and not the merchant, is the useful and valuable man. Great as the blessings of industry and commerce are, they become fatal, when they overwhelm the martial genius of a nation.

The people of North Britain were in a state of war and military exertion for a thousand years after they became known in history. During all that time they had their freedom and settlements to defend from enemies, foreign or domestic. The spirit of the times, a principle of just revenge, or the laws of necessity, taught them to be warlike, and perhaps barbarous. Romans, provincial Britons, Saxons, Danes, Normans, and English foes, made frequent attempts on their liberty and country. When the Picts and Scots began to dispute for the empire of Albany, there was little room for the arts of peace ; nor was it possible to cultivate them with any degree of success. After the Picts had been subdued, the numerous pirates of Scandinavia, for a course of three hundred years, discouraged the Scots from minding the

business

bufinefs of agriculture or civil life. Upon the death of Alexander the Third, under whole reign the Norvegians obliged themfelves, by a formal treaty, to abftain from all future hoftilities againft the dominions of Scotland, the kingdom became a fcene of unparalleled miferies. Two fucceffive competitions for its crown, and the cruel ambition of two Englifh Monarchs, every way formidable, converted it into a field of blood and defolation. The felfifh views of two regents, during the long captivity of James the Firft, the long minorities of his fucceffors, their conftant difputes with powerful Barons or Lords, too great to be loyal fubjects; all thefe, and many more unfavourable circumftances, co-operated ftrongly in difcouraging induftry, and in encouraging violence and bloodfhed.

From thefe confiderations it follows, that the principal virtues of the nation were of the military kind. High-fpirited, enterprizing, and fearlefs of danger, they were almoft continually in the field, carrying fire, fword, and defolation into the territories of the enemy, defending their own againft foreign invaders, or fighting the battles of their Kings, Lords and Chieftains, againft rebels and competitors.

Those among the Scots of former generations who poffeffed the wealth of the times, maintained dignity of character, without pageantry. Their houfes were acceffible to the ftranger and the diftreffed. Though void of fuperb decorations and a dazzling fplendor, they were adorned with numerous bands of bold warriors, who paffed their time in thofe amufements and exercifes I have fo particularly defcribed.

I 3

THE

THE tables of the old Scottish Lords and Chieftains, however ill supplied with exotic delicacies, abounded with the true pleasure of entertainment. The real generosity and unaffected complaisance of the open-hearted host appeared conspicuously in every circumstance, and gave the highest seasoning to the repast. Next to the glory arising from martial exploits, the reputation acquired by acts of hospitality was, in those ages, esteemed the highest honour. The bards displayed the whole power of their poetical abilities in celebrating the hero and beneficent man; and they, in meriting the praises bestowed by those heralds of fame. The great men emulously strove to outvie one another in the manly virtues. A portion of the same noble ambition fell to the share of every individual, according to his rank in life. That is possibly the happiest period of a nation, when the practice of the generous and martial virtues become the amusement and object of every member of a community, in proportion to their respective situations *.

IT must however be confessed, that the national vices of those times were far from being few; nor can it be denied, that the Scots of our present times have greatly the advantage of their ancestors in many respects. Property is now under the protection of the law; and the civil magistrate possesses authority. Agriculture, the most useful of all arts, is studied, and has made great

---

* In the old Galic there is but one word for a brave and good man, and but one for a land-holder and an hospitable man; which sufficiently demonstrates the ideas the ancient Caledonians entertained concerning bravery and hospitality.

progress.

progress. Commerce is underſtood, and its advantages purſued. The mechanic and manufacturer furniſh their country with ſeveral commodities, either uſeful or ornamental. Arts and ſciences are patronized by ſome, eſteemed by all, and with ardor purſued by many. Murders, robberies, and all the outrages and barbarities, are unfrequent, and individuals enjoy that liberty which has diffuſed itſelf over the whole nation.

But notwithſtanding all theſe great and eſſential advantages, a doubt may be raiſed. Whether the virtues of our preſent times are more numerous, more ſublime, more generous and diſintereſted, than thoſe of our anceſtors, in the dark ages of barbariſm, poverty and confuſion ? If that queſtion muſt be reſolved in the affirmative, another will immediately riſe out of the compariſon ; and that is, Whether our vices are fewer, or leſs unnatural ?

No reaſonable man will deny that commerce naturally produces an inſatiable love of gain, and together with that boundleſs paſſion, all the arts of circumvention, perjuries, unmanly deceits, and groſs frauds. Avarice and luxury are inſeparable companions of riches : nor is it an eaſy matter to keep haughtineſs, inſolence and impiety at a due diſtance from an affluent fortune. The ſame ingenious arts which improve the taſte, and poliſh the manners, have a tendency to effeminate the ſoul, ſo as to prepare it for ſlavery. The refinements of good-breeding and inſincerity go too frequently hand in hand. Falſe learning may be worſe than groſs ignorance. That philoſophy which tends neither to ſtrengthen the mind, or improve the happy feelings of the heart, is worſe

I 4

than

than the inftinctive feelings of the foul of the
favage.

—— Upon the whole, it is difficult to prove, that
opulent kingdoms poffefs a greater degree of virtue, and confequently of happinefs, than the petty
ftates from which they rofe.   The queftion is of
a complex nature, and would require a longer
difcuffion than would fuit with a work of this kind.
The beft writers of antiquity have declared in favour of what we, with great impropriety perhaps,
call barbarous times.   Xenophon, towards the end
of his Cyropœdia, has difcuffed the point with
great ability.

DISSERTATION XII.

A Tradition preserved by Bede considered. A Parallel between the Manners and Customs of the Caledonians and ancient Germans.----General Reflections on the Subject.

IT was an established tradition a thousand years ago, that the Picts were the original inhabitants of the Northern division of Britain. Bede [*] says, in his ecclesiastical history, that they came to Caledonia from *Scythia*, the European part of which, according to Pliny [†], comprehended Germany. The authority of the venerable writer was never questioned on this head ; and a belief has ever since obtained that the Picts were a different race from the Gauls, who possessed the Southern parts of Britain. Though the hypothesis of deducing the origin of the Caledonians from the old Germans is improbable, on account of the distance of the two countries from one another, and the small progress that navigation must have made in

---

[*] Bede, Hist. Ecclef.
[†] Pliny, Nat. Hist. lib. ii, c. 13.

fo early a period, yet the opinion of Tacitus * on that fubject, weighed fo much with me, that I examined this fyftem with a good deal of attention.

The refult was, a parallel which I drew between the manners and cuftoms of the old Caledonians, and thofe of Germany, as defcribed by Tacitus. I am very fenfible, that all nations in their primæval ftate are very fimilar in their genius, cuftoms, and manners. Similar fituations will, no doubt, create an identity of ideas. Hunting and war feem to be the fole bufinefs of nations in rude times, and it is no matter of furprize, that there fhould arife, from thefe occupations, a great affinity not only of fome characteriftical cuftoms but even of language. It is not therefore with a defign of ftrengthening the tradition preferved by Bede, that I give this parallel to the public, being perfuaded that a fimiliarity of a few ftriking cuftoms is too feeble an argument for deducing the Caledonians from the old Germans, when common reafon declares againft a migration of this fort in fuch early times.

The military character of the Caledonians and Germans were very fimilar. As they fought with the fame fpirit, fo they ufed the fame kind of weapons; the fword, dart, and fhield. The fwords of Germany were long and unwieldy †. Thofe of Caledonia were equally enormous. It was this very circumftance that gave a fatal difadvantage to her braveft fons in the battle they fought againft Agricola near the Grampian mountains ‡.

---

* Tacit. Vita Agric. c. 26.
† Plut. in Mario.   ‡ Tacit. in Vita Agric. c. 26.

WE

WE are told by Tacitus, that the German fpear was immoderately long *; and every one converfant in the hiftory of Scotland muft know that the fpear ufed of old in that country was remarkable in point of length.

VIRGIL fpeaks of a weapon properly Teutonic, which he calls *Cateia* †. All the commentators, down from old Servius, and together with them all the compilers of dictionaries, have miftaken the meaning of that word. *Cateia* is undoubtedly of a Celtic original, and in the Galic dialect of that tongue, fignifies a *fiery dart* ‡. We learn from Cæfar that fuch darts were ufed by the Perfians, a Belgic nation of German extract ‖.

THE compofitions of their ancient bards were the only records known to the old Caledonians. In one of thefe compofitions, Cuchullin, the fame hero that is fo much celebrated in Offian's poems, is faid to have killed his friend Ferda in a miftake, with a dart *kindled into a devouring flame by the ftrength of wind* **.

THE Caledonian fhield was fhort and narrow ††. That of Germany was contrived in much the fame manner ‡‡. The authority of that excellent

---

* Ann. l. ii. p. 49. Ed. Lips.
† Teutonico ritu Soliti torquere Cateias, Æn. vii. v. 740.
‡ Bullet. Dictionnaire Celt vol. ii. p. 608.
‖ Tacit. de moribus Germ.
** That is, by a blackfmith's bellows. The words in the Galic original, are *Gathbulig* and *Craofach-dhearg*, words of the fame import with Cæfar's *jaculum fervefactum*, and Virgil's *Cateia* or *Ga-tie*, i. e. *Gath* or *Cath*, a dart, and *tei*, of fire. The only difference is, that the Galic words are more poetically turned.
†† Herod. l. iii. 47.
‡‡ Tacit. An. lib. iii. p. 47. Vit. Ag. c. 36.

writer,

writer *, who seems to have studied the real character of the two nations better than any other,
has decided this point.

The Germans painted their shields with beautiful colours †. The old Britons adopted that
custom. The rhimes of our ancient bards speak
frequently of *shields stained with red.*

Dio relates that the Caledonians upon whom
Severus made war were armed with that sort of
dagger, which the English call *Durk*, and the
Welsh, Irish, and Scots, *Bidog*. This appears
likewise from an antique stone dug out of the remains of Antonine's wall, and preserved among
the curiosities belonging to the university of Glafgow. On that stone are exhibited two Caledonian
captives, and each with a *Durk* hanging down before him.

I cannot say whether all the Germanic nations used this kind of dagger ; but the Saxons
certainly did, if we may credit Windichindus, an
author born of Saxon parents ‡ ; and it deserves
notice, that the picture of a Saxon soldier, as it is
drawn by that author, is in every one of its lines
like that of a Highlander of the last age, or genuine Caledonian.

Herodian, in his description of these barbarous nations of Britain, who fought against Severus, takes occasion to observe, that they reckoned
helmets and coats of mail absolute incumbrances.
The country they inhabited was full of lakes,
morasses, and inaccessible fastnesses, and that was
the reason, according to him, why they used no

---

* Tacitus.   † Seneca, in Apololocynthosis.
‡ See Cambd. Brit. Art. Saxons.

such

ſuch inſtruments of defence* But the true reaſon ſeems to have been either a brave contempt
for ſuch unmanly impediments, or a natural attachment to the cuſtoms of their forefathers. The
Germanic Nations, in Trajan's time, had very
few coats of mail, and ſcarce any helmets †. If
we go back beyond that period, it may be preſumed they had none at all.

U p o n a compariſon of the weapons uſed by
the Gauls with thoſe of the Germans, it will be
eaſily found that the difference was very conſiderable : and hence ſome might infer, that the Caledonians borrowed the faſhion of their arms from
the latter rather than from the former.

T h e ſhields of the Gauls were long, and their
darts ſhort. To prove this aſſertion ſeveral paſſages might be quoted from ancient authors. But
one authority is ſufficient ; that paſſage in the
Æneid, where, among a great variety of very
beautiful figures, the picture of a Gauliſh ſoldier
is ſo finely drawn by Virgil ‡.

T h e armies of the old Germans were made
up of ſeparate tribes. Their battalions conſiſted
of men who had a natural connection with each
other, men who had the ſame common intereſt in
view, were engaged in the ſame purſuits of glory,
and ſtrongly cemented by an inviolable attachment
to the ſame chieftain. Tacitus, who probably

---

* Herod. lib. iii. v. 47.
† Tacit. de mor. Germ. p. 437. Ed. Lips.
‡ Galli per dumos aderant
  Duo quiſque alpini coruſcant
Gæſa manu, ſcutis protecti corpora longis.
    Æneid viii. v. 660, &c.

understood

underſtood the art of war, as he undoubtedly did the art of thinking juſtly, ſeems to give his hearty approbation to this part of the German diſcipline*.

" In a day of battle, ſays, that author, the Chieftain thinks it highly diſhonourable to yield. His warriors follow his path in the field with the moſt undaunted emulation and vigour. To die for him is their utmoſt ambition. But to ſurvive his death, and to leave him dead in the field, are actions of everlaſting infamy and diſgrace. The Chieftain fights for victory, the warriors for the Chieftain †."

The Caledonians of Agricola's time were made up of ſeveral different tribes, and theſe headed by independent Chieftains or Kings. Galgacus was no more than one of theſe petty ſovereigns. An univerſal monarchy was unknown in North Britain till the ninth century ; and after that form of government was eſtabliſhed there, every diſtinct tribe or ſmall nation fought, in a day of battle, under its own Chieftain or Lord. Theſe Lords and Chieftains were accounted the common fathers of the nations or communities at the head of which their birth and merit had placed them. They were the great protectors of all, the hope and dread of every individual, and the common center of union, being equally dear to their kinſmen, their vaſſals, and their clients. It is natural to believe, without having recourſe to hiſtory, that their friends and dependents would have riſqued their lives in the ſervice of their Chieftains with greater zeal and alacrity than any hireling

----

* Tacit. de mor. Germ. cap. 7.
† Tacit. ib. cap. 14.

ſoldier

foldier will be apt to do for a Prince who happens to wear an imperial Crown.

AMONG the Germans there was a powerful nation diftinguifhed by the name of Arians, of whom we have the following account. " The Arians are peculiarly fierce, and they ftudy to heighten their natural ferocity by the help of art, and favourable opportunities. Their fhields are black, their bodies are painted, and they make choice of the darkeft nights for fighting their battles. The confequence is, that by the horrible appearance they make, and by the dreary afpect of their death-like armies, their enemies muft be greatly terrified : nor can any of thefe ftand out againft fuch new, and one may fay, infernal objects; for the eyes of men are firft of all overcome in battles *."

IT is needlefs to fay that the Caledonians painted their bodies like the Arians, and with the fame defign : nor will it be denied that the Britons of the South were once addicted to the fame cuftom. Were we to admit the German extraction of the Picts, we might alfo fuppofe that this cuftom travelled Southward from Caledonia.

IT is an opinion generally received, that the firft inhabitants of South Britain came thither from Gaul. The vicinity of the two countries, and that clofe fimilarity which the Romans found in the religion, language and character of the refpective inhabitants of the two countries, are the arguments with which Tacitus endeavours to eftablifh this opinion ; and thefe arguments are more than plaufible. But whether the ancient inhabitants of South

---

* Tacit. de mor. Germ. cap. 43,

Britain

Britain came in general from the Belgic, Celtic, or Aquitanic divifion of Gaul, is a point which neither hiftorians nor antiquaries have determined. That they came from the Belgic Gaul is undoubtedly the moft probable hypothefis. But fhould it be fuppofed and allowed, that the three feveral divifions of Gaul fent their feveral colonies into this ifland, it will be difficult to prove that any of thefe colonies could have imported the fafhion of painting their bodies. Their mother country was an abfolute ftranger to a cuftom fo barbarous when they became firft known to the Romans. It is therefore not improbable that the cuftom of painting faces and limbs, to ftrike the enemy with terror, arofe firft from the fuperior barbarifm of the Caledonians, and travelled Southward to the Britons, who had come in a later and more civilized period from Gaul.

The inhabitants of the Southern and Northern divifions of Britain muft have had fome intercourfe, either in a hoftile or a friendly way. And fhould it be fuppofed that the Brigantes of South Britain were more than once intimidated by the horrible figures imprinted on the bodies of their Northern enemies, and of courfe vanquifhed in feveral battles, it was natural enough for them to affume the fame artificial ferocity which had given their enemies 'fo manifeft an advantage. The fafhion of painting, being thus introduced into South Britain, was probably diffufed in a courfe of ages, over all that part of the ifland, and the fooner fo that it had been practifed with fuccefs by the Brigantes, a people remarkably brave, numerous and powerful.

SHOULD the fuppofition now made be thought not abfurd, it will be afked in the next place, how this barbarous cuftom of painting was introduced into Caledonia? It is difficult to fay, unlefs it arofe, as I have faid, from the fuperior barbarity of a people living in a mountainous country. The abettors of the Germanic extraction of the Caledonians might draw a plaufible argument from fo characteriftical a cuftom. The Arians of Germany, and the Caledonians of Britain, were men of much the fame character. Each of thefe nations was wild and ferocious. Each of them took care to heighten their innate ferocity by the help of art. Both nations exerted their whole ftrength of ingenuity, in giving themfelves the moft dreadful afpect poffible; and to attack their enemy in the night time was one of thofe military arts which they practifed in common *. It would therefore be a more rational fyftem, to derive the original of the Caledonian Britons from the German Arians, than to draw their defcent from the *Agathyrfi*, according to the opinion of Stillingfleet and Boece †,

---

* Tacit. ut fupra, et in Vita Agric.

† 'The Agathyrfi were fettled in a divifion of Sarmatia, at no fmall diftance from the fea *. The Geloni, another nation who ufed paint in Sarmatia, lay to the Eaft of the Boryfthenes. It is not therefore eafy to fuppofe that either the Agathyrfi or Geloni could tranfmit their cuftom of painting, or tranfport themfelves into Britain. The feas that lay neareft to them, were the Palus Mæotis, the Euxine, and the Baltic: neither can it be reafonably fuppofed that they had any tolerable knowledge of navigation; and if the practice they made of painting was a good foundation for the ftrange conjecture made by Boece, a fimilar practice that prevailed among thofe Ethiopians in the army of Xerxes † will furnifh any one elfe with another genealogical account of the Caledonians equally authentic.

* Vide Celt. Not. Orb. Ant. in Sarmatia.   † Herod, lib. vii. c. 69.

K

CÆSAR

CÆSAR has drawn a parallel between the Gauls and Germans. Upon comparing the manners and cuſtoms of thoſe two great nations with thoſe of the Caledonians, one may eaſily perceive that the cuſtoms of the latter bear a much nearer reſemblance to the old Germans than to the Gauls.

" THE Germans, ſays Cæſar, differ greatly in their manners from the Gauls. They neither have Druids to preſide in religious affairs, nor do they mind ſacrifices. Their whole lives are employed either in hunting or in cultivating the arts of a military life. They inure themſelves early to toil and hardſhips. They are clad with ſkins or ſhort mantles made of fur, ſo that a great part of their bodies is naked. To agriculture they give little or no attention. Their food conſiſts principally of milk, cheeſe, and fleſh. The only perſons among them who have a property in land, are their magiſtrates and Princes. Theſe give annually to the tribes and families who aſſociate together under their protection, as much ground as they think proper, and where they ſee moſt convenient. In the enſuing year theſe great men oblige their dependents to ſhift their ſettlements."

" WHEN a German nation is engaged in a war, either defenſive or offenſive, they inveſt the general to whom they commit the management of it, with a power of life and death. In time of peace they have no public magiſtrate : the Chiefs of the ſeveral diſtricts and Clans diſtribute juſtice and decide controverſies among thoſe under their juriſdiction. Robbery is attended with no degree of infamy, if committed without the territories of the nation to which the robber belongs : nor do theſe men ſcruple to affirm before the world, that

in

in order to exercife the youth, and to put a ftop to the growth of effeminacy, that practice muft be not only indulged, but encouraged. In their public affemblies when any of their Chieftains undertakes to go at the head of fuch an expedition, thofe who give their approbation to his defign rife up before the affembly, enlift themfelves in the fervice, and are applauded by the multitude. They who break their engagements are reckoned traitors * and deferters : nor do they ever after recover their former honour †."

" THE Britons of the North, fays Dio, till no ground, but live upon prey, hunting, and the fruits of the wood. They dwell in tents, naked and without fhoes. They take peculiar pleafure in committing depredations. They endure hunger, cold, and every kind of hardfhip with wonderful patience ‡."

THE principal lines of this picture are extremely like thofe of the original we have been juft now viewing; and the more we compare the accounts which ancient authors have given of the refpective nations, the more we are ftruck with their fimilarity in genius and manners. Dio has indeed obferved that the Caledonians went naked; but it may be prefumed, that he meant no more than that they were poorly clad. This is all that Eumenius, the panegyrift, has faid concerning the

---

* One would think that Cæfar, in this paffage, copied the manners of an American tribe of Indians upon a like occafion. This is the very method ufed by them in their affemblies, when they refolve on a war. There is a wonderful fimilarity between all nations in the firft ftage of fociety.

† Cæf de Bel. Gal. lib. vi. cap. 21, 22, 23.

‡ Dio, lib. lxxii.

 habits

habits of thofe Picts who fought againſt the Britons of the South, before Cæſar invaded this iſland : and Cæſar himſelf has told us that thofe who inhabited the inland parts of Britain in his time were cloathed with ſkins *. Whatever the opinion of Dio may have been on this ſubject, it is certain, that the Caledonians could hardly ſecure their lives againſt the natural ſeverity of their climate, without ſome ſort of cloathing, notwithſtanding all their conſtitutional vigour and acquired hardineſs.

IT muſt be acknowledged that Herodian likewiſe ſeems to make the inhabitants of North Britain a naked people. His words are, " Theſe barbarians are ſtrangers to the uſe of cloaths, but they trim their bellies and necks with iron trappings, being poſſeſſed with a belief that iron is ornamental and a ſign of opulence, in the ſame manner that gold is eſteemed by other nations. They mark their bodies with a variety of figures reſembling many different animals. For this reaſon they take care not to cover their bodies, for fear of concealing theſe figures †.

BUT this author has told us in the paſſage immediately preceding that now quoted, that theſe barbarians were far from being totally naked, the greateſt part only of their bodies being ſo ; and that muſt in all probability have been true.

THE Greeks and Romans knew very little concerning the habits of the Caledonians, excepting thoſe they wore in a day of battle. Upon ſuch occaſions they were indeed very ſlightly clad, if

---

* Cæſar de Bel. Gal. lib. v. cap. 14.
† Herod. lib. iii. cap. 47.

cloathed

cloathed at all. Before the engagement began they threw away their upper garments, and marched up to the enemy having only a piece of thin ſtuff wrapped about their middle. The Highlanders of Scotland inherited the ſame cuſtom ſo late as the battle of Killicranky, in which they fought in their ſhirts, having laid by their plaids and ſhort coats before the action began. The old Germans behaved in the very ſame manner upon ſimilar occaſions.

THOSE who are very meanly or thinly clad are in common converſation called naked. Agreeable to this uſual form of ſpeech, Virgil adviſes the Italian farmer whether in ploughing or ſowing his ground to work *naked* ; that is to ſay, without that part of his garb that was no more than a real incumbrance to him *.

BESIDES the ſkins of beaſts worn by the Caledonians, like the more barbarous inhabitants of Britain and Germany, there is reaſon to believe that they imitated the latter in another part of their habit. The Germans wore woollen mantles, and theſe ſometimes party coloured, though generally otherwiſe. A mantle of the latter kind was by the Romans called *Sagum*, and a party-coloured one either *Sagum* or *Braccæ* promiſcuouſly. The only garment of an ordinary German was, according to Tacitus, a mantle tacked together with a *Fibula*, or if that ſhould be wanting they uſed a pin †. The *Fibula* was a buckle or ring made

---

* Nudus ara ſere nudus.   VIRG.

† Tegumen omnibus ſagum, fibula aut ſi deſit ſpina conſertum. Cærera intecti, &c. Locupletiſſimi veſte diſtinguuntur. Stricta et ſingulos artus exprimente §

* Tacit. de mor. Germ. p. 442.

                          of

of a thin plate of filver, brafs, or iron, with a
needle running through the middle and joined to
the buckle at one end. But if the perfon who
wore the mantle was too poor to afford the fibula,
a fkewer made either of wood or bone was formed to anfwer its ufe. The buckle or fkewer kept
the two upper corners of the mantle together.

I⊤ muft be allowed that the writers of ancient
hiftory are filent as to the garb worn by the Caledonians, Picts, and Scots : but in a matter of this
kind, we may fafely depend on the faith of tradition, efpecially when fupported by immemorial
cuftom ; and we are informed by both, that the
moft ancient inhabitants of North Britain were
clad with a *Sagum* tacked together about the neck
with either a pin or buckle. If the *Sagum* was of
one colour, it was called, in the language of the
country, *Plaide* : if party-coloured or ftreaked
w th different dyes, it was called *Breaccan*.

Varro obferved that the word *Sagum* is of
Celtic extract. The word *Braccæ* is fo likewife.
In the Galic tongue, which is perhaps the moft genuine branch of the old Celtic, *Saic* fignifies a
fkin or hide. The Germans, like many other
uncivilized nations, covered themfelves with fkins
before they began to manufacture woollen ftuffs ;
and as *Saic* was the name of their original garb,
it is highly probable, that after the woollen mantle was introduced in its p'ace, they gave it the
well known name of their former covering. This
conjecture is fo much the more plaufible that the
form of their mantle was in a great degree fimilar to that of their old covering.

I⼀f we confult either lexicographers, or the writers of notes critical and explanatory, we fhall find

fome

ſome difficulty in ſettling the preciſe meaning of the word *Bracca*. But every Highlander in Britain knows that the *Bracca* was an upper garment of diverſe colours. The very word is to this day preſerved in the Galic language, with the addition of only a ſingle letter, and, in the ſame language, any thing that is party-coloured is conſtantly diſtinguiſhed by the epithet *Breac*.

BLUE was the favourite colour among the Caledonians *, or at leaſt the moſt prevalent. That their women of quality uſed blue mantles may be concluded from a paſſage of Claudian †, as well as from tradition.

THE only or principal difference between the dreſs of the males and females was, that the mantle of the latter flowed down to their ankles, as it did among the women of Germany. The uſe of the *Fibula* was common both to the men and the women of Caledonia *.

K 4

IT

---

* Solin. cap. xxxv.
† Inde Caledonico velata Britannia monſtro
Ferro Piſta genas, cujus veſtigia veriit
Cærulus, oceanique æſtum mentitur amiſtus.
Claud. Imprim. Con. Stil.

In this paſſage Britain is perſonified by the poet, and is painted in the cheeks, and clad with a blue mantle in the Piſtiſh manner. It is hardly poſſible to make ſenſe of the words without taking them in this view.

I have it from very good authority, that a large ſilver buckle, once worn by Robert Bruce, King of Scotland, was till of late in the poſſeſſion of Macdougal, of Dunolly, a gentleman in Argyleſhire. Bruce, after the fatal battle of Methven, found himſelf under the neceſſity of flying to the Highlands, attended by only a ſmall band of truſty friends. Macdougal, of Lorn, one of the anceſtors of the gentleman now mentioned, being in the Engliſh intereſt, attacked that illuſtrious Prince in his flight, and
overpowered

IT would be no difficult matter to carry the parallel between the Germans and Caledonians much further. Thofe who have enquired with care into the primæval ftate of North Britain, will fee the comparifon in a much ftronger light, upon perufing, with attention, that admirable treatife of Tacitus concerning Germany and its inhabitants. There is certainly a ftrong uniformity between all nations in a barbarous ftate. The fimilarity muft be much more apparent between nations origi ally fprung from the fame fource. But it evidently appears to any one acquainted with the early hiftory of the Germans and Caledonians, that the conformity between them, in point of cuftoms and national manners, is much more ftriking than between the Caledonians and Britons *. This feems greatly to favour the opinion of Tacitus, and the tradition preferved by Bede. But it muft be confeffed, that nothing decifive can be faid on this head, though I intend to do all juftice to the fyftem of the fuppofed Germanic extraction of the Caledonians.

THE great objection againft the fyftem is, that as in that early period wherein North Britain was peopled, the art of building and navigating veffels muft have been either totally unknown, or very imperfectly underftood in Germany, it is much

---

overpowered him with fuperior numbers. Bruce performed prodigies of valour, in a narrow pafs where he pofted himfelf fingly till all his friends were out of danger ; but he was forced at length to give way, and in his retreat loft his upper garment, or at leaft the buckle with which it was faftened. This fcuffle in which Bruce was thus worfted, is fung by Barbour, an old Scottifh bard.

* Sir William Temple.

more

more probable that the firſt inhabitants of Caledonia came rather from the Southern diviſion of the iſland, than from any part of the Northern continent, at the diſtance of ſeveral days ſailing from any part of Britain *.

THIS indeed is a very plauſible argument, and difficult to be obviated ; at the ſame time it is not eaſy to aſcertain the period of time in which the Germans could firſt venture to commit themſelves, with ſafety, to the ocean.

WE know from good authority, that the *Suiones* of Germany had very conſiderable fleets, either in the Baltic or in the Northern ocean, in Trajan's time † ; of conſequence it may be preſumed, that they knew the art of building and navigating ſhips much earlier. The Teutones, who fought againſt Caius Marius, muſt have had ſome tolerable veſſels to tranſport themſelves and their families to Germany from the Northern parts of Scandinavia, when they went upon their celebrated expedition towards the South of Europe. This being the caſe, there is but little abſurdity in ſuppoſing that the anceſtors of the ſame Teutones, or of the Suiones, or of ſome other maritime nation in the Weſtern part of Germany, might have ventured upon a voyage to North Britain, five or ſix hundred years, at leaſt, before the Suiones made ſuch a conſiderable figure at ſea in the reign of Trajan. It does not appear that the Gauls underſtood ſea affairs much ſooner than the Germans. If the Phænicians made early voyages to the coaſt of Gaul, the ſame love of gain that carried them thither would have led them likewiſe to the maritime

---

* Innes, Crit. Eſſay, p. 71. † Tacit. Lips. p. 450.

parts of Germany ; and nothing could hinder the Allemans, any more than the Gauls, from learning the more fimple branches of fhip building and navigation.

I⊤ may indeed be faid that the Gauls might have ealily learned the art of building fhips from the Phocœans of Maſilia, who were fettled among them, and confequently might have underftood fea affairs much earlier than the Germans. But South Britain muft have been peopled, if we can judge from appearances, before the Phocœans pofſeſſed themſelves of the Maſſilian diftrict of Gaul, an event which happened about five hundred years before the birth of Chrift *.

Wⵏ⊤ɦoʊ⊤ admitting an early knowledge of navigation, it is difficult to account how the Belgic Gauls tranfported themfelves into Britain. They certainly could not ftow themfelves, their wives, children, and cattle, in *Currachs*. They muft, in fhort, have veſſels of a larger and better conftruction. Should this be allowed, what could hinder the anceftors of thofe Saxons, Friefians, Normans, and Oftmans, who harraffed the Southern parts of Europe in after ages, from having veffels equally good with thofe of Gaul, or from making voyages into a country at the diftance of a few days failing ? The Saxons infefted the coaft of Britain under the reign of Diocletian ; and if we can give credit to Saxo Grammaticus, the Danes invaded Britain feveral ages before the Roman enfigns were difplayed there. But be that as it will, it is certain that the maritime nations of Germany and Scandia were very bold adventurers

---

* Juſt. lib. xliii. c. 3.

at fea, before the Roman empire began to decline; and they may have been fo much fooner,
though the Greek and Roman hiftories are filent
upon that head.

I f it fhould be faid, that the firft Belgic colonies made their way into Britain in *Curachs* or
boats made of wicker and ox hides, it may be
anfwered, that thefe *Curachs* muft then have been
confiderably larger than thofe ufed for many ages
by feveral barbarous nations upon rivers and narrow
founds. The Belgic colonies who tranfmigrated
into Britain, had originally cattle to carry along
with them in their tranfports : and there is
no reafon to believe that the ancient inhabitants
of Britanny, Normandy, or Picardy, had more
fkill to build veffels fit for a national migration,
or more courage to ufe them than the ancient inhabitants of Holland, Friefland, Weftphalia, Saxony, or Denmark. It is true, the latter lay at a
greater diftance from Britain : But if the Britons
of Lucan's time ventured out into the ocean in
Curachs *, the old Germans might have likewife
done fo. Should they even be too timid or un-
fkilful to make at once a crofs voyage to Caledonia, it was always in their power, after coaft-
ing the Belgic Gaul and South Britain, to arrive
at laft in the Northern divifion of this ifland.

F r o m the parallel drawn between the Germans
and Caledonians, and the obfervations I have made
on the fuppofed ftate of navigation in thofe times,
it muft be owned that there is fome additional
ftrength given to Bede's tradition, and the remark
of Tacitus. But after all, the Gaulifh defcent of

---

* Lucani Pharf. lib. iv. ver. 130, et feq.

the

the Caledonians is the moſt natural and the leaſt liable to objections. In the obſcurity which involves ſo early a period, probability muſt take place of all arguments drawn from the ſimilarity of manners and cuſtoms which invariably ſubſiſts among all barbarous nations; at the ſame time, I am actually of opinion, that the Caledonians and Germans deſcended originally from the ſame Gauliſh ſtock.

The Gauls who firſt poſſeſſed themſelves of Britain, might eaſily, at the ſame time, ſend colonies beyond the Rhine. In a courſe of ages the inhabitants of Gaul, as they poſſeſſed a fine climate and ſoil, naturally formed themſelves into regular governments and communities, and made a more rapid progreſs towards civilization than the Celto-Germanic colonies they ſent beyond the Rhine, and which, from the nature of the country they poſſeſſed, muſt longer remain in a ſtate of barbarity. In proceſs of time the Gauls, no doubt, from an increaſe of numbers, ſent ſucceſſive colonies to Britain. The firſt coloniſts, from the preſſure of thoſe new comers, gradually migrated to the North, till at laſt they poſſeſſed themſelves of the inacceſſible mountains of Caledonia. There they not only found ſecurity to themſelves but to their original cuſtoms and language, which, from the ſimplicity of a life ſpent in hunting, ſuffered very few innovations. The northern Germans, certainly, from ſimilar circumſtances, gradually had moved towards the Baltic, and had the ſame opportunities of preſerving the ancient cuſtoms and language once common to the great Celtic ſtock. Thus the reſemblance between the old Germans and Caledonians is better accounted for, than from

a

a deduction of the latter from the former in an after age.

A s the Gauls, as I have above said, made a
quicker progress towards civilization than their
colonies in Britain, and beyond the Rhine, so their
language and manners suffered a more rapid
change. The arts of civil life introduce among
mankind a new form of ideas, and of course new
words and new manners. To this, and this alone,
must be ascribed the difference between the Caledonians, and the Gauls and Britons of the South,
in point of the construction of their language,
and the diversity of a few national customs.

DISSER-

DISSERTATION XIII.

Of the Degrees and Titles of Honour among the Scots of the Middle Ages. Of obsolete Law Terms in Regiam Majestatem.   Of the Merchetæ Mulierum.

THE Galic dialect of the old Celtic was the common language of the greatest part of Scotland, from time immemorial, down to the eleventh century.   The Scots who lay to the South of Clyde and the Forth had, for several ages before the æra now assigned, a good deal of intercourse with the Saxons of Bernicia and Deira. That division of Scotland was, at intervals, subject to a Saxon government *.   Some of the Scots Kings were Lords of Cumberland, before their accession to the throne, and kept their little courts in that part of England.   From these circumstances we may conclude, that the Saxon tongue prevailed in the Southern division of North Britain for a considerable time before it crossed the Firth of Edinburgh, in its progress to the North.

* Bede.

TOGETHER

TOGETHER with the language, cuftoms and laws of the Saxons, Malcolm Canemore introduced Saxon or French titles of magiftracy and honour, unknown till then in Scotland.

BEFORE that time North Britain, like other un-polifhed countries, may be fuppofed to have been very defective in its laws. Hector Boece, and fome other Scottifh hiftorians, have given the word an abftract of fome excellent laws made by Kenneth the Second and Macbeth : but their authority on this head is extreamly queftionable. There is another body of laws which are commonly attributed to Malcolm, the fecond of that name, who in the year 1004 mounted the throne of Scotland : but our ableft antiquaries have been much divided on this fubject. The learned Sir John Skene, and Sir James Dalrymple, are pofitive that thefe laws ought to be afcribed to Malcolm ; but Dr. Nicolfon, Bifhop of Carlifle, Dr. Hickes, and before them, Sir Henry Spelman, contended for fixing them to a later period. I have thrown at the bottom of the page Spelman's own words *.

MAL-

---

* " Skene begins the laws of Scotland with thofe of Malcolm the Second. But it is far from being clear that the laws which go under that King's name are fo ancient. They contain many words and terms which belong to a more modern age : befides, they refer to cuftoms, and names of offices, which belong to a later period. Skene likewife attributes to David the firft thofe four books which are intitled, Regiam Majeftatem Scotiæ. This Monarch, according to his calculation, began to reign in the year of Chrift 1124, or about the twenty-fourth of Henry the Firft. But Randolph de Glanville did not write his treatife concerning the laws and cuftoms of England, till after the twenty-fixth of Henry the Second's reign, that is, not till the year 1180 ; and they who compare this book of Glanville's, and the Regiam Majefta-

.tem

Malcolm MacKenneth, or the second King of Scotland of that name, was cotemporary with Canute. He was long at war with the Danes and English; and it is not likely that he borrowed these titles of honour from either of those nations. It is much more probable that his great grandson Malcolm Canemore imported them from England. In the MacAlpine or MacKenneth laws mention is frequently made of earls *, among the barons. Sir James Dalrymple infers from this circumstance, that we had that degree of honour in Scotland during Malcolm the second's reign †.

---

tem of Scotland, will readily find such an agreement and similitude in them, that they must conclude one of the two was copied after the other. But I allow others to determine whether we have imported our system of laws from Scotland."

" If it is impossible to prove that the feudal law was established in England before the Norman conquest, it is therefore far from being probable that the same feudal law was known in Scotland about sixty years before that epoch. However ancient the league between the French and the Scots may have been, it may be doubted whether Malcolm the Second had intercourse enough with that, or any other Continental nation, to learn the constitution of their government, or to know even their titles of dignity and honour, so as to transfer them into his own kingdom. It is hardly credible that he could have been the author of those laws which give exact descriptions of the offices of chancellor, justiciary chamberlain, steward of the houshold, constable, marischal, sheriff, provost, baillies of burghs, together with the privileges and jurisdiction of barons. " The Britons, says Cambden, disown the name of barons: nor is there any thing said with regard to it in the Saxon laws. The first mention of this title that I have met with, is in a fragment of the laws made by Canute the Great†" See Spelman's Glossary, under the words Lex Scotorum.

     † Britannia, under the article, Degrees of all England.

   * Collections, p. 146.
   † Comites.

But

But the argument is not conclufive, till it is admitted that that Monarch was the author of the
MacAlpine laws ; and if the ancient copy to which
the learned knight appeals ; be a fufficient authority to afcribe thefe laws to Malcolm MacKenneth,
the old tradition which attributes them to Mac-
Alpin, is an argument equally good for making
them much more ancient.

EARL is originally a Danifh word, which
anfwers to Conful, Comes and Dux, of the Latin
ufed in the middle ages *. Dalrymple infers, from
two or three conclufive authorities, that we had
Comites and Vice-comites in Scotland before the
reign of Malcolm the Second †. But he allows that
this title of dignity was not hereditarily annexed to
families, till the time of Malcolm Canemore. The
Scots hiftorians accordingly tell us, that MacDuff,
Thane of Fife, was the firft that obtained the
hereditary title of Earl to his family.

Buchanan ‡ fays, that there was no title of
honour in Scotland fuperior to that of Knight, excepting thofe of the Thanes and Jufticiaries, before the reign of Malcolm the fecond. But it is
not even certain that there were gentlemen of the
equeftrian order in Scotland fo early ‖ Cambden
and Spelden fuppofe, that the origin of this dignity muft be inveftigated among the ancient Germans. They quote the following paffage from

---

* Spelm. Gloff. under the word Eorla.
† Collect. p. 146.
‡ Rer, Scot. lib. 6. cap. 52.
‖ We find no great mention of this order till Malcolm the
Third's time. Henry Firs-Emprefs was fent from England to
receive the honour of knighthood from David the fon of that
Prince.

L

Tacitus :

Tacitus: " Among the Germans, it is never cuftomary for any man to carry arms till the community have firft given their approbation. That done, one of the principal nobility, or the young man's father or relation, adorns him with a fhield or javelin, before a public affembly. This ceremony confers the fame dignity among them that the gown does among the Romans. Before their youth receive this honour, they are reckoned only a part of a private family; but from that day forth they are confidered as members of the commonwealth *"

BEFORE the titles of Barons, Earls, Dukes, Marquiffes and Vifcounts were imported from foreign countries, all the degrees of honour known in Scotland were, as far as I can learn, the King, the Lord, the Tanift, and the Tofhich; together with thofe belonging to offices, civil and ecclefiaftical. Barons came in with the feudal law. The word Earl is of a Danifh extract; and the language of the Danes was unknown here till after the middle of the ninth century. Robert the Third created our firft Dukes, and James the Sixth our Marquifes, Vifcounts and Baronets.

THE ancient Scots or Highlanders call the fovereign *Ri*; the old Britons or Welfh *Rhuy*; the modern French *Roy*; the Italians *Re*; and the Spaniards *Rey*. From this fimilarity of founds, and identity of fenfe, we may reafonably infer, that the *Rex* of the Latin is derived from the Celtic, and had originally the fame idea affixed to it which is conveyed by the correfpondent names in the feveral dialects of that language.

* Tacitus de mor. Germ. cap. 13.

THE meaning of *Ri* is a ruler; and among the ancients the idea of deſpotiſm was not annexed to regal government. This opinion only obtained in the Eaſt. The Celtic nations limited the regal authority to very narrow bounds. The old Monarchs of North Britain and Ireland were too weak, either to controul the pride and inſolence of the great, or to reſtrain the licentiouſneſs of the populace. Many of thoſe Princes, if we credit hiſtory, were dethroned, and ſome of them even put to death by their ſubjects; which is a demonſtration that their power was extremely circumſcribed. They were not in poſſeſſion of treaſures, to keep ſtanding armies, or to corrupt thoſe whoſe avarice might induce them to be inſtruments of tyranny.

NEXT to the King were thoſe great landholders who are called *Lords* in Engliſh, *Lairds* in Scotch, and *Tierna* in the ancient Galic. It it very probable that the Galic *Tierna*, or the Welch *Teyrn*, was the firſt title of ſupreme dignity among the Celtic nations *.

THE Highlanders and Iriſh frequently addreſs the Supreme being under this name; and hence it may be concluded, that their anceſtors had no conception of power ſuperior to that of the *Tierna*. From the ſame conſideration we may likewiſe infer, that originally every one called Tierna was an independent Prince. It was only after many ſuch Lords had become the vaſſals of mightier

---

* Tierna is derived very probably from *Ti*, *The one*, by way of eminence, and *Ferran*, *Land*. *Ferran*, in the oblique caſe, produces *Eran*. So that *Tierna* is the ſame with *Tieran*, *A man of land*, or *a great proprietor of land*.

                    Princes

Princes, that this name was given to perfons in a ftate of fubordination. As the Romans formed their *Rex* out of the Celtic word *Ri*, fo the Greeks derived their Τυραννος from Tierna. The word Tyrant was originally no more odious, in the language of that nation, than King is in that of England. It were an eafy matter to fhow that fome excellent Princes were ftiled Tyrants in Greece, and agreeable to that mode of expreffion in ancient times, Æneas gives the very fame title to the good old Latinus.

The third name of dignity among the Scots of ancient times was *Tanift*, or *Taniftear*. This word has been confounded with *Thane*, which occurs frequently in the hiftory of Scotland. Buchanan fays, that before the reign of Malcolm the Second, *Thane* was the higheft title immediately after that of King. His explication of the word is, the Governor of a country, or the King's Lieutenant in a certain divifion of his dominions *. Every one converfant in the hiftory of Scotland has read of Banquho, Thane of Lochaber, MacDuff, Thane of Fife, and Somerled, Thane of Argyle.

The appellation of Thane was known in England, and common there for feveral ages: nor was it difcontinued till after the Norman conqueft. In the Saxon tongue, *Thane*, *Theger*, and *Tain*, fignified a Servant or Minifter †.

The Irifh had their *Tanift* ; and in their language the meaning of that word is, the fecond perfon, or fecond thing ‡. It is not probable that

---

* Præter Thanos hoc eft præfectos Regionum. Buchan. in Milcolm.

† Spelman's Gloffary, under thefe words.

‡ See Lhoyd's Irifh Dictionary.

they

they borrowed the title from the Englifh, as, not-withftanding of Bede's allegation concerning the friendly difpofition of the Irifh towards the Saxons of the fixth and feventh centuries, they had a mortal averfion to the Englifh ; and before the conqueft of Ireland by Henry the Second, the title of Tanift became obfolete : it may therefore be prefumed that Tanift is an ancient Galic word.

In the fettlement of fucceffion, the law of Taniftry prevailed in Ireland from the earlieft accounts of time. " According to that law, fays Sir James Ware *, the hereditary right of fuccef-fion was not maintained among the Princes or the Rulers of countries ; but the ftrongeft, or he who had moft followers, very often the eldeft and moft worthy of the deceafed King's blood and name, fucceeded him. This perfon, by the common fuffrage of the people, and in the lifetime of his predeceffor, was appointed to fucceed, and was called *Tanift*, that is to fay, the fecond in dignity. Whoever received this dignity, maintained him-felf and followers, partly out of certain lands fet apart for that purpofe, but chiefly out of tributary impofitions, which he exacted in an arbitra-ry manner ; impofitions, from which the lands of the church only, and thofe of perfons vefted with particular immunities, were exempted."

The fame cuftom was a fundamental law in Scotland for many ages. Upon the death of a King, the throne was not generally filled by his fon, or daughter failing of male iffue, but by his brother, uncle, coufin-german, or near relation of the fame blood. The perfonal merit of the fuc-

---

* Antiq. and Hift. of Ireland, chap. 8.

L 3

ceffor,

ceffor, the regard paid to the memory of his immediate anceftors, or his addrefs in gaining a
majority of the leading men, frequently advanced
him to the crown, notwithftanding the precautions
taken by his predeceffor.

— · The hiftory of the Saxon heptarchy, or that
of the Englifh monarchy, down to the time of the
conqueft, fhews, that the law of Taniftry was
very often the rule obferved in the fucceffion of
Sovereigns. No great regard was paid to hereditary right : the King's brother was frequently preferred to his fon ; a baftard Prince fometimes took
place of a legitimate one ; and the will of the
laft reigning Sovereign had more than once excluded the lineal heir.

It is plain that the law of Taniftry had a
natural tendency to embroil families, countries
and kingdoms. In all the places where it prevailed, domeftic feuds, provincial infurrections,
and national wars, muft have been unavoidably
frequent. But as the Scots and Irifh, and almoft
every other Celtic nation, made arms the great
occupation of life, they thought it highly
inexpedient to intruft the direction of the ftate to
infants, minors, or unexperienced youths. With
them it was the moft effential confideration to have
a brave and difinterefted Prince, who had been
inured to war, and who could lead them into the
field, infpire them with fpirit, and fupport them
with conduct. They confidered the King at once
as the fubject and leader of the community.

In Ireland the law of Taniftry not only determined the regal fucceffion, but likewife extended
to every great eftate poffeffed by a fubject. The
Lord of every country, and the Chief of every

Sept

Sept was fucceeded, not by his fon or next heir, but by the Tanift, who was elective, and who frequently procured his election by force of arms[*]. In Scotland the cafe was much the fame, till the eftablifhment of the feudal law, and in fome places long after that period.

In the Highlands and Weftern Ifles the Tierna's next brother claimed a third [†] part of the eftate during life, by virtue of a right founded on an immemorial cuftom. It is now above two hundred years back fince the Taniftry regulation, and the difputes confequent upon it, prevailed in the Highlands. There have been fome inftances of it much later.

Toshich was another title of honour which obtained among the Scots of the middle ages. Spelman imagined that this dignity was the fame with that of the Thane [‡]. But the Highlanders, among whofe predeceffors the word was once common, diftinguifh carefully in their language the *Tofhich* from the *Taniftair*, or the *Tierna*. When they enumerate the different claffes of their great men, agreeable to the language of former times, they make ufe of thefe three titles, in the fame fentence, with a disjunctive adverb between them.

In Galic, *Tus, Tos,* and *Tofhich,* fignify the *beginning,* or *the firft part* of any thing, and fometimes the front of an army or battle [‖]. Hence the Name *Tofhich* [¶] ; that is to fay, the General,

---

[*] Sir John Davis's Hiftor. Relations of Ireland.
[†] Trian Tiernis.
[‡] Spelm. Gloff under the word Thane.
[‖] See Lhoyd's Irifh Dictionary.
[¶] The Moguls or Calmachs give the name of *Taifha* to their heads of tribes, and that of *Contaifha* to their Great Chan.——

L 4

Can

or Leader of the van. The interpretation now given of the word Toſhich is confirmed by the name of a conſiderable family in the Highlands of Scotland—the clan of M'Intoſh, who ſay, that they derive their pedigree from the illuſtrious Mac Duff, once Thane, and afterwards Earl of Fife. MacDuff, in conſideration of his ſervices to Mal-

---

Can itſelf is the ſame with the *Caen* of the Galic, ſignifying *Head*, and metaphorically the head of a family ; ſo that *Cantaiſka*, or grand Chan, would be expreſſed by a Highlander *Cantoiſbich*. Here it is worthy to remark the connection between the old Mogul or Tartar language and the Celtic. This connection offers ſome kind of preſumption that they ſprung from the ſame original ſtock. The great river Oxus, called by the Tartars *Am*, which, riſing in mount Imaus, once diſcharged itſelf in the Caſpian ſea, but now, having changed its courſe, falls into the lake of *Aral*, naturally divides Aſia into almoſt two equal parts. The Tartars, and ſome other Eaſtern nations, called that diviſion which lies to the South-weſt *Iran*, that to the North-eaſt *Turan*, which are plainly Celtic words. *Iran* is compounded of *Ier*, South-weſt, and *ran*, diviſion ; and *Turan*, in the ſame manner, is compoſed of the two words *Tua* and *ran*, which ſignify the Northern country or diviſion. See *Abul Ghazi's* Hiſt. of Tartary, vol. ii. p. 541.

It were eaſy to purſue the ſimilarity between the Tartar and Celtic languages much farther. I ſhall give one other inſtance. The great Zingis Chan, firſt Emperor of the Moguls, being one day hunting, and perceiving a ſolitary tree, exceeding tall and beautiful, he ordered his ſons to inter him under it, after his death ; which they accordingly executed with all the requiſite ceremony. There grew, in time, ſuch beautiful trees about the tomb, and in ſuch numbers, that an arrow, ſhot from a bow, could hardly find a paſſage through them. From that circumſtance, they have given to that place the name of *Barchan Caldin*; and all the Princes of the poſterity of Zingis Chan who ſince then died in thoſe provinces, have been interred in the ſame place. *Barchen Caltin* is perfectly underſtood by every Scots Highlander : it ſignifies a beautiful thicket of birch and hazel trees.——Hiſt. of Tartary, vol. ii. p. 145.

colm

colm Canemore, obtained a grant, which gave him and his heirs a right of leading the van of the royal army on every important occasion. The Chieftain of the clan that is descended from this great Earl is stiled *Mac in Tosbich* in Galic, that is to say, the Son of the General.

OCHIERN, or Ogetharius, is another title of honour mentioned in the ancient laws of Scotland. Spelman, copying after Skene, says, that the *Os-chiern* is a person of the same dignity with a Thane's son ; because, in the laws of Regiam Majestatem, the *marcheta* of a Thane's daughter is equal to the marcheta of an *Ochiern*'s daughter *, as the *Cro* of a Thane was the same with that of an *Ochiern*. The word is undoubtedly a Galic one, contracted from *Oge-Thierna*, that is, the young Lord, or heir apparent of a landed gentleman. It is likewise not improbable that the Thane of our Regiam Majestatem is the Tanist, or the person who possessed the third part of a great Lord's estate †.

THE *Brehon* or *Britbibb*, may be ranked, without any impropriety, among the old Scottish titles of honour. The Brehons were, in North Britain and Ireland, the Judges appointed by authority to determine, on stated times, all the controversies which happened within their respective districts. Their courts were usually held on the side of a hill, where they were seated on green banks of earth. These hills were called mute hills. It may be presumed that the Brehons were far from being

---

* Two kids, or twelve pennies.

† Ogetharius is derived from Oig-thear, that is, a young gentleman.

deeply

deeply fkilled in the intricate fcience of the law, which they profeffed. By converfing with the ecclefiaftics in their neighbourhood, they learned fome fcraps of the canon law, but knew little or nothing of the civil. The cuftoms which prevailed in the land wherein they lived, and the opinion of the times, were generally their rules of decifion. The office belonged to certain families, and was tranfmitted, like every other inheritance, from father to fon. Their ftated falaries were farms of confiderable value.

By the *Brehon* law even the moft atrocious offenders were not punifhed with death, imprifonment, or exile, but were obliged to pay a fine, called *Eric*. The eleventh or twelfth part of this fine fell to the Judge's fhare: the remainder belonged partly to the King, or Superior of the land, and partly to the perfon injured; or if killed, to his relations.

We learn from Tacitus, that the fame cuftom prevailed among the ancient Germans. After he had obferved that they hanged traitors and deferters on trees, and that perfons, either cowardly or infamous for impurity, were drowned in miry lakes, he adds, " Men guilty of crimes lefs fcandalous, were, upon conviction, fined in a number of cattle. A part of this fine was paid to the King or common-wealth, and another portion of it was given to the perfon injured, or to his neareft friends."

In Scotland the fame cuftom prevailed, till within three or four hundred years ago, and in fome divifions of it much later. In our laws of Regiam Majeftatem, we find it enacted, That one who, riding through a town, rides over and kills

any

any of the inhabitants, is to pay a proper ranfom, no lefs than if he had wilfully deftroyed him *. The name given to the ranfom in the law is *Cro* and *Galmes*. The *Cro* of every man is afcertained, in the fame inftitutes, according to his quality or birth. The *Cro* of an Earl is one hundred and forty cows. The *Cro* of an Earl's fon, or Thane is an hundred cows. The Cro of a plebeian, or *villain*, is fixteen. The *Cro*, *Galmes* and *Enach* of all other ranks and orders of men are particularly defined in thofe laws.

Spelman has judicioufly remarked, that thefe three barbarous words are of Irifh extraction. But he did not recollect that the Galic of Scotland was much the fame with the language of Ireland, and that the words were originally Britifh. They certainly had once a place in the law of Scotland, though their true meaning has not been yet fettled. The wealth of the ancient Scots, efpecially towards the North, confifted folely in cattle. In the language fpoken there, *Cro* fignifies Cows, and *Croo* a fheepfold or Cow-pen. Agreeable to this explication of thefe two terms, a murderer is ordered by our old laws to pay the *Cro* of the perfon whom he had killed, that is, to pay the ftated equivalent for his life, in cattle taken out of the flayer's pen or fold.

GALMES is a Galic word, and means a Pledge, or Compenfation for any thing that is carried away or deftroyed †. In the fame language, *Enach* ftands fometimes for the Englifh word Bounty, and fometimes for an Eftimate or Ranfom.

---

* Regiam Majeft. lib. 4. cap. 24.
† Gial, in the Galic, is a Pledge, and Meas an Eftimate.

C R O,

CRO, Galmes and *Enach* are perhaps fynoni-mous terms, according to the common language of the Scottifh law, which is full of fuch tauto-logical expreffions. If there is any real difference between thefe words in the cafe before us, they fignify three diftinct fines ; one payable to the King, or Superior of the perfon flain ; another to his children ; and a third to his *Cinea*, or the tribe to which he belonged. Agreeable to this diftinc-tion of fines, the old Saxons of England obliged murderers to pay three different ranfoms, the *Fredum* to the King, the *Wergelt* to his family, and the *Linebote* to his kinfmen *.

KELCHYN is another term in the old Scot-tifh law, to exprefs a mulct due by one guilty of manflaughter. In our Regiam Majeftatem †, the *Kelchyn* of an Earl is fixty-fix cows and two thirds; the Kelchyn of an Earl's fon, or of a Thane, is forty-four cows, twenty-one pence, and two thirds of an obulus or bodle ; the Kelchyn of a Thane's fon is by a fourth part lefs than that of his father; and the law adds, that a fwain, or perfon of low degree, is to have no fhare of the Kelchyn.

The learned Sir John Skene obferves, that in the ancient language of Scotland, *Gailchen* figni-fies a pecuniary mulct, to which one is made liable, for a fault or crime. Spelman differs from him only fo far as to think the word an Irifh one. Skene's conjecture is partly juft, and partly other-wife. The Kelchyn was a mulct, but not always a pecuniary one, not payable for every fault or crime. We fee the Kelchyn of an Earl is fixty-

---

* See Spelman, under thefe words.
† Reg. Majeft. lib. 4. cap. 38.

fix

fix cows, and two thirds of a cow. This fine belonged to the kinfmen of the perfon killed *, but to thofe only of principal note among them.

In the old Scottifh law, with regard to the fine paid by the murderer of an Earl, this Croo is declared to be one hundred and forty cows, and every cow priced at three Oræ. In a law of Canute the Great, quoted by Spelman †, fifteen Oræ, or Horæ, are made equal to a pound : and fuppofing the Engiifh pound of thofe days to have been twelve times as much as the Scottifh one, and the Oræ of both nations the fame, the pecuniary value of one cow would have been about five fhillings fterling. But fhould one fuppofe that the Ora of North Britain was to that of the Southern divifion, what the pounds, fhillings and pence of the former are to thofe of the latter, the price of a cow in Scotland was, at the time of compiling the Regiam Majeftatem, proportionably low.

It is certain that money was extremely fcarce in Scotland during the reign of King David the Firft. But as we cannot well imagine that a full grown cow was fold for the fmall trifle of fivepence in that period, and as it is not in any degree probable that the price of it could have rifen to five fhillings fterling, we have here one proof, together with many more, from which it may be evinced, that the laws of Regiam Majeftatem were framed in the time of David the Second, and not in th days of the firft Scottifh King of that name.

---

* Kelchyn fignifies, paid to one's kinfmen, and is derived from Gial and Cinnea.

† In voc. Ora.

In

In that part of Regiam Majeſtatem which aſcertains the different Merchetæ Mulierum, the Vacca, or large Cow, is valued at ſix ſolidi, or ſhillings. The real amount of that ſolidus cannot well be determined. If an Engliſh one, the price of a cow is conſiderably greater than the eſtimate already given : if a Scottiſh, it ſinks down to a ſmall matter.

As I have entered upon the explication of law terms, it is proper to give ſome ſolution of one of them, which, as it is now underſtood, leaves a reproach upon our anceſtors. The meaning of *Merchetæ Mulierum* is, according to ſome, founded upon a cuſtom which did great diſhonour to the ancient civil government of Scotland.

Some of our beſt hiſtorians give the following account of the introduction of the *Merchetæ Mulierum* among the ancient Scots. Evenus the Third, a King of Scotland, cotemporary with Auguſtus, made a law, by which he and his ſucceſſors in the throne were authorized to lie with every bride, if a woman of quality, before her huſband could approach her : and in conſequence of this law, the great men of the nation had a power of the ſame kind over the brides of their vaſſals and ſervants. We are told further by the ſame grave and learned hiſtorians, that this law was ſtrictly obſerved throughout the kingdom ; nor was it diſcontinued or repealed, till after a revolution of more than ten whole centuries. It was near the end of the eleventh age, that the importunities of St. Margaret prevailed with her huſband, Malcolm Canemore, to aboliſh this unjuſtifiable cuſtom. From that time forward, inſtead of the ſcandalous liberty given to every Superior by virtue of Evenus's

law

law, the vaſſal or ſervant was impowered to redeem the firſt night of his bride by paying a tax
in money *.   This tax was called Merchetæ Mulierum.

I know not whether any one has been hitherto
ſceptical enough to call the truth of this tale in
queſtion, though it wears the face of abſurdity
and fable: Twenty moral demonſtrations conſpire
in rendering it abſolutely incredible.

Evenus, the ſuppoſed author of the law, is
no more than an imaginary being. Boece and
Buchanan, with all their hiſtorical knowledge
and induſtry, knew juſt as little concerning the
Princes of Caledonia, coeval with Auguſtus, and
of the laws eſtabliſhed by them, as the other
learned men of Europe knew with regard to the
Emperors of Mexico before the time of Fernando
Cortez.

It is impoſſible to prove that any conſiderable
diviſion of Caledonia was governed by a ſingle Monarch in the Auguſtan age. But were it true that
the caſe was otherwiſe, and alſo certain that Evenus reigned in the Weſtern parts of North Britain in that very epoch, it is not credible that the
Scots of that age would have granted ſo very extravagant a prerogative to their King, or ſo very
uncommon a privilege to their nobility. In thoſe
early times men were too fierce and intractable
to crouch under a burden ſo inſupportable. To
a people of ſpirit, a total extinction of freedom
and property, in every other inſtance, would have
been a much eaſier yoke than the ſlavery, oppreſ-

---

* Boece ſays a merk of ſilver, Buchanan half a merk.

ſion

fion and difgrace attending fo very fhocking a proftitution of their wives, daughters and kinf-women. But had even the lower people of Scotland been the moft abject of all flaves, and uncommon patterns of paffive obedience, it cannot be fuppofed that all the nobility, from age to age, would have practifed the doctrine of non-refiftance, in fuch an amazing degree of perfection, as to permit their Sovereign to violate their honour in fo heinous a manner. We know that many Princes, befides Tarquin, were dethroned, banifhed, and cut to pieces, for attempting the chaftity of women. And we may fafely affirm, that the moft defpotic King or Sultan in the Eaft would fall a facrifice, fhould he endeavour to eftablifh the law of Evenus in that country, which has always been the fcene of the fevereft exertion of arbitrary power.

Some may fay, that the manners and opinions of men are greatly changed. But human nature was always, and will ever continue the fame, in the matter now under confideration. In vain will it be faid, that the Scots, through a long habit, became reconciled to this ignominious cuftom. The Scots certainly were not more paffive than the other brave nations of the world: and the hiftory of mankind does not exhibit a fingle inftance of fuch brutal infenfibility in any nation.

The fatyrical Gildas, who had entertained the moft violent prejudices againft the Scots, would not have omitted fuch an opportunity of declaiming againft them, with his ufual acrimony. Bede himfelf, though a writer of much greater humanity and moderation, would not have overlooked fo remarkable a part of their character, efpecially as he impeaches them, more than once, of other immoralities. It would have been more to his honour to have animadverted feverely on fo flagitious a practice, than to arraign them fo frequently of heterodoxy, for a pretended error in the trivial affair of Eafter.

If we confider the jealoufy natural to women, it is highly improbable that the queen of Malcolm Canemore was the firft royal confort in Scotland that would have folicited her hufband for a repeal of this infamous law. In the courfe of more than a thoufand years, which intervened between the pretended Evenus and Malcolm, there were no doubt many Queens whofe influence with their hufbands might have abrogated this lafcivious inftitution. — The ftory altogether wears fuch a face of improbability, that it is aftonifhing how it ever became the fubject of tradition itfelf, and much more that it has received the fanction of hiftorians.

It is however certain that the Merchetæ Mulierum were once paid in Scotland, and authorized by law. But this impofition was not peculiar to that kingdom. The Merchetæ Mulierum were, properly fpeaking, pecuniary fines, paid by the vaffal and fervant to his lord and mafter, upon the marriage of his daughter, or paid by a widow upon a reiteration of nuptials: and this cuftom obtained in every part of Britain, though with fome variation.

I cannot determine whether the brides of England or Wales were liable to this tax before the conqueft; but in the reign of William the Norman they certainly were. " A woman faith Domefday book in what ever way fhe came by

M

a husa hufband, gave twenty fhillings to the King, if a widow ; but if a maid, ten only[*]." That the grievance arifing from this hard law was univerfal, or at leaft very general, may be juftly concluded from different articles of the charter granted by Henry the firft, and from the famous Magna Charta of King John.

In the fourth article of Henry's charter are the following words : " If any one of the Barons, or of the other vaffals that hold immediately of me, fhall incline to give his daughter, fifter, niece or kinfwoman in marriage, let him fpeak to me on that fubject : but neither fhall I take or receive any thing from him for a marriage licence, nor fhall I hinder him from difpofing of the woman as he pleafes, unlefs he beftow her on my ene-my [†]."

From the immunity given in thefe words, and from the preamble of the charter, one may naturally infer, that the law of the Merchetæ had formerly prevailed in every part of England, excepting the fingle county of Kent. After King John had given the great charter of liberties to the Barons, and after that ineftimable right had been confirmed by his fon, grandfon, and great grandfon, we find, that not only villians, or the loweft clafs of people in England, were obliged to pay this fine, but thofe too who held their lands in free foccage [‡]. The fine was called Merchetum or Maritagium there, as it went under the name of Mercheta in Scotland.

---

[*] Spelman in voc. Maritag.
[†] Matth. Paris, p. 55.
[‡] Spelman in voc. Soke mancric.

IT can fcarcely be doubted that the feudal inftitutions of Scotland came originally from England.
The general fpirit of feudal laws, and the manner
in which they are expreffed, afford almoft a demonftration on that head. Malcolm Canemore
had lived long in England, and owed very great
obligations to that country. His Queen was a
Saxon Princefs, and Englifh exiles were the great
favourites of both. Malcolm's children had an
Englifh education; and after that period of time,
the Englifh language, the Englifh fyftem of religion, the Englifh drefs, and the Englifh law,
became fafhionable in Scotland. Hence it may
be inferred, that the old Scots ftood obliged to
their neighbours for the Merchetæ Mulierum, and
not to Evenus, their ideal King.

WE have no caufe to believe, whatever our
hiftorians affirm on that head, that Queen Margaret eafed the Scots from this oppreffive tax.
In Regiam Majeftatem, the Merchetæ payable
by an earl's daughter is no lefs than twelve cows,
and was a perquifite which belonged to the Queen.
The Merchetæ due by a Thane's daughter fell to
the fuperior, and was no more than a fingle cow,
and twelve pence, which fell to the collector's
fhare. The Merchetæ of every woman, whether
virgin or widow, is determined by our oldeft inftitutes, and the fine payable to the Queen was
by far the moft confiderable.

IT is very evident that Boece and Buchanan
miftook the origin and true meaning of the Merchetæ. According to the former, a Mark of filver X
was the compenfation demanded by Malcolm Canemore for the firft night of the bride; a privilege to which he and his nobles had an equal

X a Scotch Mark, about thirteen pence farthing

right.   But according to Buchanan, the very half of that pecuniary tax was all that could be required, or was given.   It is ſtrange enough that theſe two authors could have differed ſo widely in this matter ; and it is equally ſo, that they imagined the ſame ſum preciſely was exacted from every woman, whether of high or low rank, and whether a maid or a widow.   From this circumſtance it may be juſtly concluded, that neither of theſe hiſtorians examined the old laws of their country*.

---

* With regard to the etymon of the word Mercheta, or Merchetum, none could be more improper than that offered by our learned countryman Skene. It carries indeed too much immodeſty in it to be laid before any delicate reader. It is very probable that the tax under conſideration was paid in England before it was impoſed in Scotland. We ſhould therefore look out for the true etymon of the Mercheta in England. The Merchetum was ſurely a pecuniary fine, and amounted at firſt to a Mark, Thoſe who have ſtudied the hiſtory of ancient coins know very well that Marks of ſilver and gold bore very different values in different countries, ages and nations †. The Engliſh Mark conſiſted of thirteen ſhillings and four pence ſterling. The Mark of Scotland was no more than a twelfth part of that ſum. The Burgundian ounce was the eighth part of a Mark ; and a Scottiſh Mark was juſt an ounce. The Daniſh Mark ſeems to have been equivalent to two denarii, or two pence ; and in ſome countries the Mark was equal to eight ounces. In ſhort, whatever the original amout of the Merchetum may have been, in all probability its etymon muſt be *Marca*, *Marcha*, or *Marchata*, three words of the very ſame meaning.

† See Spelman, under the word Marca.

DISSERTATION XIV.

Of the Bards.

A MODERN writer of some eminence has attempted to prove that religion was the true source of poetry. According to him, it was very natural for a person who possessed a warm imagination and a good heart, after contemplating the marvellous works of that Great Being who is the Creator and Sovereign Lord of the universe, to feel the strongest emotions of admiration, gratitude and love. Filled with the idea of this grand object, he would soon endeavour to express the awful impression he felt in language. Words falling short of his conceptions, he would strive to supply that want with the tuneful sounds of some musical instrument. Delighted with the harmony of agreeable sounds, he would exert his whole strength in adding to his vocal praises the same numbers, measure and cadence, which had been expressed by the action of his hands, in playing on the instrument*.

---

* Rollin, Bell. Let. Vol. I. book ii. art. i.

We

WE are told by the moſt ancient of all hiſtorians, that the harp and organ were known in a very early period, and it is natural to think that there had been ſome poetical compoſitions before Tubal invented thoſe inſtruments. Vocal muſic was certainly prior to the invention of inſtruments of muſic. There is no reaſon therefore to ſuppoſe but the numbers, meaſures and cadence of verſe, were known before words were adapted to the tone of an inſtrument.

THE moſt ancient ſpecimens of poetry now remaining were dedicated to the honour of the divinity. The two ſongs of Moſes, and that of Debora, are entirely in that ſtrain. The praiſes beſtowed on men and women in the latter are introduced epiſodically, and have a manifeſt reference to the main ſubject. The lamentation of David over Saul and Jonathan is in a different ſtile. Religion has little or no concern in it. The heroic exploits and untimely fate of theſe two great Princes make the whole burthen of that ſong.

WE may take it for granted, that the art of of verſification was known and much practiſed before Moſes wrote his triumphal ode. But whether the firſt poetical eſſay was employed in the ſervice of God or in honour of ſome great man or wonderful natural object, it is impoſſible to ſay. Poetry is the triumphant voice of joy or the broken ſighs of ſorrow and melancholy. The extreams of thoſe paſſions are moſt violent in the earlieſt ſtage of ſociety before the faculties of the human mind are regulated by advanced civilization, the feelings of the heart are ſtrong: and ſtrong feelings always produce that ſublimity of expreſſion

which

which we call poetry. The variety of the life of the favage affords him opportunities of viewing natural objects in their moſt awful and ſtriking form; therefore even his common converſations are expreſſive of the deep impreſſions of his mind, and his language is metaphorical and ſtrong. In advanced ſociety, the cultivated ſtate of the mind gives riſe to abſtracted ideas, which are too jejune and ill underſtood to conſtitute that ſublimity of expreſſion which is ſo remarkable in the poetical compoſitions of early ages.

THE poets of the Celtic nations were univerſally called bards by antient writers. The bards celebrated in verſe the great actions of heroes, and men of high dignity and renown. Without encroaching on the province of another order of men, they could not employ their genius on religious ſubjects.

A PASSAGE of Ammianus Marcellinus deſerves our attention. " After the inhabitants of " Gaul, ſays he, had been gradually poliſhed out " of their original barbarity, the ſtudy of ſome " valuable branches of learning made a conſide- " rable progreſs among them. The Bards, Eu- " bates, and Druids, gave birth to that ſtudy.

" IT was the buſineſs of the bards to ſing the " brave actions of illuſtrious men in heroic ſong, " and their poems on theſe ſubjects were accompa- " nied by the ſweet modulations of the lyre. The " Eubates made deep reſearches into the nobleſt " and moſt ſublime properties of nature : and they " endeavoured to expreſs their ſpeculations on that " ſubject in verſe. But the Druids, men of a " more elevated genius, and formed into ſocieties " agreeable to the rules laid down by Pythagoras,

M 4

" acquire

" acquire the higheſt pitch of honour by their
" enquiries into things ſublime and unknown, and,
" deſpiſing all that belongs to the human race in
" this lower world, they made no difficulty of
" affirming that ſouls are immortal *."

Many learned writers among the moderns have been of opinion that the Druids, Eubates and Bards, were three different orders of prieſts. But it requires a clearer proof than ancient hiſtory can furniſh, to ſhew that the Bards took any greater concern in ſpiritual affairs than the laity of their country.

It is plain from Strabo's teſtimony †, that the Eubates were prieſts and much employed in phiſiological diſquiſitions. But unleſs we ſuppoſe that they publiſhed poetical compoſitions on religious ſubjects, it is difficult to know how to diſtinguiſh them from the Druids in the preceding paſſage of Ammianus. The Druids compoſed in verſe, but never publiſhed any of their compoſitions.

---

* Per hæc loca hominibus paulatim excultis, viguere ſtudia laudabilium doctrinarum, inchoata per Bardos et Euhages et Druidas: et Bardi quidem fortia virorum illuſtrium facta, heroicis compoſita verſibus, cum dulcibus lyræ modulis cantitarunt: Euhages vero ſcrutantes ſumma et ſublimia naturæ pandere conabantur. Inter hos Druidæ ingeniis celſiores, ut auctoritas Pythagoræ decrevit, ſodalitiis aſtricti conſortiis quæſtionibus occultarum rerum altarumque erecti ſunt; et deſpanctantes humana pronuntiarunt, animas immortales. Ammian. lib. xv. circa finem.

I have taken the liberty of tranſlating our author's *pandere,* to expreſs in verſe. *Pandere* is a poetical word, and though ſometimes found in proſe writers, is never uſed in a profaic ſtile. In the ſenſe of that word now under conſideration it almoſt always conveys the idea of a pomp of diction, and a harmony of numbers.

† Lib. iv. p. 302.

Οὐάτεις,

Οὐάτεις, *Vates, Eubates, Euhages,* and *Eubages,* are words of exactly the fame meaning, and diver-fified only in the orthography by the vicious pronunciation of original authors, or the blunders of tranfcribers. Thofe to whom the name belonged were a Celtic order of priefts, philofophers, and poets, thought to have been prophetically infpired. Though the office is no more, the title has been hitherto preferved in the name of an Irifh tribe, and in that of a Scottifh clan, once confiderable, and not yet extinct *.

LUCAN has indentified the Vates and the Bard †: but he is the only claffical writer who has confounded thefe two names together. Virgil, Horace, Tibullus, Propertius, Ovid, and others, fpeak of the Vates with great refpect, and have given that title to themfelves, as well as to the moft eminent poets of Greece; but not one of them has thought of doing the fame honour to the more ignoble race of Bards.

---

* Among the old Irifh families of note in the county of Mayo, Cambden reckons that of MacVadus ‡, and in the Weftern Ifles of Scotland are fome called MacFaid. In the Galic and Irifh languages, *Faid* fignified a Prophet ‖.
As the Hibernian and Hebridian Scots had clans among them who drew their origin and appellation from fome eminent *Faids* or prophetical poets, fo they had others who derived their pedigree from Bards famous in their day. Every one belonging to the clans defcended from thofe, was, after his poetical anceftor, denominated *Mac-i-Bhaird,* that is to fay, the fon of the Bard; and according to the genius of the Saxon language, which generally fubftitutes the German W in place of the Celtic Bh, the Mac-i-Bhairds go under the name of Ward, in the South of Scotland, and fome parts of England, the Mac being rejected.
† Lib. i. ver. 247, &c.

‡ Hib. Com. Maio.
‖ Lhoyd's Irifh and Englifh Dictionary.

THE poet and prophet are co
Their profellions are nearly allied.
fupernatural infpiration is common
certainly without a large portion o
taking that word in its original fe1
them could fucceed fo well as the
The conceptions of both rife to th'
vellous, and pathetic; their langua
animated, magnificent, full of trop
way removed from profaic diction.
prophet's bufinefs to utter prediction
affumes the fame character occafional
that he fpeaks the language of the G'

IT was for this reafon that the
the name of Vates indifcriminately
and poets. This emphatical word
more, they borrowed from the old
Vates of Gaul certainly exercifed
function. Strabo fays fo exprefly in
which I have already referred. A
forms us, that the Vates was a po'
dignity to the Bard. This opinion '
is ftrengthened by the authority of V

QUINTILIAN remarks, that Virgi
arly fond of old words, when proper
five. This admirable poet was born :
in the Cifalpine Gaul. He therefor
been much better acquainted with tl
guage than any writer of his time. B
it will, it is plain that he makes a di
tween the Bard and the Vates.
eclogue, Lycidas confeffes, or rather
tle, that he himfelf was a poet, and
his own making, but one formed b'
at the fame time he had too much

imagine that he had a right to the name of Vates, though the shepherds were pleased to honour him with that title.

" Incipe si quid habes : et me fecere *poetam*
" Pierides, funt et mihi carmina : me quoque dicunt.
" Vatem pastores, sed non ego credulus illis :
" Nam neque adhuc Varo videor nec dicere Cinna
" Digna, sed argutos interstrepere anser olo-res *."

Servius, and some other commentators of great reputation, have done a manifest injury to this passage. Dr. Martin, after having given a long and learned note on it, concludes that the proper signification of Vates is, a poet of the first rank, a master of the art, and one that is really inspired. He had said before that *Vates* seems to be an appellation of greater dignity than *Poeta*, and to answer to the Bard of the English. In this last opinion he has been followed by another learned translator.

If I understand the English language, Bard is not a title of greater dignity than poet ; notwithstanding two eminent English writers are of that opinion. The title of Bard, no doubt, is sometimes given to men deservedly celebrated for their poetical genius ; but the present mode of expression seems to have affixed an idea of contempt to that name. But in whatever degree of esteem the name of Bard is or may have been held, it is certain that Vates never lost its original dignity.

Some Celtic Bards treated, it is true, of theological subjects in their compositions. We are

------

Virg. Eclog. ix. ver. 32, &c.

told

told by Tacitus *, that " the Germans celebrated
" Tuisto, an earth born God, and his son Man-
" nus, in poems of great antiquity." He adds,
a little after, that the same nation had poems of a
very different strain ; poems calculated solely for
inspiring their warriors with courage in action.
Those martial songs were of the composition of the
Bards, as appears from the name of Barditus,
which was given to that species of poetry. This
name was borrowed from the Germans themselves.
Tacitus does not say that the religious poems of
the Germans were the productions of the Bards.
The contrary is rather insinuated. These theological pieces were the work of a more venerable
race of men, of the Eubates of Marcellinus,
who investigated the most mysterious arcana of
nature.

THE Eubates or the Vates of Strabo were the
disciples of the Druids ; and it is not improbable
that the Vates composed the numerous poems
which those great teachers of all the Celtic nations
communicated to their followers †.

THE translator of the poems of Ossian has in a
great measure explained the reason that there are
no traces of religion to be found in the works of
that illustrious Bard. To the arguments produced
by that ingenious gentleman I beg leave to add
one more, which rises naturally from the observations I have just made on the subject. Though all
the Celtic nations were in a manner full of Gods
and superstition, their Bards could not employ
their genius in the service of any divinity without

---

* Tacit. de mor. Germ. cap. 2.
† Cæsar de Bell. Gall. lib. vi. cap. 14.

going

going out of their own proper fphere. Heavenly themes belonged to the Vates, another order of men, of a more dignified and facred character.

THOUGH religion is an univerfal concern, yet in every age and country there we.e perfons fet apart whofe more peculiar bufinefs it was to praife and addrefs the divinity. According to the Chriftian fyftem, every one is under an obligation to celebrate their creator, though there is an oider of men whofe more immediate employ it is to deal in matters of religion. The old Celtic nations did not fo much take the bufinefs off the hands of the prieft as we do : the *Faids* or Vates had no competitors in the province of theology. The Bard fung merely mortal fubjects : hymns and anthems belonged folely to the more dignified race of *Faids*. Offian, therefore, though one of the firft men of the ftate, could not, fuch were the prejudices of thofe times, interfere with religious fubjects, without a manifeft breach on the peculiar privileges of that branch of the Druids called the Vates. It is to this caufe, and not to the extinction of the Druids, I attribute the total filence concerning religion in the poems of Offian. Religious enthufiafm, of whatever kind it is, takes too much hold of the human mind ever to be eradicated ; and it may be fafely affirmed, that it is a prejudice impoffible to be removed, even by the fevereft exertions of power †.

IT

---

* The learned differtator might have added, that nothing is capable of removing one religious enthufiafm, but the fuperior abfurdity of another fyftem of the fame kind, or an immediate revelation from heaven. The feeble ray of reafon can never difpel that hazinefs which fuperftition has naturally thrown over

the

IT is idle to attempt to inveſtigate the etymon of Bard. Nothing can be more trivial than the opinion of thoſe who derive it from Bardus, an imaginary King, who, according to Beroſus, reigned over the Gauls and Britains, and was the inventor of poetry. Bard is undoubtedly Celtic; and being a monoſyllable it is vain to hope to trace it to any root.

---

the human mind. Accuſtomed to look through this groſs atmoſphere, our ideas of ſupernatural things are ſtrangely magnified and confuſed, and our diſtempered dreams, on that ſubject, make deeper and more permanent impreſſions than any material objects can do. If in an age when we can bring the wiſdom of former times to the aid of reaſon and philoſophy, we are almoſt incapable of diveſting true religion of the trappings of ſuperſtition, it is much more improbable, that, in a barbarous period, the human mind could extricate itſelf from the chains of ſuperſtitious fanaticiſm. Dr. Macpherſon, therefore, has accounted better for the ſilence concerning religion in the poems of Oſſian, than the tranſlator has done, by the ſuppoſed extinction of the Druids.

It is certain, that ſeveral tribes of American Indians have apparently no ſigns of religious ſuperſtition among them. This neither proceeds from groſs ignorance nor from the refinements of philoſophy; for the firſt has been always known to create more ſyſtems of enthuſiaſm than the ſcepticiſm of the latter has been ever able to deſtroy. It muſt be aſcribed to the ſerenity and unchangeableneſs of the climate of the more inland and Southern parts of North America, which preſerves an equal diſpoſition of mind among the natives, not ſubject to the ſudden reverſes of joy and melancholy, ſo common under a more variable ſky. Superſtition delights to dwell in the fogs of iſlands, the miſt of mountains, and the groſs vapors of a fenny country. Theſe circumſtances throw a melancholy over the mind that is very productive of vain and ſupernatural fears and pannics. It was from this cauſe, perhaps, that Britain was anciently the principal ſeat of Druidical ſuperſtitions; and on the ſame account, though from other circumſtances, it now poſſeſſes true religion in its purity, it will, in a courſe of ages, revert to that gloomy enthuſiaſm ſo ſuitable to its moiſt air and variable climate.

A CERTAIN

A certain modern hiftorian is of opinion, that it was from the ignorance of the old Celtic nations, and their contempt of letters, originally rofe the Bardifh compofitions of Europe. It is certain that poetry had a great reputation among the Celtic nations, long before they knew the ufe of letters. It is even probable that poetry was known to the Celtes before their tranfmigration from Afia into Europe. We are to look for the origin of poefy much farther back than that ignorance and contempt of letters which prevailed among the European Celtes, after they became great nations, and objects of attention to Greece and Rome.

In Gaul the Bards were held in great efteem. They had contributed greatly to polifh that nation out of its primæval barbarity. The Spaniards alfo, and more efpecially the Celtiberians, had the fame high refpect for that order of men : nor is it improbable that thofe old poetical compofitions, of which the *Turdetans* boafted fo much, were the works of their Bards *. Ancient Germany had the greateft veneration for her Bards. Poetical records were the only annals known in that extenfive country, and in them only the actions of great men were tranfmitted from generation to generation. Thofe oral chronicles prevailed over all that country through many ages. Charles the Great found barbarous poems of very high antiquity among his German fubjects, and ordered copies of them to be made †. The German Saxons of a

---

* Strabo, lib. iii. p 204. Edit. Amflet.

† Barbara et antiquiffima carmina, quibus veterum regum actus et bella canebantur fcripfit, memoriæque mandavit. He

later

later age could not be perfectly reconciled to Chriftianity till the Holy Scriptures were rendered into verfe, fuch a permanent hold had their prejudice in favour of the Bards taken of their minds.

The Northern Europe had the fame profound refpect for its Scalds, fo poets were called in Scandinavia. The fcalds were the fole recorders of great events. The Danes and Norwegians have no records older than the twelfth century, and the Swedes fall even fhort of the Danes in the antiquity of their writers of hiftory ‡. Saxo Grammaticus, who flourifhed in that age, has frequent recourfe to the authority of the Scalds who preceeded that æra ; and Joannes Magnus, archbifhop of Upfal, appeals to them continually in his hiftory of the Goths.

Torfæus relates that the Scalds were accounted perfons of very confiderable importance in Norway, Denmark, and Sweden. They were retained by monarchs, were invefted with extraordinary privileges, and highly careffed. In the court of that great Norwegian monarch, Harald Harfager, they had the honour of fitting next to the King himfelf, every one of the order according to his dignity. If we can depend on the authority of Saxo, Harnius gained the crown of Denmark by the ftrength of his poetical abilities : an illuftrious perfon of this profeffion was in the fame country exalted to a matrimonial alliance with one of it's Princes †.

---

calls them *Barbara*, becaufe they were written in a language which he did not underftand. Eginhard, in Vita Car. Mag. c. 29.

‡ Torfæus, in Orcad præfat.

† Idem, ibidem.

THE *Kymri* of Britain were remarkably fond of Bards. Every one of their Princes had his laureate ; nor could any man of quality fupport the dignity of his rank, without having one of that faculty near his perfon. From the vaft number of poetical manufcripts written in their native tongue, which the Welfh have hitherto preferved, it may be concluded that poetry was in very high eftimation among their anceftors †.

AMONG the ancient Cambro-Britannic Bards, Taliefin and Lhyvarch held the firft place for the felicity of their poetical genius. They flourifhed in the fixth century, and a confiderable part of their productions is to this day extant. Taliefin was cotemporary with the great Maglocunnus, and was highly favoured by that Prince. He was dignified by his countrymen with the title of *Ben-Bairdhe*, or the chief of the Bards.

IT is needlefs to prove that the Irifh had the greateft value for poetry. Never did any nation encourage or indulge the profeffion of Bards with a more friendly partiality. Their nobility and gentry, their Kings, both provincial and fupreme, patronized, careffed, and revered them. The Bards of a diftinguifhed character had eftates in land fettled on themfelves and their pofterity. Even amidft all the ravages and exceffes of war, thefe lands were not to be touched, the poet's own perfon was facred, and his houfe was efteemed a fanctuary.

EVERY principal Bard was in the Irifh tongue called *Filea* or *Allamb Redan*, that is to fay, a *Doctor in Poetry*. Each of the great Fileas or

---

† Tit. vii. p. 239.

Graduates

Graduates had thirty Bards of inferior note constantly about his perfon, and every Bard of the
fecond clafs was attended by a retinue of fifteen
poetical difciples.

IF any faith can be given to Keating, many
other extraordinary advantages and immunities
were annexed to the office of Bard, befides thofe
which arofe from the extravagant munificence of
private perfons. It was ordained by law that all
Bards fhould live at the public expence for fix
months in the year. By the authority of this law
they quartered themfelves upon the people
throughout the ifland from Allhallow tide till May
*. This heavy annual tribute was of a very old
ftanding, and for that reafon the Bards who were
authorized to exact it, were in the language of the
country called *Clear-hen-chaine*, that is, the fong-
fters of the ancient tax.

THE very ample privileges conferred on the
Bards, and the blind refpect paid to their perfons,
made them at laft intolerably infolent. Their
avarice alfo kept pace with their pride. Their
haughty behaviour and endlefs exactions became
an infupportable grievance to the nation. The
numbers of thofe ftrollers increafed daily. Such
as inclined to fpend their time in idlenefs and
luxury joined themfelves to the fraternity, and
paffed under the character of Bards. In the reign
of *Hugh ain Mearach*, fays Keating, that is, in the
latter end of the fixth age, a third part of the
people of Ireland went under that title, and claimed
the privileges annexed to the order.

* Keat. Gen. Hift. of Ireland, Part ii. pages 25, 26.

IT is a juft obfervation of Claudian, that every one who performs actions worthy of being celebrated by the mufe, is always fmitten with the love of fong. The fame of the hero will foon die, unlefs preferved by the hiftorian, or immortalized by the productions of the poet. Barbarous times have produced very few tolerable hiftorians; but all ages indifcriminately, and all countries where military merit fubfifted with a confpicuous luftre, have produced Bards famous in their generation.

THE ancient inhabitants of Caledonia were very warlike, and of courfe fond of fame. Such as had remarkably fignalized themfelves in the defence of their country, were, no doubt, proud of patronizing the beft Bards of the times in which they lived. Cambden's immenfe erudition has difcovered that Galgacus was celebrated by the poets of South Britain *; and therefore it is likely he was highly extolled by the Bards of his own country. We are told by Tacitus that Arminius, the great deliverer of Germany, was in his own time fung by the Bards †. Every Celtic nation took care to perpetuate the memory of all their patriot heroes in their poetical annals. The laureates, if I may call them fo, of every community were obliged by their office to pay a juft tribute of fame to the benefactors of the public; even crowned heads and warlike Chieftains thought it no difparagement to their high rank to exercife their talents in the poetical eulogiums fo common in thofe times.

THE princes of Scandinavia valued themfelves much on their poetical genius. Four Norwegian

---

* See his Britannia, under the article Caledonia.
† Tacit. Annal. lib. ii. cap. ult.

monarchs,

monarchs, and a Danifh King, diftinguifhed themfelves remarkably in that way. Thefe were Harald Harfager, Olaus Trygvinus, Olaus the faint,
Harald the imperious, and Ragnar Lodbrach *.
The great men who held of thofe monarchs, emu-
lated their mafters in difplaying the fire and vigour
of their genius in a ftudy fo fafhionable in thofe
romantic ages.

The Caledonian Princes of ancient times were
animated by the fame fpirit. We know that
James the Firft was an admirable poet for the age
in which he lived. Some Galic rhimes compofed
by his coufin german, Alexander, the famous Earl
of Mar, have been hitherto preferved. The Highland Chieftains contended frequently in alternate
verfe: nor have all thofe poetical dialogues perifhed. The apoftle of the Pictifh nation, and
the old Scottifh miffionaries were remarkably fond
of the mufes, and frequently couched their facred
leffons in fong.

The public has lately received the works of
Offian, the fon of Fingal. The impartial and men
of tafte have read them with admiration, and fen-
fibly felt the true language of natural and fublime
genius. Thofe who affected to defpife the compofitions of ancient times have been confounded
and mortified by the impartial voice of Europe in
the praife of thofe poems. The candid part of
the nation, though fome of them perhaps were at
firft prejudiced againft the genuinenefs of the
work, have been agreeably furprized to find that
their fufpicions were abfolutely groundlefs.

---

* Torfæus, in Orcad. præfat. ad Lect.

It

It has been a queſtion with ſome whether Oſſian was a Caledonian or Iriſh Bard. Aſia and Europe, in a remote age, contended for the honour of having given birth to Homer. It is therefore no matter of wonder that North Britain and Ireland ſhould emulouſly claim a particular right to the great poetical ſun of their dark ages. They have formerly contended for much ſmaller prizes. The queſtions whether Sidulius, the poet, whether Cataldus, the biſhop of Tarentum, whether St. Aidan, St. Finan, St. Adamnan, and many more wrongheaded monks, belonged more properly to the ſacred iſland than to the wilds of Caledonia, have been agitated with all the keenneſs and zeal incident to national diſputes of that kind.

The editor of Oſſian's works is very able to defend his own ſyſtem. When objections worthy his notice are raiſed, he will certainly pay them all due regard. If he will ſit down gravely to confute the groundleſs and ill connected objections which have been raiſed by ſome people in the cauſe of Ireland *, it is deſcending too far from that dignity of character which he has already acquired. For the poetical errors of his author, if he has committed any flagrant ones, the tranſlator is no ways accountable. But if Oſſian's compoſitions do honour to that dialect of the Celtic language, in which they have been wrote, to that Celtic nation which produced the Bard, and to human genius itſelf; the editor has an indiſputable title to great praiſe, for bringing to light ſuch a monument of the poetical merit of the ancient Bards.

---

* See Mr. O Connor and Dr. Warner on this ſubject.

Among.

AMONG the feveral arguments from which it may be concluded that the author of Fingal was a Caledonian, the language he ufes is a decifive one. The genuine Irifh poems which are to be found in books, and the little Irifh fongs which are brought into the Highlands by ftrolling harpers from Ireland, are in every other ftanza unintelligible to a Highlander.—But the language of Offian's compofitions is eafily underftood by every one who has a competent knowledge of the Galic tongue.— If fome few of the words are uncommon, or become obfolete, it is no more than what muft have been naturally expected in a work fo ancient. It is aftonifhing what a purity and fimplicity of language prevails over all the works of this poetical hero, while the Galic compofitions of the laft century are dark, affected and confufed *.

WHETHER Offian flourifhed in the third, in the fourth, or in the fifth age, is a point difficult to difcufs. His poems are undoubtedly more ancient than any extant in the Celtic tongue, and the genius of the diction, of the arrangement and fentiment, gives a ftrong internal proof of their genuinenefs and high antiquity †.

BESIDE the Bards appointed by authority in Caledonia, the Princes, great Lords, and petty Chieftains, afpired much after the reputation arifing from a poetical genius. It was impoffible that all the numerous effays produced, could be deftitute of merit. Every clime, however diftant from the fun, is capable of producing men of true genius. The thick fogs of Bœotia, and the cold

---

* See Lhoyd's Irifh preface to his Irifh Dictionary.
† Dr. Blair's Critical Differtation on the Poems of Offian.

mountains

mountains of Thrace, have given birth to illuftri-ous poets, while the fcorching fands of Africa have remained languid and filent.

THERE is great reafon to doubt the doctrine advanced by Martial, that there will be no want of poets equal to Maro, if there fhould be pa-trons as munificent as Mecænas: at the fame time it is certain, that when the love of poetry in a na-tion confers upon thofe who have a genius that way, rewards of honour, profit, and repu-tation, their compofitions will be numerous, and fome of them worthy of public attention. The old Caledonians were as bountiful to their poets as their pofterity the Irifh were. Lands were ap-propriated to the eminent Bards, and became he-reditary in their family. Many diftricts in the Highlands ftill retain the name of the Bard's ter-ritory *.

ABOUT a century back one of the Highland Chieftains retained two principal Bards, each of whom had feveral difciples who were his infepar-able attendants. The Chieftains of former times, if led by choice, or forced by neceffity, to ap-pear at court, or to join thofe of their own rank, on any public occafion, were attended by a nu-merous retinue of vaffals, and by their moft emi-nent poets and ableft muficians. Hence it was that in the fpacious hall of an old Celtic King, a hun-dred Bards fometimes joined in concert. Keating informs us that there was no lefs than a thoufand principal poets in Ireland during the reign of one monarch.

---

* The fecond title of the noble family of Athol is taken from lands appropriated to a Bard. *Tullybardin* is compounded of *Tulloch*, a hillock, and *bardin*, bards.

WE of modern times may perhaps condemn this ftrange tafte of our barbarous anceftors. We may blame them for retaining and loading with wealth and honours fuch numerous bands of rhimers, a race of ufelefs, infolent, and flattering men. A flur of this kind is unjuftly thrown on our progenitors, till we remove a prevalent folly of the fame kind from among ourfelves. Our great men, to their honour be it faid, give but little encouragement to poets, or that flattery which is natural to the mufe. But our courts are full of worthlefs fycophants, the halls of our Lords with pimps and parafites. Flattery feeds on the folly of the great without the merit of being cloathed in the ftrength of fentiment, or in the harmony of numbers.

BUT to return back to the regions of antiquity: the martial exploits of great men were fung by the Bards in epic poems, and tranfmitted from one generation to another. They exerted the whole force of their genius in perpetuating the memory of departed heroes, in exciting the nobles to walk in the fame paths of activity and glory, and in roufing up their nation to fupport its dignity and to cultivate the generous and manly virtues. Praife throws around virtue attractive charms. Nothing tends more to raife fentiments of magnanimity in the heart than the nervous and glowing exhortation of the poet. It follows, therefore, that the Bard was the great and fuccefsful inftructor of the barbarian, and had in fome meafure a right to be held facred.

HISTORY informs us, that men of that character have done the moft important fervices to ftates overpowered by a victorious enemy, or enflaved

flaved by Tyrants. Tyrtæus, though a very de-
fpicable perfon in his appearance, faved Lacedæ-
mon from utter ruin, and by the ftrength of his
poetical abilities * ; and Alcæus, by employing
the fame talent, refcued his country from the hands
of cruel ufurpers †.

We are told by Quintilian ‡, that Alcæus was
rewarded with a golden plectrum for his great fervices. Horace, for the fame reafon, afligns him
a place of diftinguifhed honour in the Elyfian fields:
and to give us a juft idea of this patriot poet's
merit, he throws around him a numerous crowd
of ghofts, attentively hearing thofe fpirited war
fongs which contributed fo much to expel the enemies of liberty out of Lefbos.

Plato, who was a declared enemy to the order in general, gives the title of a moft divine
poet to Tyrtæus, and pronounces him at the fame
time a wife and good man, becaufe he had in a
very excellent manner celebrated the praifes of
thofe who excelled in war ‖. There is fomething
in the character of Tyrtæus which feems to refemble that of a Celtic Bard. He was a poet and
mufician at once. The inftruments on which he
played were the harp and that kind of martial
pipe which the Lacedemonians ufed inftead of the
trumpet of other nations.

The chief Bards of North Britain, like thofe
of other Celtic nations, followed their patrons into
the field, and were frequently of fignal fervice. It
was their bufinefs and cuftom, upon the eve of a

* Juftin. lib. iii. cap. 5.
† Horat. Carmin. lib. 2. od. 13.
‡ Inftitut. lib. x. cap. 1.
‖ De Repub. lib. 1.

battle,

battle, to harangue the army in a war song compofed in the field. This fpecies of a fong was
called *Brofnuha Cath*, that is to fay, an *infpiration to war*. The poet addreffed a part of this
perfuafive to every diftinct tribe, fhewing them the
rewards of a glorious death, and reminding them
of the great actions performed by their anceftors.
He began with a warm exhortation to the whole
army, and ended with the fame words. The exhortation turned principally on the love of fame,
liberty, and their Prince. " The Germans, fays
Tacitus, have poems which are rehearfed in the
field, and kindle the foul into a flame. The fpirit with which thefe fongs are fung predicts the
fortune of the approaching fight ; nor is their manner of finging on thefe occafions fo much a concert of voices as of courage. In the compofition they ftudy a roughnefs of found and a certain
broken murmur. They lift their fhields to their
mouths that the voice, being rendered full and
deep, may fwell by repercuffion *.

THE fate of battles depended not a little on
the encomiums and invectives of the Bards. To
be declared incapable of ferving the fovereign in
any military ftation is now deemed an indelible
reproach. To incur the fatire of the Bard, by a
cowardly behaviour, was reckoned in former times
the laft degree of infamy and misfortune.

WE are told by a Norwegian hiftorian †, that
in time of fea engagements, if near the coaft, the
Scalds of Norway were fometimes landed in a
fecure and convenient place, and ordered to mark

---

* Tacit. de mor. Germ. cap. 3.
† Torfæus, in Hift. Rerum. Orcad. vid. præfat.

every event diftinctly, fo as to be afterwards able to relate them in verfe. The fame author informs us, that Olaus, the Saint, had in a day of action appointed ftrong guards for his three principal poets, after giving them inftructions of the fame kind.

WHEN a great and decifive battle was fought, the Bards were employed in doing honour to the memory of thofe gallant men who had facrificed their lives in defence of their country, and in extolling the heroes who had furvived the flaughter of the day *.

A JUDICIOUS Roman poet obferves that many brave men who lived before Agamemnon were buried in oblivion, unlamented and unknown, becaufe they had the misfortune of wanting a poet to celebrate their memory †. This obfervation is in fome meafure juft. But it may be doubt-

---

* In the year 1314, Edward the Second, of England, invaded Scotland at the head of a very great army, having, according to all human appearance, reafon to expect an abfolute conqueft of that kingdom Full of this imagination, he ordered the prior of Scarfborough, a celebrated Latin rhimer, according to the tafte of thofe times, to follow his troops all the way to Bannockburn. He intended to employ this eminent poet in immortalizing his victory; but fortune declared for the enemy, and the prior was found among that immenfe number of prifoners which the Scots had made : the ranfom demanded for his life was, a poem on the great fubject he had before him. He gave a fpecimen of his fkill, but it was invita Minerva, though he fucceeded wonderfully well in the judgment of times not remarkable for delicacy of tafte. Another learned monk was appointed by the Scots to eternize their victory in verfe ; and though Apollo was as niggardly in his aid to him as he had been to the Englifh Carmelite, we have reafon to believe that his compofition was much admired.

† Horat. Carmin. lib. 4. od. 9.

ed

ed whether heroifm is more ancient than poetry, and whether any illuftrious perfonage of the remoteft ages of the world wanted his Bard. It is certain that the works of many eminent poets have perifhed altogether, and with them the renown and even the names of thofe mighty chiefs whom they endeavoured to eternize. At the fame time it is evident, that of all the monuments which ambition is able to raife, or the gratitude of mankind willing to beftow, that reared by the mufe of a genuine poet is the moft expreffive, the moft durable, and confequently the moft to be defired. The works of Phidias and Praxiteles, once thought everlafting, are now no more. The fainteft traces of the magnificent Babylon cannot now be inveftigated. The famous Egyptian pyramids, though ftill extant, have not been able to preferve the name of the vain monarchs by whom they were conftructed. But the ftructures which Homer has built, and the monuments which Virgil has raifed to the memory of illuftrious men, to Gallus, to Mecænas, and Auguftus, will perifh only together with the world.

Though the beft of Roman poets had a contempt for Ennius, yet the elder Scipio, with all his learning and tafte, had a greater refpect for him than Auguftus had for Virgil himfelf. The old Calabrian Bard was conftantly near that *thunderbolt of war*, and we are told by Cicero, that a marble ftatue was erected for him in the burial place of the Scipio's *. It therefore is no matter of wonder that Celtic Kings and Celtic Lords fhould have patronized the poets of their own times ; a

---

* Oratio pro Archia Poeta.

race of men whofe compofitions, however rough or unpolifhed, kindled the foul of the warrior to attempt great actions, and promifed the hero a perpetuity of fame.

THE more ancient Bards were greatly fuperior to thofe of later ages, yet mere antiquity was not the real caufe of that fuperiority. In times more remote, true merit was the Bard's only title to favour. In after days the office became hereditary, and an indefeafible right was the circumftance which rendered his perfon and character facred. It was only after the feudal law took place, that the proper reward of genius and great actions became the birthright of unworthy perfons.

No people, however barbarous, could have imagined that the lineal heir of an eminent poet fhould inherit the natural enthufiafm or acquired talents of his predeceffor. But the general cuftom of en tailing almoft every office in certain families, and perhaps an extraordinary regard paid to the memory of fome excellent poet, fecured the poffeffion of the grant of land to the pofterity of thofe bards whofe merit had acquired them that lucrative diftinction from their fuperiors.

DISSERTATION XV.

Of the Western Islands of Scotland.---Accounts given of them by the Writers of Rome.---Of their ancient Names, Ebudes, Hebrides, and Inchegaul. Subject to, and possessed very early by the Scots of Jar-ghael.

THE disquisitions of antiquaries are incapable of those ornaments which, in the opinion of the world, constitute fine writing. To trace the origin of a nation through that darkness which involves the first ages of society, is a laborious task, and the reputation attending the success of a very inferior degree. The antiquary is no more than a kind of pioneer, who goes before, to clear the ground, for the construction of the beautiful fabric of the historian. In this dissertation I enter into the dissection of words, the investigation of etymons, and into an inquiry into the ancient state of islands now very unimportant in the British empire. Should this trivial subject discourage any reader, let him turn to another section.

THE geography, as well as internal hiſtory of the Northern Europe, was little known to the writers of Greece and Rome. The uncultivated and barbarous ſtate of the Celtic nations diſcouraged travellers from going among them. The Romans met often, on their frontiers, hoſtile nations, to whoſe very name, as well as country, they were abſolute ſtrangers.—Involved in a cloud of barbariſm at home, the inhabitants of the North were only ſeen when they carried war and deſolation into the provinces of the empire ; and conſequently the accounts given of them by the hiſtorians of Rome are vague and uncertain.

THIS ignorance of the true ſtate of the Northern diviſion of Europe afforded an ample field for fiction, and encouraged pretended travellers who had a talent for fable, to impoſe upon the world the moſt abſurd tales, with regard to the ſituation, hiſtory and inhabitants of the barbarous regions beyond the pale of Roman empire. Strabo complains frequently that Pythias the Maſſilian, and other travellers, cou'd not be credited, in the account they gave of their voyages, which looked more like a poetical fiction, than a faithful narration of facts. Pythias, though a man in the moſt indigent circumſtances, had the vanity to ſay, that he had travelled over all the Northern diviſion of Europe, to the very extremities of the world : " A ſtory, not to be credited," ſaith Strabo *, " though Mercury himſelf had told it." He pretended to have viſited Britain in the courſe of his peregrinations, and with great gravity gives a very circumſtantial deſcription of that iſland.

---

* Lib. ii. p. 163.

He

He also fays, that he made a voyage to Thule, the remoteft ifland belonging to Britain, at the diftance of fix days failing from it, in the fkirts of the frozen ocean. He is candid enough to own that he was obliged to others for the hiftory which he gives of that place; but he does not hefitate to affirm that he himfelf had feen it. It was a place, according to him, which was neither earth, fea nor air, but fomething like a *compofition of all of them*, fomething refembling, to ufe his own expreffion, the *lungs of the fea*, fomething, in fhort, totally inacceffible to the human fpecies. Such is the ridiculous account which the Maffilian traveller gives of Thule, and from which the idle tales of fucceeding authors concerning that ifland feem to have been taken.

Solinus defcribes Thule as an extenfive tract of land, inhabited by a race of men, who, in the beginning of the vernal feafon, fed, like their cattle, upon grafs or ftraw, lived upon milk in fummer, and laid up the fruits of their trees in ftore for their winter provifion *. But his authority will not be greatly refpected by thofe who know what he has faid of men and women, whofe feet were contrived like thofe of horfes, and whofe ears were long enough to cover their whole bodies.

Strabo owns that thofe who had feen the Britifh Ierna had nothing to fay concerning Thule, though they gave fome account of other fmall iflands on the coafts of the Northern Britain. We learn from Tacitus, that Domitian's fleet, after the reduction of the Orkney ifles, defcried Thule; a place which till then, faith he, lay concealed un-

---

der

der fnow and an everlafting winter *. The truth
of this fact refts upon the veracity of the perfon
from whom Tacitus received his information.

PTOLEMY is fo particular in his account of
Thule, as to inform us, that it lies in fixty-three
degrees N. Lat. and that the longeft day there confifts of twenty-four hours †. There is no place
near the Britifh ifles to which this, or any other
defcription given of it, can agree better than to
Shetland. But after all that has been faid upon
the fubject, with a confiderable expence of erudition, by Sir Robert Sibbald and others, there is
reafon to conclude, with Strabo, the moft judicious of all ancient geographers, and one of the
beft hiftorians and critics of remote times, that
the hiftory of Thule is *dark, dubious* and *unau-
thentic* ‡, and that every thing told by Pythias
concerning it is a fiction.

THE ifles of North Britain have been divided
by fome ancient geographers into two claffes,
and by others into three. The firft of thefe claffes
confifts of the *Ebudes* and Orcades. The fecond
comprehends the *Hemodes, OEmodes,* or *AEmodes,*
together with the two juft mentioned. An exact
defcription of places then fo little known, cannot
be expected from thefe writers ; but their volun-
tary errors admit of no excufe.

PLUTARCH relates, upon the authority of one
Demetrius, who feems to have been employed by
the Emperor Adrian to make geographical obfer-

---

* Difpecta eft et Thule, quam hactenus nix et hyems abde-
bat. Vita Agric. c. 10.
† Lib. viii. c. 2.
‡ Strabo, lib. iv. p. 308.

O

vations

vations and difcoveries, that fome of the Britifh ifles were confecrated to Demi-gods .—That *Saturn*, bound with *chains of fleep*, is confined in one of them, under the cuftody of *Briareus*, and that feveral inferior divinities are his conftant attendants.

SOLINUS writes with great gravity and feeming precifion concerning the inhabitants of the Ebudes, their manner of living, and their form of government., " They know not," fays he *, " what corn is : they live on fifh and milk only. " The ifles of the Hebudes are feparated from one " another by narrow founds, and by reafon of " their contiguity are governed by one King. " This Monarch has no property.—He is fup- " ported at the expence of the public.—He is " bound by eftablifhed laws to rule according to " the principles of equity. Left he fhould be " tempted by avarice to commit any acts of op- " preffion, poverty confines him within the rules " of juftice.—He has no perfonal intereft to pro- " mote.—He has no wife, that can with any pro- " priety be called his own : any woman for whom " he conceives a paffion muft be at his fervice.— " Hence it is, that he has neither hopes nor de- " fires with regard to children, to whom he can- " not claim a peculiar right."

MANY ancient writers of hiftory and geography have taken a boundlefs liberty of inventing marvellous ftories, in their defcriptions of the manners and cuftoms of diftant nations ; and Solinus feems, in his defcription of Thule and the other Britifh ifles, to have indulged his fancy in that

---

* Solin. Polyhiftor. cap. 35.

refpect

respect with much freedom. Some eminent critics have observed, that this author copies, in a servile manner, after Pliny the elder ; but he has rejected his authority with regard to the number of the Ebudes and of the Orkney isles. According to Pliny*, the Orcades amount to forty, and the Hebrides to thirty ; but Solinus reduced the number of the Hebrides to five, and of the Orcades to three wretched isles, overgrown with rushes, or made up of horrible rocks or naked sands, and totally destitute of inhabitants.

I f Solinus flourished, as is commonly supposed, after Tacitus had published the life of Agricola, or the history of his own times, it is surprizing that he could have been a stranger to the works of that excellent writer, and totally unacquainted with the story of the voyage performed by Domitian's fleet round Britain, and the conquest made of the Orcades during that voyage. Solinus is one of those ancient geographers who divided the isles of North Britain into two classes only—the Hebudæ and the Orcades.—Ptolemy follows very nearly the same division. But Pomponius Mela, after informing us that there are thirty Orcades, placed at small distances from one another, observes that there are seven OEmodæ lying over against Germany †, which are probably the isles of Shetland.

Salmasius and other critics believe that the Ebudæ of Ptolemy and Solinus are the OEmodæ of Mela. The great similarity of the names, and the silence of the last of these writers with respect

---

* Nat. Hist. lib. iv. cap. 16.
† Mela de situ Orb. lib. iii. cap. 6.

to

to the Ebudæ, and of the other two with regard
to the OEmodæ, seem to justify this opinion. But
Pliny's authority is against it. That author di-
stinguishes the OEmodæ from the Hebudes, with
the greatest clearness and precision * ; and he could
not have been misled by either of the other two
geographers. He wrote before Ptolemy, and after
Mela.

It is matter of some wonder that the ancient
writers of geography, who flourished before the
reign of Domitian, could have known more concerning the Orcades, than Solinus, who flourished
after Tacitus wrote his history. Pomponius Mela
was cotemporary either with Julius Cæsar, or
rather with Claudius. This we have reason to
conclude from a passage in that part of his work
where he attempts to give an account of Britain*.
But supposing Mela to have been cotemporary
with the last of these Emperors, rather than with
the first, one will be still at a loss to find out
how he could have learned that there were islands
to the North of Britain, which were called Orcades,
and which were separated from one another by
narrow friths, and were thirty in number. We
learn from Tacitus, that before Agricola's time it
was a problematical question, whether Britain was
an island or part of a continent; and it is not
probable that any foreign ships had sailed to the
Northern extremity of it before the period he
mentions. The Carthaginians are the only peo-

---

† Nat. Hist. lib iv. cap. 16.

* Britannia qualis sit, qualesque progeneret mox certiora et
magis explorata dicentur: quippe tam diu clausam aperit ecce
principum maximus, &c. Mela de situ Orb. lib. iii. cap. 7.

ple

ple who can be fuppofed to have made fuch a
voyage; and it was not confiftent with their max-
ims of policy and commerce to have made public their difcoveries. It is plain, however, that
Mela and Pliny had received diftinct information
concerning the name and number of thefe ifles.
Thefe authors differ indeed as to the precife number of the Orcades: one of them makes them
thirty, and the other forty. But this difference
is not material, if we confider that there are no
lefs than forty Orcades, including the *Holmes*, and
not more than thirty, if we enumerate thofe only
which are or may be conveniently inhabited.

BUCHANAN was totally at a lofs with regard to
the origin and meaning of the word Orcades.
Cambden attempted to explain it very ingenioufly:
he quotes an old manufcript, which was afterwards
publifhed by Father Innes, where it is derived
from *Argat*; that is to fay, according to the author of that little tract, above the Getes: but he
rejects this etymon, with good reafon, and conjectures that the name in queftion is derived from
" *Arcat*, or above *Cath*, a country of Scotland,
" which, from a noted promontory there, is called
" *Cathnefs*."

THE juftnefs of this etymon is founded on a
fuppofition that the modern *Caithnefs* was called
Cath, before *Mela*'s time at leaft. But were that
fuppofition well grounded, and were it certain
that inftead of *Carini* in Ptolemy, we fhould read
Catini, which Cambden fuppofes, in order to help
out his conjecture, I am ftill apt to think that the
Word *Orcades* fhould be derived from another
fource. The old Scottifh bards call Orkney *In-
che-Torch*, that is to fay, the *Iflands of whales.*

One

One of two things muſt have been the foundation of the name : either whales of an enormous ſize were frequently ſeen around the Orkneys, which indeed is ſtill the caſe; or thoſe old Caledonians who ſaw theſe iſles at a diſtance, compared them to theſe monſtrous ſea-animals. Agreeable to the laſt of theſe ſuppoſitions, the Highlanders of Scotland call the Orkneys *Arc-have*, that is to ſay, the *Swine* or Whales of the ocean*.

I SHALL now endeavour to throw ſome light on that part of the ancient hiſtory of Britain wherein the Hebrides are more particularly concerned; a ſubject hitherto almoſt entirely neglected, though not abſolutely unworthy the attention of the curious.

PTOLEMY and Solinus comprehend five iſles under the general name of Ebudæ or Hebrides. They are enumerated by the former; and the names he gives them are *Ricina, Maleos, Epidium*, the Weſtern and the Eaſtern Ebudæ. In Cambden's opinion *Ricina* is *Richrine*, an iſle which lies much nearer the coaſt of Ireland than that of North Britain, and belongs to the county of Antrim. But as Richrine was too inconſiderable an iſle to have deſerved Ptolemy's particular notice, amidſt ſuch a vaſt number of other iſlands omitted by him, and as Cambden's opinion is founded ſolely on remote affinity of names, there is, I

---

* In the Galic language *Orc, Arc,* and *Urc,* ſignify a Sow. *Torc* likewiſe ſignifies a Sow. The old Scots called the whale commonly Muc.Mhara, i. e. the ſow of the ocean.

For a full and diſtinct account of the Orkney iſles the reader may conſult the works of *Torfæus*, a Norvegian hiſtorian, and Mr. Wallace, a learned Miniſter of Kirkwall.

think,

think, more reason to believe, that the *Ricina* of the Egyptian geographer, and the *Riduna* of Antonine's itinerary, is rather the *Arrin* of Scotland: so they who speak the Galic call an extensive island near the mouth of the Clyde, which is the property of the family of Hamilton.

CAMBDEN thinks that the ancient *Epidium* is the same with Ila; *Maleo:*, Mull; the *Western Ebuda*, Lewis; and the *Eastern Ebuda*, Sky. But if Ricina is the same with Arran, it is far from being improbable that *Epidium* is the island of *Bute*, which lies near it; *Ey Bhoid*, that is, the isle of *Bute*, in the Galic language, being much more nearly related to *Epidium* in its sound than Ila. I have no objection to Cambden's opinion with regard to *Maleos* and the larger *Ebudæ*.

PLINY is the oldest author who has made very particular mention of the *Ebudes*; and if we consider their number only, he speaks of them with much greater accuracy than any of the ancients. According to him, there are no less than thirty isles of that denomination. If all the islands in the Deucaledonian ocean, and all the *holms* adjoining to them, should be comprehended under the general name of Ebudæ, there are certainly more than three hundred of that class: but a vast number of the *holms* are too inconsiderable to deserve a writer's notice; and sixty at least of the isles which are of some consequence, may be justly reckoned appendages to the principal ones. — We cannot therefore blame Pliny for want of exactness in that part of his British topography which relates to the *Ebudes*. Some writers of the middle ages, who had occasion to understand the subject perfectly, inform us, that these isles were thirty two

O 4

in number, and the old natives call them twenty four to this day.

WE can hardly guefs what commodities could have been exported from Ireland in an early period, excepting live cattle, hides, and flaves. However, Tacitus informs us, that merchants frequently vifited that ifland, which, for that reafon, was better known to the Romans of his time than Britain. There muft have been a confiderable intercourfe between the Irifh and the inhabitants of the Ebudæ in thofe times. They were undoubtedly at that time the fame nation, in point of language, manners and cuftoms. Pliny learned from fome merchant of his own country, very particularly, the length and breadth of Ireland. The fame perfon, or any other employed in the trade to Ireland, might have had a pretty exact account of the Ebudæ from the Irifh, or even fome of the natives of thofe iflands, as no doubt they ventured often to Ireland in their *Curachs*. Agricola had not difplayed the Roman Eagles in the Northern divifion of Britain when Pliny loft his life; and we are told by himfelf, in the very chapter where he fpeaks of the Ebudes, that the arms of the empire had not penetrated further than the Caledonian foreft. It may therefore be concluded, that he received the account he gives of thefe ifles as I have above fuppofed.

IT is difficult to inveftigate the meaning or etymon of the name Ebudes, as the prefent inhabitants have no fuch term of diftinction in their language. Camden's fuppofition was, that it ought to be derived from the fterility of the foil, or the total want of corn in thofe iflands; *Eb-eid*, in the old Britifh language, fignifying a place void of corn. To
fupport

support this conjecture, he quotes Solinus, who informs us, in a paffage already mentioned, that the inhabitants of the Ebudes knew not the ufe of corn.

This etymon, however plaufible, is far from being fatisfactory. The Caledonians of the third century were, according to Dion, abfolute ftrangers to tillage, as much as the inhabitants of the Ebudes, cotemporary with Solinus, could have been. Even the inland Britons of the South knew not agriculture in Cæfar's time. It may be therefore afked, with great propriety, why the ifles on the weftern coaft of Caledonia, and no other part of Britain, fhould be characterized by a want that was common to Britain in general?

Some of the Ebudes, it is true, are very barren; but many of the Weftern iflands were formerly among the moft fertile and plentiful tracts of land in North Britain. It would therefore be equally proper, with Cambden's etymon, to call them *Ey-budh* in the Britifh, or *Ey-biod* in the Galic, that is, the *Iflands of corn*, or metaphorically the *Ifles of food*. The truth is, neither Camden or I can give any fatisfactory etymon of the *Ebudes*.

The old appellation of *Ebudes* has, by writers of latter ages, been changed into *Hebrides*; a name utterly unknown to the more ancient writers of monkifh ages, as well as to the old Greeks and Romans. The following conjecture may account in fome meafure for this change*.

* The name of Hebrides may probable have originally proceeded from an error in fome tranfcriber, who miftook the *u* in Hebudes for *ri*.

OF all St. Patric's difciples, excepting perhaps Columba, *Bridget* had the good fortune of acquiring the higheft reputation. Her miracles and peregriniations, her immaculate chaftity, conftant devotion, and high quality in point of birth, made her very famous in Britain and Ireland. The feveral divifions of Britain concurred very zealoufly with Ireland, the country that gave her birth, in treating her character with a moft fuperftitious refpect. Through a courfe of ages fhe was thought a perfon of too much influence in heaven, and confequently of too much importance upon earth, to be tamely relinquifhed to the inhabitants of Kildare, who piqued themfelves upon the peculiar honor of having her body interred in their ground. The Irifh of Ulfter challenged that honour to themfelves. But the people of Britain would never cede a property fo invaluable : the Picts were pofitive that her remains lay buired at *Abernethy*, the capital of their dominions ; which *Nectan* the Great, one of the moft illuftrious of their King's, had confecrated and made over to her by a royal and irrevocable donation*.

THE Scots, after having annexed the Pictifh territories to their own, paid a moft extravagant homage to the relics of Bridget in Abernethy †. But the inhabitants of the Weftern ifles exceeded all the admirers of this female faint, excepting perhaps the nuns of *Kildare*, in exprefling their veneration for her. To Bridget the greateft number of their churches were dedicated : from Bridget

---

* See Innes in his Crit. Effay, Append. Num. 11.
† Boeth. Scot. Hift. lib. 9. Lefl. in Rege 47.

they

they had oracular refponfes; by the divinity of
Bridget they fwore one of their moft folemn oaths:
to Bridget they devoted the firft day of February;
and in the evening of this feftival, performed many
ftrange ceremonies of a Druidical and moft fuperftitious kind.

From thefe confiderations we have reafon to
fufpect, that the Weftern ifles of Scotland were,
in fome one period or other during the reign of
popery, put under the particular protection of St.
Bridget, and perhaps in a great meafure appropriated to her; as a very confiderable part of England was to St. Cuthbert. The name of this
virgin-faint is, in Galic, *Bride*; and *Hebrides*, or
Ey-Brides, is, literally tranflated, the Iflands of
Bridget.

The reafon why the Ebudes of ancient times
were in latter ages called *Inchegaul*, is more obvious. We have had occafion to obferve that the
old Scots of Britain and Ireland gave the name
of Gauls to all foreigners indifcriminately. They
affixed to that name the fame idea which *hoftis* expreffed in the language of the more ancient Romans. *Hoftis* at firft fignified a *ftranger*, afterwards an enemy, either public or private, and
confequently a perfon to be detefted and ab-
horred.

DERMIT, the provincial King of Leinfter,
betrayed Ireland, his native country, into the
hands of the Englifh; and therefore the old Irifh,
in order to brand his name with an everlafting
mark of infamy, called him *Dermit na ngaul*, that
is, *Dermit of the ftrangers*, or the friend of a
foreign nation, and confequently his country's enemy. The ancient Scots of Britain ufed the word

Gaul

Gaul in the same acceptation, and their posterity continue it to this day.

The English were not the only foreigners of whom the Irish and Scots of former times had reason to complain. The *Normans* and *Easterlings* often molested them: they came from a remote country in a hostile manner, and therefore had the opprobrious appellation of Gauls affixed to them. The wars of the Irish against the Scandinavians are, by an Hibernian historian, who wrote on that subject, called the wars of the Gadelians against the *Gauls**.

The Western isles of Scotland were long subject to the Norwegians. The Scots of the Continent, who had a mortal aversion to those foreign interlopers, gave the name of *Inche Gaul,* or the Islands of strangers, to the Ebudes.

We have already examined Solinus's account of the Ebudes, and his romantic description of their inhabitants. All the other old geographers who have made particular mention of these isles, have said nothing concerning the inhabitants: nor am I able to recollect that any Greek or Roman historian, who has written concerning the affairs of Britain, hath touched that subject. What the Scottish historians have told us concerning the first colonies settled in these isles, concerning the country from which they emigrated, the manners and customs of the inhabitants, and that state of anarchy in which they lived, till blessed with a monarch of the Milesian race; all this, I say, rests entirely on the veracity of Irish sennachies, or the ill-founded suppositions of historians.

---

* Keat. Gen. Hist. Part. II. pag. 50.

We have reason to believe that the Ebudes, as they were diftant from one another, and feparated by dangerous founds, were for a long time poffeffed by different tribes, and governed by different chiefs. It does not appear from authentic hiftory, that thefe chiefs depended on the Kings of Albany, whether Pictifh or Scottifh, if any fuch King's exifted, till after the Romans left this ifland.

But whether we date the origin of the Scottifh monarchy from Bede's *Reuda*, or from *Fergus* the fon of *Ferchard*, or from *Fergus* the fon of *Eirc*, which is indeed the moft probable hypothefis, it may very reafonably be prefumed, that foon after the eftablifhment of that monarchy, the Ebudes were annexed to the continental territories of the Scots. A clufter of iflands, thinly inhabited, diftitute of ftrong-holds, altogether unprovided for defence, and incapable of affifting one another, muft have fallen an eafy prey to any powerful invader. The Ebudes, however inconfiderable they may be thought now a-days, would be a very confiderable addition to the petty monarchy of the Scots of Albany, and could not fail to be an object worthy their acquiring.

At whatever period the ifles may have been annexed to the Scottifh kingdom, the inhabitants perhaps would be inclined to embrace a proper opportunity to fhake off their yoke, and to difturb the government of their new Lords. The hiftory of thefe iflanders in latter ages, and the vindictive fpirit of every conquered people, render this opinion probable. But there cannot be any foundation for the circumftantial account which Boece and Buchanan have been pleafed to give us of grand
rebellions

rebellions in the Ebudes, during the reigns of Caractacus, Corbredus, Ethodius, and other ideal Scottish Kings. It is certain, notwithstanding all the pains taken by Abercromby to prove the contrary, that *Caractacus* never reigned in North Britain, and that *Corbredus*, *Ethodius*, and other royal persons of the same imaginary existence, have fought their battles against the chiefs of the Ebudues only in the fabulous annals of our historians. The accounts they give of a *Donald of the isles*, so old as the times of the Romans, bear about them the apparent mark of a modern invention.

DONALD was a name very common among the Islanders; and two of that name, who were both of the great family whose power was once more than equal to that of the King, over all the Ebudes, were extremely famous. These were Donald earl of Rofs, who fought a battle, fatal to Scotland, against an army raised by Robert duke of Albany, during the captivity of James the first in England; and *Donald Balach*, who obtained a signal victory over the earls of Mar and Caithnefs, wounded the first of these noblemen, killed the other, and made a great slaughter of the King's army under their command. The public calamities produced by these battles, and the devastations committed by the two Donalds, seem to have led our historians, who were very ill informed concerning the affairs of the Ebudes, into a notion that all the lords of the isles went, from the earliest ages, under the same detestable name.

When the Kings of Scotland possessed no other territories than those upon the Western coast of

Albany,

Albany, we may take it for granted that they frequently vifited their dominions in the Ebudes. Being involved in perpetual wars, either with the Britons, Saxons, or Picts, it was neceffary for them to fecure the leading men of the ifles to their intereft. Without a fuppofition of this kind, it is difficult to comprehend how the Scots could have fubdued the Picts, or defend themfelves againft the Saxons. When Aedan King of Scots, invaded Northumberland, at the head of a numerous and gallant army, he received no affiftance from the Picts, and had no Irifh auxiliaries to fupport him in that expedition. We muft therefore conclude that the Iflanders, among whom Adamnan informs us Aedan had been inaugurated, made a confiderable part of that numerous army which he led into England.

ALL the Scots hiftorians affirm, that the Weftern Ifles made a part of the Scottifh dominions, from the earlieft accounts of time, to the death of Malcolm Canemore in the year 1093. On the demife of that prince, fay thefe hiftorians, his brother *Donald Bane* formed a defign of mounting the throne ; and to fupport, by foreign aid, his title, which was far from being juft, as the old law of *Taniftry* had been abolifhed, he implored for this purpofe the affiftance of *Magnus* the *Barefooted*, King of Norway, and obtained it, upon ceding all the Northern and Weftern Ifles of Scotland to that Monarch. Magnus took immediate poffeffion of thofe ifles, and the fucceffors of *Donald Bane* in the throne of Scotland did not for a long time recover them. Orkney and Shetland remained in the poffeffion of the Norvegians to the year 1468, when James the third of Scotland married the

daughter

daughter of Christian the first of Denmark, and got possession of those islands, until the portion of the Queen should be paid. Even the Ebudes likewise were subject to the Norvegians, till Alexander the third, King of Scotland, after having given a signal defeat to the Norvegian army at *Air*, in the year 1263, re-annexed them to his dominions.

In this manner, and in these different periods, if the unanimous consent of Scottish writers could be depended on, did the crown of Norway acquire and lose the western isles. But the Norvegian historians give a very different account of the matter in almost every material circumstance. Shetland, Orkney, and the Hebrides, were according to them, subdued by their nation in a more early period than that assigned; and the Scots owed the restitution of those islands more to the negotiations of a treaty, and a sum of money, than to the force of their arms.—A discussion of this point will naturally comprehend the history of that Norvegian dynasty which went under the name of the kingdom of Man; which I shall briefly give, in the succeeding dissertation.

DISSERTATION. XVI.

The History of the Norwegian Principality of the isles, commonly called the Kingdom of Man.

IN the close of the preceding dissertation, I pro-mised to give a brief history of the Hebridian principality of the Norwegians, commonly known by the name of the kingdom of Man. In the account I am to give, I shall follow more the digressive manner of the antiquary, than the regular narration of the historian. If I shall be able to throw a new and stronger light upon the subject, I shall attain my purpose, and leave the palm of fine writing to men of greater abilities.

ABOUT the year 875, according to the annals of Norway, written by historians appointed by authority *, Harold *Harfager*, or the *Fairhaired*, one of the greatest heroes of Scandinavia, obtained a decisive victory over many independent Princes who disputed his title to the throne, and was declared King of Norway. Some of these Princes,

* Torfæus in Orcadibus, p. 10 & 11.

P

who

who had been defpoiled of their dominions, took refuge in the Scottifh ifles, and uniting their forces there, made feveral defcents upon the dominions of Harfager. Harold, exafperated by thefe frequent incurfions, refolved to carry his arms to the retreats of the invaders. His progrefs through the ifles was irrefiftible ; and while he purfued his enemies from place to place, he made a total conqueft of Man, the Ebudes, Shetland and Orkney. From that time forward, all the Iflands became fubject to the crown of Norway, and continued fo, with little interruption, for many ages. The writer from whom I have taken this account, informs us further, that Harold often invaded the Continent of Scotland, and fought feveral battles there with great Succefs : and to corroborate the teftimony of the old *Iflandic* hiftorian from whom he had this relation, he appeals to the rhimes of two ancient poets of Scandinavia, who celebrated that monarch's actions in Scotland in heroic fongs.

It is certain that a powerful army of Scandinavian pirates infefted the Eaftern coaft of Scotland about the time now affigned, and committed the moft cruel devaftations, under the conduct of two famous brothers, *Hinguar* and *Hubba*. Conftantine the Second, King of Scots, marched a-gainft them in perfon, and twice gave them battle. In the firft action he obtained the victory, but in the fecond he was defeated, taken prifoner, and beheaded. This event happened, according to the Scottifh hiftorians *, in the 879 ; and as Harold Harfager reigned at that time, the authority of the bards, to whom Torfæus appeals, feems to

---

*Fordun, Boece, and Buchan. in vita Conftant. II.

deferve

deferve credit. It is true, the enemies by whom Conftantine was killed are by our hiftorians called Danes : but that is an objection of no force : the pirates who infefted the different kingdoms of Europe in the ninth century are, by different writers, ftiled Norvegians, Danes, Getes, Goths, Jutes, Dacians, Swedes, Vandals, Livonians, and Frieflanders ; their armies being compofed of all thofe nations. As the countries from which thefe inundations of plunderers came, lay either to the Eaft or North of the European kingdoms which they infefted and harraffed, they went under the more general denominations of Eafterlings, Oftmans, or Normans.

It appears evidently from the annals quoted by Sir James Ware *, that in the year 735, the Normans laid wafte a great part of Ireland, and the ifland of *Richrine*, which is reckoned by fome one of the Ebudes. Three years after this devaftation they infefted Ulfter and the Hebrides ; and it is not probable that Orkney, which lay in their way, could have refifted their fury. In the year 807, continues Ware, the Danes and Norwegians, landing in the province of Connaught, deftroyed Rofcommon with fire and fword. At the fame time *Cellach*, abbot of I-collumcille, fled into Ireland for fafety, after the enemy had murdered a confiderable number of his people. He did not return to Scotland for feven years : and from that circumftance we may take it for granted that thefe favages made themfelves mafters of *I-na*, at leaft, and probably of all the other Weftern ifles.

---

* Antiquit. of Ireland, page 57.

About

ABOUT the year 818, *Turgefius*, by fome called a Dane, and by others a Norwegian, invaded Ireland. This famous adventurer, after a long feries of piratical defcents and flying battles, ufurped at laft the fovereignty of the whole ifland, ruled the miferable inhabitants with a rod of iron, made dreadful maffacres of all the ecclefiaftics he could feize, and committed their books to the flames.

THE Irifh were revenged of this cruel tyrant, but had not ftrength enough to fhake off the yoke of flavery under which they groaned. New fupplies of hoftile Troops came yearly from Scandinavia, which, with the adherents of Turgefius, maintained the war with fuccefs againft the divided natives. About the year 850, they poffeffed themfelves of Dublin, and the parts of Leinfter adjacent to that capital *, from whence the Irifh were never able to drive them.

THE greateft Monarch that ever held the fcepter in Ireland, prevailed, in the year 1014, with the greateft part of the provincial Kings to join their forces to his own, and to attempt a total expulfion of the common enemy. Sitricus, who was at that time King of the Dublinian Eafterlings and Normans, ufed every poffible precaution to make head againft this powerful confederacy. He entered into a league with the King of Leinfter, procured a body of auxiliaries from him, and received a great acceffion of ftrengh from the Danes of Man and Inchegaul. After vaft preparations had been made on both fides, the contending nations met at laft near Dublin, and fought the obftinate and

---

* Ware's Antiq. of Iel. p. 58.

bloody

bloody battle of *Cluain-tarf*. In that fatal conflict the Irish loft the illuftrious *Brian Bore*, their fovereign, together with his fon and grandfon, befides fome provincial Kings, a vaft number of the nobility, and many thoufands of the common people *.

Sitricus retired, and maintained his poft in Dublin, with the fhattered remains of his army. The preparations made by that prince before the battle, and the fupplies he received from Man and Inchegaul, afford a clear demonftration that the Scandinavians were poffeffed of thefe ifles before the æra affigned by the Scottifh hiftorians; and the Irifh annals, from which Ware has taken the account he gives us of thefe things, are more to be depended upon, with regard to the time at leaft in which the Ebudes became fubject to the crown of Norway, than the accounts followed by Buchanan, Boece and Fordun.

We know that the Normans made confiderable acquifitions in France, and the Danes in England, about the fame time that Turgefius became fo formidable in Ireland. We learn from Fordun, that the Danes infefted the Eaftern coaft of Scotland before the end of the ninth century. It is not probable, therefore, that the Hebrides, which lay in their way, could have been entirely overlooked by thefe free-booters, in the courfe of their ravages. Thefe ifles, difcontiguous, and thinly inhabited, incapable of affifting each other with powerful fuccours, and lying at a great diftance from the feat of the Scottifh kingdom, could make little re-

---

* Ware's Ant. &c. p. 63. Keating's Gen. Hift. of Irel. Part 2. page 64.

P 3

fiftance

fiftance to a torrent which at that time carried almoft all Europe before it. The Monarchs of Scotland could not have relieved their Hebridian fubjects, nor repoffefs themfelves of their conquered iflands : they had fufficient employment elfewhere ; the Eaftern provinces of their kingdom muft be defended from the frequent invafions of the fame barbarous enemy, or from the infurrections of the lately conquered Picts.

The moft authentic hiftory of the revolutions which happened in the Weftern ifles, is contained in the *Chronicle of Man*, as far as it goes. This fmall piece has been preferved by Cambden, in his Britannia. It was written by the monks of Ruffin, an abbey in Man, and is probably older, by a whole century, than Fordun's Scotichronicon. Thofe who examine the tranfactions of thofe times with attention, will difcover fome chronological errors in the Chronicle of Man ; but thefe errors are owing to the negligence of tranfcribers, as they are manifeftly inconfiftent with the truth of facts related, and with the æras affigned in other parts of the Chronicle.

This ancient record begins thus : " In the year 1065, died Edward, King of England, of bleffed memory. He was fucceeded in the throne by Harold, the fon of Godwin ; to whom Harold Harfager, King of Norway, gave battle at Stainford-bridge, The victory fell to the Englifh, and the Norwegians fled. Among the fugitives was Godred, firnamed *Chrovan*, the fon of Harold the Black from Iceland. This Godred coming to the court of Godred, the fon of Syrric, who reigned in Man at that time, was entertained by him in an honourable way. The fame year William the

Baftard

Baftard conquered England ; and Godred, the fon of Syrric, dying, was fucceeded by his fon Fingal."

THE King of England who died in the year with which the Chronicle begins, was *Edward* the *Confeffor*, a prince highly extolled by monks, who derived extraordinary advantages from his pious liberality. It is well known that Edward aflifted *Malcolm Canemore* in recovering the throne of his anceftors, which had been ufurped by Macbeth, and that Malcolm, for years, carried on a war a-gainft the Norman conqueror and William Rufus, his immediate fucceffor. Malcolm died in the year 1093, about thirty years before Godred, the fon of Syrric, left the kingdom of the ifles to his fon Fingal, and confequently thirty years be-fore Donald Bane made the pretended donation of the Ebudes to Magnus of Norway. This dona-tion never exifted ; for it manifeftly appears from the Chronicle of Man *, and other concurring re-cords, that the Norwegians had occupied the Weft-ern ifles long before Donald Bane mounted the throne of Scotland, and before *Godred Chrovan* took poffeffion of the dynafty of the ifles.

GODRED was a powerful prince. He fub-dued a great part of Leinfter, annexed Dublin to his empire, and reduced the Scots, according to the Chronicle, to fuch a ftate of dependency, that

---

* The authors of this chronicle, and after them other writers, were miftaken in calling the Norwegian King flain in the battle of Stainford-bridge, Harold Harfager. We learn from Torfæus and others, that the true name of that prince was Harold the im-perious. Harfager lived in a much earlier period. The fame Chronicle writers, or their copyift, muft have committed a blun-der likewife in making the year 1066 the year of Godred Chro-van's acceffion to the throne of Man.

P 4

he

he would not permit them to drive more than three nails into any boat or veſſel they built. Ware quotes a letter of Lanfranc, archbiſhop of Canterbury, wherein that prelate called Godred King of Ireland *. He died, after a reign of ſixteen years, at *Yle*, or Iſla, and was ſucceeded by his ſon Lagman.

Torfæus, following the annaliſts of his country, labours hard to prove that *Magnus* the *Barefooted* dethroned *Godred*, bound his ſon Lagman with iron fetters, made an abſolute conqueſt of the Weſtern iſles, and beſtowed them on his ſon, *Sigurd*, with the title of King †. But the Chronicle of Man places the expedition of Magnus into the Weſtern parts of Scotland, and into England and Wales, in the year 1098, twenty years after the death of Godred, and eleven after the death of his ſon and ſucceſſor, *Lagman. Simon Dunelmenſis* agrees with the chronicle in the æra here aſſigned ; and if any regard is to be paid to the Scottiſh hiſtorians, the acquiſition made of the Weſtern Iſles by King Magnus, muſt have happened ſoon after the death of *Malcolm Canemore.*

Torfæus, after a long diſcuſſion of the chronological difficulties ariſing out of theſe contradictory accounts, rejects the authority of the chronicle, confutes Buchanan, finds fault with ſome of the writers of his own country, and prefers at laſt the teſtimony of Ordericus Vitalis to all others. But if we follow that author's ſyſtem, the firſt expedition of Magnus into the Weſtern ſeas of

---

* Antiq. of Irel. p. 65.
† Orcades, p. 71, 72.

Britain

Britain took place in the fifth year of William
Rufus, that is, in the year 1092. According to
this calculation, the Norwegian monarch muft have
feized on the Ebudes before the death of *Malcolm Canemore*, and confequently *Donald Bane*
could not have been guilty of the infamous ceffion which has hitherto done fo much injury to
his memory.

Magnus the Barefooted, might have fufficient
provocation to invade the Ebudes in a hoftile
manner, though fubject to the crown of Norway
before his time. Many of the piratical Eafterlings
and Normans, who infefted the Britifh ifles, after
the time of Harold Harfager, were originally independent of the Norwegian crown, or rendered
themfelves fo. Turgefius, and his fucceffors in Ireland, were fovereign Princes. The Earls of Orkney, though much nearer the feat of that empire
to which they were vaffals, made reiterated attempts to fhake off all marks of fubjection :
and that the Kings of Man endeavoured frequently to render themfelves independent, will appear
in the fequel.

We learn from the chronicle *, that one *Ingemunde* was fent by Magnus to take poffeffion of
the Hebudes, in quality of King. But the chiefs
of the ifles, finding that this man abandoned himfelf wholly to the moft fcandalous exceffes, to luft,
avarice, and cruelty, confpired againft him, and,
without regarding either his perfonal dignity or
the authority of his conftituents, fet fire to the
houfe where he was lodged, and deftroyed him,
together with his whole retinue. It was probably

____

* Chronicon. Manniæ, ad an. 1097.

with a deſign of revenging this inſult, that Magnus undertook the expedition already related. But whatever may be in this conjecture, it is plain, from the commiſſion with which *Ingemunde* was inveſted, that the Kings of Man had aſſerted their independence, or had refuſed to pay the ancient tribute.

AFTER the death of *Lagman*, the ſon of Godred, who had taken the croſs and died in the holy land, *Murchard O Brien*, King of Ireland, ſent, at the deſire of the nobility of Man, one of his friends who was a perſon of royal extraction, to act as Regent in that iſland, during the minority of Olave, the brother of their late ſovereign †. Here we have another clear proof that the Princes and great men of the Weſtern Iſles had withdrawn their allegiance from their old maſters, the Kings of Norway.

MAGNUS the Barefooted, only recovered the territories which one of his remote forefathers had acquired, and which one of his more immediate anceſtors had loſt. He ſubdued all the Scottiſh iſles from Shetland to Man, and according to ſome hiſtorians, added the fruitful peninſula of Kintire to theſe conqueſts : he carried his victorious arms into South Britain, and made himſelf maſter of Angleſey, in ſpite of the united efforts of the two brave Earls who led a numerous army againſt him. He was unqueſtionably one of the moſt powerful Princes of his time, and preſcribed what laws he pleaſed to all thoſe whoſe ſituation made them obnoxious to his intemperate rage, or to the luſt of his boundleſs ambition. The Welſh felt the

---

† Chron. of Man.

dreadful

dreadful effects of his barbarous power, and therefore courted his friendfhip with a multitude of pre-
fents.   He obliged the Scots of Galloway to furnifh him with timber, at their own expence, for
the ufe of his bulwarks.   He fent his fhoes to
Murcard, King of Ireland, and commanded him
in the moft peremptory manner, under the pain of
his difpleafure, to carry them on his fhoulders, in
the prefence of his ambaffadors, on the anniverfary
of Chrift's nativity.   The Irifh nobility received
this infolent meffage with becoming fentiments of
difdain and indignation : but *Murcard* was too
wife to provoke the refentment of a conqueror
whofe power was equal to his pride, and told his
friends that he would eat the fhoes of the Norwegian monarch, rather than fee any one province in
Ireland deftroyed.   Accordingly he paid homage
in the difhonourable way prefcribed by the haughty
Magnus, entertained his ambaffadors with a royal
magnificence, and difmiffed them with the higheft
expreffions of refpect for their mafter.

It does not appear from any authentic record,
that Magnus came near the Eaftern coaft of Britain
in either of its divifions.   His troops cou'd not
therefore have been of great ufe to *Donald Bane*,
had any one of his nephews difputed the crown of
Scotland with him : and indeed it appears to me
more probable that Donald, upon the demife of his
brother, poffeffed himfelf of the throne by virtue
of the old *Taniftry* right, or that, according to
fome Englifh hiftorians, he was elected king,
than that he owed his crown to the aid of a foreign
ally.

Donald's

DONALD's immediate predecessor in the throne, though a great Prince, had disobliged the nation by many unpopular actions. He had introduced the English language, dress, manners, and religion, in a country at that time full of the most violent prejudices against every thing which came from a quarter so hostile. His obstinate attachment to the interest of his brother in law, Edgar Atheling, involved the nation in a series of wars more expensive and calamitous than profitable or glorious. The large estates which he had settled on some noble exiles who followed the fortune of that weak Prince, must have greatly exasperated the Scottish nobility, and alienated their affections from his family. He had been overmatched by the conqueror of England, and grosly insulted by his successor, William Rufus. His heir apparent, Prince Edward, had perished unfortunately with Malcolm at Alnwick. The rest of his children by Queen Margaret were under age, and that Princess, already worn out by the austerities of a superstitious life, overwhelmed with grief, survived her husband and son but a few days.

ALL these circumstances conspiring together must have made it easy for Donald Bane to possess himself of the throne vacant by the death of his brother, without purchasing the aid of a Scandinavian potentate, so much at the expence of his country and his own reputation. His pretensions to the crown were opposed only by a law neither ancient nor ever much regarded; and the distractions at court in consequence of so many unhappy events, afforded him the most favourable opportunity of asserting his claim. The conclusion I
would

would draw from what has been faid on this fubject, appears to me to be perfectly juft : that our
hiftorians were ill informed with regard to the
manner how, and the time when the Weftern Ifles
fell under the dominion of Norway.

AFTER Magnus the Barefooted had, through
his temerity, loft his life in Ireland, Olave, the
fon of Godred, recovered his paternal dominions,
and reigned over the ifles forty years. Olave was
a Prince of a peaceable difpofition, diftinguifhed
greatly by the religious virtues of the times, and
extremely liberal to ecclefiaftics. He was educated
in the court of Henry I. and was on good terms
with the monarchs of England throughout his life.
He lived in amity with Ireland; and it does not
appear that thofe Kings of Scotland, who were
his cotemporaries, difputed his title either to Man
or the Ifles.

SELDEN complained that *Olaus* and *Aulave*,
Amlaff and *Anlaphus*, are names which breed
great confufion in the Englifh hiftory; but thefe
names feemingly different appear to me to be the
fame. The fennachies of the ifles call the Olave,
of whom we are now fpeaking, *Aula* or *Ambla*, in
Latin, *Amlavus*, *Anlaphus*, or *Olaus*; and they
diftinguifh him from other Princes of the fame
name by the title of *Ambla Dearg mac Ri Lochlin*,
that is to fay, *Red Olave, the King of Lochlin's
Son.* Godred, the father of Olave, was from
Scandinavia, which is called Lochlin by the inhabitants of the Highlands and Ifles.

IT is the opinion of fome that *Lochlin* and *Denmark* are words of the fame import : but it appears
to me rather that *Lochlin* and *Scandinavia* are fy-
nonimous terms. *Harold Harfager*, and Magnus,
the

the Barefooted, were Norwegian Princes, and the iſlanders give no other appellation to thoſe great conquerors, nor to other *Normans*, who held their anceſtors under ſubjection for many ages, than that of *Lochlinich*.

In the Galic language, *Loch* ſignifies a great collection of water, whether ſalt or freſh, and *lan* full. *Lun* is the name of a certain bird remarkably voracious. The Baltic might have been very properly called *Lochlan*, if it neither ebbs nor flows ; and many different countries, particularly Scotland and Ireland, experienced that from this ſea ſwarmed an immenſe number of pirates, who by an eaſy and juſt metaphor might have been compared to birds of prey and of paſſage. But whatever the etymon of the word *Lochlin* may be, it is certain that all the adventurers who came from the Baltic, or from the Northern ſeas, and the countries bordering upon them, whether Norwegians, Swedes, Finlanders, Ruſſians, Livonians, Poles, Pomeranians, Danes, Frieſlanders, or Icelanders, were by the Iriſh and Hebridian Scots called *Lochlinich*.

It has been thought a matter of wonder that Scandinavia, ſo barren in every other reſpect, ſhould have been ſo very fertile of men, as to pour forth whole inundations of rovers almoſt every year from the latter end of the ſeventh century, at leaſt, till the thirteenth.

Some ingenious writers have endeavoured to account for this extraordinary phænomenon by reſolving it into the effects of polygamy. A plurality of women were, by the laws or cuſtoms of Scandinavia, confined to the bed of one man, if we believe theſe writers ; and hence it was that the

inhabitants

inhabitants multiplied almoft beyond belief. A country in this fituation, which did not abound with the neceffaries of life, could not but fend numerous colonies abroad in queft of either plunder or fettlements: and fuch colonies, confifting of adventurers hardy, enterprifing, lawlefs, poor, and determined to make their fortune or perifh in the attempt, muft have carried defolation far and wide.

But it is by no means certain that polygamy was eftablifhed either by law or cuftom among the ancient Scandinavians. The Germania Magna of the old geographers comprehended at leaft the Southern coaft of the Baltic, together with its ifles. Mela and Tacitus feem to extend it much farther *; and Cluverius is pofitive that Norway, Sweden, and every region lying to the North of the Baltic, made a part of that immenfe tract of land. The *Suiones* of Tacitus are undoubtedly either the Norwegians or the Swedes, or perhaps both: and the Æftii of the fame author are by Archbifhop Ufher †, and other eminent critics, called the progenitors of thofe pirates, afterwards ftiled Eafterlings and Oftmans.

Tacitus, who feems to have made the manners and cuftoms of the Germans his particular ftudy, informs us, that every one of that nation, excepting only a fmall number of the chief or leading men, contented himfelf with one wife, and that of all the barbarians in the world, they were the ftricteft obfervers of the matrimonial

---

* Mela, lib. iii. cap. 3. Tacit. de mor. Germ. cap. 45.
† See Ware's Antiquities of Ireland, chap. 24.

laws

laws ‡.　We have therefore reaſon to believe, that the *Suiones*, *Æſtii*, *Cimbri*, *Teutones*, and other nations, of whom the Normans and Eaſterlings of after-ages muſt have been deſcended, had not a plurality of wives in his time; and it does not appear from good authority that polygamy became faſhionable among the poſterity of theſe nations, in the period intervening between the time of Tacitus and the introduction of chriſtianity.

But even allowing, without any neceſſity, that polygamy was common in Scandinavia, ſtill it is doubtful, from the hiſtory of nations who give into that cuſtom, whether a plurality of wives increaſe population or not.　As the males of Scandinavia were always engaged in war at ſea, there is indeed reaſon to believe that the accidents from enemies, and thoſe ariſing from a rude navigation, carried off a greater proportion of them than of the males of any other nation; and therefore it may be ſuppoſed that a greater number of women fell to the ſurvivors.　But, when we conſider that the women of the North always attended their huſbands and friends in their expeditions, we muſt allow that they were ſubject to the ſame accidents with the males.　In this way therefore it is impoſſible to account how the Northern Europe could cover the Southern diviſions of it with ſuch deluges of barbarous adventurers.

The old Norwegians and Swedes, before their converſion to Chriſtianity, were addicted to piracy, and eſteemed it a glorious occupation.　The wild

---

‡ Severa illic' matrimonia, nec ullam morum partem magis laudaveris: nam prope ſoli barbarorum ſingulis uxoribus contenti ſunt, exceptis admodum paucis.　Tacit. de mor. Germ.

tribes who lived near the gulphs of Bothnia, Finland, and Livonia, followed the fame practice. The maritime nations inhabiting the Southern coaft of the Baltic were led by the example and fuccefs of thofe rovers to try their fortune in the more wealthy divifions of the South of Europe. If to thefe numerous nations of plunderers we add thofe of Denmark, Holftein, Saxony, and Friefland, all the way to the mouth of the Rhine, we do not make the country of thofe Northern rovers, who have done fo much mifchief in former ages, more extenfive than hiftory affirms. It is alfo extreamly probable that thofe who dwelt in the more inland diftricts of the kingdoms of the North joined the freebooting inhabitants of the fea coafts in their expeditions. In a divifion of Europe fo extenfive, it could have been no difficult matter to mufter up fwarms of adventurers, fome thirfting after glory, others rendered defperate by poverty, and all of them animated by the fuccefs of their neighbours or predeceffors in emigrations of the fame kind.

I⊤ may alfo be fufpected that the piratical Eafterlings and Normans, who committed fuch devaftations in the lower Germany, France, Britain, Ireland, and other places, were not fo very numerous as they have been reprefented. Inftead of making war in a regular manner, they generally invaded one particular divifion of a country near the coaft, in flying parties, gathered all the fpoils they could carry away, and deftroyed every thing elfe. They were compofed of feveral bodies independent of one another, and no fooner was one band gone than another came. By this means the countries expofed to their ravages had

Q

fcaice

scarce any refpite from their incurfions : this circumftance muft have greatly fwelled the idea of
their numbers in the minds of thofe who were fo
cruelly haraffed by them ; and as they made a
conqueft of fome countries, the writers in the intereft of the old natives, to fave their credit in
fome meafure, would perhaps have afcribed thofe
conquefts to the numbers of the enemy, rather
than to their fuperior bravery.

To leave this digreffion, for the hiftory of the
dynafty of Man. *Olave*, King of the ifles, after
a long and peaceable reign, was treacheroufly flain
by his own nephews : he was fucceeded by his fon,
Godred, whom he had by the daughter of *Fergus*,
Earl of Galloway, the moft powerful fubject in
Scotland at that time.

GODRED had failed to Norway before his
father's death, and did homage to King *Hinge*. In
his abfence the three fons of his uncle *Harold*
feized on his dominions, and divided them among
themfelves. But the ufurping affaffins foon met
with the fate their crimes deferved. *Godred* returning from Norway, afferted his title to the
kingdom of Man, caufed one of the fons of Harold to be executed, and agreeably to the inhu-
man cuftom of thofe barbarous times, put out
the eyes of the other two *.

Soon after *Godred* had recovered the inheritance of his anceftors, the Eafterlings of Dublin
invited him over into Ireland, and made him their
King. Elated beyond meafure by this great acceffion of power, he began to rule tyrannically in
his own dominions, and regardlefs of juftice and

---

* Chron. Man. ad ann. 1143.

the

the laws, deprived the nobles of their estates. The most powerful among them, *Thorfin*, the son of *Oter*, to gratify his revenge, entered into a league with *Somerled*, the famous thane of Argyle, and after wresting many of the isles out of *Godred*'s hands, by the assistance of that powerful chief, erected them into a separate kingdom for *Dugal*, the son of his new patron.

The Chronicle of Man calls *Somerled* Prince of *Heregaidel*, and informs us further, that he had married a natural daughter of King *Olave*, and consequently *Godred*'s sister. By that lady he had four sons : *Dugal*, of whom came the *MacDougals* of Lorn ; *Reginald*, the progenitor of all the *Mac Donalds* of Scotland and Ireland ; *Angus*, an ambitious lord, whose great power and numerous offspring became extinct in a short time ; and *Olave*, of whose actions or issue neither history nor tradition have recorded any thing memorable.

The King of Man, upon receiving intelligence that Thorfin and Somerled had seized on a part of his dominions, equipped a considerable fleet, and putting to sea went in quest of his enemies [*]. Somerled met him with a fleet consisting of eighty sail : after an obstinate fight, attended with great slaughter on both sides, they patched up a peace, having agreed to divide the kingdom of the isles among them. From that day, saith the chronicle, may be dated the downfal and ruin of the kingdom of Man.

Either Somerled's ambition was very high, or Godred's perfidy provoked him soon to recommence hostilities ; for he invaded Man with a new

---

[*] Ad. ann. 1156.

fleet

fleet about two years after the partition treaty had
been concluded. Godred, unable to maintain his
ground, abandoned the ifland, fled to Norway,
and laid his grievances before the fovereign of
whom he held his dominions by a feudal right.
He remained in Norway for fix years before his
reprefentations had any effect. At length he obtained a confiderable fupply of forces, and returning to Man, defeated his brother Reginald, who
had taken poffeffion of the ifland in his abfence,
and re-eftablifhed himfelf in his kingdom †.

SOMERLED was killed before this revolution
happened. Intoxicated by repeated victories, and
his vaft acquifitions, he had formed a defign, if
we believe the Chronicle of Man, to conquer all
Scotland. Having, in confequence of that extravagant project, equipped a fleet of one hundred
and fixty fail, he landed a numerous army near
Renfrew in Clydefdale. Here, faith the chronicle, he was, through the juft vengeance of God,
vanquifhed by a fmall number, and he himfelf,
together with his fon and a vaft multitude of his
people, flain *.

THE Highland fennachies give a very different
account of Somerled's death and character. According to them, this powerful thane had received
many infufferable provocations from the minifters
of King *Malcolm* IV. a Prince weak, unexperienced, and entirely under the direction of his fervants. The vaft extent of Somerled's eftate on
the continent, to fay nothing of the acquifition he
had made in the ifles, filled thefe minifters with

---

† Chron. Man. ad ann. 1164.
* Chron. Man. ubi fup.

a polia political jealoufy, and tempted their avarice at the fame time. Refolved to humble fo formidable a fubject, and to divide his lands among themfelves, they compelled him, by a long feries of attrocious injuries, to take aims in his own defence. The King's counfellors attainted him and *Gilchrift*, Earl of Angus, the ableft general of that age in Scotland, was fent with a great military force to render that urjuft fentence effectual; but Somerled fought the Earl, though with an inferior army, and the victory remained dubious. This happened during the minority of Malcolm.

AFTER that Prince had taken the reins of government into his own hands, his minifters, enraged by a difappointed ambition, made it their chief bufinefs to convince him that it was neceffary to annihilate the overgrown power of Somerled, or at leaft to reduce him to a ftate of mediocrity. The force of an argument fo fpecious, concurring with the facility of his own temper, prevailed eafily with the King to favour their defign. But to have fomething of a plaufible pretence for commencing hoftilities, it was agreed in council, that a perfon invefted with a public character fhould be fent immediately to propofe to the Thane, that in order to procure a remiffion of his crimes from the King, he fhould renource his right to the lands held of him on the continent, and fatisfy himfelf with his poffeffions in the ifles.

SOMERLED was tooconfcious of his own ftrength, and too tender of his undoubted right, to acquiefce in a propofal no lefs injurious to his character than prejudicial to his intereft. Incapable of difguifing his fentiments, and fired with a juft indignation, he drew his fword; and told the mef-

Q 3

fenger

fenger that " He would fooner terminate the dif-
" pute with that weapon, than tamely furrender
" any part of his property."   After returning fuch
an anfwer to a meffage fent by his fovereign, he
had reafon to believe that a violent ftorm would
immediately gather, and burft upon him : he
therefore armed his numerous vaffals in Argyle-
fhire and the ifles, procured a confiderable body
of auxiliaries from Ireland, and determined to
carry the war into the country of his unprovoked
enemies. He landed with an army of fifteen
thoufand men in the Bay of St. Laurence, now
Greenock, and marched directly to Paifley, where
the King's troops were encamped. But before he
could bring them to an action, he was moft bafely
affaffinated by *Maurice Mac Neil*, one of his nephews, whom the King's generals found means to
bribe. This is in fubftance the account given by
the Highland fennachies of Somerled's difpute
with his fovereign, and of the unhappy end of his
life, which was the confequence of it. His followers, fay the fennachies, betook themfelves to
their gallies, upon receiving the news of their leader's fate, and returned home without fuffering
any confiderable lofs.

THE account given by the Scottifh hiftorians
of this matter, agrees neither with the Chronicle
of Man, nor with the relation now given. According to them, Somerled's ambition knew no bounds,
and his luft of power was infatiable. Led by the
dictates of thofe paffions, he formed an audacious
defign of extending the limits of the principality
he had by very indifferent means acquired, at the
expence of his fovereign. Malcolm IV. a minor,
had mounted the throne of Scotland upon the
death

death of his grandfather, David the Saint; and Somerled taking advantage of the minority, rebelled in the very beginning of this reign. He put himfelf at the head of a numerous army, confifting partly of his own vaffals, and partly of lawlefs perfons, whom the love of plunder or a confcioufnefs of guilt had driven from all quarters to his ftandard, and laid wafte thofe divifions of the kingdom which lay next his own principalities. But the celebrated *Gilchrift* *, Earl of Angus, being fent with an army to oppofe him, gave him a total defeat, and obliged him to fly for refuge into Ireland.

MALCOLM's reign was full of troubles. Henry II. of England, taking advantage of his pacific difpofition and mean genius, forced him to furrender the towns and countries which his anceftors had poffeffed in South Britain. A ceffion fo inglorious provoked the refentment of the Scottifh nation, and became the foundation of a dangerous infurrection. To pacify the malecontents, Malcolm was under the difagreeable neceffity of declaring war againft England. But he carried on and concluded that war in a way which gave little fatiffaction to his people. The alienation he made of Northumberland, and a fcandalous pufillanimity which appeared in every part of his conduct, rendered his perfon and authority contemptible.

THE inhabitants of Galloway, defpifing this feeble adminiftration, revolted openly, and thofe of Murray followed their example. In the midft of fo many commotions and civil wars, which had

* There was no Earl of Angus called Gilchrift in that age. See Dalrymple's Collect. p 392.

deftroyed

deftroyed the braveft foldiers in the nation, Somerled's genius was too enterprizing to remain un-
active. He had returned from Ireland, whither
the unfuccefsful battle already mentioned had driven him, and harraffed for fome time the coafts of
Scotland with piratical depredations. In a conjuncture fo full of tumult and public confufion, he
foon collected a large body of men, with whom he
made a defcent upon the left fide of the river Clyde,
and penetrated as far as Renfrew : but being too
intent upon plunder, and too little folicitous about
his own fafety, he was furprized and his followers
cut to pieces. Some writers relate that he himfelf
was taken prifoner, brought before the King, and
executed like a common malefactor ; others will
have it that he and his fon fell in battle. Buchanan
places thefe events about the year 1163.

I think there is reafon to believe that both
the Scottifh hiftorians and Highland fennachies
have committed a number of errors in their contradictory account of this powerful chief. Had
his birth been obfcure, and his original fortune
low, as thefe hiftorians pretend, it is difficult to
comprehend how he could have raifed himfelf to
the thanedom of Argyle, or why the public fhould
have recognifed his title. The Chronicle of Man
calls him *Prince of Heregaidhel* *, at the time of
his marriage with the daughter of King Olave. It
does not appear that this marriage gave him a
right to any part of the ifles, though Abercromby †
concurs with the Highland genealogifts in an opinion of this kind. *Olave* was fucceeded by his

---

* A corruption of Jar-ghael, that is to fay, the country of
the Weftern Caledonians.

† Mart. Arch of the Scots nation, vol. ii. p. 440.

son Godred, and the posterity of Godred inherited the greatest part of Olave's dominions, for a whole century after Somerled had been killed near Renfrew.

It is hard to determine whether Somerled gave the first provocation to his sovereign, or received it from the ministers of that prince. It is not improbable, that after he had acquired so vast an addition of power in the isles, he aspired to be independant towards the latter part of his life. If his whole army, as is alledged, a very small number excepted, was cut off near the river Clyde by an inconfiderable body of royalists, it is suprising that his family should have subsisted, after his death, without any dimunition of its vast power. No advantage appears to have been obtained by a battle so decisive. The estates of the rebel were neither annexed to the demenses of the crown, nor parcelled out among court favourites. His son *Dugal* was left in the undisturbed possession of Argyle and Lorn : *Reginald*, another of his sons, was Lord of the Isles and Kintyre : *Angus* their brother, was powerful enough to fight battles by sea and land against Reginald : and *Somerled* the Second, the fourth son of Somerled the first, and an hereditary traitor, say our Scottish historians, was able to raise a new rebellion in the reign of Alexander the Second.

I suspect indeed that this Somerled the Second never existed, notwithstanding what hath been said about him by sennachies and historians. The Chronicle of Man makes no mention of him ; and the time at which we are told he revolted, looks like a demonstration that the whole story is a mere fiction. Somerled the first was killed in

the

the year 1164. The younger Somerled rebelled againſt Alexander the Second in the year 1248*. He muſt of courſe have been eighty-four years of age, when he engaged in a war againſt his ſovereign, ſuppoſing he had been born on the very day in which his father was ſlain.

ANOTHER argument from which it may be concluded, with great probability, that the real Somerled's party ſuſtained no conſiderable loſs at Renfrew, is, that the diviſion of the iſles which had fallen to the ſhare of that mighty Thane, after his firſt ſea-fight with the King of Man, remained after his death in the poſſeſſion of his ſon Reginald, and of his poſterity for three centuries. If Somerled's army had been totally deſtroyed at Renfrew, it may be very reaſonably preſumed that *Godred*, King of Man, who had been violently diſpoſſeſſed of theſe iſles about eight years before that event, would have laid hold of ſo favourable an opportunity to re-annex them to his dominions, before the ſons of Somerled could have recovered themſelves from the loſs they ſuſtained in the battle which was fatal to their father.

IT is true indeed the Chronicle of Melroſs, another old hiſtorical regiſter, agrees exactly with the account which we have in the Chronicle of Man, of the total overthrow given to Somerled's army. From it we learn, that " Sumerled, the petty King of *Eragaithel*, had carried on an impious rebellion againſt his natural lord, Malcolm King of Scotland, during the ſpace of twelve years: that this rebel, after having collected a numerous army in Ireland and other places, was, through the ven-

---

geance

geance of God, killed at *Renfrew*, together with
his fon, and a multitude of his vaffals: and that
a handful of men belonging to the fame province,
the inhabitants of Clydefdal probably, had the
fole merit of delivering the nation from this
rebel*."

Sir James Dalrymple quotes a charter belonging to the family of Innes, from which it appears
that Malcolm and Somerled once concluded a
peace, and of courfe that Somerled's rebellion
could not have been of fuch a long duration as the
Chronicle pretends. King Malcolm reigned twelve
years only, and the Thane of Argyle died before
him †.

It is more than probable that the true hiftory of
Somerled's birth and character — of his difputes
with the Kings of Scotland and Man—of his laft
great armament and death, was this :—His anceftors were perfons of confiderable influence, though
greatly inferior to him. He foon began to extend
his power—he wrefted half of the ifles out of the
hands of Godred, King of Man—he made war on
Malcolm, King of Scotland—a battle was fought,
but the controverfy was not decided.—Malcolm,
directed by his natural clemency, or more probably
by reafons of ftate, adjufted all his differences with

---

* Sumerledus, Regulus Eregeithel, jam per annos duodecim
contra Regem Scotiæ Malcolmum, dominum fuum naturalem,
impie rebellans, tam copiofum de Hibernia et diverfis locis ex-
ercitum contrahens apud Renfrim applicuiffet, tandem ultione
divina cum filio & innumerabili populo, a paucis cumprovincia-
libus ibidem occifus eft. Chron. Melros. ad ann. 1164.

† The charter was dated, *apud Pert. natali domini proximo
poft concordiam Regis & Sumerled.* Dalrymple's Collections,
p. 425.

Somerled

Somerled in an amicable way. After this agreement, the ambitious thane taking advantage of his brother-in-law's unpopular adminiftration, and the inteftine commotions confequent upon it, feized on many of thofe ifles which made a part of the Norwegian dynafty of the ifles. Two fuccefsful fea-fights eftablifhed the right which the ftrength of his arms and political intrigues had given him to that acquifition. An increafe of power fo great muft have made him the object of public jealoufy more than ever. A wife miniftry faw the neceffity of humbling a perfon already too powerful to be a good fubject ; and no doubt fome of the nobles of Scotland were willing to facrifice him to their avarice. Somerled faw the danger with which he was threatned, and took every precaution to defeat the machinations of his enemies. He formed the bold defign of rendering himfelf totally independent of the crown. He had no reafon to dread much from the magnanimity or addrefs of Malcolm ; and accordingly having collected a great body of men, not only in Argyle and the ifles, but likewife in Ireland, where he had connections, he made a defcent on Clydefdale. The King's generals took the fhorteft and moft effectual, though an ignominious way of ending the difpute. They bribed a perfon from whom Somerled could have no fears, and by his means got him affaffinated. The rebels difperfed immediately ; but the loyalifts were too weak to purfue their fuccefs. They permitted the Highlanders to retire unmolefted, and the fons of Somerled to divide his overgrown eftate among themfelves.

GODRED, King of the ifles, was obliged to yield a confiderable divifion of his hereditary territories,

riteries, as related above, and was likewife ftript
in a fhort time of the dominions he had acquired
in Ireland. We learn from the annals of that kingdom, that *Dermit nan gaul* and his fon-in-law, the
famous Earl of *Pembroke*, took Dublin, the capital of the dominions of the Eafterlings, in the
year 1170*, and that the troops fent from Man to
recover it, next year, were totally defeated, and
their leaders flain.

G O D R E D died in the year 1187, during the
winter feafon, and his body was in the following
fummer conveyed to *I-colm-cille* †. It has been
obferved already, that this King muft very probably be one of thefe Norwegian Kings, who according to the Scottifh hiftorians, lie buried in
Iona.

O L A V E, furnamed the Black, the only legitimate fon left by Godred, had been declared
heir by his father, and by the pope's legate: but
as he was too young to affume the reins of government, the people of Man made his natural brother
Reginald King in his ftead. We are told by the
hiftorians of Norway, that *Reginald* was the moft
famous warrior in the Weftern parts of Europe,
during his time ‡. It had been the practice of
fome famous pirates among the old Normans to
live for three years without entering under the
roof of a houfe which emmitted *any fmoke*. Reginald had conformed himfelf to that cuftom, and
became of courfe capable of fuftaining hardfhips
of every kind. He prudently lived upon good

---

* Ware's Ant. of Irel. chap. 24.
† Chron. Man. ad ann. 1187.
‡ Torfæi Orcades, p. 146.

terms

terms with the King's of England, and ftudied to oblige thofe of Scotland. At the requeft of *William* the *Lion* he undertook to recover Caithnefs out of the hands of Harold, Earl of Orkney, and effected it ‖. After apprehending his brother *Olave*, and committing him to prifon, for prefuming to ask a more comfortable maintenance than the mountainous and fterile ifland of Lewis could afford him, he delivered him into the hands of *William*, to prevent a civil war; and the innocent prince was kept in prifon during the life of that Monarch*.

REGINALD faw very good reafons for courting the honour of being a vaffal to the fee of Rome. The Popes of the twelfth and thirteenth ages prefcribed laws to fome of the greateft fovereigns of Europe, and fecured the intereft of thofe who committed their perfons and eftates to their protection. Reginald thought the tribute payable by his kingdom to the crown of Norway too high, and the Lord of his allegiance was at too great a diftance to defend him, if oppreffed by one of his more powerful neighbours. He therefore, like two Englifh Monarchs, his cotemporaries, fubjected his kingdom to the pope, who demanded only an annual tribute of twelve merks †.

REGINALD, though illegitimate, ftiled himfelf King of Man, *by hereditary fucceffion.* In thofe days illegitimacy did not incapacitate any perfon in the Northern parts of Europe from fucceeding his father in the poffeffion of an eftate or kingdom;

‖ Torfæi Orcades, p. 164.
* Chron. Manniæ.
† Fœdera Angliæ, tom. I. p. 234.

and

and the cafe was much the fame towards the
South.

AFTER *Reginald* had reigned near thirty years,
his brother Olave found means to re-eftablifh his
own authority in the Northern Ebudes; and having equipped a confiderable fleet there by the affiftance of his friends, invaded Man, and furprized Reginald : but he entered into a treaty with
him, and left him in poffeffion of Man, with the
regal title.

IN a little time after the conclufion of this treaty, Reginald entered into a confederacy with Al-
lan, Earl of Galloway, the moft powerful fubject
of Scotland; and accompanied by that Lord,
made an expedition into the Northern Ebudes,
with a defign of re-taking thofe territories which
he had refigned to Olave by treaty.   But the confederates found themfelves under the neceffity of
returning home without effecting any thing; the
people of Man having too great a partiality for
Olave, and too much regard for the Iflanders in
his intereft, to fight them ‡.   Soon after this un-
fucceſsful expedition, *Reginald* pretended a journey to the court of England; and to defray the
expence of it, obtained from the people of Man a
pecuniary aid, which was thought very confiderable at that time; but he went only to Galloway, in order to facilitate the execution of his
former defign, and to marry his daughter to the
fon of his ally. His fubjects, difobliged by this grofs
mifapplication of the aid they had granted, fent
for Olave, and made him King ‖.   Reginald made

---

‡ Chron. Man. ad ann. 1225.
‖ Ibid. ad ann. 1226.

two unsuccefsful attempts to difpoffefs his brother, and loft his life in the laft of them.

THE competition being ended by the death of *Reginald*, and a perfect tranquility enfuing, *Olave* went to Norway, with a defign of paying homage to his fovereign, and getting his right confirmed; but before his arrival, *Haco*, the Norwegian Monarch, had made a certain nobleman called *Husbec* King of the *Sodorian* ifles*.   This nobleman, who, according

---

* The meaning of the word *Sodor*, which has been very much mifunderftood by many learned men, may contribute to throw light on fome parts of the *Hebridian hiftory*, hitherto involved in darknefs, and apparent contradictions.—We are told by Buchanan, lib. 1. cap. 34. that the age before that in which he lived, gave the name of *Sodor* to a town in the Ifle of Man. Bifhop Brown, the author of a new defcription of that ifland, which Dr. Gibfon has annexed to the old one given by Cambden in his Britannia, fuppofes that the *Infulæ Sodorenfes* thirty-two in number, were fo called from the bifhopric of *Sodor*, erected in the ifle of Iona, which was one of them.   Thefe *Infulæ Sodorenfes* were united to *Man*, if we believe him, about the beginning of the eleventh century, and the bifhops of thefe united fees were ftiled bifhops of *Sodor* and *Man*.   But after the Ifle of Man, continues Dr. Brown, had been annexed to the crown of England, the two fees were disjoined, and Man had bifhops of its own, who ftiled themfelves varioufly, fometimes bifhops of *Man* only, fometimes *Sodor et Man*, and fometimes *Sodor de Man*; giving the name of *Sodor* to a little ifland, called by the Norwegians *Holm*, and by the natives *Peel*, in which the cathedral ftood.—(See Cambd. Brit. Gibfon's edit. page 1449.)   To juftify this explication of the word, Dr. Brown appeals to a charter granted by Thomas, Earl of Derby, to one of the bifhops of Man, in the year 1505.

I fhall not infift on the difficulty of proving that a bifhopric was erected in the weftern ifles of Scotland before the twelfth century, or perhaps before the thirteenth, nor on fome other remarks which might be made on the hiftorical relation now given; but it is certain, that after Man had fallen into the hands of the Englifh, the bifhopric of the ifles was tranflated by the

according to the Chronicle of Man, was the son of
Owmund, but according to Torfæus, the son of
Dugal,

Scots into Iona, and that the bishops who filled that see from
that period, till the final abolition of the episcopacy after the
revolution, went under the title of *Episcopi Sodorenses* : whether they or those of Man had the best right to it we shall not
now inquire.

If *Sodor* was a town in *Man*, in the beginning of the sixteenth
century, or in the fifteenth, which was Buchanan's opinion ;
or if, from that town or *Holm*, the bishops of Man and the Isles
derived their respective titles, agreeably to Dr. Brown's opinion ;
it is difficult to comprehend, why, in charters, registers, histories, and common conversation, *Sodor* should be preferred to
Man, of which it was no more than a small part. When we
take the word *Sodor* in so confined a signification, there seems to be
the same impropriety in stiling a person *Bishop* of *Sodor and Man*,
as in stiling another of the same order Bishop of *Derry and Ireland*, Bishop of *Bangor and Wales*, or Bishop of *Dumblane and
Scotland*.

The passage quoted from the Earl of Derby's grant seems to
me to be misrepresented, and by no means to imply that *Pele*,
Holm, or that small island to the West of *Man*, was the true
Sodor of ancient times.

When the Norwegians conquered the Western isles, they
sometimes changed the old Galic names of places, and gave
them new ones, abundantly descriptive. Thus to the Eastern
OEbudæ of the ancients they gave the name of *Ealand Skianach*,
or the Cloudy Island ; Sky in the Norse language signifying
a Cloud ; and to the Western OEbuda, that of *Logus*, or *Lod-
bus*, i. e. a Marshy Country, more fit for pasturage than tillage :
and when they divided these isles into two parts, agreeably to
their situation, and appointed a distinct governor to each, they
gave the name of *Sudereys* to that division of the isles which lay
to the South, and of *Nordures* to that in the opposite quarter ;
Ey or Ay, in the Norwegian language, signifying an island,
and *Suder* and *Norder* signifying Southern and Northern, when
they possessed the ancient *Cathanesia*, they gave the new name
of *Suderland* to a county in the Northern division of Scotland,
now well known by the same appellation.

Dugal, and grand-son of Somerled, was killed, in the firſt year of his reign, at the ſiege of a caſtle

---

It appears from the hiſtory of the Orkneys, compiled by an old Iſlandic writer, and tranſlated, with large additions, by Torfæus, that the explication now given of the two vocables *Nordureys* and *Sudereys*, is perfeɛtly juſt.

The promontory in Argyleſhire, which is called the *Point of Ardnamurchan*, was the boundary which ſeparated the *Sudereys* and *Nordureys* of former times from each other. To the South of that promontory lies Man, Arran, Bute, Cumra, Avon, Gid, Ila, Colenſa. Jura, Scarba, Muil, Iona, Tiree, Coll, Ulva, and many other iſles of interior note. To the North of Ardnamurchan are Muck, Egg, Rum, Canna, Sky, Raſay, Barra, South Uiſt, Benbicula, North Uiſt, and the Lewis, including Harris, together with a vaſt number of ſmall iſles. All theſe when joined together, and ſubjeɛt to the ſame prince, made up the whole kingdom of Man and the Iſles.

The Southern diviſion of the Ebudes was reckoned more conſiderable than the Northern. The ſeat of empire was fixed in the former : the Kings kept their courts in the Iſle of Man, and ſent deputies into the *Nordureys*, who reſided either in Sky or in the Lewis. When the kingdom of Man and the Iſles was divided between Godred, the ſon of Olave, and Somerled, Thane of Argyle, Ila, one of the beſt iſles in the Southern diviſion of the Ebudes, fell to the ſhare of Somerled, and became in ſome meaſure the capital of a ſecond Hebridian kingdom : for theſe reaſons the *Inſulæ Sodorenſes*, or Southern Iſles, became much more famous than the *Nordureys*, and are therefore more frequently mentioned in hiſtory. When the Norwegian writers make no diſtinɛtion between the *Sudereys* and *Nordureys*, the latter are always comprehended under the name of the former; and hence it was that the biſhops of the iſles were ſtiled biſhops of *Sodor*, though their dioceſe included all the iſles to the North of Ardnamurchan, as well as thoſe to the South. But when the *Nordureys* are particularly mentioned by theſe writers, the Southern Ebudes are totally excluded : thus we are told by Torfæus, that *Magnus the Barefooted*, ſome time before he had made a deſcent on the Southern Iſles pertaining to the King of Man, made a priſoner of *Lagman*, the ſon of *Godred Chrovan*, whom his father had made governor of the *Nordureys*. Torſæ. Hiſt. Orcad. p. 71.

in

in Bute, and his body tranflated into Iona. Immediately after his death, *Olave* reaffumed the government of his paternal dominions, and his title to the kingdom was in a little time recognized by *Haco.* He died in the ifle of Man, after a reign of eleven years, and was buried at *Ruffin*; the monks of that abby having found means to recommend themfelves to his favour more powerfully than thofe of Iona.

OLAVE *the Black*, was fucceeded by his fon *Harold :* this young Prince confiding in the alliance he had contracted with the King of England, refufed to pay homage to *Haco*, King of Norway. But that monarch, to punifh the difloyalty of his vaffal, fent *Gofpatric*, one of his favourites, in quality of viceroy, into the ifles, at the head of a great fleet. *Gofpatric* drove Harold out of all his dominions; but dying foon thereafter, *Haco* was reconciled to Harold, and reftored him to his paternal dominions, confirming to him and his heirs, under the royal feal, a right to all the ifles enjoyed by his predeceffors.

IT appears evident, from this part of the hiftory of Harold, and of his father Olave, that the Kings of Man held their dominions of the crown of Norway; and we learn from Matthew Paris *; that a tribute of ten merks of gold † was paid by thefe

R 2

vaffal

---

* Hift. Norm. p. 1000.

† Spelman, in Voce Marca, quotes an author who makes a merk of gold equivalent to fifty of filver. According to other writers to whom the fame learned antiquary refers, the merk of gold was fometimes of no greater value than ten merks of filver, and fometimes equal to nine only. But if the tribute due by the Kings of Man to their fuperior Lords of Norway, was no more

than

vaffal Princes to their fovereigns, at the time of their inveftiture ; and that this tribute became due whenever a new monarch happened to obtain the fcepter of Norway. It is likewife clear that the more ancient bifhops of *Sodor* were under the metropolitical jurifdiction of the archbifhops of Drontheim ; for though in the treaty concluded between Alexander III. of Scotland, and Magnus IV. of Norway, the patronage of the Sodorian bifhopric was vefted in the Scottifh monarchs, yet the former jurifdiction of Drontheim over it, was by a fpecial article referved to the archbifhops of that fee. Accordingly we find that King Alexander fent *Marcus*, the Gallovidian, who had been elected bifhop of Man, in the year 1275, to be confecrated or confirmed in his right by his metropolitan in Norway ‡.

HAROLD was a Prince of diftinguifhed abilities and many fhining virtues. He was highly careffed by the Kings of England, and lived in a good underftanding with his neighbours of Scotland. Haco courted his friendfhip much, and after beftowing his daughter on him in the Orkneys, celebrated his nuptials with a royal magnificence at Bergen in

---

than *ten times ten merks* of filver, and that tribute payable only four or five times in a century, King Magnus IV. of Norway, certainly made a profitable bargain when he ceded the Weftern Ifles to Alexander III. of Scotland, for a confiderable fum of money paid in four years, together with a yearly tribute or rent, commonly called the Annual of Norway.

‡ After the Ifle of Man had been fubdued by the Englifh, the bifhopric of Sodor was divided into two. That which was erected in the principal ifland, and confined to it, fell under the jurifdiction of the archbifhop of York. The other, which comprehended all the Ebudes of Scotland, and was eftablifhed at Iona, became fubject to the archbifhop of Glafgow.

Norway *.

Norway *. But while Harold was returning into his own dominions with the Princefs his fpoufe, accompanied by many perfons of eminent rank and fortune, he was overtaken by a violent hurricane near Shetland, and perifhed, together with his whole retinue. This unfortunate event happened in the year 1248, according to Torfæus ; but in the year following, if we believe the Chronicle of Man.

Some time before the death of Harold †, Alexander II. King of Scotland, a Prince of great abilities, who defired above all things to extend the limits of his empire, fent two bifhops to the court of Norway to reclaim the *Sodureys*, and the ifles to the Weft of Scotland. This is the language of the Iflandic annals, of which Torfæus has given a Latin verfion. From that paffage, as well as from many more in the fame annals, we learn diftinctly that the *Sodureys* were no more than a part of the ifles called Ebudes by the ancients. The Scottifh ambaffadors executed their commiffion with great fidelity and zeal, but were difmiffed with a categorical refufal. Haco, the fon of the Haco formerly mentioned, told them that all his anceftors, down from Harold Harfager, had an hereditary right to the Weftern Ifles of Scotland, and that he was unalterably determined to maintain it. The two bifhops, upon receiving this anfwer, had recourfe to another expedient. After reprefenting the danger attending a rupture with their mafter, they took it upon them to fuggeft to the Norwegian monarch, that Alexander, though a Prince

---

* Torfæus Hift. Orcad. p. 164.
† Torfæ. Hift. Orcad. p. 163.

of great magnanimity and power, was of too pacific a difpofition not to redeem the Ebudes with a
fum of money. But Haco replied immediately
that he was in no dread from any foreign quarter;
that he was at prefent fufficiently provided with
money; in fine, that no offer or temptation of any
kind could prevail with him to difmember a province from his empire.

It does not appear that any Scottifh King, prior
to Alexander II. demanded a reftitution of the
Weftern Ifles. During the piratical incurfions of
the Norwegians through the Deucaledonian and
Irifh Seas, it would have been no eafy matter to
recover thofe ifles, or to keep them if recovered.
The revenues arifing from them in that early period could not have been confiderable, and the attention of the Kings of Scotland was almoft conftantly employed by inteftine commotions, or by
uninterrupted wars with foreign enemies. But
Alexander, an opulent, wife, and magnanimous
Prince, being married to a daughter of England,
and in the beft underftanding with its monarch,
formed a refolution of recovering thefe ifles. After
negociations and pacific overtures had failed, he
equipped a fleet with an intention of conquering
the territories in difpute. But a violent diftemper
feizing him while engaged in the expedition, he
died without having made any progrefs in the
execution of his defign. The untimely death of
this excellent King happened in the year 1249 *.
It is furprifing that the Scottifh hiftorians fhou'd
have been ftrangers to a circumftance fo remarkable
as the vaft preparations made by King Alexander

---

* Chron. Man. Torfæ. Hift. Orcad. p. 64.

II.

II. to wreft the Ebudes out of the hands of foreign ufurpers. They have related at great length the difputes of that Prince with John, King of England; the fervices done by him to the Barons who fought againft that unhappy monarch; the fubfequent differences he had with the court of Rome, and with Henry III. together with the manner in which he quelled two or three dangerous rebellions at home: but one of the nobleft projects he had ever formed, a project which undoubtedly he would have executed, had heaven prolonged his days for any time, has by thefe writers been buried in oblivion.

" ALEXANDER, King of Scots, faith the Chronicle of Man, prepared a mighty fleet about this time †, with a view of conquering the ifles; but a fever feized him in the ifle of Kerwaray ‡, of which he died.

THE old Iflandic hiftorian, tranflated by Torfæus, gives a more particular account of this grand defign. " Alexander, of Scotland, faith that writer, actuated by a ftrong paffion of extending his dominions, raifed forces throughout all his territories, and boafted that he would not lay down his arms till he had reannexed the Ebudes to the kingdom already in his poffeffion. He alfo held forth that he would fubdue Orkney and Shetland. To fucceed the better in this undertaking, he began to tamper with one of the Hebridian Kings, *Jon* or *John*, the fon of Dugal of Lorn, and grandfon of Somerled, Thane of Argyle. Haco had

---

† That is in the year 1249.
‡ On the coaft of Lorn.

R 4

committed

committed the impregnable fort of Kiarnaburgh *, and two or three other caftles of great importance, to this John. Alexander offered him much larger poffeffions than thofe he had obtained from the King of Norway, provided he would deliver up the fort and caftles. But the Hebridian chief, in fpite of the importunities of his friends, and all the ample promifes made to him, continued faithful to his mafter. Alexander, not difcouraged by this repulfe, profecuted his defign, and invaded the ifles. But while he lay in the bay of *Rialarfund* †, faith Torfæus, after his author, he had a very extraordinary vifion and foon after died ‡.

ABOUT the time of Alexander's death, *Harold*, the fon of *Godred the Brown*, and grandfon of that

---

* The true name of the fort is Kiamaburgh ; it lay in a fmall rocky ifle near the coaft of Mull.

† The *Rialarfund* of the Iflandic hiftorian, is the ifland Kiararey near the Sound of Mull, where Alexander died. as we learn from the epitaph infcribed on his tomb, in the abby church of Melrofs. See Abercromby's Life of Alexander II.

‡ Three men approached Alexander when afleep in his bed. Thefe phantoms were St. Olaus, King of Norway, St. Magnus, Earl of Orkney, and St. Columba, abbot of Iona. The firft of thefe being a perfon of great ftature, with a red coloured face, and clad with a royal apparel, looked him full with a ftern and terrible look. The fecond was in his appearance younger, wonderfully handfome and very richly dreffed. The third, who was taller than the reft, and very violent in his manner, afked the King, in a moft wrathful tone, whether he really intended to invade the Ebudes ? Alexander anfwering in the affirmative, the phantom advifed him, at his peril, to drop that defign and return home. After the King had related this awful dream to thofe about him, the wifeft of his council diffuaded him very earneftly from the profecution of his defign : but perfifting in his former refolution, he was attacked by a violent diftemper which foon made an end of his life and rafh projeƈt together. Vide Torfæ. Hift. Orcad. p. 163, 164.

Reginald

Reginald who had formerly reigned in Man, affumed the title of King of the Ifles. But his reign
was tyrannical and fhort. Summoned by his pa-
ramount Lord to appear before him, he found
himfelf under the neceflity of repairing to Norway, and was imprifoned there for his ufurpation
and cruelties ‡.

Haco, upon receiving intelligence that his
daughter and fon-in-law, *Harold*, the fon of *Olave
the Black*, had unfortunately perifhed, committed
the adminiftration of all public affairs in the E-
budes to *John*, the fon of *Dugal*, and grandfon of
Somerled, till fome one of the blood royal could
be conveniently fent into that province †. But
John arriving in Man, affumed the regal title,
without regarding either his mafter's inftructions
or the inclinations of the people. But the people
highly provoked by this indignity, and firmly at-
tached, at the fame time, to their lawful Prince,
drove the ufurper out of the ifland, and having
foon after concerted matters with their neighbours,
declared Magnus, the fon of Olave, their King * ;
and Haco recognized his title. John, difappointed
in his ambitious views by the exaltation of a rival,
began to hearken to the advantageous offer of the
Scottifh monarch. Alexander II. had in vain employed the ftrongeft folicitations and ampleft promifes to corrupt him ‖ ; but the conjuncture was
now more favourable ; and Alexander III. had all
the fuccefs he could defire in feducing John from his
allegiance to his fovereign.

---

‡ Chron. Man. ad ann. 1249.
† Torfæ. Hift. Orcad. p. 164.
* Chron. Man. ad ann. 1250.
‖ Torfæ. Hift. Orcad. p. 164.

The

The Scottish and Norwegian historians give contradictory accounts of the manner in which the Western Isles were reunited to the dominions belonging to the crown, in the reign of Alexander III. Buchanan's account is as follows:

" In the year 1263, *Acho*, King of Norway, having approached the coast of Kyle with a fleet of one hundred and sixty ships, landed twenty thousand men near a town of that district called *Air*. His pretext for making war upon the Scots was, that some of the isles which had been promised to his ancestors by *Donald Bane*, had not been given up. These were Bute, Arran, and the two Cumras, places which had never been reckoned in the number of the Ebudes. But to one who wanted only some colour of reason for making war, it was enough that these places were islands. Acho reduced the two largest of them before any opposition could have been made to the purpose. Elated by this success, he made a descent upon *Cunningham*, and engaging in battle with the Scots, in a place called *Larges*, was overpowered by their superior numbers, and reduced to the shameful necessity of flying with the greatest precipitation to his ships. But the loss of that battle was not his only misfortune. A violent tempest destroyed the greatest part of his fleet, immediately after the action was over; and it was with no small difficulty that he made his escape into the Orkneys with a few ships that remained after that calamity. The Norwegians left sixteen thousand men in the field of battle, and the Scots five.

" Acho, overwhelmed with grief upon the loss of his army, and the death of a favourite youth, distinguished by his valour, died soon after. His
son,

fon, Magnus, who had lately come over from Norway, feeing things in a much more defperate fituation than he expected, and as he could not get any new fupplies from home before the fpring feafon, was willing to terminate the quarrel by a definitive treaty of peace. There were feveral reafons which confirmed him in this difpofition. The Iflanders were difaffected, and thofe on the continent of Scotland, on whofe affiftance his father had laid no fmall ftrefs, had entirely abandoned his intereft. *Man* had been already reduced by the enemy, and it was very probable that the other ifles were foon to follow the fame fate.

" MAGNUS was eafily determined by fo many weighty confiderations to offer a peace : but Alexander would not hearken to any propofitions made by the Norwegian ambaffadors, till it fhould be previoufly agreed that the Ebudes fhould be ceded to him, and annexed to his crown for ever. This preliminary article having been at laft admitted, a final pacification was concluded on the following terms : That the King of Scots fhould immediately pay four thoufand merks of filver to his brother of Norway, as an equivalent for the Ebudes, of which the latter made a total renunciation, and together with that fum, an annual tax of an hundred merks of filver, was to be paid by Alexander, and his fucceffors, to Magnus, and his. It was further ftipulated, that Margaret, the daughter of the former, fhould marry Hungonan, the fon of the latter, as foon as their ages fhould permit *."

IN this manner were the Weftern Ifles recovered by Alexander III. of Scotland, and upon thefe

* Buchan. Rer. Scot. Hift. lib. v.j. cap. 62, 63.

terms ceded by Magnus of Norway, if we are to give faith implicitly to the Scottish historians.

But the account given by Torfæus of the matter, after the authors of his country, and the public records kept there, is in substance this.

" In the year 1263, the petty Kings of the Sodorian isles acquainted their sovereign Haco of Norway, that *Kiarnach*, Earl of Ross, had committed the most cruel devastations in their territories, that he had destroyed many of their towns, villages, monasteries and churches, and that he had in the most barbarous manner killed all the people that fell in his way, without any distinction of age or sex. They notified further, that the King of Scots had declared he would never desist till all the Ebudes possessed by the Norwegians should be reunited to his dominions ‡.

" Haco, a Prince of uncommon abilities, and of a military genius, heard all this with a becoming indignation ; and having without loss of time fitted out a vast fleet, set sail for Scotland, on the 11th of July 1263. He arrived in Shetland on the 13th, and staid there for two weeks ; and after having settled his affairs in Orkneys and Caithness, steered his course first for the Lewis, and afterwards for Sky. Here he was joined by Magnus, King of Man, and by Dugal, one of those great Lords in the isles, who had assumed the regal title. Haco was piloted by this vassal King to the Sound of Mull, and from *Mull* to *Kiarary*. He had ordered all his ships of war to rendezvous in this isle, and here he received a considerable accession of strength

------

‡ Torfæ. Hist. Orcad. p. 165.

by

by the junction of a fleet which the Islanders had brought to his aid.

" WHILE Haco was settling his plan of operations at *Kiarary*, he detached a squadron of fifty ships to the isthmus of Kintyre, and another consisting of fifteen to the isle of Bute. The first was commanded by Magnus, King of Man, and Dugal, the Sodorian Prince already mentioned. Three or four Norwegian Captains, and one of the Ebudenfian Chieftains commanded the other. These two squadrons had all the success that could be desired. The conquest of Kintyre was finished in a short time. Two Lords who bore the greatest sway in that province delivered it up to the Norwegians, swore fealty to Haco, and brought in a thousand bullocks for the use of his army. The castle of Bute surrendered, and the whole island was subdued, and a considerable body of troops sent from it did no small damage on the continent of Scotland.

" WHILE Haco lay before the isle of Arran, after having reduced all the other Ebudes *, the King of Scots sent ambassadors to him with propositions of peace. The Norwegian monarch, after receiving several different messages in the same stile, began to listen to the overtures made, and sent two bishops and three laics of distinguished talents, invested with a public character to settle all differences. Alexander was in appearance fond of an accommodation, but insisted peremptorily that Arran, Bute, and Camray, should be restored to the crown of Scotland. Haco, unwilling to grant such advantageous terms, and perceiving that

---

* Torfæ. Hist. Orcad. p. 166.

he

he had been too long amuſed with the inſidious promiſes of an enemy, who had been ſpinning out the time with affected delays, till he could draw a more numerous army together, broke off the treaty, and recommenced hoſtilities. He had in vain made a new propoſal, that he and the King of Scotland ſhould meet in a certain place, at the head of their reſpective forces, and either ſettle a laſting peace, or terminate their differences in a pitched battle.

" Haco finding that his enemy had only made an equivocal declaration, in anſwer to this generous propoſal, ſent Magnus and Dugal of the Iſles, together with ſome more of his general officers, at the head of a fleet, corſiſting of ſixty ſail, and a numerous body of land forces, into the bay of *Skip-afiord* *. Theſe generals having landed their troops, penetrated into the country—deſtroyed all the villages around *Loknlovie*—laid waſte a country from which one of the Scottiſh earls derived his title, and carried back all the plunder they could find to their ſhips."

---

* Skipafiord is a Norwegian word, which ſignifies, according to Torfæus, the *Bay of ſhips*. In the confines of the ſhires of Argyle and Dumbarton there is a bay which is now called *Loch loung*, a Galic word, of the ſame import with the *Skipafiord* of the Norſe. Unleſs this *Loch loung* be the bay meant by Torfæus, and the writer whom he tranſlates, it muſt be the bay of *Greenock*. Each of theſe bays lies at a ſmall diſtance only from *Lokn-love*, i. e. *Loch-lomond*, a large freſh-water lake, that abounds with iſlands, agreeably to the account given of it by the Norwegian writers. The tract of land which, according to the ſame writers, gave his title to a Scottiſh earl, muſt be the county of Lennox, or ſome part of it: it cannot be either Lorn or Lochaber, as Torfæus imagined.

WHILE

WHILE the squadron commanded by Magnus lay in the bay of *Skipafiord*, a terrible tempest destroyed a great part of it—the grand fleet lying at the same time before an island, in the mouth of the Clyde it may be presumed, five transports were driven from their anchors, and wrecked on the coast of Scotland. It was with extreme difficulty " that Haco's own galley was saved. The Scots seeing so many of the Norwegian vessels stranded, came down to the shore in great numbers, and attacked them; but the Norwegians, supported by a reinforcement sent from the fleet, defended themselves with extraordinary valour, and maintained a desperate fight throughout all the night, till the Scots found it convenient to retire."

ON the following day, Haco, notwithstanding the manifest disadvantages of every kind to which his people were exposed, formed a resolution of landing, either to share the same fate with his distressed forces on shore, or to relieve them out of such imminent danger. But the chief man of his council and army persuaded him to keep the sea, and send new supplies of men to the party ashore. As the storm continued to rage without any intermission, it was not in his power to land more than eight hundred men, who had ten times their number to encounter. They fought, however, with undaunted resolution and vigour for a whole day. The enemy gave way in the evening, and withdrew to a place of safety. The Norwegians pursued them, and after having dislodged them, retired to their ships, and joined their companions.

" THE day after this engagement, Haco took up the bodies of the Norwegians who had been slain, and buried them in holy ground.—The
winter

winter now approaching, he left the isle before which his fleet lay, and steered his course for the North. In the course of his voyage through the Ebudes, he dismissed Magnus, Dugal, and several other Sodorian lords, and appointed governors over the isles and forts, of which he had made himself master. He arrived safe in the Orkneys, and died soon after at Kirkwall *."

A Norwegian historian animadverts with some degree of severity on the Chronicle of Man, as well as upon the Scottish writers, for asserting that Haco effected nothing in this expedition; and I incline to think he had great reason. It is hardly possible to believe that the battle of *Larges*, if ever such a battle was fought, was so very fatal to the Norwegians as is represented by the Scottish historians. Their loss amounted to sixteen thousand men, according to Buchanan, but twenty-five thousand, according to Boece; and neither of these writers could determine whether the Scottish army was commanded on that occasion by *Alexander the Third* in person, or by Alexander Stewart, the great grandfather of *King Robert the Second*. From that and other circumstances it may be fairly concluded, that the records, or rather perhaps traditionary reports, from which they drew their account of Haco's misfortunes, must have been very imperfect.

If the Norwegian fleet had been almost totally destroyed by a tempest; if the greatest part of Haco's land forces had been cut off in the battle of *Larges*; if the Isle of Man had been reduced by King Alexander the Third of Scotland; and if a

---

* Torfæ. Hist. Orcad. p. 166, 167, &c.

spirit

spirit of diffatisfaction generally prevailed in the other Ebudes ; all which is alledged by our Scottish hiftorians ; it is ftrange that Magnus, the fon and fucceffor of Haco, with thefe and feveral other manifeft difadvantages on his fide, could have been able to procure a peace, in every refpect more honourable to him than to the other contracting power. In vain has it been objected by Abercromby *, that Magnus would never have given up the acquifitions fuppofed to have been made of Bute, Arran and the Comras, together with Man and the other Ifles, if his father had effected any thing confiderable.—Magnus was young, a ftranger to the art of war, and of a pacific difpofition. The Ebudes lay at a great diftance from the feat of his empire. The revenue fent from thefe ifles into his exchequer amounted only to ten merks of gold, and that was paid only at the acceffion of a new monarch. The expence to which his crown had been put in the late King's time, for fecuring thefe remote and unprofitable territories, would have probably overbalanced all the duties collected there fince the days of Harold Harfager. Befides all this, we learn from a Norwegian Chronicle, cited by Torfæus, that in the year immediately after Haco's death, the King of Scotland fent fome friars to treat with Magnus concerning the Ifles ; a circumftance hardly credible, had his father's army and fleet received fo heavy a blow.

A peace at length was concluded at *Perth*, in the year 1266 ; Alexander the Third of Scotland being prefent, together with his clergy and nobles, while the chancellor of Norway and one of his

---

* Mart. Atch. vol. i. p. 323.

S

barons

barons reprefented King Magnus.   The principal articles of the treaty were, That the Kings of Norway fhould lay no further claim to *Man*, or to the *Sodorian Ifles :*—That thefe fhould for ever belong to the Kings of Scotland, with all the fuperiorities, homages, rents, fervices, and other rights pertaining to them, together with the patronage of the bifhopric of Man ; faving at the fame time to the church of Drontheim her metropolitical jurifdiction over that fee :—That the inhabitants of the ifles ceded to the crown of Scotland fhould enjoy all the heritages and privileges formerly granted to them by the Kings of Norway, without being brought to account for any thing they had done before that time in favour of their old mafters :— And that the faid inhabitants fhould be governed for the future by the Kings of Scotland, and fubject to its laws, unlefs any of them fhould incline to refide elfewhere ; in which cafe, they were to have full liberty to remove unmolefted with their effects.

On the other hand, King Alexander obliged himfelf and his fucceffors to pay, as an equivalent for the renunciation made by his brother Magnus, four thoufand merks fterling, within four years, from the date of the treaty—together with an annual penfion of one hundred merks fterling, to be paid in the church of St. Magnus in the Orkneys, by Alexander and his fucceffors, to the King of Norway and his fucceffors for ever.

We are told by the Scottifh hiftorians, that to eftablifh this peace upon the moft folid foundation, another article was inferted in the treaty, by which the contracting parties obliged themfelves reciprocally to marry *Hungonan*, the fon of Magnus, to

Margaret,

Margaret, the eldeſt daughter of Alexander. But the ſon of Magnus who married the Lady Margaret of Scotland, was not called *Hungonan*, but Eric; and he was not born till the year 1270, that is, ſour years after the peace had been concluded at Perth *. So very ill informed were the Scottiſh writers with regard to almoſt all the diſputes and tranſactions between Alexander, Haco, and Magnus †.

THEY give us a long account of the mighty feats performed in Man by Alexander, lord high ſteward of Scotland, and John Cummin, earl of Badenoch, who had been ſent thither by Alexan-

---

* See the contract of marriage between Eric and Margaret, inter Fœdera Angliæ, tom. xi. p. 1079.

† It is not improper to obſerve that Abercromby, the firſt of our hiſtorians who gave, and perhaps could have given, the Norwegian account of theſe diſtricts and tranſactions, is far from being exact in the relation of them, which he drew out of Torfæus. He was either in too great hurry, or too much under the influence of national prejudice, while tranſlating that author. His complaint, that the names of the iſles through which he made his progreſs, are very different, in the Norwegian Journal, from thoſe now given them by the Scots, is not altogether juſt; and were it more ſo, the objection would ſignify little. To thoſe who know the ſituation of the iſles through which Haco paſſed, and have at the ſame time any notion of the Galic and Norſe, the Journal is abundantly intelligible, and worthy of credit. The author of it ſeems to have aſſiſted in the expedition, and to have been a ſpectator of every place and action. He may indeed have extenuated the loſſes ſuſtained by his countrymen upon that occaſion: but ſurely an objection of greater force may be made upon the ſame head, againſt the veracity of thoſe writers who have appeared on the other ſide of the queſtion.

I add further from Torfæus, that *Sturles*, an eminent poet, cotemporary with Haco, gave a full deſcription of the expedition in heroic verſe, and that the greateſt part of his compoſition was extant in that author's time: if ſo, the Norwegian annals ſeem in this matter to be preferable to thoſe of Scotland.

S 2

der

der the Third; and of the vigorous refiftance made by Magnus, then King of Man and the Ifles, in defence of his people and crown. But the author of the Chronicle of Man, who lived in that very period, makes no mention of thefe things. After relating that Magnus, the fon of Olave, King of Man and the Ifles, died at his caftle of Ruffin in the year 1265, he adds, in the very next fentence, that the kingdom of the Ifles was tranflated in the following year to Alexander, King of Scots.—Whence we may conclude, that the Scottifh hiftorians muft have been mifled in their relation of thefe matters, as well as in the account they give us at the fame time of the conqueft of all the Weftern Ifles by the lord high fteward of Scotland, the earls of Athol, March and Carnock, together with the thanes of Argyle and Lennox. If this conqueft had been made before the treaty of Perth, it is matter of no fmall wonder that the King of Scots fhould have granted fuch extraordinary conditions on that occafion to his adverfary of Norway. If after it, one can hardly believe that the petty Kings, lords and chieftains of the Ifles, men whofe territories lay at confiderable diftances from one another, men diftracted in their councils, all too feeble to contend with a powerful Monarch in their neighbourhood, if clofely united, and all perfectly fenfible that Magnus had abandoned them for ever, could have thought of making any refiftance againft their new mafter, efpecially as their late fovereign had fecured their eftates, privileges and rights of every kind, in the ftrongeft manner. This and Buchanan's filence confidered, I am apt to fufpect, that this conqueft received all the exiftence it ever had from the invention of

Boece,

Boece, who has, in too many instances, forgotten or neglected the first rule which an historian should have in view.

We learn indeed from the little Chronicle so often quoted, that the people of Man, four years after all the Ebudes had been ceded by Magnus of Norway, to Alexander, King of Scots, fought with great spirit, though unsuccefsfully, against an army sent by that Monarch to reduce them *. From that time, till the crown of Scotland, with all the dominions pertaining to it, was extorted from the unhappy John Baliol, by Edward the First of England, the Isle of Man continued in the poffeffion of the Scots. But about the latter end of King Edward's reign, one of the family of Montacute, who was of the blood royal of Man, faith Cambden +, having raifed a body of English adventurers, afferted his right to the ifland by force of arms, and drove the Scots out of it : but having plunged himfelf into a vaft debt by the expence attending this conqueft, he mortgaged the ifland to the famous *Anthony Bee*, bifhop of Durham, and patriarch of Jerufalem. Some time after the death of this bifhop, Edward the Second made over the kingdom of Man to his favourite Peter de Gavefton ; and when that minion could no longer enjoy the grant, gave it to Henry de Beaumont, *with all the demefnes and royal jurif-diction thereunto belonging* ‡.

In the year 1313, Robert Bruce, King of Scots, after having befieged the caftle of Ruffin, which

---

* Chron. Mann. ad ann. 1270.
† Cambden, in his Continuation of the hiftory of Man.
‡ Cambden, ibidem.

was

was bravely defended by the Engliſh, took it at laſt, reduced the whole iſland of Man, and made his nephew, Randolph earl of Murray, lord of it.—Randolph, upon receiving this title, aſſumed the arms of the later Kings of that iſland. The arms of the older Kings of Man, I mean thoſe of the Norwegian race, were, a ſhip with its ſails furled, and the title in their ſeals was, *Rex Manniæ & Inſularum* *-   The arms of the later Kings were three human legs linked together.

In the unfortunate reign of David Bruce, *William Montacute*, earl of Saliſbury, recovered Man out of the hands of the *Randolph* family, and in a little time ſo'd it, together *with the crown thereof*, to *William Scrope*. Upon the confiſcation of Scrope's eſtate, Henry the IV. of England beſtowed the iſland and lordſhip of Man upon Henry Piercy, earl of Northumberland. But Piercy having been attainted, in about four years after this grant, the Iſle devolved, by the King's favour, upon the *Stanley* family. It is almoſt needleſs to add, that the earls of Derby, of that family, enjoyed the title of *Kings* and *Lords of Man*, for many ages, till the ſovereignty of it fell, by female ſucceſſion, to the family of Athol.

The vaſt Continental eſtate of Sumerled, thane of Argyle, and the large acquiſitions he had made in the Iſles, at the expence of his brother-in-law, devolved wholly, ſome time after his death, on his two ſons, Dugal and Reginald. The lordſhip of Argyle, fell to the ſhare of the former, together with the entenſive iſland of Muil,

---

* Cambden, in his Continuation of the hiſtory of Man.

and some others of inferior note. The latter had Kintyre, Ila, and several more of the smaller Ebudes. The successors of these two brothers, while the kingdom of Man and the Isles remained in the hands of Norwegian Princes, like these their allies, neighbours, and sometimes masters, assumed the highest titles, and made an extraordinary figure for many ages. We have already seen that John, the son of Dugal, the same who had revolted over to Alexander the Third, was dignified with the name of *King*. The posterity of Reginald had pretensions equally good to that appellation, and were more than equally able to support them. They accordingly bore the regal title for a long time. While the more immediate descendants of Sumerled possessed the *Sodorian Isles*, with a kind of royal jurisdiction, the *Nordureys*, or the isles to the North of Ardnamurchan, were governed by the viceroys sent thither by the Kings of Man. These viceroys or governors were generally the sons, or brothers, or kinsmen of the reigning Princes. Of one of those lieutenants are descended the *Mac Leods* ; a family once very powerful in the Northern division of the Ebudes. Their descent from the Kings of Man appears not only from tradition, and the genealogical tables of the sennachies, but likewise from the arms of the family ; one branch of the two into which it has been divided, above five centuries back, retaining the *three united legs*, and the other *a ship with its sails furled*.

BESIDES the petty Kings and powerful chieftains sprung from Sumerled and the Nordureian governors, there were, in the two several divisions of the Western Isles, many considerable families ;

some

ſome of a Scottiſh extraction, and others originally
Norwegians.   At the head of each of theſe families was a perſon of high dignity and importance among his own people.   His ordinary title
was *Tierna*, or *Armin*, two words of much the
ſame ſignification ; the firſt of them belonging to
the Galic tongue, the ſecond to the Teutonic.
We learn from Torfæus and the Highland ſennachies, as well as from many paſſages in the Chronicle of Man, that theſe *Tierns* or *Armins*, called
frequently the great men of the Iſles in that Chronicle, were much employed in the adminiſtration
of public affairs, and of the utmoſt conſequence
at the time of electing Kings and governors.

It appears from an expreſs article of the pacification of Perth, above inſerted, that Magnus
took care to ſecure the eſtates, privileges and
rights of all the great men in the Iſles, whether
petty Kings, Chieftains, or Armins.   It was provided in the ſame article, that theſe great men,
and all the other inhabitants of the iſles, ſhould
be ſubject to the Kings of Scotland, and governed
by the laws and cuſtoms of that realm for ever.
But to me there ſeems to be no great temerity in
affirming, that the Iſles were almoſt entirely independent of the Scottiſh empire, and totally unre-
ſtrained by its laws for about two centuries after
that tranſaction.   The lords and great chieftains
were abſolute monarchs within their little principalities : all the laws known among their people
were, the arbitrary will and pleaſure of their
maſters, the deciſions of ignorant brehons, the
canons made by their prieſts, abbots and biſhops,
ſome ſtrange cuſtoms deſcended to them from
their anceſtors the Caledonians, and ſome feudal
inſtitutions left among them by the Norwegians.

I T

I T does not appear that the great men of the
Ifles paid any pecuniary taxes to the government
of Scotland during the period I have mentioned,
or joined their arms with their fovereign againft
his enemies, till after the middle of the fifteenth
century. The deftructive wars, foreign and domeftic, in which the whole nation was miferably
involved during that time, put a ftop to almoft all
legal proceedings in the heart of the kingdom,
and much more in remote corners. Amidft thefe
diftractions, and the difrefpect to laws neceffarily
attending them, it could not have been expected
that Iflanders, who enjoyed a fort of regal authority at home, and had nothing to fear from
abroad, would have fpontaneoufly burdened themfelves, or their people, with any public duties.
Upon the whole, it is hard to fay how far King
Alexander III. eftablifhed his authority in the Ifles;
and after the death of that excellent Prince, and
while the fatal difputes confequent upon it did remain, the Sodorian and Nordureian lords had the
beft opportunities they could defire of enlarging
their power, and rendering themfelves independent.

A N G U S, Lord of the Ifles, was led by political reafons, as well as by motives of a more laudable kind, to engage in the caufe of Robert
Bruce. When that illuftrious Prince, after the
unhappy battle of *Methven*, had fled into the
Weftern Highlands, purfued by the force of an
Englifh Monarch, extremely formidable, and unable to fecure a fafe retreat in any other part of
his own dominions, Angus received him into his
caftle of Saddle, protected him there for fome
time, and furnifhed him with boats, to tranfport
himfelf,

himself, and his small party of trusty friends, into an obscure isle on the coast of Ireland.

WHEN fortune began to smile a little on the royal adventurer, Angus assisted him with the utmost alacrity in recovering his paternal estate of Carrick ; and when every thing was at stake for the last time, the honour and life of his sovereign, the freedom and independency of his country, the existence of his friends and fellow patriots, all in the most imminent danger of being swallowed up by a prodigious army of foreigners, he joined him at Bannockburn with five thousand men, say the Highland sennachies, and did him a most substantial service upon that occasion.

AFTER Robert had fully established his authority in every part of his dominions, he gave to Angus several marks of an extraordinary regard. However sensible the King might have been that it was highly impolitic to increase the power of a lord of the Isles, he bestowed on his old friend, perhaps from a principle of gratitude, a considerable part of the estates formerly belonging to the Cummins of Lochaber and MacDougals of Lorn, two families that had deserved very ill of him, and had for that reason been forfeited.

THE grandson of this Angus, John, lord of the Isles, adopting a very different system, abandoned the interest of David Bruce, and espoused the cause of Edward Baliol. Having obtained from that Prince, while acting the part of a Scottish King, a right to all or most of the Ebudes, after vindicating that right by the superiority of his strength, he began to aspire after a regal authority at home, and in pursuance of that design, entered into a formal alliance with that powerful

Prince,

Prince, Edward the Third of England. But returning afterwards to his allegiance to his natural sovereign, Robert the Second of Scotland confirmed all the rights of his family, whether old or recent, and gave him his daughter in marriage.——Donald his son of that marriage was the famous Lord of the Isles, who added the earldom of Rofs to the vast poffeffions left by his anceftors, fought the battle of Harlaw, to defend that acquifition, against the duke of Albany's army, and maintained his title, in spite of all the efforts made by thofe in the adminiftration of that time.

The two immediate fucceffors of Donald were either too powerful to be loyal fubjects, or too much the objects of public jealoufy and private refentment to be left in the undifturbed poffeffion of their overgrown eftates. John, the laft of thefe great lords, provoked by injuries received from the court of Scotland, either really or in imagination, deluded at the fame time out of his duty by the Douglaffes, and bribed withal by Edward the Fourth of England, who took care to feed his immoderate ambition with the ampleft promifes, exerted his whole ftrength in fubverting the eftablifhed government of his country, and in the end proved the ruin of his own family's greatnefs. He loft the earldom of Rofs, together with many other confiderable tracts of land which he had poffeffed in different parts of the Continent, and was of courfe reduced to a mediocrity of fortune, which difabled him effectually from being any longer formidable. The other chieftains and great men of the Isles, who had been long the obfequious vaffals, or at beft the impotent neighbours of Sumerled's pofterity, embraced fo favourable

an

an opportunity of afferting their liberties, procured new rights to their eftates from the crown, and
became from that time forth ufeful fubjects.

THIS vaft diminution of that almoft unbounded
power, of which the lords of the Ifles had been
poffeffed for fome ages, happened in the reign of
James the Third, and after the middle of the fifteenth century.

DISSER-

DISSERTATION XVII.

Of some Monuments of Antiquity in the Western Islands of Scotland.   Occasional Observations upon the Genius, Manners, and Customs, of the Hebridian Scots of the Middle Ages.

THE counties of Dumbarton and Argyle, were the theatre of the first campaign of Julius Agricola in Caledonia.   It is therefore probable, that considerable detachments of the Roman army passed over from the continent into some of the Southern Ebudes.   It may likewise be taken for granted, that Agricola's fleet, in its return to South Britain, through the Deucaledonian Sea, was more than once under a necessity of refitting in some of the many excellent harbours of the Northern Ebudes.   But whether the Romans took any long stay in those places or not, it is certain that they have not left any monuments of antiquity there.   The Norwegians and Druids are the only people who have left the least vestige of themselves behind them in those islands.

THE

THE circles of ftones fo often mentioned by Offian, and fo frequent in the northern Ebudes, were the works of the Pictifh Druids, and though fimple in their conftruction, are not unworthy of the attention of the curious. They were the temples in which the old heathenifh priefts, employed by our anceftors in the fervice of their idols, performed the moft folemn offices of their fuperftition. There are many of thefe temples to be met with in the Eaftern Ebuda of Ptolomy, now called the Ifle of Sky. In the language of the country they are generally called Druidical houfes ; and though the inhabitants have but a very confufed idea of Druidifm, ftill they agree in calling the circles holy places, and fometimes give them the name of temples *.

THAT the Caledonians, as well as other Celtic nations, worfhipped the fun under the name of Grannius, admits of no doubt. An infcription, not many years fince dug out of the ruins of the Roman prætenture between the friths of Forth and Clyde, is a demonftration that the fun was one of the deities of Caledonia. Grannius is

---

* About half a century back, a farmer in the ifle of Sky imagined he had very good reafons for removing his houfes from that part of his farm where they formerly ftood, to another part which he found had been once occupied by the Druids, and was confequently more aufpicious. The farmer was remarkably induftrious, and had of courfe more than ordinary fuccefs in his bufinefs. The confequence of his fuccefs was, that almoft all his neighbours removed their houfes to the confecrated hillocks and circles which tradition had named, after the Druids, nor would they permit the leaft ftone in thefe temples to be touched for fear of difobliging the genius of the place ; fo unconquerable are the remains of a once prevalent fuperftition.

manifeftly

manifestly derived from *Grian* *, the Galic word for the sun. That thofe circles of stone I have mentioned were constructed for the worship of the sun seems to me evident, from a circumstance communicated to me by a learned friend in the county of Invernefs.

In the confines between two districts of that county, called Badenoch and Strathfpey, is a very extenfive and barren heath, through which the river Spey runs. On this heath are still to be feen entire, many of thofe Druidical circles of stone. The name of the heath is Slia-ghrannas, which, literally tranflated, is the *heath of Grannius*. No perfon in that country underftood the etymon of *Slia-ghrannas*, till my friend paffed that way. The country round about this place was called of old, and by fome of the vulgar to this day, *Ghriantochd*, or the country of *Grannius*. Some people imagined that *Ghriantochd* had its name from a Highland clan called *Grants*, who poffefs that country. To me it appears much more probable that the Grants, in Galic called *Griantich*, had their name from the country, and not from a pretended *Legrand*, as the genealogifts of that tribe affirm.

In fome parts of the continent of Scotland, the Druidical holy places confift of two or three circles which have the fame common center, and

---

* Grian feems to me to be derived from *Gre* or *Gne*, fignifying the *nature*, and *thein*, the oblique cafe of *tein*, fire. In the Galic language, a confonant before an *h* or afpiration is always quiefcent, fo that *Gre thein* muft be pronounced *Gre-ein*, i. e. *The effence* or *natural fource of fire*. Should this etymon appear unjuft, the editor, and not the author of the Differtations, is to be blamed for it.

greatly

greatly refemble, though in miniature, the famous
Stonehenge in Salifbury plains. I have not feen
any fuch double or triple circumvallations in the
iflands, but have more than once obferved one
ftone broader than any one of thofe which form the
circle, ftand detached from it at a certain diftance,
This broad ftone is placed towards the Eaft, with
a cavity in the top, and a fiffure either natural or
artifical in one of its fides : thefe hollows were
perhaps intended for receiving the libations offered
to their Gods. The largeft ftones in the circumference of the Druidical circles, which I had occafion to fee in the Weftern iflands are about
three feet and a half above the ground, and near
three feet broad. The diameter of the greateft
area is about thirty feet. There is fomething
agreeably romantic in the fituations chofen for
thefe temples. The fcene is frequently melancholy
and wild, the profpect is extenfive but not diver-
fified. A fountain and the noife of a diftant river
were always efteemed as requifite neighbours for
thofe feats of dark and enthufiaftic religion.

Those large heaps of ftones which are called
Cairns in Scotland, Ireland, and Wales, are very
numerous in the Ebudes. There are no lefs than
feven fuch piles within the confines of a little village in the ifle of Sky. All cairns are not of a
fimilar conftruction. Thofe which depart moft
from the common form are called *Barpinin,* in
the language of the country ; thefe refemble the
barrows of England. The word *Barp* or *Barrow*
is originally Norwegian. *Cairn* is a Britifh word,
which fignifies a heap of ftones, either lying together in the greateft confufion, or piled up in
fome fort of order. I have feen fome of thefe heaps

that

that are three hundred feet in circumference at the bafe, and about 20 feet perpendicular in heighth. They are formed conically, and confift of ftones of almoft all fizes, as chance or the materials of the place directed. They lie generally near fmall arms of the fea which run into the land and receive rivers. They are always placed near the common road, and upon rifing grounds. The motives which induced the builders to rear up thefe piles in fuch places, were the advantage of the ftones, and a defire of exciting the traveller's admiration, and devotion. Various have been the opinions of the learned concerning the intention of thofe *Cairns*, and concerning the people by whom they were collected. Some will have them to have been made by way of trophies, or with a view of perpetuating the memory of heroes flain in battle. Some conjecture that they were monuments erected by wayfaring men in honour of Mercury, the protector of travellers. Others fancy that they were feats of judicature for the old Brehons : and others are of opinion that they were the eminences on which our old Kings ftood after their election ; fo as to exhibit themfelves to the multitude. One or two critics have imagined that they were no more than boundaries which divided the eftate of one great Lord from that of another : and many have thought that they were intended only for burial places.

THE laft of thefe opinions is undoubtedly the jufteft. The fepulchral urns always found in every Cairn that has been hitherto examined, are fufficient to demonftrate the truth of it. Thefe urns are depofited in large ftone coffins, which lie in the center of the barrow. The coffin confifts of fix rude flat ftones ; one in the bottom, two in the

fides,

fides, two more in the ends, aud another larger one above. There is fometimes a kind of obelifk which overtops the barrow, and ftands at the head of the coffin. The coffins are generally more than fix feet long, and the urns which they contain are half full of afhes and bones. The workmanfhip of thefe veffels is rather coarfe than otherwife *.

IT is a queftion whether the Cairns were reared by the Norwegians or old Britains of Caledonia: there are Cairns in the different parts of the continent of Scotland, particularly in the Highland diftricts of the counties of Aberdeen and Invernefs, into which neither the Norwegians nor Danes ever penetrated. Befides, the mountains of Carnarvonfhire have many monuments of the fame kind. It is therefore evident, that the old Britains erected fome of thefe fabrics; nor can it be affirmed that

---

* It is not above fifty years fince the Iflanders underftood that the barrows were the repofitories of the dead. Much about that time a gentleman in one of the ifles having occafion for ftones to build a houfe, broke down one of thefe old fabrics, and coming to the bottom of it, near the center, lighted on the large flat ftone which formed the cover of the coffin. Upon comparing a current tradition with the contrivance of the ftones, and the found emitted from them, he immediately concluded that here was a ftone cheft which contained a quantity of hidden treafure: full of this agreeable fancy, and dreading much at the fame time that a perfon of much greater authority in the country would infallibly deprive him of the treafure, if the fecret fhould once tranfpire, he obl'ged the workmen, by the interpofition of a moft folemn oath, to conceal the happy difcovery. After this point was fettled, and a reafonable dividend promifed to every one of the workmen, the coffin was opened with due care: but the treafure found in it gave very little fatisfaction, being no more than a fmall quantity of afhes contained in a yellow-coloured earthen veffel.

the

the Norwegians were ſtrangers to the ſame art. We are told by Pomponius Mela, that the Druids burned and interred the bodies of their departed friends *. And Sir James Ware quotes a paſſage from an ancient book of cannons, from which it appears that the old Iriſh buried their dead in the ſame manner.

We learn from the epitaph of the robber, Baliſta, and from ſeveral paſſages in other ancient authors, that malefactors were ſometimes buried under heaps of ſtones. It is certain that the barrows in the iſles were intended for illuſtrious perſons, or thoſe of the higheſt dignity among the people. The expence of time and labour, to which theſe huge piles muſt have ſubjected the builders, together with the coffins and urns found within them, leave no room for a doubt in this matter. In one of theſe barrows which I ſaw broke open, there were found four different coffins placed at ſome diſtance from a larger one in the centre. Each of theſe contained an urn with aſhes and ſome half burnt bones. The coffin or cheſt in the middle was certainly the repoſitory of a great Chieftain or King, and thoſe around belonged to perſons who were either his near relations, or heroes of a leſs exalted character.

There is a proverbial expreſſion common in the Highlands and iſlands to this day, from which we may form a conjecture of the manner of erecting theſe piles, and the uſe for which they were intended. The expreſſion is, *I ſhall add a ſtone to your Cairn* †; that is to ſay, I ſhall do your

---

memory all the honour in my power, when you are no more. I shall contribute to raise your monument. This is the language of petitioners, when sensible the favours they ask cannot in all probability be sufficiently acknowledged till after the benefactor's death. The religious belief of these times obliged every pious traveller to add a stone to the pile of the dead. The larger the stone the more to the honour of the departed spirit which was thought to hover around his heap, and to rejoice over the piety of the traveller. If the Cairn belonged to a man of distinguished merit, who died in the cause of his tribe, or was reared in memory of a famous bard, the whole community came on appointed days to increase the pile, and send it down with lustre to posterity. Hence we may account for the bulk of those little hills, tho' reared in times when carriages and mechanical engines of all kinds were little known.

Among all the monuments of antiquity found in the Western Islands, the ruinous forts, so frequent there, deserve the first notice. The irregular and uncommon construction, the similarity of their magnificent situations, and the almost unintelligible peculiarities of their workmanship, seem to render them very curious objects for antiquaries.

These forts are, in the language of the isles, called *Duns*, in that of the Norwegians, *Burghs*, and in the Irish, *Raths*. The first of these names is a Celtic word, which signifies a hill or eminence in almost all languages *. It was customary among the ancient nations to build their castles or places of defence upon high grounds, in order to

* See Bull. Dict. Celt. vol. i. p. 2.

discover

discover the enemy before he approached, and to repel his assaults with greater facility. When the inconveniences of such situations appeared, the places of defence were built in low grounds; but they still retained the old names of *Duns, Raths, Burgs* or *Bergs* *.

I T will be no easy matter to prove that the Caledonians, Piéts, or ancient Scots of Britain, had stone edifices of any kind. The case was the same with the Irish, till after the Normans were settled among them: and before Alfred's time there was scarce a royal palace, or a house for divine worship in England, built of any other materials than timber †.

Some perhaps will be surprized to hear that the piratical nations of Scandinavia should have understood any one of the arts of polished life better than our anceſtors. It is unqueſtionably certain, that the oldeſt forts on the Weſtern and Northern coaſts of Scotland were erećted by the barbarians of the Northern Europe. Tradition has hitherto preserved the names of several Norwegian chiefs, who built the moſt conſiderable forts in the E-budes ‡.

All the Norwegian towers in the Ebudes were of a circular form. The old square caſtles there are of a much later date. Thoſe Norwegians who built theſe towers muſt have underſtood the art of

---

* Casaubon, in his notes upon ſtrabo, obſerves that the Πύργος of the Greeks, the *Burg* of the Germans, and the *Brica* of the Spaniards, all ſignify a *Hill*, in their original ſignifications; ſo *Arx*, in Latin ſigniſied the top of a hill, as well as a caſtle.

+ Aſſerius.

‡ *Kynninburg, Kernburg, Boſewick.*

T 3

quarrying

quarrying, forming, and laying ſtones, in great perfection, and have uſed mechanical powers of which the iſlanders of late ages have no conception. The expence of working and carrying the ſtones to the very ſummit of a high hill, or to the edge of a dreadful precipice, through almoſt impaſſable paths, muſt have been very conſiderable, and indeed ſuperior to what can well be imagined. One of the forts which I had occaſion to view, ſtands on the edge of a rock which hangs over the ocean, and is of an amazing height. The other ſide of the rock againſt which you approach the fort, is a ſteep aſcent of more than half a mile, and all the ſtones which compoſed the fort muſt have been carried up that hill. This fort is in the Southern extremity of the iſland of Barra.

MANY of theſe ſtructures are ſtill pretty intire, and almoſt every one of them is ſituated upon a hill, commanding a very extenſive proſpect, or upon a ſmall iſland of difficult acceſs, or upon a precipice every way hideous. As they were deſtined for watch towers, as well as for places of ſtrength, they are built and connected through irregular diſtances, every one of them is in ſight of another, and they follow the windings of the ſea coaſt and valleys. The Norwegians being foreigners, and conſequently under continual apprehenſions either from the natives, or from the Scots of the continent, took care to contrive theſe fortreſſes, ſo as that the alarm in caſe of an invaſion might run immediately from one diviſion of the country to another. On ſuch occaſions they raiſed great pillars of ſmoke in the day time, by ſetting fire to a great quantity of combuſtible

matter,

matter, and at night made signals of distress by burning whole barrels of pitch.

The most curious fabric of the Norwegian kind that is to be seen in any part of the Highlands or islands is in Glenelg, within two miles of the firth which divides that part of the continent from the isle of Sky. This fabric is of a circular form, about thirty four feet high, and includes an area thirty feet in diameter. The wall is double : the inner one stands perpendicular, and that without falls in gently till it unites with the other near the top of what may be called the first story. The opening between the two walls is four feet broad at the bottom, and each of the walls is four feet in thickness; so that both, including the aperture between them, are twelve feet thick at the foundation. The stones are large and better chosen and more judiciously laid than can be well conceived. There is neither lime nor any other kind of cement in the walls, and the stones are indeed placed with so much art, and so beautifully inserted into one another, that none was necessary.

Between the two walls there are laid in a position nearly horizontal, different rows of large thick flat stones which were at first near as close to one another as the deal-boards of a floor. These united stones go all the way round the edifice, and form so many different stories of unequal heights, from six to four feet; the one story rising above the other to the part where the two walls meet. A gentleman * of that country, to whose knowledge and industry I am indebted on this subject, informed me that some of the old men in the

---

* The reverend Mr. Donald MacLeod.

T 4

country,

country who faw this Dun intire, were of opinion that the rows of flat ftones afcended in a fpiral line round the building, and fupplied a communication within the walls from the foundation to the top.

WHERE the two walls join, there is a regular row of large flat ftones four inches thick, which project horizontally towards the area, from the face of the inner wall. ·There was another row of fimilar ftones which projected in the fame manner, about eight feet above the lower tire. But the barbarity of a military man employed by the government in that country, has deftroyed this curious monument of antiquity. In this whole building nothing is more curious than the rows of windows, or window-like-apertures in the inner wall. They rife in a direct line above each other, from the bottom to the fummit of the ftructure: two of them are detached from the reft, and begin at the diftance of about thirteen feet from the foundation. It appears that there have been fix rows of the windows firft mentioned, all of the fame breadth, that is a foot and a half, but unequal in the heights, fome of them being but two, and others three feet high. There is no appearance of a window in the outer wall, nor of any other opening excepting the door, which communicates with a little circular ftone fabric called the Houfe of the Druids.

IT muft be confeffed that there are fome things in the conftruction of this and the other old towers in the iflands which cannot eafily be underftood. It is likely that the feveral wide fpaces which lay between the two walls were defigned for ftorehoufes, beds, and places of arms; but

it

it is difficult to say what might have been the intention of the windows or openings in the inner side of the walls, and of the circle of flat stones which projects from the top towards the area.

We cannot learn by tradition, or otherwise, that these buildings were ever covered above. The men had small huts within the areas, and the governor had a kind of hall for his particular use. The walls had battlements of one kind or other, to which there was an ascent either by ladders or through the passages in the middle. In times of war a centinel stood constantly on the battlements in a kind of centry box; his business was to cry aloud at certain intervals, so as to convince the enemy without, that the fort was not to be taken by surprize. The Norwegians called this centinel *Gok-man*. He was obliged, by the rules of his office, to deliver all he had to communicate in extemporary rhymes. A large horn full of spirituous liquor stood always beside him to strengthen his voice and keep up his spirits. It is little more than half a century since this Norwegian custom was last observed in an old tower belonging to a Chieftain whose estate lay in one of the remotest of the Western Islands. Torfæus says *, that the great men of Norway employed such Gok-men, not only for giving the alarm in case of danger, but likewise to inform the generous lord of the castle if they spied a vessel in distress at sea.

The boats which were used by the ancient inhabitants of the Ebudæ, ought not to be forgot in describing their ancient curiosities. We are

---

* Rer. Orcad. Histor. p. 8.

told

told by Solinus, that the Britons and Irish committed themselves to the mercy of a tempestuous sea in wicker hulls covered with cow hides *. It is not above thirty years since one of those South British boats or curachs was used in the isle of Sky : and though the Norwegians had taught the Islanders the use of building boats with wood in a very early period, yet these curachs were the only kind which they employed on ordinary occasions, till within a century back.

Some of the ancient curachs must have been much larger than those seen in late ages. Marianus Scotus speaks of three devout Irishmen, who, upon having formed a resolution of leading a life of pilgrimage, left their country with great secresy, and taking with them provisions for a week, came in a boat made of skins, without sails or oars, after a navigation of seven days, into Cornwall. We are informed by Adamnan, that St. Cormack, another wrong-headed monk, who went from Iona to the Orkneys in quest of a proper hermitage, was with all his enthusiasm wise enough to keep oars in his curach ; by this precaution he got safely through the ocean. These curachs must have been of a tolerable size, otherwise the romantic passengers could never have made out their voyages.

The curach in which St. Columba came from Ireland into Iona, must have been little less than forty feet long, if the tradition hitherto preserved in that Island deserves credit. And we are told by Sidonius Appolinaris †, that it was no more than

---

* *Vimineis Alveis.*　　　　† Carm. vii.

matter
Mr. Cottington a young Gentleman of great w——
attempting to cross the Boyne near Drogheda

matter of amufement with the Saxon pirates of his time, to crofs the Britifh fea in fuch leathern veffels. Boats made of the fame materials, were very commonly ufed by other ancient nations, particularly by the Spaniards * and the Veneti near the Po †. It was in fuch tranfports that Cæfar wafted his men over the river Sicoris, before he attacked Pompey's lieutenants near Ilerda ‡.

BESIDES thefe wicker pinnaces, the ancient inhabitants of Caledonia had a kind of canoe in which they fifhed on rivers and frefh water lakes. This kind of canoe was hollowed out of a large tree, either with fire or tools of iron. In the Galic of Scotland, a boat of that make was called *Ammir* or trough, and *Cotti* in the language of Ireland. A few of thefe canoes are ftill to be feen in the Weftern Highlands: and Virgil was not perhaps far miftaken, when he imagined that the firft experiments in navigation were made in fuch bottoms ‖. It cannot be afferted that the Iflanders had galleys, or what they called long fhips, till the Norwegians were fettled among them. After that period they furely had fuch veffels, and in imitation of their mafters, rowed about in them in queft of plunder from fea to fea through almoft all the feafons of the year **.

THE hiftories of Scotland are full of the depredations committed by the Iflanders of the mid-

---

* Strabo.   † Georg. lib. iii.   ‡ Lucan Phar. l iv.
‖ Alnos primum fluvii fenfere cavatas. Georg. i.
** The fame practice took place among the ancient inhabitants of the Grecian iflands, foon after they knew how to conftruct galleys. Thucid. lib. i.

dle

dle and lower ages. The annals of Ireland complain loudly and frequently of the Hebridian *Red Shanks.* The petty Kings of Ireland were continually at war with enemies, either foreign or domeftic, and had conftant recourfe to the affiftance of the Hebridian Scots. Mercenary foldiers have been always remarkably rapacious, and by all accounts thefe Scots were not inferior in cruelty and barbarity to any foreign allies. Whenever they met with a repulfe in Ireland, they fled home in their fhips, and plundered the South Weft coafts of Caledonia in their way : fuch was the conduct and art which they imbibed from their Norwegian conquerors.

When the Hebridian chiefs and captains returned home after a fuccefsful expedition, they fummoned their friends and clients to a grand entertainment. Bards and fennachies flocked in from every quarter; pipers and harpers had an undifputed right to appear on fuch public occafions. Thefe entertainments were wi'd and chearful, nor were they unattended with the pleafures of the fentiments and unrefined tafte of the times. The bards fung, and the young women danced. The old warrior related the gallant actions of his youth, and ftruck the young men with ambition and fire. The whole tribe filled the Chieftain's hall. The trunks of trees covered with mofs were laid in the order of a table from one end of the hall to the other. Whole deer and beeves were roafted and laid before them on rough boards or hurdles of rods wove together. Their pipers played while they fat at table, and filence was obferved by all. After the feaft was over, they had ludicrous entertainments, of which fome are ftill acted in the Highlands.

Highlands. Then the females retired, and the old and young warriors fat down in order from the Chieftain, according to their proximity in blood to him. The harp was then touched, the fong was raifed, and the *Sliga-Crechin*, or the drinking fhell, went round.

It is a great queftion with the prefent Highlanders, what liquors were drunk at the feafts of their predeceflors. They find them frequently mentioned in their old fongs under various names; but it is univerfally allowed that they were of an intoxicating kind. We are told by Diofcorides, that the ancient Britons drank a ftrong liquor made of barley, which they called *Curmi*. This furely was the drink ufed by the Albanian Britons, and old Hebridian Scots; for in their language, to this day, every great feaft is called *Curme*, as in their apprehenfion drink is the very life of fuch entertainment. Some have imagined that the *Ufkebai*, the favourite liquor of the modern Highlanders, is the fame with the *Curmi* of their forefathers; and there can be no ftrong objection to this opinion. The Gauls ufed their *Cervifia* * ; the Germans their *Humor ex Hurdeo*; and all thefe liquors are evidently of the fame origin, and made of perhaps the fame materials. But however that may have been, it is certain that the Iflanders were furnifhed with ftrong drink in a very early period; nor were they fparing of it at their publick entertainments, whether of a feftal or funereal kind. Whenever the gueft was placed in his feat, he was obliged, by the fafhion of the land, to drink off a draught of their *Water of Life*, out

---

* Plin. Nat. Hift. lib. xxii. cap. 35.

of a large family cup or ſhell. This draught was in their language called a *Drink of Uſkebai :* and the gueſt had no ſooner finiſhed that potion than he was preſented with a crooked horn, containing about an Engliſh quart, of ale. If he was able to drink all that off at a time, he was rather highly extolled, than condemned in the leaſt for intemperance.

THE births of their great men were attended with no rejoicings or feaſting by the old Hebridians. But their funerals were celebrated with great pomp, and followed with magnificent entertainments : all the Chieftains of the neighbouring tribes attended on ſuch occaſions, and came accompanied with a numerous retinue of their firſt men, and all well armed. After inviting people of ſuch rank from their reſpective habitations to perhaps a diſtant iſland, it was incumbent on thoſe principally intereſted in the ſolemnity, to diſplay the utmoſt magnificence of expence.

AT the funeral proceſſion, the men belonging to the different Chieftains were regularly drawn up, taking their places according to the dignity of their leaders. They marched forward with a ſlow pace, and obſerved great decorum. A band of pipers followed the body, and in their turns played tunes, either made for that occaſion or ſuitable to it. Great multitudes of female mourners kept as near the coffin as poſſible, and made the moſt lamentable howlings, tearing their hair and beating their breaſts. Some of theſe, after the paroxyſms of their zeal or affected grief, had in ſome meaſure ſubſided, ſung the praiſes of the deceaſed in extemporary rhimes. The male relations and dependents thought it unmanly to ſhed tears, or at

leaſt

leaſt indecent to betray their want of fortitude in public *.

IF there were any characteriſtical diverſities in genius, Manners, and cuſtoms, of the Iſlanders, when compared to their neighbours on the continent, they muſt have borrowed them from the Norwegians, who had been long their ſuperiors, and who of conſequence muſt have introduced their own taſte, faſhions, and laws, among them. Hence we may account for that diſpoſition and attachment which the inhabitants of the Ebudes diſcovered to piracy and poetry, in a ſuperior degree to any other tribe of the Albanian Scots.

---

* Fæminis lugere honeſtum eſt, viris meminiſſe. Tacitus de mor. Germ.

DISSER-

DISSERTATION XVIII.

Of the Scottish and Pictish Dominions, before they were united under one Sovereign.

H AVING shewn, in the course of the preceding differtations, that the Picts and Scots were the genuine pofterity of the Caledonians, though divided into feparate kingdoms, it is neceffary I fhould throw fome light on the extent of their refpective dominions. ———— That want of records which has involved their ancient hiftory in obfcurity, has alfo left us in the dark with regard to the real boundaries of their territories.

According to two ancient fragments of Scots hiftory, publifhed in the appendix to Innes's Critical Effay, Fergus, the fon of Erc, reigned over Albany, from *Drumalbin* to the fea of Ireland and Inchegall*. The fea of Ireland is a boundary well underftood. The Weftern iflands of Scotland, formerly the Ebudes of the Romans, are called

---

* De fitu Albaniæ, quæ in fe figuram hominis habet,

Inche

Inche Galle to this day. In the eighth century thofe iflands fell into the hands of the Norwegians, who, like all other foreigners, were called *Gauls* by the Highlanders of the Continent. *Inche* is an abbrevation of *Innis*, which in the Galic fignifies an Ifland ; fo that *Inchegalle*, literally tranflated, is the *Ifles of flrangers*. How far *Drumalbin*, the other boundary mentioned in the fragment, extends, is not yet determined by antiquarians.

THE word *Drumalbin*, literally tranflated, fignifies the *Ridge of Albany*. Agreeable to this interpretation, it is called by Adamnan, the writer of Columba's life, *Dorfum Britaniæ*, or a Chain of hills, according to the genius of the Latin tongue. Thefe hills have been confined to a principal branch of the Grampian mountains, which extends from the Eaftern to the Weftern Sea. But the true meaning of the name implies that this *Ridge of hills* muft have run from South to North, rather than from Eaft to Weft.

THE anonymous author of another fmall piece concerning the ancient hiftory of Scotland, was, according to his own teftimony, informed by Andrew bifhop of Caithnefs, who flourifhed in the twelfth century, that Albany was of old divided into feven kingdoms. All thefe petty kingdoms are defcribed, and their boundaries fettled pretty exactly. The two laft of thofe dynafties mentioned in that fragment are the kingdom of Murray, including Rofs, and the kingdom of *Arragatheil* *. According to Cambden and Ufher, the territories of the more ancient Scots were confined within

---

* Sextum regnum fuit Murray et Rofs. Septimum regnum fuit Arregaithel.

U

Cantyre,

Cantyre, Knapdale, Argyle, Braidalbain, and fome of the Weftern Iflands. Cambden believed too precipitately, that Iona was made over to Columba by Brudius, King of the Picts.

ADAMNAN, who wrote the hiftory of the life of Columba, and was himfelf abbot of Iona, relates, that the faint was courteoufly received by Conal, King of the Scots. As Adamnan has been very minute in his hiftory, it is far from being probable that he would forget Brudius, had he given fuch a benefaction to Columba.

THE author of the Critical Effay is more liberal to the Scots than Cambden and Ufher, and extends their ancient territories to a branch of the Grampian mountain which runs all the way from Athol to the fea coaft of Knodort*. But as he had very juftly expofed the miftake of Bede with regard to Iona, and as it does not appear from any other author, that either Brudius or any other Pictifh King poffeffed a foot of ground from the Glotta to the Tarvifium of the ancients, he might have given all the North-weft coaft, from Clyde to Dunfbyhead, as alfo the Cathanefia of his anonymous author, to the kingdom of *Arreghael*.

THE Galic name *Arreghael*, or rather *Jarghael* †, was, in the Latin of later ages, changed into Ergadia : and it appears from a charter granted by the Earl of Rofs, and confirmed by Robert the Second of Scotland, that *Garloch*, a diftrict which lies at a confiderable diftance from Knodort, to the North, was a part of Ergadia ‡. It is like-

---

* Near the Ifle of Sky in Invernefs-fhire.

† See a note on the word Jar-ghael, page 16.

‡ Confirmatio donationis Comitis Roffiæ Paullo Mactyre de terra de Gerloch, anno fecundo Roberti II.

wife

wife apparent, from the charters given by King Robert Bruce, to Thomas Randulph, Earl of Murray, that all the Weftern Continent, from Lochaber to *Eaft Rofs*, was comprehended within the Ergadia of the antients.

We learn from Bede ‡, that in the year 603, Ædan, King of the Britifh Scots, came againft Ordilfred, King of the Northumbrians, at the head of a very numerous and gallant army ‖. In the genealogical feries of the Scottifh Kings given by Innes, from his authentic Chronicles, Ædan, or Aidan, is the great grandfon of Fergus Mac-Eirc. It is difficult to underftand how this King of Scots could have muftered up fuch a vaft army againft the Saul of the Englifh nation *, if his territories were pent up within the fmall principality of Cambden's *Arreghael*, or even the Ergadia of Innes. So far were the Picts from lending any affiftance to the Scots, that they were engaged in a clofe confederacy with the Saxons of that time.

The Britons, it is true, were allies to Aidan, but they deferted him in the very crifis of this war. He certainly could not have any auxiliaries from Ireland, as Bede pofitively fays that the Irifh never committed any acts of hoftility againft the Englifh ; on the contrary, that they always cultivated an inviolable friendfhip with them. We therefore have reafon to believe that Aidan's numerous army muft have entirely confifted of his own fubjects; and confequently that his dominions

---

‡ Hift. Ecclef. cap. 24.
‖ Cum immenfo et forti exercitu.
* Adamn. Vita Columbæ. lib. 2.

com-

comprehended at leaſt all the Weſtern coaſt of Scotland, together with the biſhops *Carthaneſia.*

BRUDIUS, the Piƈtiſh King, who was converted to the Chriſtian faith by Columba, had a kind of royal ſeat at Inverneſs. This appears from the accounts given by Adamnan, in the life of that ſaint. From the ſituation of this royal reſidence we may conclude, that Murray, and very probably Roſs, which was of old annexed to that diviſion of Albany, made a part of the Piƈtiſh kingdom.

COLUMBA, in his journey to the palace of King Brudius, travelled over Drumalbin, or Adamnan's Dorſum Britaniæ. It is impoſſible to tell whether the ſaint went direƈtly from Iona, or from a more Northerly part of thoſe Weſtern diſtriƈts which were under his juriſdiƈtion. But as there is a ridge of high hills all the way from Glengary, where Loch Neſs terminates*, to the Frith of Taine, it is far from being improbable that Drumalbin extended that far, and that the kingdoms of the Scots and Piƈts were ſeparated by the frith and hills juſt mentioned.

ALL our hiſtorians have agreed that the inhabitants of Murray were a ſeditious and diſloyal race of men, for ſeveral ages after the Scots had reduced Piƈtavia. They rebelled frequently againſt the poſterity of Malcolm Canemore. One of thoſe Princes found himſelf under the neceſſity of tranſplanting that turbulent people into different parts of his kingdom. But it may be inferred, from

---

* Brudius had his ſeat at the end of this lake.

the

the impatience with which they lived under the yoke of a new government, that they were of the Pictifh nation, and confequently that the dominions of that people extended much farther towards the North than fome of the Scottifh hiftorians are willing to allow.

THE Picts and Saxons were alternately mafters of *Laudonia*, or thofe more Eafterly countries which lie between the frith of Edinburgh and the river Tweed. We learn from Bede, that Ofwin, brother to St. Ofwald, and the feventh King of the Northumbrians, fubdued the Pictifh nation in a great meafure, and made them tributary †. This Prince began his reign in the year 642. His fon Egfrid having formed a refolution to carry his conquefts beyond the Forth, invaded the Pictifh territories, and was cut off, with the greateft part of his army, in the year 685. A victory fo decifive produced great confequences, The Picts of that age recovered what their predeceffors had loft. The Eaftern counties, or *Laudonia*, fell immediately into their hands.

IT appears from Bede, that the Saxons continued mafters of Galloway, when he finifhed his Ecclefiaftical Hiftory. He gives an account of *Candida Cafa*, or whitehorn, where a bifhop of the Saxon nation was inftalled in his time. After Bede's death, the Picts recovered Galloway likewife, or made a conqueft of it ; fo that before the extinction of their monarchy, all the territories, bounded on the one fide by the Forth and Clyde, and on the other by the Tweed and Solway, fell into their hands.

---

† Bed. Hift. Ecclef. lib. 2. cap. 5.

UPON

Upon the whole, it seems evident, that the antient Scots, some time before the conquest of Pictavia, possessed all that side of Caledonia which lies along the North and Western ocean, from the frith of Clyde to the Orkneys. Towards the East, their dominions were divided, in all appearance. from the Pictish dominions, by those high mountains which run all the way from Lochlomond, rear Dumbarton, to the frith of Taine, which separates the county of Sutherland from a part of Rofs; and those high hills which pass through the middle of Rofs, are very probably a part of the antient Drumalbin.

DISSER-

DISSERTATION XIX.

Of the Religion of the antient Caledonians.

SOME ingenious writers have been of opinion that Druidifm was never eftablifhed in Caledonia. It is difficult to fay, why aſſertions ſo ill-founded were obtruded upon the world, if it was not to deduce the honour of the prefent prevalent ſyſtem of free-thinking from our remoteſt anceſtors. Irreligion is never one of the virtues of favage life : we muſt defcend to polifhed times for that fcepticifm which arifes from the pride and vanity natural to the cultivated ſtate of the human mind. It is not now my bufineſs to enter into a controverfy with thoſe who affirm that religion is no more than an engine of policy, and that the gods of all nations fprung from the timidity of the multitude in the firſt ſtages of fociety.

HAD the inhabitants of Britain rofe originally like vegetables out of the earth, according to the opinion of Cæfar and Tacitus, there might have been fome foundation for fuppofing that the Druidical ſyſtem of religion was never known in Cale-

U 4

donia.

donia. But as it is generally allowed that the inhabitants of both the divisions of Britain deduced their
origin from nations on the Continent, it is reasonable to think that they carried along with them the
gods of their anceftors, in their tranfmigration to
this ifland.

THAT the Caledonians, in the time of Julius
Agricola, were not totally diftitute of religion,
appears from a paffage in the fpeech which Tacitus
puts into the mouth of Galgacus; in which that
chieftain mentions both gods and a providence.
The celebrated writer alfo obferves, that after the
Caledonians were worfted in the firft action with
the Romans, far from being intimidated, or cured
of their own felf-fufficiency, they formed a refolution to renew the war with greater vigour. For
this purpofe, fays Tacitus, they armed their young
men, placed their wives and children in places of
fafety, fummoned their feveral communities together, held public affemblies, entered into con-
federacies, and confirmed their engagements with
facrifices and the blood of victims *.

DRUIDISM was certainly the original religion of
all the branches of the Celtic nation : yet Cæfar
obferves, that the Germans, who undoubtedly were
principally defcended from the great Celtic ftock,
had no druids among them. We have reafon
to differ in opinion from that great man. Cæfar
was too much ingroffed with his own vaft projects,
to enter minutely into the theological inftitutions
of the Germans. Tacitus, who made the cuftoms
and manners of Germany his particular ftudy, in-

***

* Cœ ibus et facrificiis confpirationem civitatem fancire.

forms us that priests possessed great influence in that country.

D R U I D, or rather *Druthin*, is originally a Teutonic word. Its meaning is, the servant of God, or the servant of *Truth* : *Dru* or *Tru* signify *God* or *Truth* indiscriminately. It is certain that every German priest was called *Dry*, and the Saxons of England brought that word from Germany into Britain.—The English Saxons, before their conversion to Christianity, worshipped, it is apparent, the ancient Gods of Gaul, and nearly under the same names. The *Tuisco*, or *Tuisto* of Germany, to whom the Saxons dedicated *Tuesday*, was the same with the *Teutates* of Gaul ; and the Thor of the Saxons was the Taranis of the ancient Gauls.

THE meaning of Teutates is GOD THE FATHER OF ALL BEINGS : *Dyu*, in the ancient British, which was undoubtedly the same with the language of Gaul, signifies *God*; and *Tad*, or *Tat*, in the Armorican dialect, is, to this day, the word for Father. The *Thor* of the Celto-Scythians of Germany was, as I observed before, the *Taranis* of their neighbours to the South. In the ancient language of the Scots, both the names of this divinity are retained to this day, with a small variation of the final syllables. *Torran*, among the Highlanders, is the lower muttering of thunder, and *Tarninach* * signifies the loudest peals of that awful noise.

---

* Tarninach is probably a corruption of *Nd'air neamhnach*, or *Tarnearnach*, as it is pronounced, literally signifying *Heavenly Father*; thunder being thought the voice of the supreme Divinity. Or perhaps it may be derived from *Torneonach* literally an *uncommon and wonderful noise:* or from *Nd'air-neonach*, the *Wrathful Father*.

THIS

THIS identity of religion which prevailed among the ancient Germans and Gauls, is a proof that tribes of the latter were the prevalent colonies of Germany. The Tectofages, a people of Gallia Norbonenfis, poffeffed themfelves, according to Cæfar, of the moft fertile regions of Germany. The Boii and Helvetii, nations fprung from the Gaulifh ftock, made very confiderable acquifitions near the Hercynian foreft. The Suevi were the moft powerful nation in Germany. Of the feveral tribes into which the Suevi were divided, the Senones pretended to be the moft noble and the moft ancient. Their pretenfions to antiquity Tacitus fupports with an argument arifing from the genius of their religion.

" AT a ftated time," faith the excellent hifto-
" rian, all thofe who have derived their blood
" from the Senones meet, in the perfons of their
" reprefentatives or ambaffadors. This affembly
" is held in a wood, confecrated by the auguries
" of their predeceffors, and the fuperftitious fears
" of former ages. In this wood, after having
" publickly facrificed fome unhappy man, they
" commemorate the horrible beginnings of their
" barbarous idolatry." In this paffage every one may fee the ftrongeft features of Druidifm, paint-ed in the moft lively colours, and placed in the cleareft point of light. It is unneceffary to obferve, that the Senones, who fent colonies into Italy and Germany, were originally a people of Gaul, and fettled near the Seine.

DURING the reign of Tarquinius Prifcus, that is, five hundred years before Cæfar was born, Am-bigatus, King of the Celtic Gaul, finding that his territories were greatly overftocked with inhabi-tants,

tants, fent his two nephews, Bellovefus and Sigovefus, at the head of two powerful armies, in
queft of fettlements in foreign countries. The
province allotted by the Augurs to Bellovefus was
Italy, and that to Sigovefus was the Hercynian
foreft.—Livy has preferved this piece of hiftory;
and according to Cæfar himfelf, the great univerfity and metrepolitical feat of Druidifm lay in the
country of the Carnates; the fame Carnates whom
Livy places among the fubjects of Ambigatus.

We have no reafon to believe, notwithftanding
Cæfar's authority to the contrary, that there was
any effential difference between the religion of
Gaul and that of Germany. The victorious Boii,
the Helvetii, the Tectofages and Senones, the
Celtic nations of Sigovefus, and more efpecially
his Carnates, could not have either forgot or defpifed their own religion, upon fettling themfelves
in a foreign country. They certainly would not
have difmiffed the Gods under whofe aufpices they
had been fo fuccefsful. The conquerors muft
rather be naturally fuppofed to have eftablifhed
their own fpiritual inftitutions upon the ruins
of thofe which had done fo little fervice to the
conquered.

It is univerfally agreed that Druidifm was eftablifhed in South Britain. The fuperintendant of
the whole order, it has been faid, refided there:
and we learn from Cæfar, that thofe who ftudied
to underftand the deepeft myfteries of that fuperftition, travelled into Britain. Whether the moft
learned profeffors of Druidifm taught in Anglefey,
or elfewhere, it is impofible to determine. From
the excifion of the groves of Mona, by Suetonius
Paullinus, nothing can be concluded in favour of

that

that little ifland. To make the Weftern Ebudæ the feat of thefe colleges, is as perfect a chimera as that Druidifm was not at all known in Caledonia.

The ecclefiaftical polity of North Britain was certainly the fame with that which took place among all the Celtic nations. We have the cleareft veftiges of the Druidical fuperftition in many parts of Scotland to this day. The appellation of its priefts, *Dru* and *Druthinich*, is ftill preferved. Their holy places are pointed out, and are called the houfes of the Druids by the vulgar. In the Ifles, and throughout the Continent of Scotland, are many of thofe circular fabrics of large rude ftones, within which they performed the myfterious rites of their religion.

Those circular piles of ftone are by fome called the Houfes of the Picts. This miftake arofe very probably from the fimilarity of found between the two Galic words which exprefs the Picts and Druids. The Picts are fometimes called *Cruithnich*, in the language of the Highlands and Druids always *Druithnich* or *Drui*.——The injudicious vulgar think that Fingal and his heroes, who are thought to have been giants placed enormous kettles upon thofe circles of ftone, in order to boil their venifon. Both thefe circumftances ftand as proofs of the uncertainty of oral tradition in every country.

The Romans, though feldom governed by the fpirit of perfecution, were very zealous in deftroying the Druidifm of South Britain. Claudius Cæfar endeavoured to abolifh it. The groves confecrated to that cruel fuperftition in Mona, were cut down by Suetonius Paulinus in the reign of Nero. It is reafonable to believe that other governors and emperors, directed by the fame

prin-

principle of humanity, declared war againſt the abominable rites of a ſect who offered human victims to their idols. After Chriſtianity became the eſtabliſhed religion of South Britain, in the reign of Conſtantine, the empire of Taranis and Teutates muſt have been totally ruined, or confined within very narrow limits.—But the Pagan Saxons, who, in appearance, had good reaſon to boaſt of the ſtrength of their Gods, undoubtedly re-eſtabliſhed the worſhip of thoſe divinities.

I HAVE already obſerved, that thoſe victorious infidels brought the word *Dry* from Germany. Together with the name they certainly introduced the office, being ſuperſtitiouſly devoted to *Tuiſto*, *Woden*, and *Thor*. The hiſtory of King Edwin's converſion, in Bede, and the great revolution brought about in the kingdom of Northumberland at that time, in ſpiritual matters, is a ſufficient demonſtration of this poſition. One circumſtance is ſufficient for my purpoſe to mention concerning the converſion of Edwin. After Paulinus had exhorted Edwin to embrace the Chriſtian faith, agreeably to the inſtructions he had formerly received from a perſon ſent from the inviſible world, the King ſummoned his friends and great council to have their advice and approbation. One of the councellors or Princes was the Pagan High-prieſt, or Primus Pontificum. The name, or rather title of this High-prieſt or Pontifex Maximus was Coifi, or Coefi.—I know not whether any one has attempted to explain the meaning of this word. It was, in my opinion, the common title of every Druidical ſuper-intendant of ſpiritual affairs. The Highland tale-makers talk frequently concerning *Caiffie*, or *Coiffie Dry*;—and by theſe two words they

they mean a perfon of extraordinary fenfe, fkill and cunning. *Dry* undoubtedly fignifies a *Druid*, a wife man, a prophet, a philofopher, and fome-times a magician, in the Galic:—*Coiffie Dry*, Bede's Coiffi or Primus Pontificum, ftands for the princi-pal Druid, or what fuch a perfon ought to be, a man fupremely wife and learned.

IT is needlefs to enlarge any farther on the Druidifm of Caledonia. That point has been handled at great length in another Effay *. Ger-many and Gaul, South Britain and Ireland, were full of that idolatrous fuperftition : and how could the inhabitants of Caledonia be ignorant of the religion of their anceftors and brethren defcended from the fame great Celtic fource ?

IT is, in fhort, very unreafonable to think that a nation, in any of its ftages, fhould be totally deftitute of religion : it is both unnatural and con-trary to experience to fuppofe it. Religion, whe-ther it arifes from the original preffure of the di-vinity on the human mind, or fprings from a ti-midity inherent in man, is certainly more preva-lent than atheifm : and indeed it is doubtful with me whether atheifm ever exifted in a mind that is not perfectly infane. It is a boaft of the fceptic, which cannot be believed : and it is equally incre-dible that the favage, however much his mind is obfcured, could entertain fuch an irrational idea.

THAT the Caledonians had fome ideas of re-ligion and a providence, is certain : that they were more pure in their fpiritual inftitutions than other Celtic nations, their barbarifm in other refpects

---

* The author alludes to the Differtation on the Druids, loft among Sir James MacDonald's papers.

fufficiently

fufficiently contradicts.—With the Teutates and Taranis of their Gaulish anceſtors, they probably worſhipped ſome local divinities of their own creation. That univerſal God of the heathen world, the ſun, was certainly worſhipped with great devotion in Caledonia. The inſtance I have given, towards the beginning of the preceding differtation, is demonſtrable of the honour paid to that great luminary, under the name of Grannius. The fires lighted on eminences by the common Highlanders, on the firſt day of May, till of late years, is one of the remains of that ſuperſtition.

DISSER-

DISSERTATION XX.

Of the Time in which Chriftianity was introduced into North Britain. That the firft Churches of Britain were planted by Oriental Miffionaries.

AFTER fpending fo much time in the inveftigation of the fecular antiquities of the Scots nation, it may be naturally expected that I have made fome inquiry into their ancient ecclefiaftical hiftory. My obfervations on that fubject are comprehended in this and the fubfequent differtation.

THE Chriftian religion became known in the principal divifions of Britain before the middle of the third century; yet it is impoffible to determine the particular time in which the firft dawn of the gofpel rofe on Caledonia. Tertullian, a writer cotemporary with the Emperor Severus, and confeffedly a very learned man, affirms pofitively, that the Chriftian religion had, in his own time, penetrated further into Britain than the Roman arms had done. Let us examine, therefore, the teftimony of Tertullian, and inveftigate what parts of Britain he had in his eye.

It

I t is certain, from the several different paſſages which Tertullian has quoted from Tacitus, that he had read the writings of that great hiſtorian ; and from them he certainly muſt have underſtood that South Britain had been entirely reduced into the form of a Roman province, before the end of the firſt century.

To ſay nothing of the ſucceſsful campaign Claudius Cæſar had made there in perſon, the Prætor Aulus Plantius had vanquiſhed ſome Britiſh Kings, taken many garriſons, and conquered ſeveral whole nations. Oſtorius Scapula, who ſucceeded Plantius, fought and defeated the Iceni, Cangi, Silures, and Brigantes. Suetonius Paulinus, Petilius Cerealis, and Julius Frontinus, three great generals, carried their victorious arms much farther than Oſtorius had done : and the famous Agricola had finiſhed the conqueſt of the country now called England, before he invaded Caledonia, near twenty years before the end of the firſt century.

I t is paſt all doubt that Agricola performed great things in North Britain. He ravaged or ſubdued thoſe diſtricts of that country which front Ireland. He defeated the Caledonian army on the Eaſtern coaſt. His fleet reduced the Orkney iſles. His land and ſea forces had ſpread either deſolation or terror over all the maritime places of Caledonia, but ſtill there were many corners of the country, and even whole diſtricts, which the difficulties ariſing from their ſituation, and his want of time, hindered that illuſtrious general from pervading. Theſe diſtricts may be reaſonably thought to have been the places meant by Tertullian *.

---

* Et Britannorum inacceſſa Romanis loca, Chriſto vero ſubdita. Tertul. lib. contra Judæos cap 7.

I t

IF any one, to invalidate the force of this teftimony, fhould object, that Tertullian was hafty
and dogmatical, frequently led aftray by an intemperate zeal, and too apt, like many of his profeffion, to obtrude pious frauds on the world, his
objection would have been too vague and unjuft to
deferve a confutation that would unavoidably lead
us into a long difcuffion of particulars.

BUT were it certain that this ancient writer's
character is enough to deftroy the credibility of e-
very fact that refts upon his bare teftimony, ftill
we have caufe to believe that fome of the remote
parts of North Britain were converted to the
Chriftian faith, in the reign of Severus. It is
impoffible to prove from hiftory, that no fuch
converfion happened in that period; and if it be
true that the gofpel had made its way into the
Southern divifion of this ifland long before that
time, it is probable that the fame change took
place in fome parts of Caledonia, before the middle of the third century.

CHRISTIANITY had made a progrefs amazingly
rapid over all the provinces of the Roman empire
before the end of the firft age, nor were the doc-
trines taught by that new religion confined within
the pale of the empire. It was one of the firft
principles of the primitive Chriftians to communicate their doctrine to all nations. Animated by
the warmeft zeal, they were active in propagating
their tenets; and their fuccefs was proportionable
to their pious induftry on that head. We are
told by Tacitus that there was a vaft multitude
of Chriftians at Rome *, when Nero, or fome

------

* Igitur primo correpti qui fatebantur, deinde indicio eorum
multitudo ingens, &c. Tacit. Annal. lib. 15.

fatal

fatal accident, laid that imperial city in afhes. Pliny the younger, informs the Emperor Trajan *, that great numbers of all ages, of all degrees, and of both fexes, had embraced the religion of thofe men : nor was this fuperftitious contagion, to fpeak with that author, confined to the cities only, it had fpread itfelf likewife through the villages and country. He adds farther, that the temples of the province committed to his care, had been almoft deferted, that the facred rites of the eftablifhed worfhip had been a long time neglected, and that the victims had very few purchafers till he had applied the cure of fome wholefome feverities for remedying fo great an evil.

TRAJAN invefted Pliny with a confular power over Bithynia, Pontus, and the republic of Byzantium, about the beginning of the fecond century ; and the reign of Severus comes down farther than the commencement of the third. After what has been extracted from one of his epiftles, it is needlefs to afk, whether Pliny was prepoffeffed in favour of Chriftianity, or in the humour of framing holy fictions to fupport its credit ? So far indeed was he from having taken fuch a biafs, that, though otherwife a reafonable and good-natured man, he gives the hardeft of all names to the profeffors of Chriftianity. He calls the Chriftian religion a fort of madnefs, and a filly and extravagant fuperftition. It is idle to fearch into the political motives which led Pliny to fpeak with fuch feverity againft Chriftianity. His words fhew plainly that the Chriftians were greatly multiplied in fome provinces of the Roman empire, about a

* Epift. xcvii. lib. 10.

X 2

whole

whole century before the latter end of Severus's reign.   Here then is a fact which rests upon the testimony of unexceptionable evidence, and what can hinder us from believing, upon the faith of the primitive divine, that the gospel began to flourish in Britain about the beginning of the third century ?

ALL the Scottish historians are agreed that Christianity was established in their country about the beginning of the third century, in the reign of King Donald.   The objections raised by some eminent antiquaries against the truth of this doctrine, are of little importance.   The story of King Donald is at least as well founded as those of King Lucius, and King Arviagrus, which some antiquaries endeavoured to support at a vast but useless expence of learning *.

THE Scots of former ages have, like their neighbours, carried their pretensions to spiritual antiquity extravagantly high.   Any one who perufes the famous letter of the Scottish nobility and barons to John, bishop of Rome, in the reign of Robert Bruce, will see a clear demonstration of this vanity.   In that letter, after the greatest men of the Scots nation had confidently afferted that " the King of Kings had favoured their ancef-" tors, though planted in the uttermost parts of " the earth, with perhaps the earlieft call to his " holy faith, " they affure his Holineſs, that Chrift had given another extraordinary teftimony of his particular regard to their people.   The words, rendered into Englifh, are, " Neither would our

---

* It is more than probable that what is told concerning the three Monarchs is an abfolute fiction.

Lord

" Lord have the Scots of old confirmed in the
" said faith by any other person than the apostle
" first called by himself the most worthy brother-
" german of the blessed St. Peter, that is St. An-
" drew, who was set apart to be their everlasting
" patron. Such was the will of Christ*."

As the Scots were in a perilous situation when
this letter was written to the Pope, it was undoubtedly convenient for them to draw some political advantages from the fraternal relation of St.
Peter and St. Andrew, and consequently from their
spiritual consanguinity with Rome. They took
care, therefore, to remind the sovereign pontiff,
" that those most holy fathers who were his pre-
" decessors, had with many favours and privi-
" leges strengthened their kingdom and people, as
" these had been the peculiar care and portion of
" St. Peter's brother." Nor did they forget to
draw from such strong premises a very important
conclusion. They most earnestly entreated the
Pope to remember those strong bonds of friendship. They conjured him to interpose his good
offices, so as to mediate a peace between them
and the English ; and they gave him to understand
at the same time, with great spirit and freedom,
" that if he should persist in his partiality, and
" continue to give faith to the misrepresentation of
" their foes, the Most High would lay to his
" charge all the effusion of Christian blood, and
" all the loss of immortal souls that should ensue
" upon the disputes between them and their un-
" reasonable adversaries."

---

* See Dr. Mackenzie in the Life of John Barbour.

X 3

We

WE may take it for granted, that the Scottish nobility and lesser barons had the story of their relation to St. Andrew, and consequently to his most worthy brother-German, from the learned ecclesiastics of those and former times. But churches, like nations, have frequently valued themselves upon an imaginary connexion with some illustrious founder. That of Rome, every one knows, began early enough to claim a peculiar right to the Prince of the apostolic college. Antioch had pretensions of the same kind, and perhaps a better title to the prerogative founded on it. Alexandria, though the seat of a great patriarch, was modest enough to content herself with an inferior dignity. She had only the honour of having St. Mark for her spiritual patron, a person who had no higher commission than that of an evangelist. The first bishop of Jerusalem could not with any decency be any thing less than the brother of Christ.

SOME time ago, it would have been deemed a heretical and a most dangerous doctrine in Spain to deny that the churches there were founded by James the Greater. Two centuries back, it was an article of every Frenchman's creed, that St. Dennis, to say nothing of Lazarus and Mary Magdalene, preached with great success in his country. Dennis was a member of the Areopagus of Athens; and Joseph of Arimathea was one of the great Jewish Sanhedrim. Rather than yield the post of honour to a rival nation, England thought proper in former days to ascribe the merit of her conversion to the honourable counsellor just mentioned, the same excellent person who had buried our Saviour in his own tomb *.

* Though the editor has all due respect for the judgment of the English, in points of national honour, he is far from think-

ing

THE churches of the two firſt ages, conſtantly diſtracted by the fears of perſecution, or always employed in affairs of much greater importance, never thought of drawing out of eccleſiaſtical annals or regiſters, containing the hiſtory or order of their paſtors. Euſebius acknowledges that it was extreamly difficult, for this reaſon, to inveſtigate the names of thoſe who governed the churches founded by the apoſtles *.

THE ableſt eccleſiaſtical critics have exhauſted the whole ſtrength of their erudition and fancy in ſettling the order in which Peter was ſucceeded. Clemens is one time the firſt, at another the ſecond, but generally the third in the papal liſt. Cletus and Anacletus are in the chronological ſyſtems of ſome learned annaliſts, one time identified, and at another divided into two pontiffs. Linus is by many called the ſecond Pope of Rome, and by not a few the fourth. Nothing, in ſhort, can be more full of uncertainty or more favourable to hiſtorical ſcepticiſm, than what ancient and modern writers have ſaid on this ſubject †.

HEGESSIPPUS was the firſt, who, about the year one hundred and ſixty of the vulgar æra, began to draw up catalogues of the biſhops of

---

ing a member of the Sanhedrim equal in dignity to one of the Athenian Areopagus. The Jews, though a choſen people, were by no means to be compared to the illuſtrious inhabitants of Attica; it were therefore to be wiſhed our anceſtors had taken a man of ſome higher rank than Joſeph for their ſpiritual patron; ſo our rivals, the French, would have been deprived of that pre-eminence which Dennis has given them, in this very material controverſy.

* Eccleſ. Hiſt. lib. iii. cap. 4.

† See Baſnage, Hiſt. de L'Egliſe, liv. vii. cap. 4.

                Rome,

Rome, Corinth, and other principal sees*. He was another Papias, equally wrongheaded, credulous, and visionary.

It is undoubtedly a task that exceeds the power of any one who extends his researches to Christian antiquities, to give authentic lists of the old bishops of Rome, Jerusalem, and Antioch, to ascertain the time at which the once famous churches of Carthage, and other African dioceses, were founded, and to discover their holy patrons. If this is the case, why should we make any difficulty of acknowledging that the origin of our British churches, and the succession of our oldest pastors, are totally lost in oblivion, or greatly embarrassed with inextricable absurdities.

In spite of that fond partiality which men will naturally entertain for those who seem to have done honour to their country, it is hardly in our power to believe, upon the authority of some ancient writers, that the British isles were visited by the apostles, by either one or more of that sacred body. To prove this supposed fact, Usher and Stillingfleet have quoted the plainest testimonies from Eusebius, Theodoret, Jerome, and Chrysostom. It will be readily objected, that these authors, though very learned, were bad authorities. They lived at too great a distance from the time at which the event could have happened. To obviate this difficulty, Stillingfleet urges the testimony of Clemens Romanus, a father of the highest antiquity, one who was cotemporary with the apostles themselves, and one whose name was written *in the Book of*

---

* Euseb. Hist. Ecclef. lib. iv. cap. 27.

Life *.

Life *. In one of his letters to the Corinthians, Clemens says expresly, that St. Paul preached righteousness throughout the whole earth, and in so doing went to the very extremity of the West. But these words are too hyperbolical to be literally true, and too undeterminate to be decisive in the present question. We know that Catullus, in his lampoon on Mamurra and Cæsar, calls Britain the remotest island of the West. Horace too calls the inhabitants of our island the most distant men on the face of the earth †. But Virgil gave the same epithet to the Morini of Gaul, though he knew that the Britons were beyond them, and, to speak in his own language, divided entirely from the whole world. And Horace, in another passage, calls Spain the last of the Western countries ‡. A noted cape there goes still under the name of Finisterre, or the extremity of the earth.

All this considered, it is probable that Clemens meant no more than some distant land, by the extremity of the West. It is certain that Paul intended to make a journey into Spain : so we are told by himself, in his letter to the Romans. Theodoret affirms that he went thither after his liberation at Rome. The expression in the epistle of Clemens may be applied with the strictest propriety to that country. If we extend its meaning as far as the power of words can go, we have a kind of demonstration that the apostle preached in Ireland, and preached also in Thule. So a Christian poet,

---

* Stilling. Orig. Brit. p. 38.
† Carm. Lib. 1. Ode 35.
Serves iturum Cæsarem in ultimos orbis Britannos.
‡ Carm. Lib. 1. Ode 36. Hesperia sospes ab ultima.

Venantius

Venantius Fortunatus, has affirmed, without any scruple, though with no more justice than Virgil had on his side, when he promised the conquest of the ultima Thule to Augustus Cæsar. Poets and orators have a right to speak at large. · The Christian panegyrists, who have celebrated the praises of apostles and saints, have assumed the same liberty ; nor do they deserve any severe censure for speaking agreeable to the rules of their art :. the whole blame ought to fall on those reasoners who draw serious conclusions from principles which are no more than the high flights and hyperbolical bombast of rhetoric.

But were it certain, that the testimonies of holy fathers, ancient Christian orators, and ecclesiastical historians, are arguments solid enough to convince the most unprejudiced that the apostles visited the British isles, it is no easy matter to comprehend why their ministerial labours should be confined to the countries now called England and Ireland. Archbishop Usher had a strong inclination to convince the learned world that Ireland had her share of that mighty advantage *, He has quoted, in the chapter of his Antiquities which relates immediately to his own country, a very clear testimony of Eusebius, from which it appears, as far as the authority of that writer can go, that the apostles preached in the British Isles : and who could deny that Ireland was of old reckoned one of that number ?

Stillingfleet had no great partiality for the *kingdom of saints*, and none at all for Scotland. He therefore exerted his whole strength in proving,

----

* Brit. Ecclef. Ant. cap. xvi. p. 386.

that

that the Southern and better part of Britain was the happy land where one of the apostles had exercised his function. To establish that favourite point, he availed himself of the testimonies which the learned primate had collected to his hand; taking particular care at the same time not to drop a kind hint that North Britain and Ireland enjoyed the same advantage.

THE most antient churches of Britain were founded, in all probability, by Asiatic missionaries. The conformity of their belief and practice in the affair of Easter, to that which prevailed among the Christians of the East, strengthens this opinion.

IT is well known that the celebration of Easter was one of the earliest customs which prevailed among the primitive Christians. The precise time at which that festival ought to be kept, was almost universally reckoned an affair of the last importance; and the question, what that time was, however frivolous in itself, produced high disputes, schismatical divisions, and the most disagreeable effects.

THE churches of the Lesser Asia solemnized their Easter, agreeably to the Mosaical institution with regard to the Jewish passover, on the fourteenth day of the moon, in the first month. The churches of the West, and of many other countries, took care to celebrate that feast on the Lord's day thereafter. This diversity of opinion created an infinite deal of animosity among the Christians of those times. Polycarp, bishop of Smyrna, came to Rome, all the way from Asia, to confer with the then possessor of St. Peter's chair, about establishing the peace of the church. Polycarp himself

was

was one of theſe who were branded with the frightful names of *Teſſares kai decatitæ* and *Quarto decimans.* The two pacific biſhops communicated with each other: but Polycarp, after returning home, was ſo far from giving up the point, in complaiſance to the Pope, that he confirmed the churches of Aſia in the belief of their old tradition. The quarrel was renewed under the pontificate of Victor, and became very violent, through the fooliſh management of that haughty prelate.

WE have no great concern in the ſequel of this diſpute. The controverſy, though it aroſe from a trifle, was kept alive for a long time. In ſpite of papal deciſions, and many ſynodical decrees, the Aſiatic churches maintained their old tradition and cuſtom, till the firſt general council of Niece, or rather the authority of Conſtantine the Great, ſilenced them. But the canons made by that and other councils, though ſupported by imperial edicts, had no manner of weight in Britain. The churches there followed the ritual of the Eaſtern Chriſtians, ſome of them till after the beginning of the eighth century, and ſome longer. It was in the year 710, that the Pictiſh Chriſtians renounced their error with regard to the canonical time of ſolemnizing the paſchal feſtival. So Bede has told us; and it coſt him and the abbot Ceolfrid the trouble of a very long and elaborately learned epiſtle, addreſſed to King Naitan, to reform them and their ſovereign out of that capital error *.

NOTHING is more improbable than that the light of the goſpel ſhined long in the Southern diviſion of this iſland, before the firſt faint rays of it

----

* Bed. Eccleſ. Hiſt. lib. v. cap. 21.

had

had penetrated into the Northern. The vicinity of the former to the Continent, and its conftant intercourfe with the world, would have foon made it acquainted with the new religion. In Nero's time there was a vaft number of Chriftians at Rome ; and it is well known that after the burning of that great city, they were moft barbaroufly perfecuted, as the perpetrators of the horrible crime, which many laid to the Emperor's own charge. We may take it for granted, that the news of that extraordinary event, and of the un-paralleled feverities confequent upon it, would take no long time in travelling to South Britain. The Romans had colonies and fubjects there. Human nature will always fympathize with the diftreffed. Every good heart will feel deeply for the innocent, when doomed, like the unhappy victims at Rome †, to the horrors and torments of the moft ignominious and painful deaths. On thefe accounts, the hiftory of the dreadful perfe-cution which Nero raifed againft the Chriftians muft have come foon into Britain, and brought along with it fome accounts of the religion that had afforded a pretext for committing fuch barba-rities. As that religion promifed to make its vota-ries wifer and happier men than thofe unacquaint-ed with it, that confideration likewife would have foon waked the curiofity of many. Some of the Chriftians who furvived that cruel maffacre at

---

† Tacit. Annal. lib. xiv. Et pereuntibus addita ludibria, ut ferarum tergis contectis laniatu canum interirent. aut crucibus affixi, aut flammandi, atque ubi defeciffet dies, in ufum nocturni luminis urerentur.

Rome

Rome, and many of those elsewhere who had cause
to dread the repetition of the same excesses, would
have undoubtedly taken refuge in places of greatest
security, and of consequence have fled into Britain.
The blood of martyrs has been in one sense justly
called the seed of the church ; and the first general persecution is very probably the æra from
which we ought to date the first establishment
of the Christian faith in the country now called
England.

It is far from being evident that the new religion made any considerable progress in Britain before the reign of Domitian.   In that reign Agricola
introduced the liberal arts and sciences among the
Britons of the South.   This circumstance, however prejudicial it may have been to the liberties
of that people, was a very favourable one to
Christianity.

In all the countries where the sciences are cultivated, a spirit of inquiry will naturally prevail.
The belief of former ages will no longer be the
rule of faith, in matters of any importance.   Established systems, whether of philosophy or religion,
will be canvassed with an ingenious freedom. Men,
who are made for speculation and the service of
virtue, will indulge themselves in the most rational
and exalted of all pleasures, that of discovering
those truths which are of the utmost consequence
to mankind.   They will most chearfully communicate their discoveries to the world, unless cruelly
restrained by penal laws, or courts of inquisition ;
and even the fury and vengeance of these will
hardly be able totally to silence them.   In the
height of persecution they will mutter out their

sense

fenfe of things in a corner, or open their fentiments freely among their friends. The hiftory
of ages and nations, efpecially in matters of religion, juftifies thefe obfervations. It is therefore
evident, that the introduction of the fciences and
fine arts would contribute much to the advance-
ment of Chriftianity in South Britain.

Among the liberal fciences which Agricola introduced into South Britain, the art of fpeaking
elegantly held one of the firft places. The humour of cultivating that branch of learning prevailed to fuch a degree, that the inhabitants of
Thule began to talk of hiring rhetoricians, if we
can believe a cotemporary writer *. All indeed
that we can infer from the Satires is, that a tafte
for eloquence was greatly diffufed over Britain :
and where the art of fpeaking was fo much
ftudied, it is more than probable that the art of
thinking was not neglected. In fhort, from the
fuccefsful attempt made by Agricola, to humanize
the people of his province, we may juftiy conclude, that knowledge, philofophy, and confequently a fpirit of inquiry, began to prevail in the
Roman part of Britain in a very early period.

We learn from Eufebius and others, that Polycarp, the famous bifhop of Smyrna, mentioned
above, had been St. John's difciple. He had
adopted the fyftem of the Quartodecimans; nor
could the authority of a Pope alienate him from
that party. No man, after the expiration of the
apoftolic age, was more zealous than this excellent

---

* Gallia caufidicos docuit facunda Britannos,
  De conducendo loquitur jam rhetore Thule.
  Juvenal, Sat. xv. ver. 111, 112.

prelate

prelate in propagating the Chriſtian faith. He ſealed this belief with his blood; and the only crime of which perſecutors impeached him, was his ſteady attachment to the intereſt of Chriſtianity, and the important ſervices he had done it. It was for that reaſon his murderers called him the Father of Atheiſm, the Father of Chriſtians, and the Teacher of Aſia. But his paſtoral care was not confined to that diviſion of the world. His zeal carried him much farther. He ſent miſſionaries into the very heart of Gaul, and founded the church of Lyons. Nicetius and Bothinus, the firſt teachers there, had been his diſciples †. And what ſhall hinder us from thinking that this truly apoſtolical man, and great lover of mankind, may have contributed every thing in his power to make Britain a province of the Chriſtian empire?

This, I confeſs, is no more than ſuppoſition and conjecture; but the darkneſs of the ſubject admits of no certainty: and when it is conſidered that the moſt ancient Britiſh Chriſtians of whom we have any tolerably juſt accounts, adopted Polycarp's ſyſtem with regard to Eaſter, that like him they refuſed to conform to the cuſtom of the Weſtern church, and that, in their diſputes with Italian miſſionaries, they always appealed to the authority of St. John, and the other Eaſtern divines, the conjecture is, at leaſt, ſpecious. Polycarp, who to all appearance has the beſt right to be called the founder of the Britiſh churches,

---

* See Baſnage—Hiſt. de l'Egliſe, lib. v. chap. 3.

ſuffered

fuffered death in the 170th year of the vulgar æra. It is not probable that the gofpel had taken any deep root in Britain before that time ; and if the teftimony of Tertullian can at all be depended upon, it begun to flourifh greatly in this ifland foon after that period.

Y   DISSER-

DISSERTATION XX.

Of the Conversion of the Southern Picts by St. Ninian. Of the Mission of Palladius to the Scots. Of St. Columba.

THE only guides we have to lead us through those dark regions of ecclesiastical antiquity, which are now to fall in our way, are Adamnan, abbot of Iona, and Bede, the presbyter of Girwy. Any impartial person who peruses the life of Columba written by Adamnan, and the history of the Saxon churches compiled by the Anglo-Saxon, must be of opinion that these two writers possessed a much greater degree of zeal, piety, and learning, than of sound judgment. I do not wish to be understood, from this observation, that I put Adamnan on any footing of equality with Bede.

AFTER Bede had told that Columba came from Ireland in the year of Christ 565, with a resolution of preaching the word of God to the Northern Picts ‡, he observes that those in the South had long before that time abandoned the errors of idolatry. The happy instrument by which these Southern Picts had been converted to the faith was

---

‡ Bede lib. iii. cap. 4.

Ninian,

Ninian, a faint and bifhop, who, to ufe Bede's language, had been regularly formed at Rome. It is faid further, that this worthy prelate built a church, which he took care to dedicate to St. Martin. That church ftood in a place which was called *Candida Cafa*, and the reafon why the place obtained that name, was, that it was built of ftone, a fpecies of architecture which the Britons had never known till introduced by Ninian.

BEDE has not mentioned the pontificate during which Ninian had been inftructed at Rome, nor has he afcertained the time of his preaching among the Picts. Modern writers have fupplied that defect. Smith, the lateft editor of that author's ecclefiaftical hiftory, relates †, that the founder of Candida Cafa vifited that fee in the time of Pope Damafcus, about the year 370, that he was ordained a bifhop for the propagation of Chriftianity among his countrymen, by Siricius, in the year 394 ; and that in his way to Britain he took the opportunity of waiting on the celebrated St. Martin, in Gaul.

INNES with great acutenefs has found out the Pictifh King in whofe reign Ninian acted the part of an evangelift among the heathens of Pictavia * : the name of that monarch was Druft, the fon of *Irb*, whofe reign commenced in the year 406.

ON proper examination it will appear, that the ftory of Ninian's fpiritual legation to the Southern Picts, and of his having dedicated a magnificent church to St. Martin, is attended with too many improbabilities not to feem at leaft dubious. His

---

† Smith, in a note on the chapter of Bede now referred to.
* Innes, Crit. Effay, p. 136.

having

having been regularly inftructed in the faith of
Rome, though a Britifh Chriftian, is a circum-
flance that renders it ftill more fufpicious. If
Ninian preached the doctrine he had learned at
Rome, with regard to Eafter, he made few pro-
felytes, and left no orthodox difciples among his
countrymen ; for when Auguftine, the monk, was
fent into Britain by Pope Gregory, all the Chriftians there were quartodeciman fchifmatics or heretics.   All that we know further, with regard to
the hiftory of this religious man, is, that he died
much about the time in which Palladius was fent
by Celeftine, bifhop of Rome, to exercife the
epifcopal office among the Scots.

PALLADIUS is faid to have been the firft bifhop
who was fent among the believing Scots ; and the
æra of his miffion is affigned to the year 430 *.
The Irifh claim the honour of being thofe Scots
to whom this great reformer was fent ; but there
was no confiderable number of Chriftians in Ireland
before St. Patrick appeared in quality of apoftle
there : fo that their title to the character of believing Scots cannot be well founded.

THE Britifh Scots, from the earlieft accounts of
time, have been poffeffed with a belief that Palladius was employed in their country ; and it is univerfally agreed, that he died in North Britain.   It
appears likewife that Pope Celeftine departed this
life in the year 432 † ; fo that if Palladius had
been but one year employed among the Irifh Scots,
as they themfelves relate, it is abfolutely impro-

---

* Anno CCCCXXX, Palladius ad Scotos in Chriftum creden-
tes a Celeftino papa primus mittitur epifcopus.
† Ufher's Ant. p. 424.

bable

bable that the Pope could have received the news of his great want of fuccefs before the time of his own death, in order to ordain St. Patrick to fucceed him in his office.

Of all the Scottifh faints who have been celebrated by panegyrifts, canonized by prieftcraft, and adored by fuperftition, Columba was undoubtedly the moft illuftrious. It it generally agreed that Columba was an Irifhman, and defcended of anceftors who had made a confiderable figure in that ifland. Adamnan has told us, that his father, Fedlimid, and his mother, Orthnea, were ranked among the nobility ‡. Keating quotes the rhimes of an old Hibernian bard, from which we learn that Fergus, his grandfather, was a Prince renowned in war *. Some have confounded that Prince with Fergus MacErc, the fuppofed founder of the Scottifh monarchy: but the Irifh manufcripts to which Ufher ¶ appeals, inform us, that the Fergus from whom Columba derived his defcent, was the fon of that celebrated hero, *Conal Gulbin*, and the grandfon of that famous Hibernian monarch, Neil of the nine hoftages.

Mr. O Connor afferts, that Columba rejected the imperial crown of Ireland. We know, indeed, that fome Princes have preferred the monkifh cowl to the regal diadem. We read of feveral Kings who abdicated their thrones and received the tonfure. England has furnifhed us with two of that character, and Scotland with a third: but we

---

‡ Sanctus Columba ex nobilibus fuit oriundus genitalibus patrem habuit Feidlimyd, filium Fergus, matrem Orthneam nomine.

* Gen. Hift. of Ireland, part ii. p. 32.

¶ Ant. p. 360.

Y 3

cannot

cannot readily believe that Columba either had a crown in his offer, or had the fame extreme contempt for the higheft pitch of human grandeur.

Many different Irifh writers relate that Columba was dedicated very early to the ftudy and fervice of Divinity: and nothing is more probable than that he mortified his appetites by a fevere courfe of abftinence. Aufterities of every kind, and macerations particularly were the cardinal virtues of thofe fuperftitious ages Our faint is faid to have overacted the part of a religious felf-tormentor to fuch a degree that his body was emaciated away into a hideous fkeleton. This ftory however cannot be reconciled to probability. Columba underwent many fatigues, and fome give accounts of his extraordinary vigour and healthinefs of conftitution. An old Bard quoted by Keating, affures us * that while Columba was celebrating the myfteries, or finging pfalms, his voice might be heard at the diftance of a mile and a half, which is a kind of proof that he was not fo ill fed as is generally fuppofed.

It is univerfally agreed that this faint employed the greateft part of his life in cultivating the devout faculties of the foul. He certainly was poffeffed with the moft ardent and unconfined zeal for religion. His unwearied and fuccefsful labours in propagating the gofpel among the Irifh, Scots, Picts, and Britons, afford a convincing proof of the enthufiafm, if not of the fincerity of his mind.

They who commonly pafs under the amiable name of good natured men, are feldom found qua-

---

* Keating, book ii. p. 35.

lified

lified for the execution of arduous undertakings. That pertinacity which is neceſſary to compleat difficult deſigns, is often the fruit of an iraſcible and choleric diſpoſition of the mind. Hence it may be inferred that Columba's paſſions were keen and violent, though perhaps not ſo peculiarly vindictive and hot, as bards and annaliſts have repreſented.

KEATING relates, on the faith of Iriſh manuſcripts, that Columba, to gratify his private revenge, frequently embroiled the whole kingdom of Ireland. His rage produced three long civil wars, ſo often and ſo ſuccefsfully did the iraſcible ſaint blow the trumpet of ſedition. If it be true that the firſt of theſe wars was occaſioned by the reſentment of Columba, for loſing a copy of the New Teſtament, which he claimed, and which the Iriſh monarch adjudged to another ſaint, the old tutelar demi-god of our country was certainly a moſt unreaſonable man.

THE ſecond war was founded on ſome kind of affront which Columba had received from a provincial King; and the third was carried on at his inſtigation, without any tolerable pretext at all. If theſe ſtories are authentic, the heathen may indeed aſk, *can ſuch violent tranſports of paſſion dwell in celeſtial minds**? But it cannot well be ſuppoſed that any conſiderable number of the Iriſh, however monk ridden, would have fought battles in compliance with the humour of a man ſo impotently wrathful: much leſs can we believe that heaven interpoſed, on all theſe different occaſions,

---

* Tantæne animis celeſtibus iræ. Virg. Æd. i. v. 11.

in

in his favour. Yet thofe very authors on whofe teftimony the truth of the whole ftory refts, will have it that compleat victories were granted by the *God of Battles* to Columba, in confequence of his prayers. Columba is faid to have been at laft made fenfible of his guilt by a holy perfon called *Molaife.* This man of God obliged the finner to abandon his native country, by way of penance. He enjoined him likewife, under the higheft penalties, never more to caft his eyes on Irifh ground. The felf-condemned criminal obeyed the fpiritual father with a filial fubmiffion; and fo religioufly obfequious was he to the difciplinarian's commands, that he covered his eyes with a veil while he ftayed in the ifland. Keating fupports this tale with the authority of a canonized bard.

Bede gives the following relation of the faint's arrival in Britain, and of his miniftry among the Picts. " In the year of Chrift five hundred and fixty five, while Juftin the Leffer held the reins of the Roman empire, Columba, a prefbyter and abbot, whom his manners have rendered defervedly famous, came from Ireland into Britain. His defign in coming thither, was to preach the word of God in the provinces of the Northern Picts, the Southern people of that denomination having been converted to the faith by Ninian, a long time before that period. He arrived in Britain while Brudius, a very powerful prince reigned over the Picts and the power of the holy man's doctrine, and the influence of his example, converted that nation to the faith*.

Adamnan calls this Pictifh King Bradeus, and informs us, that he ordered the gates of his palace

---

* Bed. Hift. Ecclef. lib. iii. cap. 4.

to be fhut againft the apoftle. But Columba, if we take Adamnan's word for it, removed this ob-ftruction without any difficulty. The fign of the crofs, and fome other efficacious ceremonies, made the paffage foon open to the faint. The King, upon feeing this miracle, received him courteoufly, and heard his advices with a refpectful attention. It is true, fome of his favourites confpired with the minifters of the old fuperftition in oppofing the new teachers; but the man of God, fays the writer of his life, overcame all oppofition: and by the help of fome fignal miracles, which gave an irrefiftible fanction to his doctrine, finifhed at laft the great work he had undertaken.

Soon after Columba's arrival in Britain, he fettled at Iona, and founded the celebrated abbey of that place.

Before Columba had fixed the feat of his little fpiritual empire at Iona, his character had rifen to a great height. The fanctity of his manners, the mighty power of his eloquence, the fpirit of that doctrine which he preached, the warmth and activity of his zeal, together with the benevolence of his intentions, had recommended him ftrongly to the higheft attention and refpect.

Should one collect all the miracles and ftrange tales that legends have vouched and tradition tranfmitted from age to age, with regard to this remarkable perfon, he might very eafily compile a huge volume: But a judicious reader would think himfelf little indebted to the compiler's induftry.

One of thefe traditional fictions, though fomewhat impious, is ludicrous. Oran, from whom the Cæmitery in the ifland of Iona was called
Relic-

Rælic-Oran, was a fellow foldier of Columba in the warfare of the gofpel. Columba, underftanding in a fupernatural way, that the facred buildings he was about to erect in Iona, could never anfwer his purpofe, unlefs fome perfon of confequence undertook voluntarily to be buried alive in the ground which was marked out for thofe ftructures : Oran with great fpirit undertook this dreadful tafk. He was interred accordingly. At the end of three days the grave was opened before a number of fpectators. No fooner was the brave martyr's face uncovered, than he opened his mouth and cried aloud in the Galic language, *Death is no great affair, hell is a mere joke.* Columba, who affifted at the ceremony, was greatly fhocked at the dangerous heterodoxy of this doctrine, and with great prefence of mind cried out, *Earth on the head of Oran, and prevent his pratling.* Thus poor Oran was actually buried, for pretending to difclofe the fecrets of the other world.

O u r hiftorians are generally agreed that whole kingdoms paid Columba the utmoft deference, and were determined by his advice in matters of high confequence. He became a councellor of ftate to many different fovereigns, and frequently decided the controverfies of contending powers. Aidan, King of Scots, upon receiving fome provocation from Brudius, the Pictifh King, declared war againft him. The armies of the two monarchs met near Dunkold, and fought a battle which produced a great effufion of Chriftian blood. After the action was over, Columba came to the field and interpofed his good offices, but all in vain. Aidan remained inflexible. The faint, fired with a pious indignation, reproved the Scottifh King

very

very fharply, and turned his back on him with great wrath. Aidan, fenfible of his error, caught the garment of the retiring faint, and acknowledging his rafhnefs, begged to know of him how the injury done could be expiated. Columba replied haftily, that the lofs fuftained was irreparable. This drew tears from the penitent monarch. Columba was foftned, wept bitterly, and after he had been filent for fome time, advifed Aidan to a peace. The King complied, Brudius acquiecfed in the propofals made, and a pacification immediately enfued.

In Columba's time, the hereditary, indefeafible right of Kings was a doctrine hardly known in any part of Britain or Ireland, in Scotland, the fuccefiion of the lineal heir feldom took place, till Kenneth the Third found means to eftablifh it by law. Columba was a perfon of the greateft influence in thofe difputes which generally enfued on the throne's becoming vacant. This will appear from the following ftory.

Gabhran, King of Scots, had left two fons, Aidan and Iogenanus. Columba had conceived a peculiar affection for the latter, and though the younger brother, inclined ftrongly to procure the crown for him. But a very ftrange adventure difconcerted his intention. Adamnan relates it thus. " While the holy man was in the ifland Kimbria *, he fell on a certain night into a fupernatural dream, and faw an angel of the Lord holding in his hand a tranfparent book which contained directions for the ordination of Kings †. The

* Cimbrei.
† Vitreus ordinationis regum liber.

angel

angel prefented the book to him ; upon perufing it, he found himfelf commanded to ordain Aidan King.   But his attachment to the younger brother made him decline the office.   Upon this the an- gel ftretched forth his hand and gave him a ftroke on the cheek, which made an impreffion that re- mained perfedly vifible during his life.   Colum- ba was then ordered in a very threatning manner, and under the penalty of a much heavier punifh- ment, to comply immediately with the pleafure of Almighty God.   He had the fame vifion, faw the fame book, and received the fame orders, three nights fucceffively.   At laft the obftinate faint obeyed, and went to the ifland of Iona, where he found Aidan, and laying his hand on his head, he ordained him King *."   It may be inferred from this marvellous ftory, that Columba was a perfon of great fway in ftate as well as religious affairs ; and that he was artful enough to make the pro- per ufe of the influence his fandtity gave him a- mong a fuperftitious people.

' He was frequently confulted in the perplexities of Government not only at home but abroad. His authority had particular weight in his native country.   *Aodh* or Hugh, one of the Irifh mo- narchs, fummoned his Princes, nobility, and dig- nified ecclefiaftics, to meet in parliament at *Drom- ceat.*   The principal reafon which induced him to call this great council proceeded from a very cu- rious caufe.

The Irifh nation had been for fome time moft grievoufly oppreffed by a numerous rabble of Bards, a race of men, idle, avaricious, and in-

---

* Adamn. Vita Colum. lib. iii. cap. 5.

fupportably

fupportably petulant. One of the many ample privileges which thefe formidable fatyrifts had acquired, was, an indifputable right to any boon they were pleafed to afk. This high prerogative joined to the advantage of a facred character, made the Bards fo intolerably audacious, that in King *Aodh*'s, time they had the infolence to demand the moft valuable jewel belonging to the crown. The jewel thefe mifcreants fought, was the golden bodkin which faftened their fovereign's royal robes under his neck. An outrage fo provoking incenfed Hugh or Aodh to fuch a degree, that he formed a defign of expelling the whole order out of the ifland: but as the authority of Irifh Kings was circumfcribed within narrow bounds, he was under the neceffity of calling the reprefentatives of the nation together, and of having Columba's affent before his will could have the force of a law.

COLUMBA, at the earneft requeft of the King and the Irifh nation, repaired to Dromceat. His retinue confifted of twenty bifhops, forty priefts, fifty deacons, thirty ftudents in divinity, and if we believe Keating, he was accompanied by Aidan King of Scotland. The faint was received by the affembly with fingular refpect: but fome of the Scottifh clergy, by whom he was accompanied, were treated with contempt and infolence. Columba had ample revenge of thofe who infulted his clergy, and we are firmly affured that the hand of God was vifible in the punifhment inflicted on the offenders. Struck by a judgment fo fignal, the King accommodated the affair of the Bards according to Columba's pleafure.

THERE

THERE is no neceffity for entering into any detail of the particulars of this faint's life, as they are related at large, though incorrectly, by his biographer. Upon the whole, we may allow that Columba, notwithftanding of his faults, was a man of refpectable talents, and could ufe well the afcendancy which his religious reputation gave him over a fuperftitious age.

THE boundlefs influence he had over two fucceffive Princes who filled the throne of Scotland ; the friendfhip he had contracted with King Rodoric of Cumberland ; the afcendant he had over the great Pictifh Monarch and his whole fubjects, together with the fhare he took occafionally in the adminiftration of public affairs in Ireland, feem to furnifh convincing proofs of his genius, fpirit and addrefs. He was born a man of high quality, and clofely allied to Princes but preferred the apparent humility of a religious life to the higheft fecular honours. Whether this aufterity was the effect of a defire of power, under a fanctity of character, or from real enthufiafm, is now difficult to fay, though very poffibly it arofe from both.

MANY learned authors have told us pofitively, that Columba wore the epifcopal mitre ; but he was no more than a Prefbyter. Had he been fond of a fuperior rank in the hierarchy, he might have very eafily gratified his ambition : but though he was confined within the more narrow limits of the priefty office, his authority extended much farther than that of the moft exalted dignitaries of his time.

COLUMBA is faid to have been a poet and hiftorian. That he poffeffed a talent for rhime, and exercifed it frequently, is very agreeable to the
reported

reported ſtrength and vivacity of his imagination, the prevailing humour of the time, and that friendly partiality which the Scottiſh and Iriſh bards have entertained for his memory.

We are informed by Mr. Lhoyd *, that there is ſtill in the Bodleian library at Oxford an Iriſh manuſcript, intituled, The works of Columbcille, in verſe, containing ſome account of the author's life, together with his prophecies and exhortations to Princes.

The ſame induſtrious writer obſerves, that there is in the library of Trinity College at Dublin, ſome other moſt curious and wonderfully ancient manuſcript, containing the four goſpels, and a variety of other matters. The manuſcript is called, The Book of Columb-cille, and thought to have been written by Columba's own hand.—*Flann*, King of Ireland, ordered a very coſtly cover to be given this book. On a ſilver croſs, which makes a part of that cover, is ſtill to be ſeen an Iriſh inſcription, of which the literal meaning is, The prayer and bleſſing of Columb-cille to *Flann*, the ſon of *Mailſheachnail*, King of Ireland, who made this cover : and ſhould the manuſcript be of no greater antiquity than the reign of that Prince, it muſt be about nine hundred years old †. This ſtory, however, carries with it a great degree of improbability—and it is more than probable that *this book of Columb-cille* aroſe from the pious fraud of a much later age.

---

* Catalog. of Iriſh Manuſcripts.
* Lhoyd's Archæol. p. 432.